Cooper Moon

Book Two

The Temptation

Cheryl Shireman

Published by Stillwaters Publishing, LLC
Print edition
ISBN: 1625660081
ISBN-13: 978-1-62566-008-4

Edited by Karin Cox
Ebook formatting by CyberWitch Press

Dedication

This book is dedicated to my second child, Lee Anne.

My tender-hearted and tough brown-eyed beauty.

You always make me feel so loved. That is your special gift.

You are mine.

Acknowledgments

Thank you to all of the readers who are going on this journey with me and Cooper Moon. I love writing this series. It has been so much fun. And a special thank you to the many readers who have taken the time to send me an email, leave me a message, or write a kind review. Your support and encouragement mean more to me that you will ever know. You have made my writing dreams come true.

Thank you to my wonderful team:

Karin Cox, a fantastic editor and wonderful friend.

Heather Marie Adkins, of Cyber Witch Press, who formats my books and makes them look beautiful.

Amy Jirsa-Smith, my eagle-eyed proofreader.

Thanks to all of you for all of your input and expertise!

And thanks to the writers in one of my Facebook groups (you know who you are) who came up with all kinds of crazy suggestions (most of which I cannot repeat) for the bus in this novel. You guys are great!

Chapter 1

October

Women often store treasures. Sometimes the treasures are from past lovers—prom favors, fragile dried flowers, or faded love letters worn soft from reading. Sometimes they are mementos from their children—baby curls, a pacifier, or a scrap from a tattered blanket. These precious items are tangible proof of a time fondly remembered. Proof of a past love or a past life. They are an attempt to keep memories alive.

Sally Moon had her own box of memories, although her collection brought no joy. Her box stored mementos of her husband's infidelities. Housed in a small cardboard box, tucked away in the bottom drawer on her side of the dresser, Sally's collection consisted of a suggestive note another woman had written to her husband, assorted scraps of paper with phone numbers she had found in his pockets, a barrette she once found in his truck, and a pair of black lace panties recently discovered behind their hamper.

Sitting on the bed, the box before her, Sally added another item to her collection: a note she found in Cooper's pocket a little over a month ago. Until this moment, the note had been kept in Sally's sock drawer. Now, she felt she was ready to add it to the rest. She read it once more. *I could make you happy. I love you with all of my heart.* L

She still could not believe Libby Cartwright had been so bold, had strutted right into the diner where Sally worked and given Cooper this nasty little note. Just the thought of it enraged Sally, but she still did not know what to do about it. She never did. Mostly, she just ached, haunted by the notion that she was not enough for her husband, broken hearted that he had sex indiscriminately with other women.

He assured her he was being faithful now. But Cooper had said the same thing many times, hadn't he? When she tried to remember the words of his frequent apologies, she could not. Sally only remembered him saying he was sorry. Every time.

Sally loved Cooper Moon. Even after all these years, she couldn't wait to roll over in the morning to see him sleeping beside her. It was always a little gift, opening her eyes and seeing him, knowing that her bed was the one he chose to wake up in.

Although she loved him, love was not the reason she stayed. After years of wondering, she finally realized her devotion to Cooper came down to one thing—faith. Oddly enough, the realization came to her one day while she was watching a documentary on the Holocaust. She wondered how the men and women in the concentration camps had survived such atrocities. How had they survived the days? What kept them going? When one of the prisoners was interviewed, he said, "Every day, I held onto the faith that I would be free again one day." At that moment, Sally realized faith was essential to enduring any situation. That prisoner could suffer through endless days of unspeakable horror because he had faith that one day he would be free.

Faith, Sally realized, provides the strength to overcome. The abused wife can endure beatings from her husband because she has faith he will change. The stroke victim can struggle to learn to walk and read again because she has faith in recovery. The cancer patient can endure the side effects of chemotherapy because he has faith he will regain his health. The athlete can endure grueling training because he has faith in winning. Those living in poverty look forward in faith to the day when things will be better. And Sally could endure the heartbreak of infidelity as long as she had faith that someday Cooper would change.

But now, *someday* was here, and her faith was wavering. This was it. She knew it. It was now or never. He promised he would be faithful to her now. And if Cooper couldn't be faithful to her now that he claimed to believe in God, she knew he never would be. There were no more excuses. If he was unfaithful to her now, all hope was lost.

Sally still didn't know what to make of her husband's recent conversion. She still wasn't sure if she even believed it. True, he had built a little church in their woods, and he had even had his first service yesterday. And, as far as she knew, he hadn't been unfaithful to her since his conversion back in April. He seemed to have changed. But with Cooper, you never knew.

Sally almost wished he had never said those words to her. Those words were everything she had ever hoped for. And he promised. They weren't words he said after getting caught cheating. He promised for no reason at all. Right out of the blue. He gave her everything with that promise, as if he had wrapped her dreams in a box and handed them to her with a delicate bow on top. And this time, she not only hoped he was telling the truth, she believed him. She had faith in him. Almost.

Now, when it seemed Cooper had become the man she always wanted him to be, she was most afraid. Her actions betrayed her faith. She found herself questioning him, watching his every move, sniffing for traces of perfume, looking for hints of betrayal. As he talked to her about the church or how he had spent his day, she wondered if he had been in the arms of another woman. She was obsessed with proving her faith was unwarranted, because now, she had so much to lose.

Sally could not imagine life without her husband. But she also knew that every woman has her breaking point, a point where living without him seems less painful that living with him. If Cooper cheated on her now, she would have to leave. And should that day arise, Sally knew, too, she would need these mementos, this proof, to give her the strength to walk out the door.

Dressed in faded jeans and a black tee shirt, his black hair still wet from the shower, Cooper entered the bedroom. "Are you sure you don't want to go to the bank with me?"

Sally tucked the flaps of the box in and returned it to her drawer. There was no need to make much effort to hide it; Cooper was not very curious. If Sally had seen him putting a cardboard box into his side of the dresser, she would check it as soon as he had left the room. Cooper never even glanced at the box as Sally put it away. "No. I need to get to the diner," she told him.

Cooper wrapped his arms around her waist. "Come on, Sally. How often do we get to deposit a fifty thousand dollar check?"

Sally could feel his breath on her neck. A quiver snaked through her body. She pulled away and turned to face him. "Not often enough. Could you do that every year?"

"Not unless TJ wins the World Wide Warrior competition every year."

"Are you serious? Is he going to give you another fifty thousand dollars if he wins it again next year?"

"No, Sally. I was kidding. He isn't even going to do it next year. He says he doesn't like the competition part of it. He only liked the training."

Sally shook her head, crossed the tiny bedroom of the mobile home, and withdrew a coat from the closet. "That's the stupidest thing I ever heard of. He wins the competition in the best time ever, wins a million dollars, and then decides he doesn't want to try again. Must be nice to not need money."

Cooper shrugged. "It's his choice. His life. He'll be here soon. Why don't you wait so you can at least be here when he gives us the check?"

"He isn't giving *us* the check; he's giving *you* the check. And I can't be late for work."

"Sure you can. He'll be here soon. What difference does half an hour make?"

"None—to you. You don't have a real job." Sally pushed past him.

"Sally, are you mad at me about something?" Cooper reached out and took hold of her arm.

"What would I be mad at you about?" She looked directly into the bluest eyes she had ever seen, eyes she could never resist, and she braced herself. Maybe, just once, he would tell her the truth. Tell her about the note Libby had slipped to him that night in the diner.

"Sally, if I've done something wrong, or said something to hurt you, please tell me. I feel like you've been mad at me for over a month. What's wrong?"

"Nothing. Everything is perfect. Just perfect. Right?" Sally gritted her teeth in an effort to keep from crying. It was painful enough to have her husband possibly sleeping with other women again, but when he lied right to her face it was more than she could bear. She could blame passion for his past infidelities, but every time he lied to her, it felt like a slap in the face.

Cooper pulled her into his arms. "Don't be like this," he whispered.

At the touch of his hands, Sally felt her resolve weaken. Maybe, oh maybe... His breath upon her neck caused her to close her eyes and tilt her head back. He pulled her closer, pressing his body against hers. She wanted to stay like that—

5

so close she could feel his heart beating against her body. Reminding herself that he still had not told her about that note, and maybe there was more than a note to be worried about, Sally stiffened. "Let me go. I'm going to be late." She pulled away. "You always start this as I'm headed out the door."

A few seconds later, the door slammed.

Cooper stood in the bedroom and listened, first to her car door, and then to the car pulling away on the dirt road. The bedroom suddenly seemed much smaller and darker. Their full-sized bed was pushed against one wall. A small bedside table holding a lamp, an alarm clock, and a couple of magazines sat near Sally's side of the bed. The only other furniture was a scratched dresser they had picked up on trash day from where it had been sitting by someone's trashcan. Cooper moved to the bed and tried to straighten the blankets. He wasn't very good at making the bed, but then again, he had not had much practice. Tugging at the comforter, he pulled it up far enough to cover the pillows. Two pillows on the floor had ruffled pillowcases that matched the cover. Cooper tossed them against the head of the bed. He hated the comforter. It was blue with a huge white sailboat on it. He didn't know anything about decorating, but it didn't look very good with this dark brown carpeting. Reaching over, he slid the drapes back to let a little light into the room.

Outside, he noticed most of the trees had lost their leaves, except for the stubborn oaks. Shades of oranges and browns bathed the woods. It was late October, almost time for Halloween. Snow would cover the ground soon. For some reason, the thought saddened him, but he wasn't sure why. Cooper had never disliked winter. In fact, he never gave much thought to any of the seasons; they were just part of life. But this year the oncoming winter seemed ominous, a feeling he couldn't shake. He had plenty of firewood cut for the winter, so it wasn't that. Yet the feeling remained.

He had just held his first service in the church yesterday.

His very own church, a little white building with a simple steeple. Despite a slow start, the service ended up better than he ever expected. The church was full of people. He still couldn't believe that. He was grateful, but it was more than that. He felt embarrassed. Who was he to lead a church? To collect hard-earned money? It felt wrong. And yet, he and TJ had spent the last year building the church and he had to have some sort of money to run it, so he supposed it would be okay. The money was in his sock drawer. Cooper supposed that was as safe a place as any for now. He'd figure out what to do with it later. Maybe he'd ask them at the bank today. Maybe he'd start a business account for the church.

His thoughts turned back to Sally. She was acting strange, and for the first time ever, he couldn't get her to talk to him. Lately, she seemed taut as a spring, and there was no telling which direction she'd take off in when released.

"Hey, Cooper," he heard TJ call from the living room.

"Yeah, TJ. I'm coming." Cooper turned away from the window.

TJ was standing just inside the front door, closing it behind him. "Nice and warm in here."

"Yeah. The woodstove is burning."

"Do you use the furnace at all?"

"Nope. Don't even know if it works anymore. Come on in. You want a cup of coffee?" Cooper moved to the kitchen and poured himself a cup.

"Nah. I don't like coffee."

"Neither do I. But it's warm, and Sally makes it every morning, so I drink it."

With his usual careless, energetic way of moving, which always reminded Cooper of a child, TJ wiped his feet on the rug by the door and walked the few steps to the white Formica kitchen counter that separated the living room from the kitchen. "Here's your money." He handed Cooper a white envelope. "Check for fifty grand is in there."

"Man, TJ. Are you sure you want to do that? That's a lot of money. You don't have to. You already paid for the materials to finish the church. That's more than I ever dreamed of."

"No. I want to. It feels good. I like to help people. For the first time ever, I have money to do that. I might not ever be able to do it again. Right now, that's what I want to do." TJ stretched his ropy, athletic arms behind his back and grinned.

After adding sugar and milk to his coffee, Cooper walked around the counter and into the living room. "Sit down. Take a load off, unless you got somewhere to be."

TJ unzipped his coat and sat down on the couch. "Where was Sally headed in such a hurry? Work? I passed her on the road and she didn't even wave, acted like she didn't see me. Maybe she didn't."

"How'd you get here?"

"My bike."

"Then she had to see you. It's not like there's any other traffic on a dead end road. Not much to distract her. She's on her way to work." Cooper sipped his coffee and placed it on the coffee table. "I don't know, TJ. She's been acting weird lately. I don't know what to think."

"If you ask me, everybody is acting weird lately. Since I won Warrior, you wouldn't believe how people have been. It's like everybody is my best friend now. Everywhere I go, I feel like people are talking about me behind my back, pointing at me or just staring. Asking me for my autograph. How stupid is that? And I get all kinds of letters from people telling me they need money. Half of them are probably fake. How am I supposed to know what's true and what isn't? I got a whole box of them at Jake's. I don't even open them anymore. It's too depressing."

"Yeah, I bet. Must be weird. But I guess you'll get that—winning a competition that was on TV. It's not every day someone wins a million bucks."

TJ nodded and sighed. "Sometimes I hate it. And the worst thing is, I don't know what to do with myself. For five years, I trained every day. Now, I wake up and I don't know what to do. What in the world do people do with all of their time? What am I supposed to do with today?"

"You got plenty of money to do it once you get it figured out."

"Yeah, I guess. I'm not complaining. Plenty of people got it a lot worse than me. I'm grateful, don't get me wrong, but I just feel sort of ... I don't know ... lost."

"Why don't you go to the diner and ask Lucy out? And why are you still riding a bike? Why don't you buy a car? You can't take her out on your bike."

TJ stood and moved to the woodstove, warming his hands over the top. "Having money doesn't change anything with Lucy. I'm just not on her radar."

"You'll never know unless you ask her."

"I guess I'd rather wonder than ask her out and have her turn me down."

"TJ, that's no way to live. You gotta have faith. Ask her out."

"I'm afraid she'd tell me no. I'd rather wait until I have some sort of a chance of her saying yes." TJ gazed out the window. "Won't be long and it will be snowing."

"Do something to make her notice you."

"Like what?" TJ collapsed into a chair across from Cooper and threw a leg over the arm.

"I don't know."

"Sure you don't. It's easy for you. Women just notice you. You don't have to do anything."

Cooper picked up his coffee cup and took another sip. He thought for a moment. "What does she like to do?"

"What do you mean?"

"Like, does she like to bowl or anything? You could take her bowling."

"I don't know."

"Well, talk to her. Find out. And then go do that with her. Say you like it too."

"What if it is scuba diving?"

"Come on, TJ. You're making this harder than it is."

"Easy for you to say, Cooper." *She'd say yes to you*, TJ thought. "You're better with women than I am."

"Lately, I'm not so sure about that."

"What do you mean?"

"Sally's been acting weird lately. Like she's kind of mad, but she won't tell me what she's mad about. And why do you suppose Frank Collette is hanging out at the diner all of a sudden?"

"The food?"

"I'm not so sure. Have you noticed how much he and Sally talk to each other? And he always comes in alone. Wouldn't you think he'd have a date once in a while? He's there all the time. There are other places in town to eat."

"Violet's gone. Maybe he's lonely and doesn't want to eat at home alone."

"Yeah. That's what I'm worried about."

"What?"

"Frank being lonely."

"Cooper, come on. You don't have to worry about that with Sally. She'd never cheat on you."

Cooper shrugged. "I've given her plenty of reasons to."

"But that was in the past."

"It still happened."

"Nah. Sally'd never do that."

"Yeah, you're probably right. Oh, hey, I forgot. Libby Cartwright wanted me to give you Beaulah Potts' business card."

TJ raised his brows. "When did you see Libby?"

Cooper shook his head. "No. It wasn't like that. She stopped by the diner and gave it to me while we were all watching you on TV." Cooper wondered briefly if that was why Sally was mad. Sally had seen Libby that night and been none too pleased. But Libby had only stayed for a couple of minutes, just long enough to give him the business card.

"Why would she do that?"

"She thinks you might want to buy a house now, and if you do, Libby wants you to use Beaulah Potts. I guess Libby gets a cut when Beaulah makes a sale."

"Me? Buy a house?"

"Why not? You can't keep sleeping at Jake's forever. And sleeping in the church can't be too comfortable. You have enough money to pay cash for a house. Or even build a new one."

"I never thought about that. Maybe I could build a house with a special room for Ma and a nurse."

"Well, if you decide to buy or build, give Beaulah Potts a call and tell her I gave you her business card."

"Okay. I'll think about it." TJ got to his feet.

"You leaving so soon?"

"Yeah. I think I'm going to go for a ride. I feel like I got ants crawling all over me. I need to do something."

Cooper stood too. "Okay. Thanks for the check."

"You're welcome." TJ moved to the door. "Later."

A short time later, as Cooper was driving to the bank, his thoughts returned to Sally. It didn't make sense for her to be mad about Libby. Ever since his conversion last April, he'd been faithful to Sally. For the first time in his life, Cooper was having sex with only one woman. And oddly enough, Sally seemed unhappier than ever before. He couldn't understand it. Maybe he'd ignored her too much while he and TJ spent all summer building the church. Cooper tried to remember when things had taken a turn for the worse. It seemed right around the time TJ won the World Wide Warrior contest, but that didn't make sense. It seems like that would have made Sally happy, knowing that TJ's win would also mean money for them. But, somehow, her anger seemed to be tied to that win.

He remembered Sally had been mad that Libby Cartwright had come into the diner. And maybe Sally saw Libby give him her business card, but hell, he'd thrown it away before he ever left the diner that night, so why be mad about that? And he hadn't had sex with Libby since before he believed in God. Here he was, trying to be a faithful husband, and it didn't do him a bit of good. He might as well be out screwing around, if Sally was going to walk around pissed all of the time.

Cooper parked his truck in front of the bank. The last time he'd been in here, Frank Collette had turned him down for a loan to buy First Baptist Church. Well, screw Frank Collette. True, the church he and TJ had built was just a small church, and nothing like First Baptist, but it was still a church. And now Cooper had a fifty-thousand-dollar check in his hand. And he was going to enjoy depositing that fifty-thousand-dollar check, right under the nose of Frank Collette.

"Hello," two young tellers said in unison as he strode toward the counter, both trying to get him to come to their window.

Cooper looked over at Frank's desk. It was empty. He approached one of the women, a pretty brown-eyed blonde whose name tag read Lee Anne.

"How are you today?" she asked with a smile.

"I want to see Frank Collette."

"He's not in, but we have other loan officers available. Would you like me to buzz one?" Her face was flawless with the exception of one small freckle on her forehead, which only made her more beautiful.

But her charms were lost on Cooper. He frowned and looked back at Frank's desk. "When do you expect him back?"

"I'm not sure."

"I need to see Frank. I don't want to talk to anyone else."

"Oh, I see." The young woman looked uncomfortable. "Actually, Mr. Collette is no longer with us."

"What?" Cooper put his hands on the counter and leaned toward her.

"Mr. Collette is no longer with Timber Lake Community Bank."

"When did that happen?"

"Would you like to talk to another loan officer?"

Cooper shook his head. "No. I guess I'll just deposit this." He grabbed an ink pen from the pen holder on the counter, quickly signed the check, and pushed it toward her.

The teller's eyes widened at the amount of the deposit. She started asking Cooper questions, offering all kinds of bank services, but Cooper heard little of what she said. When she paused, awaiting his response, he asked, "Why'd he leave?"

"Pardon?"

"Frank. Why'd he leave? Is he working at another bank in town?"

"I ... I don't know where Mr. Collette is."

"Did he get fired?"

"If you'd like to open an—"

"No. I don't want to open anything. We already have a checking and a savings account here. That's enough."

"But with this kind of balance—"

"Did he get fired?"

She looked back at the offices, as if afraid she might be overheard. Leaning slightly forward, she whispered, "Yes."

"Crap. I wanted him to be here."

As the young woman made the deposit, Cooper looked at Frank's desk again. While he waited, a woman sat down at the desk and began typing on a keyboard. A small vase on the corner of the desk held flowers. *Must be her desk now*, he thought.

"Thanks." He collected his deposit receipt and turned to leave. Lee Anne said something as he headed for the door, but he did not hear her. The visit to the bank was not nearly as much fun as he had thought it would be. He had so wanted Frank to see that fifty-thousand-dollar deposit.

(

Across town, Lucy Miller stood in her parents' new sunroom. Cooper and TJ had built most of it. They had been in the middle of finishing the drywall when her mother had fired Cooper.

That night, Ivy had explained to her husband, Drake. "He said he was getting the raw end of the deal." From her bedroom, Lucy had overheard the entire conversation. "He said it was too much work, building the sunroom in exchange for you processing his timber. He got nasty about it, so I fired him."

But Lucy knew that wasn't true. Cooper had been fired because he refused to sleep with Ivy. Long ago, Lucy had lost any illusions about her mother. She knew exactly what kind of woman she was: bitter and desperate. She slept around. Everyone in town knew it. Lucy supposed her father knew it too. But she also knew that Cooper didn't want anything to do with Ivy. It wasn't too hard to piece together the puzzle. Ivy had been coming on to Cooper that day, and the next thing Lucy knew, he had been fired, was gone. Her parents hired someone else to finish and paint the drywall, and then hired a couple more guys to come in and install the floor tile. Still, though, Lucy liked to be in the room. It reminded her of Cooper. But most things reminded her of Cooper.

She wondered why Cooper had not said anything about the note she had slipped into his pocket that night in the diner, when they were all watching TJ on World Wide Warrior. Some woman Cooper had called Libby had come in and given Cooper a business card. Lucy didn't know Libby, but she didn't like the look of her. Beautiful—and without even trying. Who could like a woman like that? Lucy hated that Cooper even knew such a woman. She refused to think about how well he might know her. Sally had also seen the woman give Cooper the business card, and she was plenty mad; that much was clear. Sally had been hateful the rest of the night, so hateful that Lucy had found the courage to finally let Cooper know how she felt about him. Scrawling a note on a scrap of paper, she'd then stuck it inside his jacket pocket. *I could make you happy. I love you with all of my heart. L*

Yet Cooper had still not said a word about the note. True, it had only been a few weeks ago, and the only time Lucy had seen him since then was at his church service, and it was hard to talk there, with everyone standing around. But still, Lucy thought that Cooper would have given her some sort of sign by now, a knowing look, a smile, or even another note in exchange. But, so far, nothing.

Lucy stood barefoot on the cold tile floor and looked across the backyard at a squirrel that was busy gathering acorns. If she married Cooper, he could build her a house. Their very own house. Wouldn't that be something? And she'd never be hateful to him like Sally was. She'd ask him to build a sunroom on their house that was twice as big as this one. She'd like to see her mother's face on that day. The thought brought a smile to Lucy's face.

Another thought took her smile away just as quickly. Maybe Cooper had not found the note! She had slipped it into his right jacket pocket that night at the diner, but guys were weird. Maybe he never even looked in his jacket pockets. Maybe *that* was why she still had not heard anything from Cooper!

Chapter 2

October

Jake Barnes cruised through Timber Lake, Michigan, in his squad car. The trees and streets were full of orange and yellow and red leaves, and his car kicked up a few as he drove past the courthouse square. His windows were down, even though it was a chilly day. He loved autumn, loved the cooler weather, the trees changing colors, the smell of burning leaves in the air. It reminded him of being in high school and playing football—the year they won the state championship. Frank Collette was their quarterback. Best high school player Jake had ever seen. Jake had envied Frank so much back then. He smiled at the memory. He missed those days. His biggest worry was when he was going to lose his virginity and whether they'd win the Friday night game. And by his junior year, the first was no longer a concern. He tried to remember her name but couldn't. Some girl he'd met while visiting his cousin in Chicago. Never saw her again, and now he couldn't even remember her name. Seemed a shame. He ought to at least know her name. But maybe it was better this way. Reality often dulled in comparison to fantasy. If he knew her name, he could run a check on her. Probably find out she was a meth head or something. Nah. He'd hold on to his memory, however flawed.

Everyone was out today, it seemed. Jake glanced at the clock on the dash. A little after twelve. That explained it. Everyone was having lunch. The benches surrounding the courthouse were full of people eating takeout food from the surrounding restaurants. Someone had an elephant ear stand set up on the corner and as Jake passed it and caught a whiff, his stomach rumbled in response. He couldn't believe it was lunchtime already. It seemed as if the morning had just begun. His schedule was so screwed up lately that he had no sense of time. Switching from second to first shift didn't help matters.

Two women on the sidewalk caught his attention. One of them had a nice ass. Great legs. He checked her out as he drew closer. There was something familiar in that walk. He laughed. *Now, that's bad,* he thought. *I've been checking out my own wife.* But he'd never seen those shorts, had he? And who was Melody walking with? He beeped his horn, waved.

Melody waved back and kept walking. As he slid by, he could hear her say, "That's my husband."

The other woman did not wave, just smoothed back her ponytail of dark hair. He didn't recognize her. He was glad to see Melody out of the house. Now that TJ had hired a nurse for their mom, Melody could get out without worrying about Clara burning the house down. Jake pushed away thoughts of his mother. He couldn't think about that now. If he did, he might end up with another anxiety attack. When they first started, he thought he might be having a heart attack. He wasn't sure which was worse: a faulty heart or a faulty head. Either way, he was trying to avoid thinking about anything that induced tension or anxiety, which was hard when he had over fifty-two thousand dollars in stolen money hidden in a bowling bag in his closet.

Jake spotted Cooper in his old pickup, and he and Jake

exchanged waves. *That guy,* Jake thought. *Now, there's a guy without a care in the world.* Never had a job that Jake knew of. Slept around with half the women in town while his wife worked her ass off at the diner to support him. Now he had a church. *How much time would that take out of his week? The guy was lucky if he worked ten hours a week. Must be nice,* Jake thought.

His stomach rumbled, and he regretted not taking time to eat breakfast this morning. He should have got up earlier and went to Annie's Diner for breakfast. Annie's had the best sausage gravy and biscuits. His stomach growled again. *Maybe I'll get an elephant ear during my break,* he thought as he drove away from town.

Cooper waved at Jake as he passed, then drove aimlessly about the streets. It didn't take long, not in a town with a population of fewer than ten thousand. He drove the block around the courthouse to see if he knew anyone sitting in the benches on the lawn. He didn't spot anyone he recognized, except Jake's wife, Melody, on the sidewalk.

An old guy was driving a riding lawnmower across the grass, picking up leaves with it and shooting them into a bagger. Squirrels darted about in front, playing a game of chicken. It was cold, but the sun was shining. It seemed like Cooper should have something to do or somewhere to go on such a pleasant day. He considered going home and cutting wood, but talked himself out of that in just a few seconds. The blade on the chainsaw needed sharpening, and he didn't feel like messing with it. Besides, he already had enough wood cut for winter. As he drove past the diner, he thought about stopping for something to eat, but Sally had been in such a pissy mood earlier that he didn't want to deal with her. Before long, his truck was headed to Bass Turds. He agreed with TJ completely; he didn't know what to do with *today*, either.

Before he believed in God, a day like this was a perfect

for prowling. In no time at all, he'd be lying in some woman's bed, her perfume in his nostrils, her leg thrown over him as they dozed after sex. Sometimes he missed those days. Sometimes being a Christian wasn't all it was cracked up to be. Sure, the God stuff was great, but knowing right from wrong wasn't always so fun.

A few minutes later, he was settling onto a barstool at Bass Turds. "Hey, Pete."

"Hey, Cooper. How are you today?"

"I wish I knew."

"What's that supposed to mean?"

"I don't know. Pete, I just went into the bank and made the biggest deposit of my life. You'd think that would make me happy, wouldn't ya? But, instead, I feel kind of lost."

"You want something to drink?"

"Yeah. Give me a beer."

"A beer? I thought you quit drinking."

"I did. But a beer sure sounds good. Hell, never mind. Forget it. Give me one of those crappy iced teas you sell."

"Actually, I don't sell many of them."

"There's a reason for that."

Pete left to get the tea and Cooper swiveled his barstool around to see who was there. A couple of women were seated at one of the booths. They both smiled at him. Cooper nodded and spun back around, careful to avoid making eye contact with them in the mirror that ran behind the bar. He knew they'd be watching him. Sometimes women were a pain in the ass.

Pete placed a coaster and a glass of ice tea in front of Cooper.

"You want anything to eat?"

"Maybe some wings. But not yet. I'm not hungry yet."

"So, TJ finally got his prize money from World Wide Warrior, huh?"

"Yeah."

"That's amazing—that he'd give you that much money.

Ten percent of a million dollars. Of course, I'm sure they took a big chunk for taxes."

"Yep. They sure did. He ended up with a little over half a million, but he got even more in endorsements. And you're right, it is amazing. Can't believe he did that. He's a good friend."

"Did you ever imagine TJ having that kind of money?"

"No. Never did."

Violet Collette came from the kitchen, carrying a pad of paper and a pen. "Pete, did you know... Oh. Hi, Cooper. Pete, you're almost out of ketchup. There's probably enough for today, but you'll be out by tomorrow for sure."

"Okay, thanks for letting me know."

Violet turned and walked back into the kitchen area.

"Is *she* working here now?" Cooper asked. Frank Collette's wife, Violet, was one of the women whose bed Cooper used to end up in.

"No."

Cooper looked at Pete in confusion. "Looks like it."

"No." Pete wiped at the bar with a white cloth. "She doesn't work here, although maybe she should. Maybe that's a good idea. Hell, I don't know."

"What do you mean?"

Pete glanced around the bar. Cooper was the only person seated at the bar, and the few other Monday afternoon patrons were preoccupied with eating and talking in the booths lining the opposite wall. When Pete spoke again, his voice was almost a whisper. "She's been here for a while, almost a month and a half. I don't know how to make her leave."

"What? That doesn't make sense. What are you talking about, Pete?"

"The night TJ won World Wide Warrior, this place was full. Violet was here. There were a lot of people here. A lot of strangers. Well, when she went out to get in her car, some asshole followed her outside and attacked her. Started beating on her. It would have got a lot worse if I hadn't shown up with that." Pete pointed to an aluminum baseball bat that hung behind the bar.

Cooper had always assumed it was a decoration, not a weapon. "You're kidding me!"

"No. And afterward, she was so shook up, and I felt so sorry for her, that I made the mistake of inviting her up to my apartment."

"Oh, man."

"I didn't know what else to do. You should have seen her, Cooper. She was a real mess. She was shaking like a leaf, and she couldn't even walk. I had to carry her upstairs." Pete leaned both hands against the bar.

"She couldn't walk?" Cooper asked skeptically.

"Cooper, I'm telling you, she couldn't walk. Her legs buckled right from under her. The poor little thing was a mess. So, I took her upstairs to my apartment, and she never left. I think she's afraid to go home. And here's the weird thing: Frank isn't in the house either. He's somewhere in a hotel. They broke up a while back and he doesn't even know she's here. I've heard her talk to him on the phone, and she acts like she's at home. So that house is just sitting empty. And I don't know how to make her leave."

"Just tell her to get out. It's your apartment." Cooper took a sip of tea, made a face, and set the glass back down on the bar.

"Yeah, I know. But, really, you don't understand. She's afraid. Ever since that happened, she's jumpy. She doesn't leave the apartment—ever! And lately she's been coming down here to the bar and working. I found her mopping the kitchen floor the other day."

"Are you sleeping with her?"

"No! Cooper, what the hell's wrong with you?" Actually, Pete was *sleeping* with Violet. She was in his bed every night, and had been since that first night. But they weren't having sex, which Pete knew was what Cooper was actually asking.

"Hey! I was just asking." Cooper shrugged and turned his palms upward. "I know Violet. And she ain't exactly shy, if you know what I mean."

"Cooper, shut the hell up. You're starting to piss me off." Pete straightened, picked up his bar rag, and wiped angrily at the spot where his hands had been.

"What'd I say? I just asked a simple question. Anyone would assume that. A month and a half of living together with a woman who is separated from her husband. Come on. Why get pissed at me?"

Pete pointed at him. "You just don't understand. And there's no need to talk about her like that. Maybe she's changed."

"Doubt it. I'd watch your back if I were you, Pete. Did you hear what she did to Frank? She passed out hundreds of flyers saying he had a little pecker. She even walked right into the bank and passed them out. And did you know he got fired? Maybe that's why."

Pete's face darkened. "Cooper, maybe you better go."

"Are you serious?"

"Yeah, I am. Get out of here. I told you. You're pissing me off."

Cooper stood and shrugged. "Don't say I didn't warn you." He rose from his barstool and strode out.

Upstairs, above Bass Turds, Violet sat on Pete's couch and copied the list of items he needed for the kitchen. The first list was so sloppy. She didn't want to give that list to Pete. He'd never be able to read her handwriting. Sometimes, she missed her computer. It would have been nice to print out the list on a printer. Once in a while, Violet thought about going home and getting it. There wasn't much to do here during the day. Pete didn't even have a television in his apartment. There was one in the bar, but she hated going down there with so many people.

Violet had planned on going home after that first night, but that next day passed and when Pete came home after closing Bass Turds, Violet was already in bed, feigning sleep. As the days passed, the idea of going home seemed increasingly difficult.

One time, as a child, Violet was sick with a terrible case of the flu. With the passing of each day, the thought of going back to school seemed overwhelming. She knew there would be so much work to catch up on. And when she came back, she would feel so out of sorts, as if she didn't fit in anymore. Finally, after five days of illness, she recovered and returned to school the following week. It was a bit strange the first day, but by the second day, she was back into the routine, and it seemed silly that she had ever been worried about returning.

Now, though, the idea of returning home seemed more difficult with every passing day. She imagined scenario after scenario where she was home alone and being attacked by the man from the bar. Violet thought about how he might hide in a closet, under her bed, in the back seat of her car, or in a dark corner of the garage. She imagined him poised behind the front door as she returned home. In her dreams, he ripped at her clothes, punched her in the face, strangled her, and worse. Every night, she woke from nightmares, terrified.

Every night, it was Pete's voice and touch that calmed her. "It's okay, Violet. It's just a bad dream. You're okay. I'm here. You're safe," he would tell her, resting a tentative hand on her shoulder. Exhausted, and often soaked in sweat, she'd sink back against him, comforted by his steady presence.

She knew Pete would probably throw her out eventually, but until then, she was going to give him every reason to let her stay. She cleaned the apartment, and she had recently started cleaning the restaurant and checking his supplies. Violet was determined to be needed. She had nowhere else to go. No one wanted her.

Lately, she'd begun to feel that no one had ever wanted her; maybe ever since that terrible day when her father had been killed in the car crash. After that, her mother hadn't wanted her, it was clear. She had been so caught up in grief that having a child around only made matters worse. Violet knew she was nothing but a financial burden to her mother. In high school, it seemed like Cooper Moon wanted her, but she soon realized he slept with everyone. She was just another girl trying to make him love her. Then Frank, the school's star quarterback, came along, and the solution seemed clear: fake a pregnancy report from a doctor, marry Frank, and move to California where he was signed on to play football for USC. That short time in California seemed perfect, but then Frank had been injured. And by then, Violet actually was pregnant and it was too late. By the time Violet and Frank returned home, her mother had moved to Florida and remarried and Violet was stuck living in Frank's parents' basement until he finished his degree and started working at the bank. And Violet knew all along that if she had not lied about being pregnant, Frank never would have married her. Frank had never really wanted her either.

Violet finished writing out the list of supplies and placed it beside her on the couch cushion. Getting to her feet, she went to the front of the apartment and looked out the window at the street, searching for a dark sedan. That was how Pete had described the car of the guy who attacked her. Violet could hardly remember anything about it. Couldn't even remember if it was a car. Could have been a white pickup truck as far as she was concerned. She vaguely remembered the guy speeding off, but it was more of an impression, not truly a memory.

There was no dark sedan parked out front. Violet wished she could see into the parking lot beside the building, but there was no window on that side of the apartment. She placed a hand on the window ledge and wondered what to do with the rest of her day. Feeling dust, she withdrew her hand and stared at her fingertips. They were covered in a heavy black dust. The window ledge was filthy. So were the windows. Pleased that she had suddenly found something to do, Violet moved to the kitchen in search of glass cleaner and paper towels.

Chapter 3

October

October is a moody month. Sometimes warm and sunny, sometimes cloudy and cold. Like a fickle woman, she stands before the mirror, changing her clothes, unable to decide what to wear. She begins with light attire, longing to hold on to the languid heat of summer. But soon discards it, for although the sun still shines, a chill has settled in the air. She pulls on a gold blouse, but it still does not fit her mood. Frustrated, she searches for something more colorful. In a frantic fit of creation, she gathers brilliant swatches of crimson, gold, and fiery orange to create a stunning gown. She twirls breathtaking and aflame, like a little girl in front of a mirror, sending fragments of her finery to the ground. Then, coming to a halt, colored scraps at her feet, she gazes into the mirror with a satisfied smile. A smile that slowly fades. No, this isn't right either. In a huff, she shakes her limbs, sending a torrent of color to the ground. Finally, getting colder now, she grabs a drab brown sweater and decides to stay in for the night.

Surrounded by the brilliance of October, Cooper stood in the bed of his truck. He had soaked it down with water, squirted a generous amount of dish soap across the bed, and was scrubbing it with an old push broom. The garden hose hung over the side, the spray nozzle leaking slightly and spraying the bottom of Cooper's jeans whenever he got too close. The bed of the truck still smelled like oil. He had Ivy Miller to thank for that. He still couldn't believe the woman had soaked his tools and truck with oil. He shook his head as he scrubbed. Maybe that's what he should talk about this Sunday: revenge. How it was wrong, and how it always backfired on you. But, right now, Ivy seemed to be winning. He squirted a little more dish soap across the bed and scrubbed harder.

What in the world was he going to talk about Sunday? The enormity of the situation was beginning to sink in. How was he going to come up with something new to say every Sunday morning for the rest of his life! How was he going to do that? How could anyone do that? There were only so many topics you could talk about. Then what? He didn't see how he could last much more than another month.

Ever since TJ had mentioned him on television, the church had become a topic of conversation for the locals. The local news had even mentioned it. Cooper hoped the attention would die down soon. The little church could only hold so many people, and the first service was close to being full. He supposed, though, that a lot of those people just came the first time because they were curious. Maybe there'd be fewer people this Sunday. The thought occurred to him that perhaps no one would come at all. He scrubbed harder.

"Hey, Cooper." Sally was dressed for work and carrying her purse.

"Leaving for work?"

"In a minute. We need to talk first."

Cooper leaned on the broom and put his other hand on his hip. This couldn't be good. He hated conversations that started out this way. "What's wrong?"

Sally took a deep breath and shook her head. "Nothing's wrong. Actually, it's good news. Earlier this year, Annie told me she was moving to Philadelphia. She asked me to sort of oversee the restaurant, and she told me she'd pay me to do it. She said she'd give me ten percent of whatever she made from the restaurant, and I could still work as a waitress and make tips too."

"That sounds like a great idea, Sally! I think you should do it!"

"Yeah. I thought so too. I told her I would." Sally pushed a stray strand of hair behind her ear.

"That's great! I can't believe it!" Cooper dropped the broom and jumped from the bed of the truck. "We get this money from TJ, we might have a little weekly income from the church, and now you're going to be making extra money too! I'm so proud of you, Sally. Annie must trust you to be giving you so much responsibility. That's awesome!" He took Sally in his arms and hugged her.

Sally hugged back briefly and then pulled away. "Well, this is the thing. Cooper, I came home to tell you about this right away, but you were so focused on the church, and it never seemed to be the right time."

"I don't understand."

"Cooper, she came to me in May. I've been doing this for months."

"May?"

Sally nodded.

"Why didn't you tell me?"

"It just never seemed to be the right time, I guess."

"Wait. That means you have been making more money since May?"

"Yes. And there's more good news."

"What?"

"Annie has decided to sell the restaurant. And I can buy it if I can just come up with fifteen thousand dollars down. That's a great deal. Originally, she wanted twenty. But, since

I am the one buying it, she said she'd let me put fifteen down. Now that we have the money from TJ, we could put down even more than that. We could...."

"We can't use the money from TJ to buy the diner."

"I have some money saved too."

"How much?"

"Almost three thousand dollars."

Cooper's mouth fell open. "Let me get this straight." He ran his hand through his hair, exhaled, and then took a deep breath. "We've been broke all year. I've been cutting firewood and working at the Millers and have been stressed out the entire year and you have three grand saved? Are you serious?"

"Cooper, this is the opportunity of a lifetime. We could own the diner! I could run it. I already have been since May, and our sales are up by almost ten percent already! I was thinking, we could add on to the diner. You could build a family dining room to the left of the entrance door, right into the parking lot. We could put nice tables in there and hardwood floors. We could rent it out for parties and we could make a killing. Remember how packed the diner was the night TJ won Warrior? We could do that kind of stuff all the time."

"We can't use TJ's money on the diner! He gave it to me for the church."

"It isn't his money now. It's ours. And he didn't say you *had* to use it on the church. I bet he'd be fine with the idea of us buying the diner. Ask him if you want. Cooper! We could own our own business!"

"I do own my own business, Sally. I have a church." Cooper could feel his arms beginning to shake.

"No. I mean a real business—one that could make us enough money to live on. Enough to even build a house eventually. Not that little bit you're going to get from the church every week. Cooper, that isn't even enough to buy groceries. Get real. If it wasn't for TJ, you never would have even finished it!"

"And if it wasn't for TJ's money, you wouldn't be able to buy the diner!"

"Yes I could!"

"You only have three grand!"

"I could borrow the rest."

"Well, why don't you just go ahead and do that. Or have you already done that and not told me?"

"I can't believe you just said that. How many things have you not told me since we've been together? All I did was save some money for us!" Sally turned her back on him and stomped to her car. She opened the door, threw her purse onto the passenger seat, and got in.

Cooper followed. Holding the car door to prevent her from closing it, he said, "No, Sally, you lied to me when I asked you about money. Over and over again. You were saving money and telling me we were broke. My truck needed work, I needed to buy tools, and all the time you said we were broke."

Sally put the key in the ignition and started the car. "You know, it wouldn't kill you to get off your ass and get a real job! Do you know how many hours a week I work? While you're sitting here on your ass reading a Bible, your wife is out working to support you! What happened to the man being the head of the household? Isn't that somewhere in your precious Bible?" Sally put the car in reverse and stomped down on the gas, jerking the door from Cooper's hands and throwing up gravel in the process. When she hit the road, she slammed the door shut and yelled through the window. "I can get a loan from the bank!"

Sally hit the gas, and gravel pinged against the undercarriage of the car as she sped away.

"Good luck with that!" Cooper ran into the road and yelled as she made her speedy retreat.

He wanted her to come back. He wanted to yell at her, to tell her how wrong she was, tell her how mad he was. She couldn't just drop a bomb on him like this and leave! "Damn it!" he shouted after her. He turned around, fists clenched, heart pumping wildly. He kicked the mailbox post, a stout 4 x 4 that didn't give much, only leaned slightly. The mailbox door popped open and Cooper kicked the post again, although the second kick lacked the power of the first. His toes were already hurting. Cooper reached out and slammed the mailbox shut. The door popped back open. "Piece of shit!" Cooper yelled. Inside were a few envelopes. Cooper drew them out and closed the door. It stayed shut.

He threw the mail onto his truck seat, threw the broom across the yard, and jerked the hose from the side of his truck, tossing it back toward the house. He needed to drive.

Cooper sped through the country roads with no destination in mind. He couldn't believe it. How could Sally have been lying to him for so long? For as long as they had been together, ever since they met in school, Sally had never lied to him. Never. Not once. At least, not that he knew of. What else could she be hiding? He suddenly felt so stupid, even embarrassed. Here he was, walking around broke while she had thousands of dollars stuffed in her purse, or wherever she kept it.

He wondered who else knew about this besides Sally and Annie. Probably everybody at the diner. No doubt they were all laughing at him behind his back. And where did she keep all of that money? Could she have put it in the bank? He never checked the balance on either of their accounts. Never looked at the checkbook. What was the point? They had been broke for so long it was just depressing to look at the numbers. Sally had always been the one who paid the bills. Maybe she had money in the bank he didn't even know about. Cooper tried to remember where he had put the receipt the teller had given him yesterday when he'd deposited TJ's check. As he drove, he checked his pants pockets. They were empty. If Sally had been depositing money in the bank, it would show on the balance of their savings account—unless she had started her own! Could she have done that too, behind his back? Did Frank Collette know about this? Maybe that was why Frank and Sally were suddenly so chummy.

Cooper slammed the heel of his hand against the steering wheel. Frank Collette probably knew about this all along! While Cooper was in the bank begging for money to start the church, Frank probably knew all about Sally's hidden savings account! Frank probably helped her start it, and then laughed in Cooper's face when he tried to get a loan.

Cooper drove on. By the time he realized where he was, he also realized he wasn't far from Libby Cartwright's place. He wondered if Libby was home. Only one way to find out.

(

Sally was not even five miles from home when she turned around. All of that money was hidden at home, under their mattress. Cooper was mad enough to search the house for it. Better safe than sorry. She didn't care if she was late for work; she was getting that money out of the house. Relieved to see his truck was gone, Sally parked and hurried in the direction of the trailer. The hose nozzle was leaking and a small puddle was forming by the steps. She stepped over it and went inside.

On her knees, Sally pulled the last of the money out from under the mattress. As mad as Cooper was, she wasn't taking any chances. She'd worked hard for this money. No one was going to take it from her. With every dollar, she was closer to building a house for them, to getting out of this mobile home. Now, though, she wondered, would the money be better spent buying the diner? If she could buy the diner, they'd definitely have the kind of income required to build a house.

Sally looked down at the money piled on the carpet. Now where should she put it? In her purse? Cooper never looked there, but she hated carrying that kind of money around with her. Then she remembered the office safe at the diner. The only other person who had a key was Annie, and she was in Philadelphia, so that seemed like a pretty safe choice. Sally picked up the money, stacked it neatly, and dropped it into her purse. She'd keep it locked in the office at the diner from now on. Maybe she'd wrap a rubber band around it to keep it from getting mixed up with diner money.

As Sally drove back to work, her purse safely beside her on the passenger seat, she had a sinking feeling. She tried to push it away, but it wouldn't budge. She hadn't passed Cooper's truck on the road as she'd driven back, which meant he must have left home and turned away from town. Sally was just a few blocks away from the diner when she pulled into the driveway of a gas station and turned around. She had to know.

Within minutes, she was driving past Libby Cartwright's house. Cooper didn't even know that Sally knew where Libby lived. It wasn't too hard to figure out. She knew what kind of truck Libby drove, too. Sally had seen it drive past their house on more than one occasion.

Please, please, don't be there, Sally thought as she slowly drove past Libby's double-wide. She didn't want to see it. She hoped she would not. But there it was, plain as day. Cooper's truck parked in Libby's driveway. Sally didn't even bother to cry. She didn't have the energy.

(

Inside Libby's double-wide, Cooper was in the middle of a rant. "I can't believe she did this to me. I can't believe Sally would hide something like this from me!"

Libby did not bother to point out that Cooper had kept plenty from Sally over the years, including sleeping with her. Right now, she was just thrilled he was here. He was fighting with Sally and he had come to her for comfort—for the first time ever. Libby tried hard to look serious as she watched him pace back and forth, waving those gorgeous arms as he talked. In truth, she was giddy. She had to work hard to keep from laughing aloud. As he talked, she looked at his mouth and thought about kissing him. She nodded and frowned, and tried to play the concerned friend, but in reality, she heard little of what he was saying. Libby had one goal in mind—to get him down the hall and into the bedroom. It had been such a long time.

Chapter 4

October

Sally locked her money in the small safe in the diner's office. She still wasn't used to having a key to the office and the combination for the safe, but she was getting a lot more used to it. And once she was the owner, it would be her office and her safe. Sally liked the sound of that, although, at that moment, the possibility seemed unlikely.

Sally had always kept the key on her keychain, but with so much money in the safe, that made her nervous. Slipping the key from her keychain, she gazed around the office. Maybe she could hide it somewhere. It would be better, however, if she could always have the key with her. Her eyes paused on a pair of old tennis shoes she kept in the office. She'd brought them in with the intention of walking on her lunch hour, but that had never happened. By the time her lunch hour came around, all she ever wanted to do was get off her feet, not go for a walk. She crossed the room, pulled a shoestring from one of the shoes, and slipped the key onto it, tying a knot to form a sort of necklace. Placing the shoestring around her neck, she then pulled at her uniform collar until the string was hidden. She didn't want to take any chances, and this was easier than carrying keys in her pocket.

With a glance at the clock, she left the office and went into the diner, greeting customers with a smile. The place was full; that was always good. Lucy was refilling someone's coffee. The new waitress was taking an order. Things were going well—at least in the diner.

"Hey, how about a cup of coffee?"

Sally turned to find Frank Collette at the far end of the counter, the place Cooper usually sat.

Sally grabbed the pot of coffee and strode over. "Hey, Frank. How are you?" She poured coffee into a cup.

"I'm fine. How are you? Pretty happy, I'd guess." He leaned forward and whispered, "You are about to be a very successful business owner!"

Sally rolled her eyes. "Yeah, right. That doesn't seem very likely right now."

"Why not?"

Sally lowered her voice. "I shared the idea with Cooper. Told him how I've been running the diner while Annie's been away. Told him she wanted to sell it to me and that we only needed fifteen thousand dollars."

"And?"

"Let's just say he didn't like the idea." Sally watched as Lucy refilled drinks at one of the booths. "And, Frank, it doesn't make any sense at all. Cooper just deposited fifty thousand dollars into the bank. We could buy the diner now. That would be a huge down payment!"

"When did he make that deposit?"

"Yesterday. But it doesn't matter. He doesn't care what I want." Sally was not prone to tears, but she could feel them threatening. She blinked and swallowed hard in an effort to thwart them.

Frank shook his head. "You know, I probably shouldn't be saying this, but it's almost as if he doesn't want you to succeed."

Sally's brow furrowed. "But ... that doesn't make sense."

Frank shrugged. "Maybe not. I could be wrong. Funny, isn't it? If things had been a little different in high school, you and I could have ended up married."

Sally laughed and turned her body to face him. "Yeah, right! Like you even knew I existed in high school."

Frank blinked. "Are you kidding? I was crazy about you. But you were so hooked on Cooper, you never even looked in my direction."

Sally's mouth fell open. "You were crazy about me?"

"Hell yeah! You didn't know that?"

"Noooo. I didn't know that."

Frank shrugged. "It's true."

Was it possible? Frank Collette, the star quarterback and most popular guy in school, was crazy about her in school? Of course, Sally had her own little crush on him at one point, as did every other girl in school. But he had ended up with Violet, at least until they had recently split. Frank Collette could have been *her* boyfriend? The notion was just too much to take in. Was it possible? Could she have been so enraptured with Cooper that she never noticed? For some reason, the thought brought more tears to the surface. She swallowed hard.

(

Libby watched as Cooper paced back and forth, still ranting. He stopped in the middle of the room and turned to face her. "I just can't believe it! Do you know how many times I told her I needed money for lumber, or to fix my truck? And all the time, she had the money! If TJ hadn't helped me out, the church still wouldn't be finished!"

Libby crossed the room and placed a hand on Cooper's shoulder. "I'm sorry, Cooper. It's not fair. It's really not." Her voice softened and grew husky. "Sometimes I don't think Sally understands you." She resisted the temptation to add, *not like I do.* Her hand moved lightly over his shoulder. "You worked so hard on the church. It's just not fair of her to hold out on you like that." Libby leaned closer and her gaze moved to his mouth. She wanted him so much she ached. Slowly, she tilted her head up, parted her lips.

She was jolted by a gentle shove from Cooper.

"What the hell, Libby! I'm trying to talk to you. Can't you see that? I've got a problem here!"

Libby blinked, confused. "I was just…"

"Yeah, I know what you were doing." Cooper stomped to the door.

"Cooper!" Libby grabbed his arm. "I was just trying to help."

He shook free from her hand and marched out of the house.

"Cooper!" Libby held the door open and yelled after him.

He did not turn around.

Libby Cartwright watched until his truck roared out of sight.

(

Frank reached forward slowly. This was a big moment. He didn't want to blow it. He placed his hand on Sally's arm. "Don't cry, Sally. It will be all right. You can still get the diner. I can get you a loan through the bank. No problem at all. You can count on me. The bank is always happy to invest in successful local businesses. And I've got some pull there. This diner can still be yours if you want it."

"You think so?"

"I'm positive. You just have to believe in yourself. I believe in you."

Sally reached out and placed her hand on top of Frank's, just for a moment. "Thanks, Frank. I appreciate it."

This sure is easier than burning down the church, Frank thought to himself, *and a lot more effective.* "Why don't we get together tonight? You can fill out the loan papers. It won't take long."

"I don't know…"

"Hey, just fill them out. You don't have to take the money if you don't want it. Just apply for the loan and see what happens.

Sally nodded. "Okay. Let's do it." She removed her hand from Frank's and pulled away.

"You bet," Frank said with a smile.

Later that night, Frank and Sally sat in the dimly lit office of Annie's Diner. It was after hours, and the diner was otherwise dark.

Sally stared down at the loan application papers. "I don't know why I'm so nervous. It's silly. This diner is such a great deal. I'll never get this kind of opportunity again."

"Think about it this way, Sally—you aren't getting a loan for the diner. You are actually only getting a fifteen thousand dollar loan so you can give it to Annie to get started on the land contract. It's not like you're borrowing the entire amount. People borrow more than this to buy a car."

"Yes. You're right. It's just … fifteen thousand dollars seems like so much. But you're sure the bank will give me the loan? You said you could arrange it, right?"

"I'm certain of it. They value my opinion, and they are always happy to invest in the community. It just makes good business sense."

Sally chewed her bottom lip and stared down at the papers.

"Sally," Frank put his hand on her arm. "I don't want you to do anything that makes you uncomfortable. I believe in you. And I think you're right. This diner is a real moneymaker, but I'd never want you to do anything that didn't feel right." Frank's voice was low and soft. He looked into her eyes and smiled. "Maybe you should think about it a little more. Not everybody is cut out to own their own business."

Sally pulled open the desk drawer and withdrew a pen. "Show me where to sign."

Frank smiled and pointed to the appropriate lines.

"How long do you think it will take to get the money? I want to call Annie and tell her."

"Probably about a week," Frank assured her, a smile slowly spreading across his face as he folded the signed papers.

(

Lucy Miller was almost home when she realized she had left her cell phone in her jacket pocket, and her jacket was hanging on a hook near the back door of the diner. She had to work tomorrow, but she hated being without her cell phone all night. Lucy drove around the building and pulled into the employee parking lot. Sally's car was still there, and so was another car Lucy did not recognize. She got out of the car and crept up to the back door, opening it slowly. A light and voices were coming from the office. Lucy stood in the doorway and listened for a moment, trying to identify the man's voice. Frank Collette! Sally was in the office alone, at night, with Frank Collette? Gently closing the door, Lucy rushed back to her car, got in, and pulled out of the lot. She could live without her cell phone tonight after all.

Reaching over, she grabbed a CD from the pile of them scattered on her seat and inserted it into the CD player, skipping to her new favorite song. It was the song she had played for Cooper when he'd been in her car. True, he had only been in her car because he'd needed a ride home, and she wasn't sure how much of the song he had even heard, but soon it would be their song. Soon enough, he'd find out about Sally and Frank, and Lucy would be there to console him. It was only a matter of time.

She pushed the repeat button and turned up the volume. Smiling, Lucy sang all the way home.

(

Cooper pulled into his driveway and sighed. He had hoped to see Sally's car there. He wondered where she was. He picked the mail up from the truck seat, got out of the truck and slammed the door shut. It had to be after eleven by now. Even if Sally worked until closing, she should have been home.

He leaned against the bed of his pickup, which still smelled like oil. Then he walked to the road, slapping the mail against his thigh with each step. The cold night air hinted at winter's approach. Halloween had not yet arrived and Cooper wondered whether the kids would be trick or treating in snow. It happened once in a while. In Michigan, you could never tell. Usually, the snow didn't last, but it could make Halloween unpleasant. Cooper stood in the middle of the road and wondered what to do. Maybe he'd walk down to the church, sweep the floor or something. Headlights on the road diverted his attention. It had to be Sally; no one else lived this far down. Cooper sighed in relief. Until that moment, he hadn't realized he was worried she might not come home at all.

Sally drove past Cooper, pulled into the driveway, and parked. Either she hadn't seen him, which was unlikely, or she was ignoring him.

"Hey." Cooper walked up the gravel driveway and called out to Sally as she exited her car.

She ignored him and went inside. Before Cooper even reached the trailer, he saw the light flicker on in the bathroom. He imagined Sally locking the door behind her to take a shower. She'd be in bed with a towel still wrapped around her head within ten minutes.

A hissing sound caught his attention. He'd forgotten to

turn off the hose, and a small stream arched from a leak in the pipe. As Cooper turned the water off, he could hear Sally inside. *Well, let her be that way,* he thought as he stepped over the muddy spot and entered the trailer. He'd watch TV for a while. Maybe he could find a good movie. Maybe he'd even sleep on the couch, although the thought of that was not too appealing. Every time Cooper slept on it, his back ached the next morning.

Cooper sat on the couch and tossed the mail onto the coffee table. As it slid across, one of the envelopes caught his attention. He pulled it from under the electric bill. It was hand addressed to him. Brows furrowed, he flipped it over, ripped open the seal, and pulled out the sheet of white paper inside.

Send $20,000 in cash to me or I am going to the press and telling them about us. I have photos and I will use them. If I don't have the money within one week, you will be in the news. Violet Collette

There was also a P.O. box number. Cooper read the note again, and then a third time. He flipped it over to see if anything was written on the back. Nothing. He looked inside the envelope again. It was empty. Slowly, he slid the letter back into the envelope. Violet Collette was blackmailing him? He couldn't believe it. It seemed so out of character for her. But then, she had passed that note around town about Frank's pecker, which seemed out of character too. He had just seen her at Bass Turds yesterday. She had looked right at him and said hi! And all the while, this was waiting for him in the mail.

Down the hall, he heard the bathroom door open. He hurriedly jammed the letter under one of the couch cushions. The bedroom door closed. Cooper sat still and listened for a couple more minutes. Evidently, Sally was going to bed without talking to him. Cooper reached under the cushion and pulled the letter back out. He folded it a few times, stuck it into the back pocket of his jeans, grabbed the remote, and settled back into the couch. Turning on the television, he stared at the screen, not seeing a thing.

Chapter 5

October

Jake rushed as he carried the remaining baby items to the basement. It was Saturday morning, and TJ had told him the furniture store would be delivering the bed for the nurse at ten. Melody, at the grocery store, had no idea Clara's nurse was moving in today. She also had no idea that her beloved purchases from Baby Stuff were presently being stacked in a corner of the basement.

Jake deposited an armload of blankets, clothes, and stuffed animals into the crib and hurried back up the steps. He had to do it. He didn't have any other choice. His mother was getting worse and they needed a bedroom for Clara's nurse much more than they needed an empty room for a baby that did not exist. At this point, Jake was pretty sure that baby would never exist. Obviously, there was something wrong with Melody and she couldn't get pregnant. Eventually, she'd accept that fact. Or, at least, that is what Jake told himself. He wasn't sure. He sometimes wondered if she were losing her mind. Then again, he was the one having anxiety attacks. He grabbed the vacuum sweeper from the closet, plugged it in, and pushed it around the room, all the while rehearsing his speech to Melody. He needed to be convincing.

"What are you doing?"

Startled, Jake turned to see his brother TJ standing in the doorway of the bedroom.

Jake turned off the sweeper, unplugged it, and then retracted the cord. "What does it look like? I'm training for the Olympics."

"Funny. How are you going to hear the furniture delivery people with that thing running? I hope you didn't miss them."

"No. I've only been running it for a couple of minutes." Jake returned the sweeper to the closet and headed for the kitchen.

TJ followed. "Here. I've got something for you."

Jake pulled a Pepsi from the refrigerator. "You want one?"

TJ shook his head.

"What's this?" Jake asked as TJ handed him a check.

"It's every penny I ever borrowed from you, plus interest."

Jake glanced down at the check. "Holy shit, TJ! This is twenty thousand dollars!"

"Yeah. I added a little extra. Figured there was probably stuff I forgot along the way."

"You don't have to do this." Jake leaned against the counter, staring down at the check in disbelief.

"Yes, I do. I told you I would. Every time I asked you for money, I told you I would pay you back."

"Yeah, but I never thought you would."

"Thanks for believing in me."

"Come on, TJ. You know what I mean. Hell, no one ever thought you'd win Warrior. The odds were huge. You can't blame me for that."

"Yeah, I guess." TJ pulled an apple from the refrigerator and took a bite. "Where'd you put all the baby stuff?" he asked in between chews.

"In the basement."

"What'd Melody say about you doing that?"

"She doesn't know yet."

"You didn't tell her?"

Jake shook his head.

"Where is she? And where's Mom and the nurse?"

"They all went to the grocery store. TJ, really, I can't take this check." He slid it over the counter to his brother.

"Yes, you can. What good is it to win all of this money if I can't help my family out? You've given me lots of money over the years. I'm just paying you back."

"Not this much." Jake looked back down at the check. "It's so weird, you writing me a check for twenty thousand dollars."

"Ha! You're telling me! I didn't even have a checking account. The woman at the bank had to show me how to write out a check!"

The doorbell interrupted.

"Must be the furniture people," TJ said.

Less than an hour later, once the new furniture was in place, Clara, the nurse, and Melody arrived home. The nurse, as everyone referred to her, was actually named Josephine, but her friends called her Jo. Her clients rarely used her name at all. She commanded that kind of respect—and fear.

A tall black woman, she was overweight by today's standards and stronger than most men. Her voice always seemed hoarse, as if she spent a lot of time yelling, which she did not. Josephine seldom raised her voice; she did not have to. Her face was attractive, but uninviting. High cheekbones and eyes the color of milk chocolate, were positioned over full lips that might have been sensuous had they not always been pressed firmly together. Josephine faced the world jaw first, squelching any approach, discouraging casual conversation.

She had a curvaceous body, despite the extra pounds, but worked hard to hide it behind loose-fitting clothes: cheap black pants with a stretch waistband, baggy tee shirts in shades of grey, and always an extra layer of a lightweight, unbuttoned long-sleeved shirt in the summer or a sweater in the winter, also usually grey or black. It was as if she were in perpetual mourning.

All three women carried the grocery bags directly into the kitchen. TJ and Jake sat in the living room and exchanged looks.

"I think I'm going to go now," TJ stood.

"Coward! You can't just leave without saying hi to Mom."

TJ frowned. "I'll stick around long enough to say hi to Mom, but I'm not getting in the middle of this," he whispered.

"Would you please get the rest of the groceries out of the car?" Melody asked Josephine.

"No. I wasn't hired to carry groceries."

"I said please."

"Doesn't change the facts. Please or no please, I was hired to care for your mother-in-law, not to tote groceries."

Melody looked at Jake.

He said nothing.

"Fine! I'll get the freakin' groceries!" Melody stomped out the door.

Jake followed her. Within minutes, he and Melody returned and dumped the rest of the groceries on the kitchen counter.

"That nurse is a pain in the ass. I don't like her. I think we should fire her," Melody whispered to Jake as she withdrew groceries from the bags and placed them on the counter.

"She's moving in, she's going to be working full time, living with us," he said all in one breath, hoping to lessen the blow.

"What! How are we going to pay for that?"

"TJ is paying for everything."

"And where is she going to sleep?"

Jake opened his mouth but found no words.

"No!" Melody shouted, spinning on her heel and running from the kitchen. She ran the few steps down the hall to the baby's room. "No!" she screamed as soon as she saw the room, which contained only a new bed. "Where's the baby's things?"

"In the basement. It's only temporary. Just for a while, Mel."

Melody sprinted toward the basement and bounded down the steps.

Jake did not follow.

"No! No!" she screamed so loudly that everyone in the house heard.

"What in the world is Melody shouting about?" Clara asked from the living room.

"No tellin'. That woman is always just on the verge of hysteria. Wind must of blown in the wrong direction." Josephine settled into a chair and sighed. "You ask me, she could use some medication."

TJ sat beside his mother on the couch and said nothing.

"What is she yelling about, TJ?" Clara asked.

"I'm not sure, Ma."

"Probably that I'm moving into that empty bedroom. That would be my guess," Josephine said.

"You're moving in with us?" Clara asked.

Josephine leaned in Clara's direction and patted her on the knee. "I sure am. I thought it would be nice. It will give us a chance to get to know each other better."

"Does Jake know about this?" Clara asked.

"Sure, Honey. He invited me to stay. It was his idea."

"Are you going to be paying rent? I mean, I like you and all, but Jake is a policeman. He doesn't make a lot of money and I expect you aren't a light eater."

Josephine threw her head back and laughed. "Well, a truer word was never spoken. I do like my food! But we have it all worked out. It will be real nice for all of us."

Melody stormed into the living room with Jake following. "Was this your idea, TJ?"

"No. Well, sorta. I mean, Jake and I decided it was needed. Someone to be here full time. I just offered to pay for it."

"Well, isn't that just wonderful! I go to the grocery store and when I come back all of my baby's things are thrown into the basement."

"I didn't throw them, Melody," Jake said.

"Why can't *she* stay in the basement?" Melody pointed to Josephine.

"*She* don't sleep in basements," Josephine replied.

"Melody, she can't sleep in the basement. She has to be close to Mom," Jake said.

"Why does she have to be close to me?" Clara asked.

"Why don't we go for a walk, Clara?" Josephine asked. "Come on. The sun is shining. Let's get out of this house and go for a walk." Josephine got to her feet and held her hand out to Clara.

Clara frowned for a moment and then glanced at Jake, and then at TJ. She took in a deep breath and sighed. "Okay. Fine. Better than sitting here. This place has become a zoo. All this screaming and people moving in and out." She climbed to her feet, ignoring Josephine's outstretched hand. "Well, don't just stand there with your hand stuck out. Let's go," she told the nurse, and shuffled for the coat closet.

After the front door closed, Melody slumped down in the chair Josephine had been occupying and Jake joined TJ on the couch. She focused on TJ. "TJ, can't you see what's happening? I'm being pushed out of my own home. Soon, I'll be in the basement too."

"No, Mel, no," Jake said. "You aren't being pushed out. It's just crazy right now. That's all. Having the nurse here will help. You'll see. It will free up your time. You won't have to worry about Mom."

"Well, isn't that just a huge weight off of my shoulders? And all I have to do is let some stranger live in my house twenty-four hours a day. And give up my baby's bedroom. That's all. Sounds just wonderful. Freakin' wonderful." She turned back to TJ. "TJ, can't you see what I'm talking about? You understand, don't you? Why can't you buy a house and take Clara and the nurse? This is a small house. When the baby gets here, there won't be enough room for all of us. Surely, you can see that."

Jake tried to interrupt. "Melody, you're not pregnant."

Melody ignored him. "TJ, please."

TJ looked back and forth between Jake and Melody and then back to Jake. "You know, Jake, maybe Melody has a point. I could buy a house. When I'm not sleeping here on the couch, I'm still sleeping in the church, on a cot. It doesn't make much sense. Maybe I should be looking for a house."

"Yes!" Melody said. "Then everything will be back to normal."

TJ and Jake exchanged looks but said nothing.

(

Cooper's hands shook as he taped the cardboard box shut with a roll of duct tape he kept in his glove compartment. He had already written the P.O. box address on it. Now all he had to do was drop it off at the post office before five. He stared at the box. Twenty grand. Gone. Just like that.

Since receiving the note, he had thought of little else. Shock was followed by outrage. Then fear crept in. What if Violet did give naked photos of them together to the press? It would mean the end of his church. It might mean the end of his marriage. Sally was still mad at him. He didn't need this. Then fury set in. Who the hell did she think she was dealing with? He wasn't paying her any money! She probably didn't even have any photos. She was probably bluffing. He'd never seen any camera, but, of course, cameras were so small now. He could have missed a camera. Maybe she filmed them together. Who knew? She could easily get photos from that, he supposed. He imagined a video of him and Violet playing on the local news with the dirty parts blacked out or all fuzzy. The thought cooled his outrage.

Then resignation ground him down. Hell, what difference did it make? It wasn't like he had to work for the money. TJ had given it to him. Maybe he owed Violet something. He'd heard her marriage to Frank had ended; maybe he had a hand in that. He thought of Violet living above Pete's bar. Maybe she needed the money now that she was split from Frank. After a while, he started thinking maybe it wasn't such a bad thing, giving Violet this money. Maybe it'd help her make a new start. Everyone was entitled to a new start.

He dropped the box off at the post office and headed straight to Bass Turds, settling himself in his usual spot at the bar. Serving another customer, Pete glanced in his direction but said nothing. Cooper had not returned since he and Pete had discussed Violet, and Pete had told him to leave.

After a few minutes, Pete came to the end of the bar.

"Hey, Pete."

"Cooper."

"Pete, I feel bad about the last time I was in here. I'm sorry. I shouldn't have said anything about Violet. You know, I haven't talked to her in months. I don't even know her anymore. I changed, so why shouldn't I give Violet the benefit of the doubt? Maybe she has changed too. I'm sorry."

"Aw, hell Cooper. I don't blame you. Honestly, I don't know what to think about her either. Let's just let the whole thing drop."

"Sounds good to me. Is she around?"

"Upstairs. Sometimes she doesn't come down at all." Pete frowned. "For days at a time. You want something to eat or drink?"

"Yeah. Haven't ate all day. How about a burger and fries, but just give me a water to drink."

"With lemon?"

"Sure, why not? Might as well live it up." How was he going to talk to Violet about this blackmail thing with Pete here? He didn't want Pete to know about the letter. He didn't want anyone to know. Cooper didn't need this kind of publicity. If he could just talk to her, he'd tell her he mailed the money and it was okay. He wasn't mad. He hoped it would help her get a new start.

He hung around Bass Turds for a couple of hours, eating and talking to Pete, but he never did see Violet.

Chapter 6

October

Sally glanced at the clock again. She had opened the diner hundreds of times over the years, but never as the owner.

Thanks to Frank, Annie had the fifteen-thousand-dollar down payment and Sally had signed the land contract. She was surprised by how easy it was. She didn't even have to go to the bank. Frank took care of everything. The diner was hers! In two years, she had the option to buy. If all went as she expected, that is exactly what she would do. Her first payment was due in less than one month. Biting the skin on her bottom lip, she scanned the diner. The floor was mopped, ketchup and mustard bottles were filled and in place, the counter was clean, the cooks were already cooking, her waitresses were here. Taking a deep breath, Sally crossed the room, flipped the sign in the window to "Open" and unlocked the door. Five minutes early.

Cooper carried the sign down the sidewalk. He had planned to do this before the diner opened, but he had fallen back to sleep after Sally had left this morning. He hoped it was a good idea. He wasn't certain. Sally seemed so strange lately, he wasn't sure how'd she react.

He walked in less than a minute after Sally unlocked the door. "I got something for you," he told Sally.

"What's that?"

Cooper tried to keep his body between Sally and the sign, so she wouldn't see it. Walking over to a wall, he plugged the sign in, flipped the switch, and turned it around. In purple neon gleamed a huge heart, over three feet tall and wide, with *Sally's Diner* written across it. Under the heart, in red neon, was the word *Open*.

"And look." Cooper flipped a switch on the back of the sign and the red *Open* went dark. "You can turn it off and on instead of flipping that little sign in the door. And I've got a guy coming today to repaint the sign over the front of the building. It will have your name on it before noon."

"Why a heart?" Sally asked.

Cooper smiled at her and swallowed. "Because I love you. And while you're working here, every time you look over at this sign in the window, I want you to remember that."

Sally sighed. "Cooper." She put her hands on her hips and tried to remember she was mad at him.

Cooper set the sign down and leaned it against the wall. Crossing the short distance between them, he pulled her into his arms and gazed into her eyes. "Sally, I don't know what's wrong. And I don't know what you've been thinking these last couple of months, but I miss you. I miss the way we used to be. I miss you coming home from the diner and telling me about your night. I miss making love to you."

Sally tried to pull away, but he would not release his grip.

"Sally. Look at me. I'm telling you, I don't know what you are thinking, but there is nothing going on between me and Libby or anyone else. I haven't cheated on you since before I believed in God, back in April. I'm telling you the truth. I believe in God now, and I'm telling you, God strike me dead right now if I'm lying to you, I've been faithful

since last spring. I'll never be unfaithful again. I promise."
He kissed her before she could answer.

Sally stiffened, but in just seconds, she relaxed against
his body, welcoming his kiss and his embrace. What choice
did she have? For months she had suspected he was sleeping
with Libby Cartwright again, ever since she'd found that
note in his jacket pocket. But that didn't prove anything. She
had no way of knowing how old the note was. Maybe it had
been there for a long time. Sally had to decide: believe
Cooper, or continue to withdraw from him for something he
may not be guilty of? In that moment, she decided. She
would believe him. What choice did she have?

The sound of someone entering the diner broke their
embrace.

"Oh. Hi, Frank." Sally smoothed her hair back into
place. "Cooper bought me a sign. Look!" She pointed at the
sign.

"Purple, huh?" Frank said.

"Yeah. It's Sally's favorite color," Cooper said,
standing straighter and turning to face Frank.

Frank nodded. "Well, that's sure purple."

"Nothing gets past you, Frank," Cooper said. He
unplugged the sign. "I'll get this hung up for you before the
customers start coming," he told Sally.

"What do I look like?" Frank asked. "I'm a customer."

"Go ahead and have a seat, Frank. I'll get you some
coffee," Sally said, and disappeared into the kitchen.

Cooper ignored Frank at the counter and hung the sign
in the front window.

As customers trickled in, most commented on the sign.
It was a hit with the ladies, or perhaps it was just an excuse
to compliment Cooper. Either way, Cooper was feeling
pretty good about his decision to have the sign made.

After hanging the sign, Cooper took his usual spot at the
counter. When Frank got up to use the restroom, Cooper
asked, "What's with Collette? He's been giving me dirty

looks, but he's awfully friendly with you. What's with that?"

"You want the usual?"

"Yeah. But what's with him?"

"I don't know. Ask him. No, don't do that. Don't cause any trouble, Cooper. He helped me get the loan for the down payment to Annie. Without him, I probably never would have got this place. Be nice." Leaning over, she kissed him on the cheek. "And I love the sign. Thank you."

Cooper smiled. "I thought you'd like it," he told her as she returned to the kitchen. He watched her swaying hips as she walked away, and Sally smiled, knowing he would.

Later that night, TJ stood before the bathroom mirror in Jake's house. A hatchet was lodged into his skull and the surrounding hair was wet and matted with blood. More blood ran down the side of his face. He stepped back and squinted at his image, turning his head to the right and then to the left. *Maybe just a little more blood around the hatchet*, he thought. He held a small white bottle over his head and gave it a squeeze. Fake blood poured out and he squeezed the bottle until it was empty. "There. That's better," he said, satisfied. Now all he needed was some sort of old shirt. Maybe one with holes in it.

"Hey, Ma, do you know if Jake has any old shirts around here anywhere?" he asked as he entered the living room.

Clara was sitting on the couch. Josephine was nearby, dumping small candy bars into a large bowl for the trick or treaters who would soon arrive. Josephine looked up and smiled.

Clara looked up and screamed, "TJ! TJ! TJ!" Her hand flew to her mouth and she pulled back against the couch.

Stunned, it was a moment before TJ spoke. "It's okay, Mom! I'm fine. It's Halloween, remember? This is fake. It's all fake. Fake blood. Look—a fake hatchet!" He pulled the hatchet from his head, revealing that it was attached to a thin wire headband. "See! It's just fake. For Halloween."

Clara put her hand to her chest. Her body relaxed. "You scared me. Don't ever do that again, TJ."

"I'm sorry, Ma. But it's Halloween, remember?"

"I'm not stupid. I know what Halloween is," she snapped.

"You might want to consider another costume this year." Josephine dumped the last bag of candy into the bowl.

TJ looked at her in question, but suddenly understood. An hour later, the same thing could happen.

The doorbell rang and TJ replaced the hatchet and grabbed the bowl of candy. "I'll get it." It was not quite dark, but the kids were already at it. TJ opened the door and leaned down, offering the bowl to two boys outside. They looked to be about six and eight and one was dressed as a cowboy and the other as a vampire. The latter slipped out his fake teeth to say, "Trick or treat!" in unison with his brother.

A woman, probably in her early thirties, insisted, "Only one piece!" as they plunged their hands into the bowl. "And what do you say?"

"Thanks!" both boys called as they dropped their candy bars into the plastic pumpkins they were carrying. Turning, they ran to the next house.

The woman smiled. "Thank you," she said. "Cool hatchet." She turned to follow the boys.

"Thanks," TJ replied. He watched as the boys crossed the road and ran to the neighbor's, their mother close behind. TJ swallowed hard. That was him and Jake, just a few years ago, it seemed. Both racing to get to the door first, Clara following. TJ wondered where his father was on all of those Halloween nights? He couldn't remember him ever going with them from door to door. Then he remembered: his father stayed home to pass out the candy. His mother walked with them until they were too old to go, every year, rain or shine. One year, she made them costumes out of their raincoats. It poured. But they stayed mostly dry and got a ton of candy. Many homeowners told them to take two or three pieces because not many kids showed up that year. When they got home, he and Jake sorted out all of the PayDay bars and gave them to Clara. They were her favorites. At first, she protested, but then she accepted them. They sat on her bedside table for more than a month, slowly dwindling as the days passed.

One day, when TJ went into her room, he noticed the candy bars were gone. He'd had the thought to buy her one, to surprise her—a full-sized one. He'd put it beside her bed when no one was looking. But he never did. Somehow, he'd just forgotten. Funny, he thought, that the memory would come to him now, in this moment. He looked down into the bowl of candy bars. No PayDays.

Back in the living room, TJ set the bowl of candy on the table. "I'm going to go take a shower." He had been planning on going to the diner to show Lucy his costume. He knew she was working tonight, and he'd heard there was some kind of Halloween party going on to celebrate Sally's opening. Now, though, it didn't seem like such a good idea.

The doorbell rang.

"Why does the doorbell keep ringing?" Clara asked.

(

By early evening, the diner was packed, and people were standing outside in a line waiting to get in. Sally, Lucy, and two other waitresses were working as fast as they could, but they couldn't keep up. Everyone seemed in a jovial mood, though. So far, no one had complained. Witches and ghosts hung from the ceiling. Fake spiderwebs were stretched across every window. The entire diner was lit with black lighting. Sally had even run an ad in the paper. *$400 in total prize money! $200 for best costume. $100 for second and third place! Kids only! Must be under 18 years of age to enter. No purchase necessary.*

She'd given a coupon for a free kid's meal to every

entrant. So far, over fifty percent of her entrants stayed to eat—with their parents. Once they saw the decorations, they wanted to stay. Initially, Sally had anticipated losing some money on this promotion, but from the looks of it, she was going to more than cover her expenses.

Lucy pushed through the crowd, balancing four plates of food. She was working like a dog tonight, but she had to admit it was kind of fun. To top it off, she was making killer tips. She wasn't sure how she felt about Sally being her new boss, but so far, so good.

She was dressed like a pirate wench—at least that was the look she was going for—in a black wig, an off-the-shoulder dress, and black fishnet stockings. She didn't imagine pirate wenches had worn fishnet, but her legs looked great in them, so she couldn't resist. She would have liked to show a little cleavage, too, but that was impossible on a couple of counts. First, Sally would never have let her, not during a Halloween party for kids. Second, she didn't really have any cleavage, not even with the most ambitious of push-up bras. Oh well, you couldn't have everything. Her legs did look great.

Lucy smiled and placed the food on the table, much to the delight of the two children, one dressed as a spider, and the other, a fairy princess. Each of them grabbed for French fries as soon as the plates hit the table.

"Careful! They're hot," Lucy told them before leaving the table.

Peering through the window, she wondered if Cooper would stop by tonight. He'd been in this morning to drop off the sign, but she had missed him. *Maybe he'll come in tonight*, she thought. She sure wished he could see her in this outfit.

After closing, Sally drove home with her shoes off. Her feet were killing her. For the first time, she hadn't closed out; she was too tired. Instead, she had dumped the cash register drawer in the office, locked it, and left. She would go in early tomorrow and do it. Her feet hurt, her back hurt, and her legs throbbed. Sally wondered if she were coming down with something. She was never this tired. But owning the diner was sure different from just working there. It was a great night, way beyond her expectations, but so much rested on her shoulders now. Sometimes, the weight was crushing; tonight had been of those nights.

Maybe she wasn't cut out to be a business owner. Of course, when Annie was running the place, she wasn't also waiting on customers. Sometimes it all felt like too much. She was having a hard time relaxing lately. Sleep held no respite because she even dreamed about the diner. Sometimes, she dreamed she dropped food on customers; other times, that she was naked while serving, only she didn't know it. All of the customers pointed at her and laughed, but she didn't know why. Sometimes, she dreamed that Cooper and Libby were making love in one of the booths while she served food to customers.

As she turned down her road, the full yellow moon revealed itself. Centered directly above the tree-lined road, it was brilliant with fall color, even in the dark. Sally slowed down and leaned forward to gaze at the moon through her windshield. It was gorgeous. She applied the brakes, stopping the car in the middle of the road. Putting it in park, she then got out and stood beside it, leaning on the roof and holding the door open.

A whispering breeze rustled through the trees and blew a few loose leaves across the road in front of her. Yellow leaves pirouetting to the road. *Classical music should be playing*, Sally thought. *It all seems so ... orchestrated. Yes, that's the word! Orchestrated.*

She wondered whether life was orchestrated. Was there a God who had a hand in her fate, or was she just drifting about, like those leaves, liable to be blown in any direction by any random gust of wind? Sally sighed and thought back to when she was a little girl. She tried to remember what she dreamed of then, but couldn't. As a young woman, Sally had had three dreams: marrying Cooper, having Cooper's baby, and living with Cooper in a real house—a white Cape Cod with green shutters and a long porch. She always imagined the two of them rocking in chairs on such a porch. Standing there, Sally realized all of her dreams included Cooper. Every one of them. She wasn't sure that was a good thing. It gave him so much power. She'd never dreamed of having her own business, although that was the primary goal in her life right now. It was where she was spending all of her time, all of her money, all of her efforts. How had that happened?

The wind caressed her legs below the white uniform dress she wore to work. Sally reached up and released her hair from the ponytail holder that had trapped it all day long. Sliding the hair band onto her wrist, she then ran a hand through her hair. Her scalp hurt, her hair having been pulled into submission all day. *If I had not gotten the job at the diner years ago*, Sally considered. *If Annie had not met some guy and moved away, if Annie hadn't decided to sell the diner, if Frank hadn't helped me get the loan, I never would have given one moment of thought to owning a diner*. So, had she made a smart decision as a businesswoman? Or had she merely been in the right place at the right time and fell into it? Was she the wind, which pushed and determined direction? Or was she the leaf—just blown about to land in a random spot?

In the dark, it seemed as if she could just keep driving straight toward that moon. Drive on down the tree-lined road forever, following the moon's luminous path. Reality, of course, was quite different. The road was a dead end. Barriers and railroad tracks were just half a mile down the road. Right now, though, it seemed possible—to just follow the moon.

Sally got back into the car and drove the short distance

home, more exhausted than ever. As she approached the steps, she tried to ignore the lawnmower that had been sitting there since July, when it had quit running. Weeds grew up around it, and the entire yard was overgrown. She picked up a couple of pieces of firewood from the pile near the door and entered. The house was dark, which was unusual. Cooper was always awake when she came home. Sally opened the woodstove and added the two pieces of wood, enough to get them through the night. Probably more heat than they needed, actually, but it would be nice to leave the bedroom windows open and get a little breeze.

"Cooper?" she called as she closed the woodstove doors and straightened back up. Then she noticed something on the kitchen floor. Something was scattered all over the linoleum. Her first thought was that Cooper had tracked a bunch of leaves into the house—that was just like him, to make a mess and then leave it for her to clean up. But then she noticed a lit candle on the kitchen table. Turning her gaze back to the floor, she realized they were rose petals. She smiled. "Cooper?" she said again, this time softer.

"Back here."

Sally followed the trail of rose petals down the hall to the bathroom, nearly breathless in anticipation. The bathroom door was open, and soft light poured into the hallway. She turned the corner to find Cooper standing in the bathroom, a smile on his face. Lit candles were scattered about the edges of the tub, the counter, and even over the closed toilet seat. The bathtub was full of bubbles.

"I made you a bath," he said with a grin.

"Cooper, that's so sweet." Sally felt as if she were going to cry. She blinked back the tears, focused on the toilet seat full of candles. "But I have to pee." She smiled.

"Oh!" With a start, Cooper crossed the little room and scooped up the candles, setting some on the counter and pushing others backward to make room. "There. Now you're set. Go pee, and then get in the tub. I'll be right back.

There's more!"

Sally did as she was told. Pulling her hair atop her head, she slid down into the tub. *Someday, I'm going to have a huge tub,* she thought to herself. Maybe in the new house they would build with all of the money from the diner.

Cooper returned, carrying a plate. "I wanted to have some music playing for you, but I couldn't find the CD player. Where's that at?"

"Cooper, that thing quit working two years ago. I threw it away."

"Oh. Well, here. I got this for you too." He kneeled beside the tub.

On the plate was the biggest roast beef sandwich Sally had ever seen. And fries."

"It's a Big Wyoming, or something like that! Doesn't it look good?" He handed her the plate.

Sally sat up in the tub and took the plate. It was heavy. "Cooper." She tried to hold it in, but started laughing

"What?" Cooper seemed confused. "Did you already eat at the diner?"

"How am I going to eat this in the tub? My hands are all wet."

Cooper scrambled to pull a towel off the rack. "Here. You can dry them."

"Cooper. It's not just that. The sandwich is so … big. It might be kind of hard to eat in the tub."

"Oh." Cooper's disappointment showed. "I'm sorry. I just thought you'd be hungry, and this looked like something you might like." Cooper took the plate from her. "I'll go wrap it up. Maybe you can eat it tomorrow." He headed for the door.

"Cooper."

"Yeah?"

"Thanks. That was really sweet of you. I love the bath. And I'll eat the sandwich tomorrow. This was a nice surprise."

Cooper turned around. He looked like a little boy, all sheepish and adorable. "I guess the sandwich wasn't such a great idea, but I'm glad you like the bath. I love you, Sally. I love you so much."

Sally scooted further down in the tub, her knees bent, eyes closed, a smile on her face.

Chapter 7

November

Every week, the crowd grew at Cooper's little church in the woods. And every week he felt a little less nervous.

He imagined that someday he might even enjoy giving sermons, although probably not any time soon.

He stood outside the church on a bright November afternoon, shaking everyone's hands as they left, something that had become a part of his regular routine since the first service. Cooper liked that part: shaking hands and thanking people for coming. It was much easier than standing in front of everyone and speaking. Up front, he always felt so far away from them. It wasn't until this moment, standing in front of the church in the midst of all of them, that he felt as if they were all actually a part of something.

"Nice job, Cooper," Jake Barnes told him. Jake and Melody were regular attendees. So far, they had not missed a service. TJ, however, had not attended a single service after the first. He still slept in the church once in a while, but every Sunday morning, TJ was gone, his cot folded up and stored in the closet.

"Thanks, Jake. I thought maybe TJ would come with

you guys today."

"We asked him. He said he didn't want to."

Cooper nodded and forced a smile. He wondered why TJ didn't want to come to church. It made Cooper feel uneasy, but he wasn't sure why. "How's your mom doing?"

"About the same. But we have a nurse living with us full time now, so it makes things easier."

"That's good. Glad to hear it."

Jake and Melody moved on, clearing the way for others to shake Cooper's hand.

More attendees filed past; many were strangers. Very often, they told Cooper they first learned about him and the church while watching TJ win World Wide Warrior. Others said they read about him in the newspaper. Many were just curious, attended once, and never returned. Some, though, attended faithfully every Sunday.

Cooper said goodbye to the last parishioner, a tall elderly man who had been in attendance every week, since the first service. Usually, he just shook Cooper's hand and complimented him on the sermon. Today, he stood in the doorway, beside Cooper. "You do a good job, boy." The man's thick silver hair was combed straight back from his forehead and almost glistened under the sun. "Troy Born," he extended his hand.

Cooper had never seen an old guy with such thick hair. He hoped he still had hair at that age. "Thank you." He shook the man's hand, surprised by his grip.

"A fine job. Of course, you've got some to learn about the Bible, but that will come along."

"I hope so. I'm sure trying."

"Sure you are." Troy reached out and patted Cooper's shoulder. "That shows. And it's what's most important—the trying. If your heart isn't in it, it doesn't matter how much you know about the Bible. And I can see that your heart is in it. Yes sir, I can see that."

"Thank you."

"I used to be a preacher."

"You did?"

"Sure did. Years ago, in a little Baptist church in southern Illinois. It was a small town and I was the only preacher."

Cooper nodded and smiled, wondering what time it was. TJ had asked him to ride along while Beaulah Potts showed him a house today. TJ was probably waiting for him by now. He didn't want to be rude, but he needed to check the time.

"Yep. I was the only game in town, and it was a lot of responsibility. Sure was. The problem was, I had five kids to feed and I couldn't live on a preacher's salary. Sure, I got some chickens and some vegetables here and there, but it couldn't buy shoes for the kids or put gas in the car—"

"That's true." Cooper felt bad cutting the guy off. He told himself he'd make an effort to talk to the guy next week after church.

"So, I had to give it up. We moved to Michigan and I got a job at a factory. Paid a lot better, and we were able to build us a nice little house. Three of the kids went on to college."

"Well, that's good. That's something to be proud of."

"I don't know. Sometimes, late at night, when I'm sitting home alone—my wife died a couple of years back— when I'm sitting home alone in that house we built, I wonder if I'm going to hell."

His words finally caught Cooper's full attention. "But why?"

"I was responsible for that town, for all the souls in it. And when things got tough, I left." Unexpectedly, the old man's blue eyes filled with tears. "There's not a day of my life I have not regretted that."

"But you had to provide for your family."

"The Lord provides; I didn't trust that. When it comes down to it, it was a simple matter of faith. And I fell short. How many of those people in that town are going to go to hell because I wasn't there to lead them to Christ? I was responsible for them." He shook his head. "I'll never know, at least not in this life."

"Do you really believe that?"

"Why, of course I do. It says so right in the Bible. Look it up."

"Where at?"

"If I'd just trusted, had faith, maybe things would have turned out different. You remember that, boy. Trust in the Lord and he will provide."

Cooper wanted to ask where he had read that in the Bible again, but he had to leave. "It's never too late, you know. Maybe you could go back to it, start preaching again? I'm sorry, I hate to cut this short, but I gotta meet someone. But, I'll see you next Sunday, okay?"

"Oh, sure. I'm sorry. Didn't mean to keep you. You enjoy your day, boy." He raised his hand in a wave and shuffled to his car, a dusty silver Buick, the only car left in the graveled parking lot beside the church.

Cooper waited until the old man had started his car. He had already forgotten his name; he felt bad about that. "See you next Sunday," he called. Then he turned and went back into the church, locking the door behind him. As he walked through the church, turning off the lights and picking up a couple of scrap pieces of paper from the floor, he wondered if the old guy knew what he was talking about, wondered how the guy's wife had died. Cooper also wondered about his own wife. He had never been lonely, but now, although surrounded by so many people every Sunday, he felt lonely most of the time. Before, there had always been a woman ready to welcome him into her arms and into her bed, but now, since he had started believing in God and started being faithful to his wife, Cooper only had Sally. Lately, that didn't seem like enough.

The night he had surprised her with the bubble bath was great. They'd made love and talked for hours afterward. But, within days, they slid back into their rut. Sally barely spoke to him. He'd asked plenty of times if she was mad at him. Had he said or done something to hurt her feelings?

Her answer was always the same: "Why would you ask that, Cooper?"

Has Violet contacted her? he worried. *Even after I paid her off?* Cooper felt that things would be better if only Sally would come to his services. Then, she could see his heart. He wanted to share the church with her, wanted her to be a part of it.

She still had not been to one of his services—not a single one! She always said she had to work, but he knew she could have taken some time off if she wanted to. She was running the place now, which meant she was in charge of scheduling.

Cooper turned out the last light, walked out the back door, and locked it behind him. It didn't seem to make much sense to lock the church. If someone wanted to break into it, they could just knock out a window, but he locked it anyway; might as well.

When Cooper and TJ pulled into the driveway of the house, Beaulah was already waiting for them in her car, along with another woman.

Cooper parked his truck beside Beaulah's white Cadillac, and the woman looked over at him.

"Shit," Cooper said to TJ as he turned the truck off. It was Libby Cartwright.

"What?"

Libby opened the car door and the first thing Cooper noticed was her bare leg extending from behind the door. She wore black high heels and a dress.

"Shit!" Cooper said again. "I really don't need this right now." He opened the truck door and got out.

"Hi, Cooper," Libby said.

"Hey, Libby." Cooper tried to avoid looking at her.

Beaulah appeared from behind the car "Hello, Cooper! How are you?"

"Great. How you doing, Beaulah?"

"Oh, never better. This is my new assistant, Libby Cartwright."

Libby smiled and stuck out her hand.

Nope, he wasn't going to fall for that. Libby had such sweet little hands. "Yes. I know her."

TJ joined them.

Beaulah looked back and forth between Cooper and Libby, and then turned her attention to TJ. "Well, let's go check out the house, shall we?" Beaulah walked between them up to the front door. There was a lock box on it, and she struggled with it a few minutes before it opened. "There! Let's go in!"

The house was a large two-story brick home set on five acres.

"Why are the owners selling?" Cooper asked.

"They've moved. They built this house right before the recession got really bad. They both had great jobs and could easily afford it, but they both lost their jobs last year. Now they're upside down on the mortgage."

"Where are they?" TJ asked as they entered a tiled two-story foyer.

"He got a job in Denver, so they moved last month."

"It's a beautiful house, TJ." Cooper ran his hand over a piece of woodwork. "Gorgeous woodwork. Look at these joints."

They walked through the foyer, through the living room, and into the kitchen.

"Granite counter tops," Cooper said.

"Is that good?"

Cooper shrugged. "They're expensive. I guess it just depends on what you like, TJ. I like granite."

"You'll never get a better bargain. They have to sell. They're making payments on this house and paying rent.

And, I am telling you this because I have their permission to do so: they want whoever buys this house to know they loved it. This isn't a house they're trying to dump; it's a house they didn't want to lose. They loved this house and they're hoping the new buyers will too."

Libby crossed the kitchen and ran her fingers over the granite counter. "Beautiful."

Cooper looked at her, and then quickly away. "Nice big sink."

"How much do you suppose it takes to heat a house this big? And what about the electric bill? How much is that a month?" TJ asked.

Libby spoke up. "I can get that information and get back to you."

Cooper looked at Libby more closely. Had her hair grown? He didn't remember it being so long. And what would you call that color? He never knew. Sort of brown, sort of red, kinda wavy and falling down over her shoulders. Cooper remembered burying his hands in her hair as he kissed her, how it fell down on both sides of his face in a silken tent when she was on top of him.

"Cooper? Cooper?" TJ repeated.

Cooper pulled himself back into the conversation. "Yes? I'm sorry, what? What did you say?"

"What do you think? Do you think I should buy it?"

"I don't know, TJ. It's a huge decision. You'd have to get an inspector in here and check everything out, but from what I see, it's a well-built house and it's been taken care of. If there is nothing structurally wrong with it, it looks like a great deal. But it's a huge commitment. I'd give it some thought if I were you."

Libby laughed and they all looked in her direction. It seemed an odd reaction. "Cooper might not be the one to ask about making a commitment. He likes to keep his options open, right Cooper?" Libby smiled sweetly at him.

Cooper's gaze rested on Libby's mouth and then

returned to her eyes. "It's not that I don't want to make commitments, I just don't want to over commit. I'm trying to make the right decisions now. I'm thinking about all of the consequences. I haven't always done that in the past."

Libby's jaw tightened and her eyes narrowed. "I think I'll wait in the car. It's a bit stuffy in here." Her heels echoed in quick snaps on the tile floor.

Beaulah smiled, but it looked more like a grimace. "Well, why don't I leave the two of you alone in here so you can look around and talk? I'll be out in the car waiting, with Libby."

After Beaulah left, Cooper and TJ revisited every room in the house. As they walked, they talked.

"Do you even want to buy a house, TJ?" Cooper asked as they inspected the master bedroom. "You don't seem very excited."

"Well, it is a nice house."

"No, I mean, do you want to buy any house? Not just this one. Do you want to be a homeowner? It can be a lot of work. This place has a huge yard. A long driveway to shovel in the winter."

"I don't know. I guess. More than anything, I'm just thinking about Mom. If I buy this house, Mom and the nurse can move in here. It would take some of the pressure off Jake and Melody."

"Why do you think Jake is under pressure?"

"Well, Mom's sick and that house is just so small. All four of them in it; they're bound to get on each other's nerves. And I'm there most of the time. Plus, I think Jake worries about money a lot. This would help take some of the burden off him."

"What about you? You, yourself, do you want a house? If it wasn't for your Mom being sick, would you be buying a house?"

A sliding glass door led from the master bedroom out onto a patio. "Honestly, Cooper, I can't even imagine living in a house like this. But I guess everybody has to grow up, right?"

"There's another option."

"What?"

"Why don't you just add on to Jake's house? He has a huge yard. You could just extend the hall at the end of the house and add two bedrooms with a bathroom in the middle. The nurse and your mom could stay in there. Maybe you could even add a little sitting room with a television, so everyone isn't always on top of each other."

"How much would something like that cost?"

Cooper shrugged. "Let me think." Running his hand through his hair, he looked down at the carpet. "Maybe fifty grand. Maybe less."

"Really?"

"Yeah. And you'd be adding value to Jake's house, which would help him out if he ever sells it, and you wouldn't have to buy a house just yet. Doesn't make sense to buy a house if you don't want to."

"We could build it, you and me!"

"Yeah, I guess we could."

"I'd pay you, Cooper. Then you'd be making some money too. This might be a good deal for everyone."

"Well, not everyone," Cooper said.

"No?"

"Not Beaulah. She's hoping to sell this house to you."

"Yeah. I feel bad about that. But I think you came up with the answer. That's a great idea, Cooper! Let's do it."

Outside, Cooper got into his truck while TJ jogged over to Beaulah's car and told her he would not be buying the house.

Cooper kept his eyes focused on the house. He did not look in Libby's direction, but he could feel her eyes on him while he sat there.

"Okay." TJ got back into the truck. "Let's go tell Jake the good news."

Cooper put the truck in gear and pulled out of the parking lot, refusing to look in his rearview mirror. Still, as he drove, Libby was the only thing he could see.

Chapter 8

November

After church, Jake dropped Melody off at home and headed over to Danny Bennett's house. Danny had called earlier and Jake figured either Danny had bought a new TV he wanted to show off, or something was wrong. Jake hoped it was a new television. He was sure Danny had not seen him take the money from the drug bust house, but he still always felt a little uncomfortable around him now.

Jake walked in without knocking. Danny was sitting in the living room, watching a football game.

Nope. Same television. "You don't even lock your doors?" Jake asked, as he sat down. "You never know what kind of lowlife might walk through the door."

"You can say that again," Danny said with a smile. Getting up, he left the room and returned with a beer for Jake. "So, how are ya, Jake? Did you go to church this morning?"

Jake unscrewed the lid of the beer bottle and took a long drink. "Yep. I'm telling you, you should go. Cooper does a good sermon. Not boring like regular church."

"Nah. I'd rather watch the game."

"Where's Becky and the girls?"

"At her mom's house. They went for a visit."

"How'd you get out of that?"

"Told her my back was hurting and I needed to lie down, stay flat on my back."

"Man. That's just not right."

Danny shrugged. "She knew the game was on today. She didn't buy it, but it gave her something to tell her parents."

"You got the life, Danny. I'd trade you right now."

"How's your mom doing?"

Jake shook his head. "Not good." He opened his mouth to add something, but decided against it. He shook his head again. "Not good. So, what's up with you? Why am I here? Not that I'm complaining. I wouldn't mind sitting here the rest of the day, watching the game and drinking your beer."

"Have at it, brother. You're always welcome. I ain't going nowhere. We could get pizza later, if you want."

"Sounds good. But, what's up?"

"You know that meth bust we did over on Miller Street?"

Jake nodded. He could feel his heartbeat quicken. He took a breath.

"One of the sleazeballs we put in jail owned the house."

"So?"

"Claims a hundred grand was taken from the house during the bust."

Jake thought, *No, not a hundred grand, a little over fifty-two grand.* "They have a hit out on all of us."

"Yeah, I know. The Captain already told us."

"Yes. But apparently the guy's brother lives in the house right next door. And word on the street is that the brother is not only out to get us, but he's also taking over where his brother left off. Back to cooking meth. Not in the house. Somewhere else, location unknown, but supplying all the same old customers. In other words, we didn't accomplish much."

Jake took another swig from his beer. "We never do."

He had to return that money. There had to be a way. He didn't want it in his house anymore. He hadn't spent a dime of it, and it was going to stay that way.

"We just need to be watching our backs more than ever. Especially since this guy's brother is in the picture. He's got a record. Attempted murder. But he got off on some technicality. From what I hear, he's nobody to mess with."

Jake picked at the label on his beer bottle. "So, this is what you called me over here for?"

"No." The commercial break ended and Danny turned his attention back to the television. "I just wondered if everything was okay with you. You don't seem like yourself lately. To tell you the truth, I'm worried about you, buddy."

"Well, ain't that touching? When did you become such a Nancy?"

"Kiss my ass, Barnes. And then tell me what's going on with you."

Jake laughed. "Well, my mom is losing her marbles. My wife blames me 'cause she can't get pregnant. We're living from paycheck to paycheck. House needs a roof. Melody's car needs tires. We got a full-time nurse living in our house—a woman who is not the most pleasant person in the world. Other than that, life is good."

Danny stared at Jake a moment before he spoke. "I know that must be tough, dealing with your mom especially. I can't even imagine. But if it were more than that, if something was really wrong, you'd tell me, wouldn't you?"

Jake moved forward in his chair and leaned toward Danny. "All right, I'll tell you," he whispered. "I'm having an affair."

Danny's eyebrows arched.

Jake nodded. "Yeah. It's true. And I can hardly keep up. I met this girl at the gas station about a month ago. Blonde. Gorgeous. Only twenty-two. I couldn't resist."

"Shit, Jake. What are you thinking?"

"I know it's wrong, but I couldn't resist. We get back to her house and I find out she's a twin. She has a sister, and she is just as hot. Both of them can't keep their hands off me. Now, it's all I can do to keep up, but, hell, you gotta give 'em what they want, right? Who am I to withhold my charms?"

"Aw, hell. You're an ass, Barnes. Here I am trying to talk to you and you go and act like an ass."

Jake finished his beer and stood. "You gotta admit I had you going for a minute there!"

"Like some young thing would want your sorry ass. Let alone two young things."

Jake placed his empty bottle on the coffee table and started for the door.

"Where you going? I thought you were gonna watch the game with me?"

"Nah. I better go. The twins are waiting."

Danny tossed a throw pillow in Jake's direction and just missed his head. "Get the hell out of here. Let me enjoy my game."

Jake laughed and swatted the pillow away. "Later, man."

He had to get rid of that money. But how would he get rid of fifty-two thousand and not leave a trace? There had to be a way. He just wasn't thinking clearly. There had to be a way.

Chapter 9

November

Cooper dropped TJ off at Jake's and headed straight for Bass Turds. Sundays were slow, but people still filtered in and out of the dark bar. Cooper sat at the bar and ordered a hamburger.

Pete put Cooper's order in and then returned with his drink, a root beer. "How'd your church service go today?"

"Good. It was good."

"I still can't believe you have a church."

"Me neither. Especially today."

"What's that supposed to mean?"

Cooper sighed. "I don't know, Pete. Sometimes I feel like a fraud."

"How so?"

"This old guy stayed back today and he was talking about how, as a preacher, I'm responsible for other people's souls. And the thought of that just scared the hell out of me. How am I supposed to carry around that kind of weight on my shoulders?"

"Maybe you don't have to."

"What do you mean?"

"I don't know, but just because some old guy says it, doesn't mean it's true. Doesn't make much sense to me. Seems like we should each be responsible for our own soul."

"I don't know what to think. Maybe I should look it up in the Bible and see if it is actually in there."

"Not a bad idea. This has really got you down."

"It's not just that. Something is up with Sally. That doesn't help matters."

"What's with her?"

Cooper took a sip from his glass. "I don't even know. It's like she's got something bothering her, but she won't tell me. I'm doing everything I can, but something still seems to be wrong. That's the thing. Before, when I was screwing around on her, she always had reason. But, Pete, I swear, I haven't been with another woman since that night in here when I started believing in God."

"No shit?"

"It's the truth, although it's not always easy."

"Especially with your track record."

"I'm being serious here, Pete. I've got a problem."

"What's the problem?"

Cooper shrugged. "Libby Cartwright."

"Ah. Yes. That could be a problem. Most men would like to have that problem."

"Today, Beaulah showed TJ a house. I rode along to look at the house and Libby was there too."

"TJ is buying a house?"

"I don't think so. I think he is going to add on to Jake's house instead. Add a couple of bedrooms for his mom and the nurse."

Pete nodded. "Good idea."

"Anyway, Libby was there, and she was looking at me. I could tell what she was thinking. Me and her, we used to have some pretty wild times. And she looked so good and smelled so good. My mind started wandering. And, I tell you Pete, it was all I could do to come here instead of drive right over to her house."

"You're here; that's got to count for something."

"But, I wanted to go to her house. Sometimes, I just feel like a failure."

"Ah, we all have those days."

"I don't know. Lately it feels like I have more than my share." He took another drink. "Are you sure this is root beer? Where's the foam?"

"It's out of the fountain. There's no foam."

"I like it out of a mug with foam on top. This tastes like crap."

"Go somewhere else and get your root beer."

Cooper looked around. "Where's Violet?" He wanted to talk to her about the blackmail note.

"Hasn't come down yet. She might not. Sometimes she doesn't. Let me check on your burger and fries. I'll be right back."

"Okay." Cooper swiveled his stool and inspected the bar. What were all of these people going to do after they finished eating? What did people do with their time? Being faithful to Sally left him with too much time on his hands. He swiveled back and rested his arms against the bar. He supposed he should start on next week's sermon, but that didn't sound like much fun.

Pete soon returned with Cooper's burger and fries. "You know what your problem is, Cooper?"

"Which one? Right now, I've got so many I can't keep track."

Pete set the plate down in front of him. "You're too damned good looking."

Cooper laughed. "Well, Pete, I didn't know you rolled that way."

"I'm serious. Women are just drawn to you. I've seen it plenty of times. You don't even have to do anything but walk into a room. And that's gotta be tough to give up."

"It seems like it'd be easier now. But it isn't. Before,

honestly, I didn't even think I was doing anything wrong. It didn't seem like that big of a deal. Now, I feel terrible about all that. I hate that I hurt Sally like that. But, even knowing that, it doesn't stop me from being tempted." Cooper shook his head and then ate a french fry. "And I'm preaching on Sunday mornings. What a hypocrite."

"Nobody's perfect, Cooper. Not even preachers. All you can do is try, and help others to try."

"I'm not so sure."

"You must be doing something right. I hear your church is growing. Unless…"

"What?"

"It's not all women, is it?"

Cooper laughed, and choked on a french fry. He coughed and laughed several minutes before stopping. Finally, he was able to catch his breath, stop laughing, and stop choking. "No, Pete. They're not all women."

"That's good. I thought maybe you were laying hands on them or something. Trying to heal them."

Cooper shook his head and laughed again. "Nope. Just praying for them." *And paying off their blackmail threats*, Cooper thought.

(

Beaulah Potts was tempted just to let the phone ring. No one ever called her on the house phone anymore. It was probably something about the church. Someone wanting something. She placed a hand against the garage wall to balance herself and slipped her shoes off. The phone still rang. Sighing, she walked into the kitchen and crossed the living room to pick it up.

"Hello."

"Hello, Beaulah. This is Ivy Miller."

Beaulah immediately regretted her decision to answer the phone. "Hello, Ivy. I'm sorry, but you caught me in the middle of something."

"Oh, I won't keep you long. I didn't notice you at church this morning. Were you ill?"

"No. I had to show a house."

"On Sunday? The Sabbath?"

"What do you need, Ivy?"

"Well, I'm sure you must have heard the sermon on Saturday, then?"

"I didn't make it to church this weekend." Beaulah gritted her teeth. "I was visiting my friend Clara on Saturday. She's having a tough time right now."

"Well, it was just brilliant, I tell you. Just brilliant. One of the best sermons I've ever heard Pastor Potts deliver. And I was thinking, maybe we should get together, the women of the church, and discuss this problem."

"What problem is that?"

"Cooper Moon and that silly church of his! I'm sure you and Pastor Potts have discussed it among yourselves, and now that Pastor has gone before the congregation and come out against that man, I think we women of the church should take it to the next step. Maybe we could do a boycott of Annie's Diner. You know his wife works there."

"Perry … Pastor Potts spoke out against Cooper Moon's church?"

"Yes! And it was something. A real barn-burner. Talking about the wages of sin and how a wolf can come in sheep's clothing and how we have to be on the lookout. I tell you, it gave me goose bumps at one point. Now, I think it's up to us women to pick up the charge and move ahead. There are misguided souls going to that church every Sunday. I hear he has over two hundred people already. Now, that's just wrong. Left unchecked, this could get completely out of hand. With a man like that leading the church, it's hard telling what will become of them. Oh, I'd like to be a fly on the wall for one of those services. Maybe that's what we should do! Maybe we should send in one of the women on a Sunday and…"

Beaulah heard the garage door go up. Perry was home. "I have to go, Ivy." She hung up the phone and walked toward the kitchen.

Perry carried his laptop case and had a smile on his face. "Beautiful morning for November, isn't it? I love that sunshine. How did your showing go?"

"You did a sermon against Cooper Moon this morning?"

"Well, no, not exactly. I talked about sin and how we can be easily misled."

"Did you mention his name or his church?"

"Yes, but only as an example of how we can be misled if we are not—"

"I can't believe it. I can't believe you'd do it. How can you do such a thing? Who do you think you are?"

Perry pushed past her into the living room and set his laptop down on the couch. "I have a responsibility to the community to—"

"Says who? Who died and made you God?" Beaulah was close behind him, leaning toward him as she talked. "Perry! Do you realize what you have done? You don't know a thing about that church. Why in the world would you do such a thing?"

"Members of the congregation have come forward and complained."

"Who?"

"Ivy Miller."

"Ivy Miller! Ha! That's a joke. That woman spends more time with her pants off than on. Who is she to be throwing stones at anyone?"

"Beaulah! It's not like you to say something like that."

"Perry! You just stood in front of the entire congregation and disparaged a man and a church, and you're worried about me saying something unkind about Ivy Miller!"

Perry waddled to the refrigerator, pulled out a gallon of

milk, and placed it on the counter. "It wasn't just her. Others have complained. I have a duty to the congregation."

"Duty! Ha! You're worried about the competition. That's all that's wrong with you." Beaulah watched Perry retrieve a glass from the cupboard.

"Beaulah! What has gotten into you?" Perry turned to face her. "You've never talked to me like this before."

"And you've never stood before the entire congregation and trashed a man."

"I didn't trash him." Perry turned his back to her again and poured himself a glass of milk.

"You might as well have."

"You weren't even there. How can you even judge?" He replaced the milk and then went to their snack cupboard and pulled out a bag of chocolate cookies.

Beaulah raised her voice. "Well, I'll be there next weekend. And I'm telling you, Perry Potts, if I hear one word mentioned about that man or his church, I'm coming back here and packing all of your clothes. I won't have it."

Perry slammed the cookies down on the counter and faced his wife again. "You can't tell me what to preach in my own church! I'm in the middle of a series! What has gotten into you? Is this part of you going through the change? I don't even recognize you!"

"This has nothing to do with menopause. It's about what's right and what's wrong. And this is wrong. And I don't recognize you either. The man I married never would have done such a thing. Never!" Beaulah strode to the door, grabbed her purse and shoes, and rushed out the door barefoot.

Perry stood there, mouth agape, wondering what in the world had gotten into her.

Chapter 10

November

Three pregnancy test strips were lined up across the edge of the bathtub. Three different brands, yet they all indicated the same thing.

Positive.

Melody sat on the toilet and stared at them. All three could not be wrong—it was impossible. Her hand moved to her still-flat belly. She was pregnant. Pregnant! And no one else knew. It was her little secret.

Melody couldn't believe it. She looked at the results once more. Yes! She was pregnant, after all of this time. Maybe it was the walking. Ever since she started walking with her friend, Brandy, she had felt better. Maybe she was more relaxed right now, with the added exercise. Maybe that did the trick!

Someone knocked on the bathroom door. "How long are you going to be in there? Miss Clara has to use the bathroom."

Melody frowned at the door. This was her moment. She had been waiting for so long. And now she was being rushed through it by Josephine. It wasn't fair! "I'll be out in a few minutes!"

"You've been in there over half an hour. Are you having some sort of problem?"

"Noooooo. I'm not having *some sort of problem*. This is my house and my bathroom. I'm allowed to be in here."

"Fine with me. But if Miss Clara has some sort of accident, I won't be the one to clean it up. That's for sure."

Through the closed door, Melody flipped the nurse off—something she would never dare do to her face. Gathering up the pregnancy tests, she stuffed them into the pocket of her pants, threw open the door and went into her bedroom. "There! It's all yours!" she yelled.

After closing her bedroom door, Melody pulled the pregnancy tests out of her pocket and lined them up on the bed. They were proof. She really was pregnant! At this very moment, a baby was growing inside her. She thought of Jake and wondered how she should break the news. She wanted it to be very special. It couldn't be here in the house, not with the nurse and Clara lurking about. Maybe they could go out for a fancy dinner, maybe this weekend. But, no, that was too far away. She couldn't wait that long.

Scooping up the pregnancy tests, Melody then picked up her purse off the dresser, dropped the tests inside, and made for the front door. "Going out. Be back later," she called over her shoulder. *July.* She counted as she bounced to the car. *She'd have the baby in July.* Once in her car, she pulled her cell phone out of her purse and called Jake. "Where are you at?" she asked.

"I'm working."

"I know that. I mean where?"

"Anderson Street. Not far from Bass Turds. Why?"

"I want to talk to you."

"Talk."

"No, I mean, I need to talk to you. In person."

"Melody, if this is about Mom, I just don't have time right now. Can't it wait until I get home tonight?"

"It's not about your mom. And, no, it can't wait until you get home tonight. I'm on my way now. I will meet you in the parking lot of Bass Turds in ten minutes."

"Okay. But I don't have long."

"It won't take long."

"Okay. See you soon."

"Bye." Melody dropped the cell phone back into her purse and drove down the street with a smile on her face. This was it, the moment she had dreamed of for so long. She was going to tell Jake she was pregnant. She would remember this moment for the rest of her life. He would too. They would probably tell the story to the baby when he or she was old enough to understand. It would become part of their history as a family—a real family.

Melody beat Jake to Bass Turds, parked, and turned off the car. Jake pulled in less than a minute later. Melody had his car door open before he even put the car in park.

"Whoa!" Jake said as she got in and sat down. "What's got you so excited? Did we win the lottery?"

"Better!" Melody reached into her purse and wrapped her hand around the three pregnancy tests. "Close your eyes and hold out your hands."

"This better be a lottery ticket."

"Do it! Close your eyes and hold out your hands."

Jake closed his eyes and cupped his hands in front of him.

Melody placed all three pregnancy tests into them. "Open your eyes!"

Jake looked down. "What's this?"

"Pregnancy tests!"

"Why are you giving them to me?"

"They're positive! Positive! We're going to have a baby!"

Jake jerked his hands apart. Two of the tests fell to the floor of the squad car while the other tumbled into his lap. He quickly brushed it onto the floor. "You peed on these! I can't believe you put them in my hands!"

"Oh my gosh, Jake. That was over an hour ago. They're dry now!"

"Yeah, but jeez! You put them right in my hands!"

"Did you hear what I said? I'm pregnant."

Jake wiped his hands against his uniform pants. "That's great, Mel. That's really great. But I wish you hadn't put those things in my hands. That's gross."

Melody sat back in the seat. "I can't believe you. I tell you I'm pregnant and all you can do is complain about some imaginary pee on your hands."

"It's not imaginary."

"What are you going to do when you have to change a diaper?"

"Well, I'll be working most of the time, so I probably won't have much chance to change diapers."

Melody glared out the car window. This was not going as planned.

"I'm sorry, Mel. You just caught me off guard." Jake reached over and pulled her into his arms. "It's great news. The best news ever. We're going to have a baby."

Melody pulled away and pouted. "You don't seem very excited."

"I am excited! But, like I said, you caught me off guard. I wasn't expecting this today. That's all. I'm really happy."

She reached for the door handle. "I'm going home. I'm tired."

"Mel, don't be like that."

"I'm fine. I'm just tired. I'll see you tonight." She opened the door to her car.

Jake rolled down his window. "Hey! What am I supposed to do with these test things? Can't you take them with you? Come on, Mel!"

Melody ignored him.

She drove toward home, but she didn't want to go there. She was so tired of someone always being home. Now that

Clara, the nurse, and TJ were all living there, she never had a moment alone. She'd like to go home and take a long bath. That would be nice. Maybe play some soft music. Have a snack afterward. Or maybe even while she took a bath. Once, she had sat a bowl of grapes on the edge of the tub and ate them while bathing. That was nice. She wondered why she had never done that again. She reminded herself to get grapes next time she went to the store. Maybe she'd go buy some now. She didn't have anything else to do.

Melody drove to Walmart, but she didn't get out of her car. She didn't feel like going in. She tried to talk herself into opening the car door, crossing the parking lot and walking inside, but couldn't, not even with the promise of a stroll through the baby section—this time even really pregnant. She just wasn't in the mood.

Melody sat in Walmart's parking lot and stared into the distance. It started to snow. Tiny flakes that made you blink and look again, wondering if you were imaging them. She liked winter. It let you withdraw from the world. It was easy to blame the weather for staying in. It was accepted. She loved it best when there were blizzards. Then she would stay home watching old movies and drinking hot chocolate. Jake always had to work, no matter what the weather. She found herself wishing for bad weather every winter.

Of course, she wouldn't be able to walk in the winter. And she'd miss her walks with Brandy. Maybe they could walk at the YMCA. They had an indoor track. She pulled her phone out of her purse. Brandy! She didn't know yet!

An hour later, Melody and Brandy were sitting in Benjamin's Ice Cream shop, both with a hot fudge sundae before them. Brandy's two-year-old son was intently licking an ice cream cone.

"Sorry I had to bring him. Couldn't get a babysitter on such short notice. Now tell me, what's the big news?"

Melody smiled. She had only known Brandy for a

relatively short time, only a couple of months, but they had become close and Melody had shared her anguish over getting pregnant. "Well, I have news." Melody pulled the cherry off her sundae and ate it, relishing the moment. "Very good news."

"What? Come on! Give!"

"I'm pregnant!"

Brandy squealed, jumped from the booth, and rushed to give Melody a hug.

Melody hugged her back and almost dropped her spoon in the process. "Isn't it great?"

"Oh, Melody! That's freakin' awesome! I'm so happy for you!" Brandy returned to her chair. "When are you due?"

"Well, I haven't been to the doctor yet, but I'm pretty sure it's July."

"A summer baby. Oh, that's just freakin' awesome. You'll have it before it gets real hot. That's good. I didn't have this one until October, and let me tell you, August and September were miserable. I'm so happy for you!" Brandy took a spoonful of ice cream. "What'd Jake say? Was he shocked?" She reached over and wiped away the ice cream her son had smeared from nose to chin.

"He's so excited. We both are."

"Did you tell your parents yet?"

"I left a voicemail for my dad. He was at work. But, yeah, I told my mom. She cried. I knew she would. She'll probably be sending all kinds of presents from Arizona. That's how she is." Melody was surprised by the ease of the lie. She felt slightly guilty, but this story was so much better than the truth.

"Man, that's awesome. That's just freakin' awesome. You'll probably want to go out and buy all kinds of baby stuff now."

"Oh, I already did! Before I was even pregnant I bought enough stuff for the entire nursery." Melody grinned and continued eating her ice cream. When the baby's things had been delivered to her house, she and Jake had had a huge argument about it. But now, it seemed like a good idea. She had bought a lot of the stuff on sale, and now they actually needed it.

"When did you do that?"

"Back in August. I was kinda down one day and went for a drive, ended up at a baby store in Kalamazoo and bought tons of stuff. Tons. I'm already all set!"

"Man, that must have been fun. But expensive too, huh?"

Melody shrugged. "Nothing is too good for my baby."

"Do you want a boy or a girl?"

"Oh, either would be fine. But I know it's a girl. I can just tell. I feel it."

Brandy nodded. "I was the same. Knew I was carrying a boy the whole time. Already had his name picked out before he was ever born." She took the spoon out of her son's left hand and put it into his right. "There ya go," she told him. "Eat with that hand."

Melody grinned. Soon, she'd have a little one too. This was great, sharing the news with Brandy. It was so good to have a friend. She hadn't had one in years. "I'm going to name her after my mom. She'd like that."

"Aw, that's a cool idea. What's her name?"

Melody froze, a spoonful of ice cream halfway to her mouth. "I can't remember!" She blinked, and stared at the table between them for a moment. Raising her gaze back to Brandy, she seemed stricken. "I can't remember. How is that possible?"

Brandy laughed. "Oh no! You've already got baby brain. Don't worry about it. That happened to me too. Out of the blue, I couldn't remember stuff. It was weird. Like the kid sucked all of my brains out. Ha! It will pass. That's not the worst of it. Wait until you start running to the bathroom every five minutes to pee. And morning sickness, wait until you get that!"

Melody was calmed by Brandy's words. She brought the ice cream to her mouth and ate it, trying, once again, to remember her mother's name. *Oh well*, she told herself, *it isn't that important. And not that surprising. The woman has been dead for years.*

She'd remember later. Melody swallowed the last of her ice cream and smiled. "Bring it on! Bring it all on! I can't wait!" she said. In that moment, Melody could not remember when she had ever been so happy, and it was only going to get better.

Chapter 11

November

Libby sat down at the bar. "Hey, Pete."
"Hey, Libby. How's it going?
"Okay. How's it going with you?"
"Can't complain. Bloody Mary?"
"Sure. Sounds good."

Pete mixed the drink and placed coaster and drink before Libby. "I hear you're selling real estate with Beaulah Potts."

"Trying to—tough market."

"Yeah, that's for sure. Is anyone selling or buying at all?"

"Yeah, but we still haven't had a closing. I think Beaulah's been concentrating on the wrong people. The way I see it, Timber Lake is divided into three kinds of people. The first are those who come here for some reason, like a job or marriage. They're not sure what they're doing. They might leave. They might stay. They are the toughest to deal with, because they haven't made their minds up yet. So, unless they accidentally come across a house for sale that they fall in love with, they aren't likely to be customers. The second are those who were born here and are gonna die here. They're dug in. They buy and sell, but not very often. They see no reason to move unless they need a bigger house."

"And the last kind?"

"The ones who hate it here. Maybe they were born here, maybe they moved here for some reason, but they all want to get out. I think we should be concentrating on those people. We could even make ads targeting them. They already want to sell, why not give them a nudge? We could even hook them up with another real estate agent in another location and get a cut when they buy a new house."

"Sounds like a plan."

"Tell Beaulah that."

"She doesn't like the idea?"

"I don't know. I haven't told her yet. She works differently from me. She's more passive. Kind of waits for customers to come to her. I mean, I like her and everything. I love working with her. She's been great with me, and I've already learned so much, but we could be doing a lot better."

Pete moved to the other end of the bar, refilled some drinks, and then returned to Libby. "So which one are you?"

"What?"

"Which one of the three? Have you dug in, are you undecided, or do you want out?"

Libby smiled but did not answer. "Violet here?"

"She's upstairs. Why?"

"I heard she was living here now. I want to talk to her."

"About what?"

Libby smiled. "Boy, Pete, you sure are turning into one nosy bartender." She poked a finger at the olive floating in her drink.

"It's just that she's not feeling so well."

"She's sick?"

Pete hesitated. Maybe he should tell Libby. She was a woman. Maybe she could go upstairs and talk some sense into Violet. Make her come downstairs. Convince her there was nothing to be afraid of. "Are you guys friends?"

"No. Not really. Beaulah did a comp on Violet and Frank's house a while back. Now that they're split up, maybe they're ready to sell. I wanted to talk to her about that."

"Oh," Pete said in a quiet voice.

"Maybe I could just go upstairs and talk to her?"

Pete wiped at the spotless mahogany bar with a rag. He took a breath. Exhaled. "Yeah. Maybe that would be okay."

Libby frowned. "Is she contagious or something?"

Pete shook his head. "No. She just doesn't come down much…"

"Okay if I take my drink up?"

"Sure. Walk through the kitchen then up the stairs in the back corner."

Libby took another sip of her drink. "Thanks."

No one answered the apartment door, so Libby knocked harder. Stepping back, she looked for a doorbell. There was none. "Violet?" she called through the closed door. She could hear someone moving about on the other side. "Violet?"

"Who is it?"

"Libby Cartwright. I wanted to talk to you for a few minutes, if that is okay."

"Is anyone with you?"

"No."

"Does Pete know you are up here?"

"Yeah. He said I could come up."

The door opened and Violet peeked through the crack, the deadbolt chain making a line across her face. "What do you want?"

"Can I come in?"

Violet leaned closer. "You're alone?"

Libby nodded. "Yes. Just me."

The door closed. Libby stood there waiting. Just when

she was certain Violet had decided not to let her in, she heard her remove the chain and the door opened a crack. Libby waited for a couple of seconds and then pushed the door open with her hand and walked through.

The apartment was Spartan but neat—something Libby had not expected from Pete. Although, he was always wiping that crazy bar of his, so maybe he was a neat freak. Or maybe this was Violet's handiwork. Libby expected the latter.

She took a seat opposite Violet, who was perched on the edge of the couch. Libby had first seen Violet in Bass Turds years ago. She had been with Frank, who was quite the looker back then. They were an attractive couple, hard to miss. Now, though, Violet looked very different. She wore a sweatshirt and sweatpants that looked like they belonged to Pete; Violet's small frame was lost in them. Her face looked pale and drawn, as if she were sick, or had been for a long time and was just recovering. "Is this a bad time? Pete said you weren't feeling very good."

Violet's hands crawled over each other in her lap, one exploring the other with nervous fingers, then switching roles, as if she wanted to verify all of her fingers were intact. "No."

"So, this is a bad time?"

"No, I mean, I'm not sick. It's an okay time, I guess. What do you want?"

"I can come back. No offense, but you don't look so good."

Violet's hand went to her hair. She pushed a strand behind her ear. "I haven't showered yet today. I've been busy … cleaning the apartment."

Libby looked around. The apartment was clean, that was for sure. Almost sterile. And no TV or radio in sight. The only sound coming through the closed windows was the muffled traffic below. Libby didn't know what to say. "Pete needs a pet or something. Maybe a bird. It's pretty quiet up here."

"We used to have a Saint Bernard, but it died. Something was wrong with its heart."

"Up here, in this apartment?"

"No. I mean me and Frank. We used to have a Saint Bernard."

"Oh," Libby said. She remembered Beaulah telling her about the dog. It had slobbered all over her clothes when she did the comp for Violet. "Oh," Libby struggled to find some sort of segue, some way to ask Violet about selling her house. "Dogs are nice."

Violet smiled back, although it looked as if it required a great deal of effort.

"Uh, I heard that you and Frank split up, so I thought you might be interested in selling your house. Beaulah Potts told me she came over and did a comp for you a while back. That's probably a great place to start. The market hasn't changed much since then. We could get you listed quite quickly if you're interested."

"Oh. No. I wouldn't be interested." Violet shook her head. "It's Frank's house. I guess it always was. Isn't it funny how you can live somewhere for years and never feel at home?" Violet's voice trailed off, as if she were thinking about something. She stared at the carpet.

Libby waited a moment, thinking Violet was going to add something, but she did not. "So, Frank would be the one to talk to?"

"Yes."

"But you are willing to sell? If that's what he decides?"

Violet shrugged. "It's his house. It's up to him."

"So, you've signed off on the house? I'm sorry. I don't mean to pry; I'm just trying to understand."

"No. I could though. If he wants me to. If he brings me papers to sign. I don't care."

Libby was done here. But still she hesitated on the couch. Part of her felt like reaching out to Violet, asking her if she wanted to go for a walk or maybe even just have a cup of coffee downstairs. But another part of her was uneasy. Violet seemed crazy, and Libby was afraid of crazy. She grew up with crazy. She'd seen what crazy was capable of. Fighting the impulse to reach out to Violet, she stood. "Okay. Well, thanks." Libby hurried to the door. As she moved down the steps, Violet said something, but Libby didn't hear her. She didn't want to.

She stopped at the bar on her way out. "Pete, you don't have a gun up there, do you?"

"No! Why would you ask that?" Pete seemed outraged.

Libby knew crazy and guns were a bad combination. She fought hard to push away the vision of her bloodied parents. "Pete, I'd get her out of here if I were you. That's all I'm saying. Something about her isn't right."

"What's that supposed to mean?" Pete called after her as she left. Libby did not turn to answer.

Violet got up from the couch and picked up Libby's drink. She had tried to tell Libby that she'd forgotten it, but Libby didn't hear. After washing and drying the glass, Violet set it on the table. Maybe she'd take it down to the bar later. She crossed the room and looked through the window at the street below. A dark sedan was parked in front of the bar. Violet held her breath. Was that him? Could it be? Had he come back for her? While she pondered the possibility, the car pulled out of the parking spot and she glimpsed an elderly woman in the passenger seat. Violet started breathing again.

Chapter 12

November

"Cooper, I need a favor." Sally walked into the kitchen, her hair still wet from the shower.

Cooper was standing near the sink, a cereal box in his hand. He smiled. This was good; maybe it meant Sally was done being mad at him. He hated when things were bad between them. "What do you need, Sally? Anything. Just let me know what it is."

"I need you to build an addition onto the diner for me."

"For you?"

"Yeah, I want to add a family dining room onto it. If you'll build it for me, it would cut all of the labor costs. The diner is a good bet. The bank can see that. It's just good business. An investment in the community." Sally was stretching the truth just a bit. She had not heard back from Frank yet, but he had assured her, over and over again, that it was almost a done deal. "And now I need you to start on that addition."

"When?"

"Right away."

"I can't do it right away. I already told TJ I'd put an

addition on Jake's house. And we've got to get the foundation poured before the ground freezes, which won't be long now."

"How long will it take you to build their addition? How big is it?"

"It's pretty big. Two bedrooms, a bathroom, and a sitting area in one of the bedrooms. It will take a while."

"I knew it! I swear, Cooper, I can never count on you for anything!" Sally moved to the counter, unzipped her purse, and began digging for her car keys.

Cooper put the cereal box down on the counter and moved beside her. "Sally, I didn't say I wouldn't build it. I just said I can't do it right away. I have to finish Jake's addition first."

"And that's more important than my business—a business that could bring in money?"

"I'm getting paid to do the addition at Jake's."

Sally pulled her keys out of her purse and faced him. "Cooper! You're not getting it! That family dining room could double my business. We could actually have a real income, something we could count on. Don't you see that?"

He closed the distance between them and placed his hands on her upper arms. "Yeah, I see what you are talking about, and I'd like to help you, but I have to get this addition done first."

Sally pulled away. "Someone else *always* comes first!" She stormed to the door. "I'm going to work," she said, slamming it behind her.

Cooper followed her from the mobile home. "Sally, why are you acting like this?" he called after her as she hurried to her car.

Sally opened her car door and glared over the roof. "I bet if Libby Cartwright wanted you to do something for her, you'd do that quick enough! Frank's right—you don't want me to succeed!"

"Sally!"

Sally got in, slammed the door and turned the ignition. Her tires spun as she sped from the drive.

"Sally!" Cooper yelled at the dust.

Chapter 13

November

Across town, in Eagle Bluffs Subdivision, another argument was flaring.

Ivy Miller walked into the living room and shook a spiral bound notebook at her daughter, who was sitting on the couch, doing homework for one of her classes at Beaver Creek Community College.

"Why are you writing Cooper Moon's name in your notebooks?" Ivy asked her daughter.

"Why are you snooping in my stuff?"

"Answer the question! Why are you writing Cooper Moon's name in your notebook—with little hearts all around it."

"It's none of your business! You have no right to be looking at my stuff! It's my room, and my stuff!" Lucy jerked the notebook from her mother's hands.

"I wasn't snooping. I needed a piece of paper. And it's my house! You don't pay the mortgage!"

"Neither do you; Dad does! You don't do anything but sleep around! That's why you don't like Cooper—he turned you down!"

Ivy slapped Lucy across the face, startling both of them. For a moment, neither said a word. Then Lucy ran past her mother, screaming, "I hate you! I hate you!" as she bolted out the door.

Ivy had never hit her daughter before. She had sworn she never would, but she just had. She remembered screaming the same words at her own mother.

Ivy never knew her father. For as long as she could remember, a photograph of a handsome dark-haired man had sat on her bedroom dresser. Little Ivy used to tell the photo goodnight every night before going to bed. She waited for him to visit her, but he never did. For a few years, when she was very young, he sent her Christmas and birthday presents, but after a while, those stopped.

By the time Ivy was ten, she started looking to the photograph as a means of escaping life with her mother. That dark-haired man could take her away from the endless parade of her mother's boyfriends, who floated in and out of their tiny apartment in some sort of drug- or alcohol-induced daze. The late night drinking, the shouting, the sound of bottles and glasses being hurled against the wall. Slamming doors and squealing tires. Afterward, her mother's rants. Or, worse, the sound of her softly crying down the hall. At such times, Ivy huddled in her bed, looking at the photo of her father and praying for rescue.

One night, just after she turned fourteen, someone came into Ivy's bedroom in the middle of the night. Ivy was woken by rough hands grabbing at her pajamas. She screamed and kicked against the unknown assailant, who smelled of beer and body odor. The light flipped on, and Ivy's mother was standing in the doorway. One of her mother's boyfriends, whose name Ivy could not remember to this day, pushed himself off Ivy and sat on the edge of the bed.

"What's going on in here?" Ivy's mother demanded.

"She's a tease. She's been coming on to me. Now, all of

a sudden, she starts screaming," he slurred.

Ivy clutched her blankets to her body, confused, disoriented. She struggled to grasp what had just happened. Was it a dream? She clenched her fists and dug her nails into her palms to wake herself. No. It was not a dream.

Her mother rushed to the bed, grabbed the man by the arm and pulled him to his feet. "Get out of here! Get out of here!" She pulled him from the room and pushed him down the hallway.

As she listened to the man stumble out of the house, Ivy clutched her blankets and rocked back and forth. Tears slid down her face. She began to shake violently. The front door slammed and her mother returned to Ivy's bedroom. Ivy longed for the comfort of her arms.

"What the hell happened here?" her mother demanded from the door.

"I woke up and he was in here, pulling at my clothes." Ivy's voice trembled.

"And just what have you been up to behind my back?"

Ivy shook her head in disbelief. "Nothing! Nothing! I was sleeping…"

"Why would he just come in here? He must have had good reason!"

"No! No! You don't understand!"

"Oh, I understand plenty."

Ivy got out of bed and rushed to her mother, still longing for her comforting embrace. "No, Mom. I was sleeping. I never did anything! He's disgusting!"

That was when her mother slapped her. "This is your fault," she screamed! "He was talking about marriage! Now that will never happen, just because you decided to wag your ass in front of him!"

Ivy pulled back, horrified at her mother's words, shaking her head in disbelief.

"I'll never ever be married, and it's all your fault! It's always been your fault!"

"You were married to Dad…"

Her mother ran across the room and picked up the photograph of Ivy's father. "Ha! Your precious father! This isn't your father! You want to know who this is? It's my cousin! He died not long after this was taken. I don't even know who your father was. This is just a picture of my dead cousin in a frame! That's all. You don't even have a father. You never did!" Her mother threw the framed photograph against the wall, breaking the glass. "Get out! I want you to get out! Take your shit with you and go! I never want to see you again. You're nothing but a weight around my neck. I'm leaving, and I swear to God you better be gone when I get back or there will be hell to pay." She spun, stomped down the hall, and slammed the front door. Ivy listened as her car raced down the street.

Endless tears sliding down her face, Ivy trudged into the kitchen and gathered all of the paper grocery sacks she could find. She filled them with her clothes and shoes, all the while avoiding looking at the broken photograph frame on the floor. There was not enough room for all of her clothes and belongings. She only had five sacks, and they were already full. Ivy did not own a suitcase. She didn't know what to do. She sat on the edge of the bed and cried harder. More than two hours later, when her mother returned, she was still sitting there, still crying.

Her mother stormed into the room, screaming, "What did I tell you? What did I tell you? Get out! Get out of my house!" She smelled of beer. She began pummeling her child with her fists. Still dressed in her pajamas, Ivy grabbed two of the full grocery sacks and ran to the front door. Her mother followed, beating her daughter's back with her fists. "Get out! Get out!"

Ivy fell, dropping one of the bags and spilling half of its contents. She scrambled to her feet while her mother kicked her. Grabbing the now half empty bag, Ivy hurtled out the door. Barefoot, running wildly down the street and clutching the paper sacks, she screamed, "I hate you! I hate you! I hate you!" She never saw her mother again.

Ivy walked back into Lucy's room. Carefully, tenderly, she pulled the sheets up on Lucy's bed. She straightened the blanket, and then the comforter. She fluffed the pillows and put them into place. At Lucy's dresser, Ivy picked up a small teddy bear and propped it against the pillows on the bed. Then she picked up her daughter's dirty clothes from the floor and left the room.

(

By the time Lucy reached the diner, she had calmed down. She had become accustomed to her mother's outbursts, her erratic behavior, her odd thought patterns. This morning, though, it was too much, attacking Cooper like that. Lucy parked behind the diner and turned the ignition off. She was over an hour early. There was no hurry to get inside. Luckily, she had a dirty uniform in the back seat of her car. Someday, she thought, she'd have to get around to cleaning her car out.

Her mother had never slapped her before; maybe it was time to leave home. Lucy had thought about it before, but they had always been passing thoughts. Now it seemed like the time had come. Even as she thought about it, Lucy felt guilty. Her mother needed her, Lucy knew that. She had no one else. Ivy had no friends, no family, and most of the time, no husband. Lucy was all she had. Tears welled in Lucy's eyes. She already regretted telling Ivy she hated her. She did not. Lucy loved her mother. Flawed, selfish, immoral, and sometimes mean Ivy—Lucy still loved her. And she knew her mother loved her too, she just didn't always know how to show it.

She withdrew her cell phone from her purse.

The phone only rang twice before Ivy answered, "Hello?"

"Hi, Mom. I'm sorry."

"I'm sorry too, Honey. I wasn't snooping in your room. I don't do that."

"I know, Mom. And I don't hate you. I was just mad. I shouldn't have said that.

"I know."

"I love you, Mom."

"I know. I love you too, Lucy."

"I'll see you tonight when I get off work."

"What time do you get off?" Ivy asked.

"I close tonight. Not until nine."

"Okay. Let's watch a movie when you get home. I'll go to Redbox and find something good."

"Do we have any popcorn?"

"I think so. If we don't, I'll buy some while I'm out."

"Okay, Mom. That sounds great."

"I love you, Lucy."

"I love you too, Mom."

Chapter 14

November

Perry Potts placed a cup of coffee on his desk and settled into the chair in his home office. Turning on his computer, he waited for it to boot up. Two days a week, he worked from home. He loved those days. He didn't answer the home phone, and he didn't answer his cell, unless it was Beaulah. The days were his and he used them to work on his sermon. True, he occasionally snuck in a few games of online solitaire and spent some time snacking, but mostly he researched and wrote his sermons. There were always leftovers in the refrigerator for lunch, and if he got stuck, he could go into the living room and watch a little television. Now that Beaulah worked, he had the house to himself. It was perfect.

He used to try to write his sermons at church, in his office, but it was just impossible. Even if he put the "Do Not Disturb" sign on the door, people never respected it. Someone was always dropping in with some sort of problem. Or sometimes, they just wanted to chat. Perry resented it. It was as if they didn't understand he had to work during the week. Did they think those sermons wrote themselves? So, a few years back, he started working one day a week from home. Then, last year, it became two. He was thinking about making it three, but he thought that might be pushing it too far. The congregation liked to see him in his office.

Perry checked his personal email, looked at the church's Facebook page (which no one ever used), and read a few stories in the news. He thought about playing a quick game of solitaire but talked himself out of it. No, he had to get to work. He pulled up Google and stared at the screen, thinking about the topic for this week. He was doing a series about avoiding the traps of the world. It started off with a bang. The first sermon was brilliant. He had them in the palm of his hand. Perry thought about the things of the world that tempted people: the entertainment industry, computer games, and sports. Then he thought about his brother. Mostly, he tried not to, but this morning, Harry came to mind like an almost forgotten dream. Perry wondered where he was living now. Probably in a mansion somewhere on a beach. Perry had lost track of Harry's football career over the years. Or, perhaps more accurately, he had chosen to ignore it—to avoid it—for years. He had not seen his family since he left for college. He did the math. That was over forty-seven years ago. How could that be? Perry did the math again. That was it! Forty-seven years. How could that much time have passed?

Perry's hands hovered over the keyboard. He'd been tempted before, but he'd always been able to fight it off. What would it hurt? Really? No one would know. Quickly, he typed *Harry Cotts football* into the Google search bar and hit return.

Almost five million entries came up. Perry rolled his eyes. It figured. The last time Perry looked, a search of his own name brought up less than twelve thousand hits. He started clicking and reading. He learned his brother had enjoyed an outstanding college career and was picked up after graduation by the Denver Broncos. There were articles about the money, the fame, the promise of the new young player. And then Perry read about the injury that ended Harry's career in his third year with the team. An injury? All these years, Perry never knew anything about an injury. Perry sat back in the chair and stared at an old picture of his twin wearing a Denver Bronco uniform. He was so young. Had they ever been so young?

Moving back to the keyboard, Perry searched for more information. He read through several pages of articles before coming across a small one about Harry now living in Florida. Perry tried to remember. Hadn't he read somewhere that Harry lived in Palm Beach? Perry could not remember if he had actually read that or just imagined it. It had been so many years ago. Harry would be sixty-five years old, the same as Perry. Perry found that hard to imagine. When he thought of his brother, he remembered the eighteen-year-old he had last seen. He wondered if Harry's hair had turned grey? Had he put on weight? Did he knees hurt in the morning, too?

It was odd. Perry had so little connection with his past life. He never thought of himself as Perry Cotts, even though it was his real name. Still, from deep within, something tugged at him. Tension crept over his shoulders. No, it was for the best. It wasn't as if he had purposely changed his name intentionally to deceive people. The college did that. They were the ones who made the mistake, a simple typo. Yet that simple typo had allowed him to step out of his brother's shadow, allowed him to lead a church as respected pastor, Perry Potts. No longer Harry Cotts' fat little brother. It was predestined. Ordained. Yes, it had all been part of God' will. He was sure of that. Certain. Almost certain. Almost.

Not bothering to shut down the page, Perry reached over and turned the power off on his computer. Maybe he'd watch a little television.

Chapter 15

November

Melody was lying on the couch, covered by a heavy blanket, a cool washcloth across her forehead. She had spent the morning vomiting. Josephine was cooking pancakes for Clara and the aroma filled the house. Melody was afraid she might have to make another run for the bathroom.

Dressed in his police uniform, Jake stood beside her. "I gotta go back to work, Mel."

"I don't even know why you bothered coming home." She refused to remove the washcloth from her eyes to look at him.

"You called and said you didn't feel good. I wanted to check on you, but I can't stay. You know I have to work. Do you want me to get you anything? Maybe something to drink?"

"No. I told you! I've been puking constantly. Why would I want to drink something?"

"Maybe some ice chips to chew on? I've heard that helps."

"No. Just go. You don't care." Melody left the

washcloth over her eyes and waved him away.

"I do care! You know I do. But I have to work. How are we gonna pay the bills if I don't work? Hey, speaking of … did you pay the credit card bill yet?"

"Noooooooooo. Should I do that in between puking?"

"No. I don't mean this second. But if you get the chance, could you write them a check later today? And we do need to keep the spending down to a minimum this month, if we can. We spent more than normal last month."

"It takes more groceries with more people."

"Well, yeah, but it wasn't just groceries. Anyway, could you pay that today?"

"Yes! I'll pay it! Go!"

Jake leaned over and kissed her forehead. "I hope you feel better. I'll see you tonight. Call me if you need me."

"What good does it do? I did call you. You're still leaving."

"Mel. You're being unreasonable."

"Whatever. Go, Jake. Someone is probably running a stop sign somewhere."

Melody listened to him walk across the room and out the front door. He was never there when she needed him. Never! Oh, but let his mom break a fingernail and he'd come running. Here she was, unable to eat, barely able to walk she was so weak, and right out the door he goes, off to play cops and robbers. It was getting old.

"Turn on the exhaust fan!" Melody yelled in the direction of the kitchen. "Those pancakes stink!"

"If the smell is bothering you, get up and go for a walk. Wouldn't hurt you to get up and get out of the house!" the nurse yelled back.

"I'm sick!"

"You ain't sick; you're pregnant! And if you'd get up and go for a walk instead of lying there thinking about how sick you are, you'd probably feel better!"

Melody pulled the blanket over her head and pressed

her hands to her ears until Josephine's muffled voice sounded like it was coming from a radio or a television in another room, turned on low volume and indiscernible. The words were just sounds, and barely sounds. It was dark under the blanket, especially with her eyes closed. She was so tired. She wanted to take a nap, but she tried that yesterday and Josephine kept making loud noises. Melody was sure it was on purpose.

Her cell phone rang and Melody reached out from under the blanket, blindly fumbling on the coffee table until her hand reached the phone. Pulling it under the blanket, she answered, "Hello."

"Hey, Melody. It's Brandy. Want to go for a walk? I've got a babysitter, so I'm ready to go."

"No. I called you earlier and left a voicemail. Didn't you get it? I don't feel good."

"Nope. Didn't get it. That's weird. Hmmm. What's wrong? Flu?"

"Morning sickness, I think. But I've had it all day, not just this morning."

"Yeah. I don't know why they even call it that. It can come any time of the day. You sure you don't want to give it a try? Maybe going for a walk would make you feel better."

"No. Really, I feel terrible. I think I'm going to take a nap."

"Okay. Well, take care. Maybe we can give it a try tomorrow, or the next day. Give me a call."

"Okay. I will."

Melody laid the phone down by her leg on the couch. She was getting hot under the blanket, but she didn't want to come out. She just wanted to sleep—in her house, by herself. There was always someone here. She never had the house to herself anymore. If she could just be alone, maybe she'd feel better. *It's no wonder I'm sick*, she thought. *Who wouldn't be, under all of this stress?*

She remembered the night she got angry at Jake and

went for a drive—the night she bought all of the baby stuff in Kalamazoo, and got a hotel. It was wonderful. Going there and taking a hot shower, putting on that white fluffy robe afterward, and crawling into that bed under a thick comforter.

Melody sat up on the couch and pushed the blanket from her head. "I'm going out," she yelled, grabbing her phone. No one answered. She hurried toward her bedroom and then searched for her small overnight bag in the closet. There it was, right next to Jake's bowling ball bag. She grabbed it and hurried to her dresser. In haste, she threw in a clean pair of pajamas and some clean underwear, added some toiletries and makeup from the bathroom, grabbed her purse, and headed for the front door. She didn't even look as she passed the kitchen.

Less than an hour later, she was stepping from a hotel shower and reaching for a fluffy white robe.

While Melody was checking into a hotel, Jake was looking in his rearview mirror. Someone was following him. He was sure of it. He had already turned a couple of times, and the car was still there. Looked like two guys were in it, but it was hard to check them out and not be obvious about it. As he drove through town, he started looking for a place where he could pull over real quick. He'd let them pass him and then get their license plate number and pull them over.

It had to be related to the money he had hid in his bowling ball bag. Had to be. Jake glanced in his rearview mirror again. They looked relatively young—in their twenties. Was there more than two of them? Was someone in the back seat? He wondered how long they had been following him. Had they followed him from his house? He didn't think so. He thought about Melody and his mom at home. "Damn it!" This was his fault, all his fault. One stupid decision and now he probably had some piece of shit drug dealers harassing him. Who knew what they had in mind.

He looked for a spot to pull over but couldn't see one.

He imagined pulling over and then the car pulling past him. A gun pointing out the window and shooting him as the car passed. His heart started beating harder, his breath quickened. Jake recognized the signs of the oncoming panic attack and tried to take a few deep breaths. He looked into his mirror again. The driver had something in his hand. What was he doing? What was it?

The squeal of car tires and the honking of a horn caught Jake's attention. He slammed on his brakes, coming to a halt just inches from the passenger door of a car that was moving through the intersection. Halfway into the intersection, through a red light, Jake jerked his head to the right, looking for more oncoming traffic. A dump truck was headed straight for him. Slamming his car into reverse, he looked behind him. The car that had been following him was gone. Jake stomped on the gas and the squad car lurched backward just as the dump truck entered the intersection. Jake pushed on the brakes and changed out of reverse, now positioned safely behind the red light, the sound of the dump truck's horn reverberating through his body.

Chapter 16

November

L ibby Cartwright had never been particularly ambitious,
but now she worked with one goal in mind: Cooper
Moon. As soon as she had enough money in the bank,
she was going to go to Cooper and tell him her plans. The
two of them would move away from here, anywhere he
wanted to move. They could get a little place together, and
Libby would sell real estate. The more she worked with
Beaulah, the more she realized she could sell real estate on
her own. Just in the short time she had been Beaulah's
assistant, she had brought Beaulah eight listings. True, none
of those had sold yet, but if even half of them did, that'd be a
nice amount of cash for Beaulah.

She cut and pasted a link to one of the listings onto
Beaulah's new Twitter account. She used the same link on
Facebook and even added a picture. Before she became
Beaulah's assistant, Beaulah didn't have a Facebook or a
Twitter account. Now, she had 4,832 followers on Twitter
and 4,111 friends on Facebook! Not bad. People were
beginning to ask questions about the listings, and calls had
increased. Beaulah had at least three showings directly

related to Libby's postings on Facebook. Still no sales, but it was a start.

Beaulah had no idea how to use either Facebook or Twitter, but luckily, Libby was a quick learner who had picked up both of them in no time. Now, she spent hours each day building Beaulah's social network platform. Today, she was going to open a Pinterest account for Beaulah, too. Libby enjoyed working from home, but it all took so much time. Sometimes, it felt overwhelming. Computers were supposed to make everything easier, but to Libby's thinking, they made things harder. Sure, you could reach millions of people, but the glut of information felt like a cascade of rushing water. Everyone was "friends," but no one ever really talked to each other anymore. Texts and tweets had replaced phone calls and face-to-face contact. In an effort to become more social, we have become less so, Libby thought. It was odd, but true. It was sort of fun posting as Beaulah and watching the list of her friends and followers grow, but Libby couldn't imagine doing this as herself. She didn't understand it. Why did people want other people to know what they were doing, where they were doing it, and whom they were doing it with? And really, who wanted to see all of those pictures? Personally, it felt invasive to Libby. A silly waste of time. But others used it, so she could see the value in connecting with those people, at least as Beaulah.

Between the social media outlets and Beaulah's new website, Libby could work for hours and never leave her house. Luckily, Beaulah trusted her. Libby kept track of all of her hours. Of course, she still hadn't made a dime, but Beaulah promised to pay Libby as soon as she had a sale. And Libby was determined that Beaulah was going to have a sale! If she had to work night and day, every waking hour, Beaulah was going to have a sale. It was a lot of effort, but Libby kept reminding herself that every skill she learned was a skill she could use once she and Cooper moved and she had her own real estate license.

Later that afternoon, Libby was waiting in the office for Beaulah when Barb Harris approached her. Libby had seen Barb in the office, but had never spoken to her. If not for Barb, Libby would never have got the job with Beaulah in the first place. Libby had originally applied for the position of assistant to Barb. But the receptionist had later told her that, upon seeing Libby's beat up old truck, Barb had told her to tell Libby that Barb had been called out unexpectedly. Beaulah had overheard the entire exchange, which is why she hired Libby. Initially it had angered Libby, even hurt her feelings, but it was good to know what kind of person Barb was. Now, Libby wouldn't turn her back on her, that was for sure. And it only made Libby even more determined to help Beaulah with her sales. She'd love to see Beaulah outsell Barb; that would be revenge enough.

"Waiting for Beaulah?" Barb asked. She looked as if she had just stepped from the salon. Her big blonde hair was teased into a halo and sprayed into submission. False eyelashes were in place and Barb's blood-red lipstick matched her nail polish. She wore an expensive-looking white silk blouse and slim-fitting black skirt. Libby resisted looking down at her shoes. It was well known in the office that Barb had a penchant for designer shoes. She went on and on whenever anyone noticed her shoes, always mentioning the designer and hinting at the exorbitant cost.

Libby wouldn't give her the satisfaction of noticing them, although she had to admit, grudgingly, she'd probably sneak a peek when Barb walked away. She pulled her feet back up against the couch, hoping Barb wouldn't notice her own shoes, which cost less than twenty dollars from PayLess. "Yes. I'm waiting for Beaulah."

"I don't think we've formally met." Barb leaned over and extended a manicured hand. "I'm Barb Harris. I'm sort of the big gun in the office."

"Oh?" Libby said as she took her hand. Soft and warm, with no grip. Libby hated it when women shook hands like that, as if their wrists were broken. Libby gave Barb's hand an extra squeeze and a hardy shake. "Great to meet you."

Barb pulled her hand away. "I see Beaulah has a new website. And she's on Twitter and Facebook now. I assume that's all you."

Libby smiled but said nothing.

"You know, I could use a new assistant. I hired one, but she didn't work out. With all of my closings and new listings, I just don't have enough time in the day. I could use someone sharp to take care of my social media, run some errands here and there for me. Maybe put up and take down my signs."

Libby resisted the urge to tell her what to do with her signs. "Actually, I love working with Beaulah. I can hardly keep up! You better be careful. She might just be the big gun here before too long. Besides, how could I help you out? I drive that junky old truck. And you wouldn't want me showing up to work in that, now would you?"

Barb gritted her teeth and parted her lips, a sort of smile. "Well, best of luck to you. Maybe you'll be able to get a new truck once Beaulah makes a sale. Of course, it's been years and she hasn't made one yet. But, I'm sure with you on board, that's all about to change, right?" Barb flashed her teeth in a smirk and didn't wait for an answer. She spun on her expensive heels and strutted off toward her office down the hall.

Libby gritted her own teeth and resisted the urge to jump from the couch and knock Barb on her ass. Instead, she flipped her off. She instantly regretted it. Her head pivoted quickly to see if anyone saw. The receptionist was the only other person in the lobby. She and Libby exchanged looks, and she gave Libby a thumbs up. Libby smiled. It was good to know someone else in the office couldn't stand that old windbag.

Libby promised herself that if Beaulah ever did make a sale, Libby was going to use her part of the money to buy

Beaulah an expensive pair of shoes—that'd shut Barb up. But as soon as the thought formed, Libby realized it was flawed. Beaulah didn't care about expensive shoes and Libby couldn't afford to spend any money on shoes. As sad as it was, Barb was right. Libby's first priority should be getting a new truck, or maybe a car this time. She and Cooper couldn't leave town in either of their trucks, not if they wanted to get very far. And Libby did want to get very far.

Chapter 17

November

Violet had not left the two-story building that housed Bass Turds and Pete's apartment since the night she had been attacked in the parking lot. Although their relationship had remained platonic and they each stayed on their sides of the bed, Violet loved sleeping beside Pete. It was the only time she felt completely safe. And now, after a few months, Pete was beginning to do little things for her. She once mentioned she did not like pulp in orange juice; Pete quit buying juice with pulp, even though he preferred it. Violet was always cold at night, so Pete bought a new blanket and put it on her side of the bed.

Every morning, Violet made them breakfast. They sat at a tiny table overlooking the street in front of the building. Violet made Pete eggs and toast, just the way he liked them. Eggs over easy and wheat toast lightly buttered. At first, Violet did things for him just so he would let her stay. She figured the more she did, the harder it would be to kick her out. But then she started enjoying cleaning the apartment and surprising him with little things like washing the windows or cleaning the grout in the bathroom. Things that felt like little gifts. Violet felt she owed him so much. When Pete found them, her little gifts, he always seemed so appreciative. Violet loved that about Pete, the way he noticed and was grateful for everything.

On this particular morning, as they sat at the little table and watched the street traffic below, Pete cleared his throat, as if about to speak. Pete didn't talk a lot during breakfast, so this caught Violet's attention.

"Violet, it's been a few weeks since … since you've been staying here."

Violet looked down at her plate. Suddenly, she felt ill. She could not eat another bite. She put down her fork. He was going to throw her out now. She could feel her pulse in her neck and she suddenly found it difficult to swallow.

Pete continued. "And I've noticed you haven't been out of the house. Your car hasn't moved from the parking lot. Have you been anywhere at all?"

Violet shook her head.

Pete cleared his throat again. "Violet, that's not good for you. I know you're probably scared after what happened, but that was just a one-time thing. I never saw that guy before, and I haven't seen him since. It was an out-of-state license plate. I think he was just passing through. He's gone. You're safe."

Violet fidgeted with the napkin in her lap.

"Violet, I think you need to get out of the house."

Here it comes, she thought. She tried to swallow again but could not.

"I think maybe you should go and talk to someone. Maybe a counselor or something. I'm sure Frank's insurance would pay for it, and if it won't, I will."

Violet looked up at Pete. "You'd do that?"

"Sure. If your insurance won't pay for it, I will."

"You really want me out of here, huh?"

Pete looked down at the kitchen floor for a few moments before he spoke again. Slowly, he lifted his head and looked directly into Violet's eyes. "No. I don't want you to leave." He took a deep breath, and then exhaled. "I don't want you to ever leave." He looked away and stared at the refrigerator. Minutes passed. The hum of the refrigerator suddenly seemed very loud. Cars passed by on the street. Somewhere, a dog barked. Finally, he looked back at Violet.

She had tears in her eyes. "I don't want to leave either. Ever."

Pete smiled. He wanted to reach across the table and take her hand, but he was afraid it might scare her. Everything seemed to scare her now. Violet smiled back. Another car passed. The dog barked again, and the refrigerator hummed, although it now seemed like a happy song to Pete. "But you still need to go talk to someone. It seems like maybe you're afraid to leave the house now, and I think that's just going to get worse until you talk to someone and get things figured out."

"I don't want to. I don't want to talk to some stranger. That won't help."

"Well, how about this? Let's just start small. How about we start going to church? I've been wanting to check out Cooper's church. Will you do that with me? Will you go to church with me on Sunday?"

Violet nodded. "Yes. I'll go. As long as you're there with me, I'll go."

"Okay then. You have a date," Pete said, and they both smiled.

Chapter 18

November

Ivy Miller's feet made little padding noises against the hardwood floor as she walked around the dining table, fussing over the table settings. She set out the expensive china on the expensive placemats and was using the expensive silverware. She even used the expensive glasses, despite hating how they felt against her lips. She liked drinking out of plastic glasses better, although Ivy would never admit that to anyone. She glanced at her watch. Six fifteen—too soon to light the candles. Drake promised he'd be home by six thirty. She couldn't remember the last time he was home before eight.

Ivy inspected the table again. It was gorgeous. She remembered the day they had bought the dining set. They had driven to Kalamazoo and spent the entire day going from furniture store to furniture store. Finally, they had come across this one, a gorgeous, dark cherry double pedestal leaf table with high-back upholstered chairs. It extended to 112 inches, and that day in the store it was fully extended, a stunning table setting in place. Instantly, they both fell in love with it. Ivy stood beside Drake, smiling and imagining the family meals they would eat on this table. They'd have three or four kids, and every night they'd eat together—on this table. It was perfect.

But reality fell short. Initially, Drake and Ivy ate at the table, both sitting together at one end for late-night dinners, the table stretching across the dining room. Then Lucy came along and Ivy realized the difficulty of waiting until eight o'clock to eat dinner with a toddler. By the time Lucy started school, it was easier for Ivy to have two dinners on the big table: one with Lucy after school, and then one with Drake when he came home. Eventually, though, Drake came home later and later, and it didn't seem worth the bother. By the time Lucy was in grade school, Ivy and Lucy abandoned the table and ate dinner every night in front of the television. Now, with Lucy in college and working, the table gathered dust. Most nights, Ivy ate alone in front of the television.

Ivy hated to be alone. The first thing she did every morning was turn on the television, just for company. She couldn't stand a quiet house. For just a moment, Ivy thought of her mother, who always hated to be alone, too. The sound of the garage door sliding up broke the memory. Ivy hurried to the living room and turned off the television. Moving to the kitchen, she checked the cherry cobbler in the oven. Everything else was done and waiting to be served—ham, homemade macaroni and cheese, green bean casserole, and mashed potatoes, all of their favorites. And cherry cobbler. She'd even made a trip into town to buy some vanilla bean ice cream from Benjamin's Ice Cream Shop. It would be great on the cobbler.

Lucy rushed through the door and ran past the kitchen. "Just gonna take a quick shower! Five minutes, tops!"

"Okay! Hurry up." Ivy smiled. She tried to remember the last time all three of them had eaten together, but could not. Even when they were all home at dinnertime, a rare occurrence, they usually ate in front of the television.

Her cell phone rang. Ivy ignored it. *No*, she thought to

herself, *not tonight. Not tonight!* She stood in front of the oven and watched the timer count down. The phone rang again. "Damn it!" Ivy said, before even looking at the phone. "Let me guess, Drake, you can't make it. Or you're going to be late."

"I'm sorry, Ivy. Really. I was walking out the door when I got a call. It's a huge order. I have to take it. Normally, I wouldn't, but everyone has left. I gotta talk to this guy."

"Why can't he just call tomorrow?"

"Ivy, you just don't understand. This is a huge order. This guy is a contractor and if I work for him I might get all of his future business. All of it! Could mean a real difference to us."

Ivy hung up. *A real difference*, she thought. *Great.* Maybe they could build an even bigger, even nicer, house for her to sit home alone in. The phone rang again. She picked it up, turned off the volume, and dropped it in a drawer.

(

From his office at the sawmill, Drake dialed again, and again. The third time, he left voicemail. "I'm sorry, Ivy. I really am. But I'm doing this for us, for our future. Can't you see that? I'll be home as soon as I can. But, honestly, it will probably be a couple of hours." He paused and searched for the right words. "I'm doing my best here, Ivy. Can't you see that?"

He hung up. He knew the answer to the last question. No. She couldn't see it. Maybe she could at first. When he first started the business, they used to lie awake at night and talk about plans for expansion. She seemed so excited back then. And when he started coming home late after a long day of work, she often had a meal waiting for him. She'd sit at the table with him and he'd tell her about his day. Eventually, as late nights become the norm instead of the exception, he'd come home to find a plate of cold food waiting for him in the refrigerator. Eventually, even that disappeared. Drake would return to find her watching television or already in bed with a book. They exchanged a few words and both went to sleep at eleven. The next day, he'd get up and do it again.

He couldn't remember exactly when it happened—when being at work started to feel more like "home" than home itself. The years passed. The days got longer. Eventually, he heard the rumors about Ivy sleeping around behind his back. At first, it hurt, but after a while, he had to admit it was a bit of a relief. He had no energy for sex anymore. Everything was poured into work. Everything. As long as she was discreet, who did it hurt? He hated to admit it, but he didn't care anymore. Initially, he had the best of intentions. As the business grew, he imagined how his success would benefit the family—a nicer house, more luxurious cars, expensive clothes for Ivy, a college education for Lucy. But eventually it became more about making the business bigger and better. And it was never enough. No matter what the bottom line was, it was never enough.

A few years ago, during a fight, Ivy had shouted, "What good does all this money do us? We don't even like each other anymore!" It wasn't until that moment that Drake realized it was true. He didn't like Ivy, and she didn't like him. And for the life of him, he didn't understand how that had happened.

(

"Mmmmm. Something smells good." Lucy was dressed in pink flannel pajamas, with her wet hair combed straight back. She crossed the room and wrapped her arms around her mother. "Thanks for doing all this work, Mom. Smells so good! I'm starving."

Ivy hugged her back. "Pajamas, already?"

"Yes! They're so cozy. You should put pajamas on too!

And we'll make Dad change into pajamas as soon as he walks in the door. It will be fun."

"He called…"

"Let me guess. He has to work."

Ivy did not respond.

"It's okay. Me and you will have a great dinner without him. His loss! Go put on your pajamas."

Ivy said nothing, but Lucy sensed she was considering it.

"Come on, Mom. Go change!" Lucy gave her mother a gentle push. "Go on! I'll find something to watch on TV, some old movie or something. Go change!"

Ivy laughed. "All right! But find something I'll like too."

Shortly afterward, they were watching *The Wizard of Oz*, the only thing they could agree on. They had both eaten too much, so Ivy was surprised when Lucy suggested they move on to the cobbler and ice cream.

"Ugh! I'm so full!"

"Me too, but it smells so good. Come on! We'll just have small bowls. Let's eat it while it's still hot. It's better that way, with the ice cream melting down the sides."

Both clad in pajamas, they ignored the dirty dishes strewn about the kitchen and filled clean bowls with cobbler and ice cream. They had put away the leftovers, but hadn't bothered with anything else. "You sure you don't want to load the dishwasher?" Lucy asked.

Ivy shook her head as she scooped ice cream from the carton. "I'll get them in the morning."

"I feel bad, though, leaving you with all of the mess. I have class in the morning."

"Since when do you feel bad about dirty dishes?" Ivy asked and then laughed.

"I do feel bad. I'll help you. We can do it right now."

"No. Let's eat our cobbler. The dishes can wait. I just want to hang out with you."

Lucy wrapped her arms around her mother from behind and rested her chin on her shoulder. "You're a good mom."

Ivy said nothing for a moment. Then, paused in the middle of scooping another scoop of ice cream, she said, "No, truly I'm not. I try to be, but I'm not."

Lucy tried to spin her mother around to face her, but Ivy resisted. "Mom, that's not true. You are a good mom."

"No. Let me say this," Ivy insisted. "I want you to know. I ... I never had much of a role model, I guess. My mom kicked me out of the house when I was just a kid, and the truth is, I just don't know how to be a mom. But I'm trying. It's important to me."

Lucy tried to spin her mother around again, but Ivy held on to the counter, refusing to move. "Mom, I'm so sorry," Lucy whispered over her mother's shoulder. "You never told me that. Is that why you never talk about your childhood?"

Ivy nodded. "I guess."

"Jeez, Mom. That's horrible. How old were you?"

"Fourteen."

Ivy straightened and went back to scooping ice cream. "I haven't seen her since, and I don't want to. I don't even know if she's still alive. It doesn't matter. It's over, in the past. I just wanted you to know that I'm doing the best I can, but I want to do better. I'm really trying."

Lucy reached up and gave her mother's shoulders a gentle squeeze. "I love you, Mom."

Ivy closed the box of ice cream and dropped the dirty spoon in the sink. "I love you too." She turned, finally, to face her daughter. "Come on. Let's go see what happens to Dorothy."

Chapter 19

November

Cooper and Sally sat on the couch, watching television, but both were lost in their own thoughts and noticed little of what was happening on the screen.

Sally was wondering if she should redecorate the diner—nothing too expensive, but something to change things up a little. Maybe she'd give it a fifties sort of look, or maybe buy a juke box and new uniforms for the waitresses—poodle skirts and those black and white shoes. What were those called? Sally frowned. She couldn't remember.

Cooper glanced sideways at Sally. Why was she frowning? What was she thinking about? *Has Violet contacted her*, he wondered. *Has she sent naked pictures to her? Is that why Sally has been so distant lately? Would Sally keep quiet about something like that? Maybe she would.* Or maybe it was something else. Cooper reached out and took her hand in his. "How are things going at the diner?"

"Fine."

"Anything new?"

"I'm thinking about adding fried green tomatoes to the

menu. Do you think people would like that?"

Cooper shrugged. "I don't know. I like 'em. You could give it a try. If they don't sell, just take them back off the menu."

"But that would cost money. I'd have to print up new menus."

"Just put a little paper insert into the menu advertising the fried green tomatoes. Or get a little chalkboard, like you see in the movies. You know, with the daily special written on it. Then you could try out new stuff and see if people like it. It would be easier than changing the menu."

Sally nodded. "That's not a bad idea."

A commercial break came on. Cooper picked up the remote and muted the sound. "Sally, if something was bothering you, you'd tell me, wouldn't you?"

Sally sighed. "Cooper, why are you always asking me what's wrong lately? Are you up to something? Is there something *I* should be worried about?"

"No! Not at all! I just … you just … you just seem so distant, that's all. Like you're always thinking about something else. Like right now, while we were watching the movie, what were you thinking about?"

"I was trying to remember the name of those black and white shoes. You know, the kind girls used to wear in the fifties."

Cooper's face scrunched up in disbelief. "That's what you were thinking about?"

"Yeah. What are those called? I can't remember."

"Is it Frank?"

"What?"

"Is something going on between you and Frank?"

Sally laughed. "Now *that's* funny! So, let me get this straight, because I'm sitting here thinking about shoes, I must be having an affair with Frank. Is that what you are saying?" She stood up. "That's pretty good, Cooper, especially with your track record." She turned from him and strode toward the bedroom. "That takes a lot of guts, accusing me of that. I'm going to bed."

"I wasn't accusing you. I was asking. Hey, come back. I'm sorry. I didn't mean to make you mad."

Cooper heard the bedroom door close. *Well, that went well*, he thought. He walked over to the door, grabbed his coat from off the floor where he had thrown it when he came home, and stepped outside. It was colder than he thought. Zipping his coat, he walked to the woods. He could see his breath. He turned up his collar and shoved his hands into his pockets.

He loved the woods, this piece of land; he'd grown up here, in the same mobile home he and Sally lived in now. His parents had left the mobile home and eighty-four acres to him. Cooper hadn't even known they had a will, but not long after they were killed in a car crash, he had inherited the place. Nineteen, and on his own. The mobile home wasn't much. In truth, he supposed it wasn't worth much at all, maybe two thousand dollars, maybe three if they threw in the woodstove. But the land, the land made him feel rich. He didn't see how anyone could live in the city. He needed this piece of land. Just walking on it made him feel better. He wondered what people in the city did? He'd never been to New York City, but he wondered what they did when they felt like going for a walk. How could you walk and think with all those people, all that traffic? Maybe they took a cab to Central Park. He'd seen the park on TV before, but it, too, always seemed so full of people. He needed nature, but he needed it in isolation. Walking in a park with a bunch of people just wasn't the same. Cooper needed to be alone, just him and the trees.

He looked skyward, hoping to see some stars through the trees, but the night was too dark and cloudy. No stars shone through. He crept along cautiously. Even though Cooper knew the woods by heart, it was dark enough that he might trip over something.

As a child, he had played in these woods. He and his buddies had built a fort out here and used to swing from the trees on ropes. One day, he had been out here with Johnny Small and Mark Wagner, playing, when one of the ropes had snapped and Mark had broken his arm. Cooper continued walking and shook his head at the memory. They were such dumb kids. The same night Mark broke his arm, Cooper and Johnny had been straight back on the rope swing again. They'd just tied a knot in the rope where it split and kept on swinging. *It's a wonder we didn't kill ourselves*, Cooper thought.

Another time, they had the idea of making a parachute and jumping from a tall old oak. Johnny had brought an old sheet from his house and the boys tied ropes to all four corners and took turns jumping from the oak, holding onto the ropes until Johnny broke his leg on a particularly spectacular jump.

One night, when the boys were barely twelve, Johnny had stolen a bottle of whiskey from his dad's liquor cabinet and they had all taken turns chugging from the bottle. It had seemed fun at first. There was much laughter—until the vomiting began. When their parents had found out, Johnny and Mark were forbidden to visit Cooper's house again. Eventually, though, the boys had found their way back to the fort in the woods. Once their teen years came, they'd gotten better at hiding their drinking. At one point, one wall of the fort had been used to display empty bottles. Eventually, they had grown bored with looking at the bottles and had taken them out and thrown them off an overpass, watching them smash onto the road below with delight. It wasn't until years later that Cooper had realized they probably passed out a few flat tires that night.

Cooper reached the fort and stood below it, gazing up. He hadn't been in it in years. He couldn't even remember the last time. A series of short two-by-four boards were nailed to the tree as a makeshift ladder. Cooper reached up and pulled on one. It seemed sturdy enough. He stepped on one and pulled himself up. It held. He continued up the tree. When he reached the top rung, he wished he had thought to bring a flashlight. It was too dark to see much. Cooper scooped some leaves and debris from the entrance to the fort and crawled inside. It was a simple box-shaped structure built next to a tree trunk, with a couple of sturdy branches supporting the floor. The roof was a hodgepodge of discarded lumber and worked fine unless it rained. They had talked about putting shingles on the roof, but they never did.

Cooper looked around the fort. It was smaller than he remembered, and higher up. There were lots of cracks he could see through. He scooted further in, noticing something carved in one of the boards. It was his name ... and something else. He ran his hand over the board and squinted. Reading it brought a smile to his lips. Yes. He remembered now. The last time he'd been here was with Sally. It was in high school. He'd brought her out here to show her the fort. He ran his hand over the words. *Cooper Loves Sally.* He'd forgotten about that. He wondered if Sally remembered. Maybe he'd take it back to the house to show her. He tugged on the board, but it was firmly in place. He tugged again. Nope. It wasn't coming off, not without a hammer. Maybe he'd bring her out here and show her. But he couldn't imagine Sally climbing up here. It smelled bad—damp and dusty. And it was probably full of spiderwebs. Maybe it wasn't such a good idea, bringing Sally out here. He crawled back over to the door and sat in the opening, his legs dangling.

The tree creaked and groaned as a wind blew through. Cooper held his breath for a moment, but the fort held. He imagined the headlines: Local Man Killed When Tree Fort Collapsed. *That'd be embarrassing,* he thought.

He wondered whatever happened to Johnny and Mark. Last he heard, they'd left for college, maybe Western, in Kalamazoo? He couldn't remember. He wondered if they were married, if they had kids, if they were even still alive. He couldn't believe he was forty. How was that possible? Cooper didn't feel forty. But, then again, he didn't know what forty felt like. He felt the same as he had when he was twenty. But the mirror told him different. He'd seen a few grey hairs lately, which bothered him. Cooper was surprised by that response. He wasn't vain—well, maybe a little—but the thought of his hair turning grey was depressing. It had always been so black. It was part of who he was. He remembered one time in high school when he was walking down the hall and a girl had called out, "There he is, that wild black-haired Cooper Moon."

One day his hair would be all grey. Cooper couldn't believe that. It just didn't seem right, his hair changing color like that. Didn't seem right at all.

It was getting colder. Cooper didn't remember it being so cold in the fort. They used to play out here all winter long. Of course, that was usually during the day when the sun warmed the fort, even through the trees. As he sat there, snow began to fall. He'd seen a few flakes here and there this winter, but this was the first real snow of the season, enough to stick. Cooper sat there, growing colder by the minute but enjoying the spectacle. The snow seemed to float down instead of fall, as if there were barely enough weight in each snowflake to make it to the ground. He watched until the floor of the woods was covered in white. His footprints would be the first to walk across that snow. Hundreds of years ago, maybe someone else walked across these woods on a snowy night like this. He liked the thought of that. That was the thing about land—it was living, in a way that seemed even more real than his life. This land had witnessed thousands of years, maybe millions, and it would be here long after he, Cooper Moon, was gone. This land. These trees. He wondered what would happen to it after he was gone. It was a shame he and Sally never had a baby; that would have given him someone to pass it along to. He'd hate for someone to come in and clear the woods for lumber. But, really, after he was gone, what difference would it make? The thought was beginning to depress him.

He wondered if people in heaven could look down here and see what was going on, if his own parents could see him right now in this silly fort. That thought depressed him even more. Maybe it was time to go home.

Looking down, Cooper tried to remember how they used to get down. There must have been some sort of handhold or something up here, but he couldn't find it in the dark. He turned around and tried to find the first board down with his foot. With half of his body hanging from the fort, he searched for the rung using both feet. Finally, his right foot hit the board and he stepped down. That's when he remembered they did have a handhold—an old rope they used to hold onto for the first few steps. Well, he had no idea where that was, so he'd just have to hang on to the floor of the fort. He stepped down with his left foot and found the next rung.

His legs were shaking, which disgusted him. He'd been in and out of this fort thousands of times. What was wrong with him? A couple of steps down and he could reach the rungs with his hands. More steadily now, he made his way to the ground. Rubbing his hands together to wipe off the dirt, he looked up at the old fort. It had to be at least twenty feet off the ground. *It's a wonder we didn't kill ourselves*, he thought again as he walked back to the trailer, doing his best to ignore his trembling legs.

Chapter 20

November

Melody stretched across the couch, a cool damp washcloth on her forehead, her eyes closed. She had spent the morning throwing up again. Weak and tired, she just wanted to nap, but instead, she had to listen to not only the ramblings of Clara and her nurse but also to the constant sound of construction as Cooper, TJ, and Jake worked on the addition. If Jake hadn't been home, she would have gone to the hotel for a quiet day of sleep. Lately, she'd been sneaking off one day a week—it was heavenly. Eventually, she supposed it would catch up with her, especially when Jake saw the credit card bill, but until then she was going to enjoy her hotel naps. She had even started ordering room service, and that was the best. Room service and a pay-per-view movie. She had missed so many new releases that it was fun to catch up. Now, she almost couldn't stand to be in her house. She wished she were in the hotel right now, wearing that pristine white robe. Instead, she had to lie here on the couch while Clara and the nurse watched *The Price is Right* and saws whined in the background.

"No! No! That's way too much," Clara told the

television as a woman bid on a refrigerator.

"I don't know. Refrigerators can be mighty pricey, especially big stainless steel ones like that one," Josephine said.

"Not a penny over twelve hundred dollars," Clara insisted.

Melody moaned, wishing all of the noise would just go away. She felt so sick, and no one even seemed to care. They all went about their business as if she did not exist. Even Jake was outside with TJ and Cooper, instead of being in here taking care of her.

The price of the refrigerator was revealed. "Eleven ninety-nine!" the announcer said.

"Told you!"

"Miss Clara, you sure know your prices," Josephine said.

"I've watched this show for years. I don't like the new guy as much as Bob Barker. He just isn't as good. I don't know how he ever got on here. I guess he used to have a TV show or something. I think they should just bring Bob back."

Melody sighed. Clara could remember how much refrigerators cost but had tried to take a bite out of a candle this morning. "Could you please lower your voices? And maybe turn the TV down a bit?" Melody asked.

"Why don't you go back to your own bedroom?" Josephine said. "That'd make more sense than sprawling out on the couch right here in the middle of everything."

"It's too noisy back there. They're working right on the other side of the wall. I'd never be able to rest back there."

"Seems like it'd be better than lying here in the living room like you was dying."

"I'm pregnant. I've had morning sickness all day."

"I had five kids, and I had morning sickness too, but I never spent one minute lying on a couch and feeling sorry for myself."

"I'm not feeling sorry for myself. I'm trying to feel

better."

"Seems to me you'd feel better if you'd just get up and do something. Get up off that couch and go do some housework. The bathrooms could sure use some cleaning, especially since you spent the morning throwing up in one."

(

Outside, the foundation had been poured and the men were working on framing up the addition. The weather was supposed to get colder the following week, so they were hoping to have the addition enclosed before then.

"How's it going, Jake? Arrest anyone interesting lately?" TJ asked in between swings of his hammer.

"Nah. Just the same old speeders and drunk drivers." Jake cut boards while TJ and Cooper hammered. The result was constant noise. They talked in between the whine of the saw and the erratic thumping of the hammers.

"Do you arrest a lot of drunk drivers?" Cooper asked.

"More than I'd like."

"Seems like we ought to have a better system. Free cab service if you're drunk, something like that."

Jake turned to Cooper. "Yeah! I've thought the same thing! I even sort of came up with an idea. We could have a bus that would go to the bars to pick up people. That way we could haul a lot of people at once. An old school bus, maybe."

"That's a good idea," TJ said. "It could have a stereo system, so you could play music, kind of make it fun to ride the bus home. Name it something cool."

"Who would buy the bus, though?" Cooper asked. "The city?"

"Yeah, that's the problem. I don't think the city would ever do it. They make money ticketing drunk drivers, and they don't have that kind of money to spend."

"Maybe one of the bars," TJ suggested.

"Yeah," Jake agreed. "But it needs to be a bus that

could make the rounds to all the bars. Why would one bar buy a bus everyone used?"

"Yeah. Doesn't make sense," Cooper said.

"Hey!" Jake turned to Cooper. "What about your church? That is exactly the kind of thing a church could do! It would sort of be a public service."

"Yeah, maybe."

"You could have some sort of fundraiser," Jake said. "Churches do that kind of stuff all the time. I'd help you. I could probably get some donations for you from some of the guys. None of us like arresting drunk drivers."

"How much do you suppose a used school bus would cost?" Cooper asked.

"I bet you could get one for less than fifteen grand," Jake said. "There can't be that much of a market for used school buses, can there?"

"We could paint it a cool color," TJ offered.

"I have to admit, this sounds like a pretty good idea," Cooper said. "And it does seem like the kind of thing a church should do. If you guys will help me figure out how to get it started, I'll do it. Wait a minute ... who would drive the bus? That's going to cost us some money, paying a driver."

"We could ask for donations from the passengers, not charge them anything, but just tell them they can donate a few bucks if they want. And we can pay for the driver and the gas with the donations."

"How many people can ride on a bus?" Cooper asked.

Jake shrugged. "Maybe fifty. I don't know. But let's just figure twenty people a night. If they each paid two dollars, that would be forty bucks, which should be enough for gas and the driver. I don't know, maybe that's not enough."

"How would they get their cars the next day?" Cooper asked.

"I don't know. That's their problem."

"Maybe we should charge five dollars for the ride," TJ said. "If people have enough money to sit in a bar and drink until they are drunk, they ought to have five dollars to avoid getting arrested for drunk driving. That way, we'd have enough for upkeep and repairs. And maybe we could offer to pick them up at their house and take them to the bar too. That way, they wouldn't drive their car at all. Kind of a limo service to and from the bar. If we made it fun, people might like that. I could see groups of friends doing that together."

"I could volunteer to drive at first," Jake offered. "Maybe we could start it as a weekend thing. In fact, maybe we'd only offer it on the weekends. There might not be enough business during the week. We could do it Friday and Saturday nights. Ten bucks a head for a ride to and from the bars. Or five dollars if you just want a ride home. If it doesn't work out, we could just sell the bus and give the money back to the people who donated."

"Maybe," Cooper said. "Maybe."

Chapter 21

November

Pete and Violet sat in the parked car in the driveway. "You have to go in and at least get some clothes. You can't keep wearing my sweatpants and tee shirts," Pete told Violet.

Violet stared through the windshield of Pete's truck. It was her house, and it was only a few steps away. She had the keys in her hand. It shouldn't seem so difficult, but it did.

"I could go in with you if you want," Pete offered.

"Would you?"

"I think it'd be better if you went in by yourself, but yeah, I'll go in with you."

It was early Saturday morning, a little before eight. Most of the subdivision was not awake, or barely so. Only one person noticed Pete and Violet, and he stood at his kitchen window peering outside, watching their every move. Bill Monroe had lived in Woodland Trace from the beginning. His house was the very first one built in the subdivision; as such, he felt a sense of ownership over the community. He had the phone number of every one of his neighbors and was always on the lookout for something not quite right. Today seemed like such a morning. Somebody was at the Collette's house, and he didn't recognize them. Bill reached for his cell phone and quickly called Frank.

Unaware that he was being watched, Pete got out of his truck and opened the passenger side door for Violet. "Come on. Let's get your stuff."

Violet exited the car slowly, her head ducked down. It seemed such a tremendous chore. The sleeves of one of Pete's pale grey sweatshirts were rolled up, and the shirt hung loosely from her petite frame over a pair of too-big black sweatpants rolled up at the bottom. Her hair was pulled back in a ponytail and she wore no trace of makeup. Violet, pale, scared and buried in fleece, approached the front door and inserted her key. It opened, surprising her somewhat, although she did not know why. When she stepped inside, the house seemed bigger than she remembered. Violet started down the hall for the guest bedroom, but stopped after just a few steps to see if Pete was following her. He stood in the foyer. "Come with me," she said.

"Okay. But it feels kind of weird, walking around in Frank's house when he isn't here.

"It's my house too." Violet no longer felt that was true.

With Pete following, she walked into the guest bedroom, pulled two suitcases from the closet, and moved back to her bedroom. After placing the suitcases on the bed and zipping them open, Violet grabbed handfuls of clothes from the bedroom dresser drawers and threw them into one of the suitcases."

"Not much of a packer, huh?" Pete asked with a smile.

Violet did not answer. The look on her face was grim and determined. She moved to the closet and pulled clothes from hangers, dropping them into the suitcases. Soon, both suitcases were full, but many of her clothes still hung in the closet. In the nearby bathroom, she grabbed an armload of toiletries and makeup and dumped them into the suitcase, atop the clothes. Then she closed both bulging suitcases and zipped them shut. "There," she said.

"That's it? That's all you're taking?"

Violet looked around the room and nodded. "Yes. That's it. Oh, one more thing." She took one of the suitcases from the bed while Pete grabbed the other. He followed her down the hall and across the living room to a desk in one corner of the room. Violet opened a drawer and pulled out a big photo album. "Photos of Rachel Ann," she said.

"What the hell's going on here?" Frank walked through the door, glancing between Pete and Violet.

Violet stared at the floor. Silent.

Pete waited for her to say something, anything, but she did not. Finally, he stepped forward. "Violet has been living in my apartment for the last couple of months, and she has decided to stay there, but she needs some clothes."

"So, you've been screwing my wife?"

"No!" Pete took another step toward Frank and then stopped himself. "No. Not at all. We're ... I ... She's had a tough time, and she just sort of moved in."

"What in the hell is wrong with you?" Frank asked Violet. "Why are you dressed like that?"

Violet continued to stare down at the floor.

"How long have you two been living together?" Frank asked Pete.

"Since September."

"You've been living with him for two months while I've been staying in a hotel for eighty bucks a night! Are you kidding me?"

Violet said nothing, just clutched the photograph album and the handle of her suitcase.

"Well, I'm moving back in. Right now! It's a good thing Bill called me. I wouldn't have even known this. You could have told me. And why don't you answer your cell phone?"

Finally, Violet spoke up. "The battery is dead. I don't use it anymore."

"Then I'm canceling the service."

"I don't care. Go ahead."

"Why are you acting so weird? You look like hell. Are you sick?"

Violet shook her head and walked past him to the front door, suitcase in tow. "I'm taking these pictures of Rachel Ann. I'll have copies made for you as soon as I can afford to." She walked out the door.

Pete followed her down the sidewalk and put both of the suitcases into the bed of his pickup.

Frank stood in the driveway. "Don't think you're coming back here after shacking up with him!" he yelled as Violet got into Pete's truck.

"I don't want to." Violet closed the door.

Frank stood there, a puzzled look on his face, as Pete backed the truck down the driveway. Just before they reached the street, Pete put the brakes on and drove back up to the house, stopping in front of the garage, close to where Frank was standing. Violet rolled down her window. "Frank," she said softly. "I'm sorry."

"For what?"

"For everything, Frank. For everything." She rolled up her window, Pete backed down the driveway, and Frank watched as his wife pulled away.

Chapter 22

November

On Sunday morning, Cooper approached the podium in his little church and spotted the old preacher in the second row. Cooper smiled at him, trying to remember his name. Troy—that was it! Troy. Cooper then spotted Pete and Violet in the front row. Pete smiled and waved, and Violet even managed a small smile. Flustered, Cooper dropped his index cards and had to kneel on the floor behind the podium and try to sort them back into order. He had not numbered them; he'd never make that mistake again.

His cards gathered, Cooper stood before the church and tried to calm himself. He couldn't believe Violet had the guts to show up at his church when she was blackmailing him. He tried to avoid making eye contact. "Welcome, everybody. Looks like another full house. If we keep this up, we are going to run out of room, but I guess that's a good problem to have."

The crowd clapped, someone whistled, and another man yelled, "Praise God!"

Cooper tried to smile, but that was difficult with Violet sitting in the front row. Why was she here? Was this some sort of threat?

Cooper cleared his throat. "Today, I'd like to talk about compassion. I looked it up and the word compassion is in the Bible eighty-two times. I don't know about you, but it's something I don't always think about. Maybe you don't either. We are so busy with our own lives that we don't always see someone else's pain. Someone cuts you off in traffic, and you immediately get mad, maybe you flip them off, or cuss them out. But, you never know what kind of day that person just had. Maybe they're coming from a doctor's appointment and they just learned they had cancer. Maybe they're hurrying to a hospital to be with a loved one who is dying. Maybe their wife or husband just left. Maybe they just lost their job." Cooper looked right at Violet. "Heck, maybe an old girlfriend is blackmailing them!"

The congregation laughed, Pete laughed, but Violet did not even crack a smile.

Cooper tried to remember his next point, but could not. He looked down at his cards.

"Jesus spoke about compassion. In Ephesians 4:32 he said, 'Be kind and compassionate to one another, forgiving each other, just as in Christ God forgave you.' But that can be a hard thing, especially if someone is deliberately trying to hurt you." He looked at Violet again. No response. Nothing. He had to look down at his cards again. He couldn't remember anything.

"I know I've been forgiven by God, because the Bible tells me that. But I've been forgiven by lots of people in my life, too. Especially my wife."

The congregation laughed, but Cooper did not even smile.

"I don't deserve that forgiveness, but she forgives anyway. And I think maybe that's how we're supposed to be. We're supposed to forgive, whether someone deserves it or not. God forgave us, so we're supposed to forgive others. Going back to my example of someone cutting you off in traffic—that has probably happened to all of us, and it always makes us mad. But would you be mad if you knew that person was speeding to a dying loved one? Probably not. You'd be understanding and forgiving. But, the thing is, we never know what someone is going through. We never know what kind of pain they're suffering. So, when someone cuts me off, now I tell myself maybe they're going to a loved one, or maybe they just had a terrible morning. I try to give them the benefit of the doubt. Instead of getting mad, I try to have compassion."

Cooper looked down at his cards again. He had another verse written down, but couldn't remember the point it was supposed to illustrate. He muddled his way through the rest of the sermon, certain it was his worst one ever. Afterward, as he stood outside thanking people for coming, Pete and Violet approached him. "Great job, Cooper! I have to tell you, I didn't think you had it in you. I never expected something like this. We enjoyed it, didn't we Violet?"

"Yes," Violet said. She reminded Cooper of a rabbit, crouched down, as if she were afraid someone might discover her. Obviously, she was feeling guilty.

"Thanks, Pete. I was a bit distracted today. Not my best Sunday."

"Well, we think you did just great, and we'll be back next Sunday. Right, Violet?"

"Yes. Thank you, Cooper." She reached out to shake Cooper's hand.

In disbelief, Cooper took her hand and shook it. He had to hand it to her: she had guts.

Beaulah sat in the front row of her husband's church. In the last week, they had barely spoken to each other. Now, she sat there, hoping he would back down from his attack on Cooper and his church. In her heart, however, she knew he would not. It was one of the things that drove her crazy about Perry, and one of the things she used to love the most.

She sat there, staring straight ahead and preparing for the worst.

The band sang four songs while the congregation stood and joined them in singing. Then the lights lowered and a video played. It was a clip from a movie, some comedy Beaulah did not recognize. The clip showed a man in bed with a woman when his wife walks through the door. He jumps from the bed, falling in the process. When he gets to his feet, he keeps saying, "This isn't what it looks like!" as his wife rushes out the door.

Beaulah braced herself. This was not going to be good.

As Perry walked onto the stage, the stage lights shone upon him. In the dark, the congregation settled into their seats and listened in anticipation.

"Not much of a husband, was he?"

The congregation laughed.

"I don't think I'd get away with that with my wife. How about the rest of you fellas?" More laughter. "And yet." Perry looked down at Beaulah and took a deep breath. "Right across town, we have a church full of people who are being led by such a man—an adulterer, a liar, and a man with no seminary education whatsoever. Yet, he is leading a flock."

Beaulah stood up, gathered her purse from the seat, and walked the distance down the aisle to the exit. She could sense people watching her; she knew Perry was.

He raised his voice. "As a spiritual leader of this community, I would be remiss if I did not bring this to your attention. These poor souls are being misled by an unfit man."

Beaulah, still avoiding making eye contact with anyone, reached the door. "It is a sin. A sin, I tell you! We are responsible for the souls we lead. How can I stand by idly while these poor souls are led astray by this wolf in sheep's clothing!"

Beaulah pushed the exit door open with the heel of her

hand, marched through the foyer, and stepped out into the November sun. The weather was turning cold. A light snow covered the parking lot. She got into her car and drove home, her face wet with tears.

Once there, she gathered every suitcase they owned and packed all of Perry's clothes into them. Moving to the bathroom, she then filled a cardboard box with his toiletries, and stuffed both of his pillows and a blanket into a clean trash bag. She retrieved a couple of heavy cardboard boxes from the garage and walked into Perry's study. Pulling the books he used for research from the shelf, she then dropped them into the boxes. One by one, Beaulah carried suitcases, bags, and boxes back out to her car, put them into the trunk, and then drove back to the church.

She called ahead and asked Perry's assistant, "Would you send someone out to help me with some boxes? Tell them to bring a cart. I'm at the side entrance."

Quickly, efficiently, Beaulah and a young man she did not recognize loaded Perry's clothing and books onto the cart. "Thanks," she told him. "Please take all of this to Pastor Potts' office."

Beaulah got back into her car and drove home. She refused to cry this time. She was already thinking about dinner. Maybe she'd have ice cream. The thought brought a little smile to her face. It was a start.

That night, Perry settled into the leather couch in his office. It wasn't bad. Beaulah had packed his favorite pajamas. Actually, he was rather comfortable. He even had a small television in his office, so it wouldn't be so bad. Maybe he'd go to Walmart tomorrow and buy a bigger one. He rearranged his pillows, pulled the blanket up over his shoulder, and settled in for the night. The television remote was in his right hand and in his left hand was a bowl of microwave popcorn. *We'll see who wins this war*, he thought, as he tossed some popcorn into his mouth and turned up the volume on the television.

Chapter 23

December

"You've got a ton of money in the bank, when are you going to buy a car?" Cooper asked TJ.

"I don't have a driver's license."

"Why not?"

"I don't know. I used to have one. Had one when I was sixteen. But I never had money for a car, and then I started training for Warrior and riding a bike everywhere, and a car just didn't seem necessary. The license eventually expired. Maybe I'll get one."

"I didn't know you ever had a license. I thought you didn't know how to drive a car."

"I know how to drive a car! Does everyone think that?"

"I don't know. I guess. Probably."

TJ laughed. "Man, this town must really see me as a weirdo."

"Yeah. Pretty much." Cooper pulled up in front of the diner and double parked. "Good luck."

"Thanks for dropping me off. I appreciate it."

"If she says yes, how are you going to take her out without a car? You going to pick her up on your bicycle?"

"I thought I'd just ask her to drive."

Cooper laughed. "TJ, let's get you a car. I'll help you find one."

"Okay. I guess I better go renew my driver's license. All right, I'll see you later."

"You want me to come back and pick you up?" Cooper asked.

"No. I'll figure something out."

"You sure?"

"Yeah."

"Good luck."

"Thanks, Cooper." TJ got out of the truck and headed for the diner. He sat at one of the booths and scanned the diner for Lucy. She was supposed to be working today. Why wasn't she here? This was beginning to seem like a waste of time—until Lucy, carrying a couple plates of food, walked through the doors that led to the kitchen. She smiled in his direction. TJ picked up a menu and tried to look at it.

He watched over the top of his menu as Lucy put the two plates down at another booth. When she turned to him, he looked back down at the menu, pretending to concentrate.

"Hey, TJ. What's up?" Lucy came to his booth.

"Not much. Just thought I'd come in and have some lunch. How are you doing?"

"I'm here. So, you know."

"Yeah. I think I'm just going to have the cheeseburger platter."

"Really?"

"Yeah. Why?"

"You usually don't eat that much."

"I'm not training anymore."

"Okay. Is the coleslaw okay or do you want something else?"

"It's okay."

She turned and walked back into the kitchen before TJ could say anything else. He put his menu back in the holder and gazed out the window. How was he supposed to ask her out if she was only at the booth for a few minutes? TJ drummed his fingers against the table. What if she said no? He was finally getting up the nerve to ask Lucy out, but what if she rejected him? It was still possible that she might say yes, but once she rejected him, how would he ever have the nerve to ask her a second time?

TJ watched the traffic through the window and tried to think of the right words. He was so lost in thought, that when Lucy came to deliver his meal, TJ jumped in response.

"Sorry. Didn't mean to scare you," she said with a laugh.

So much for looking confident, TJ thought to himself. He took a deep breath. "Hey, I was thinking about going to the movies Saturday night. The ten thirty show. You want to go with me? I mean, if you're not working."

Lucy placed the platter on the table before TJ. "The movies?"

"Yeah. Why not? Might as well. If you wanna."

"Well, I only work till eight on Saturday."

TJ did not bother to tell her that he already knew her schedule. And he had asked Sally. "Oh, well, that would work out then, if you want to go."

"Me and you? To the movies? Like a date?" Lucy asked.

TJ felt his throat tighten. "Oh, no, not really a date, just going to the movies."

"Oh. Okay, then. Sure. Sounds good."

"Want to just meet here after work?" TJ asked.

"No. I'd have to go home and shower. But we could meet here later. How about ten?"

"Sure. Sounds good. We could just walk to the movies from here. Only half a block. That'd give us plenty of time to get popcorn and buy tickets."

"Okay. Sounds good." Lucy moved on to another booth.

TJ smiled and looked down at his plate. *She said yes!* He and Lucy were going on their first date. But then he remembered what she'd said. *Like a date?* And then he had said: *no, not really a date*. Then she said: *Oh. Okay, then.* He wondered what that meant? If he had said it was a date, would she have said no? TJ frowned and he stuffed a french fry into his mouth, his elation slowly fading. Did she only see him as a friend? Why didn't he just say it: Yes! Like a date!

He chewed his french fry and looked out the window. *Idiot!* He shook his head. *Oh well, better than nothing*, he thought. It was a step in the right direction.

He hoped it didn't snow Saturday. TJ imagined walking through a howling snowstorm with Lucy. Cooper was right: he really did need to get a car.

Chapter 24

December

Jake, Melody, TJ, Clara, and Josephine were all gathered in the living room, watching an old John Wayne movie. It was Jake's choice. The Duke was his favorite, and he never missed a movie if one was playing on his night off.

TJ slouched in the corner of the couch, his legs stretched out before him. He had been in a bad mood ever since Lucy said she'd go to the movies with him. All he'd had to do was say: "Yes, it's a date." But he hadn't, so now everything was still up in the air. Had she only said yes because she thought it was not a date? Or was she interested in him? TJ supposed he'd find out Saturday, but it sure seemed a long time away.

Clara sat beside TJ, in the middle of the couch, crocheting a baby blanket. Evidently, Clara had decided the baby was going to be a girl, because she was crocheting a pink blanket. The last week had been a good one for Clara. A stranger observing her would have seen no sign of her illness. Even her own family had wondered whether she might be getting better?

Only Josephine knew better. She'd seen it before, the

heartbreaking ebb and flow of Alzheimer's. Good days that made the hopes of loved ones soar, followed by bad days that felt like reality had slapped you in the face. Josephine had learned to float with the waves, enjoy the good days and deal with the bad. But it was a lot easier when you weren't dealing with your own loved ones. Josephine wasn't going to waste one minute watching a John Wayne movie, so she sat on the other end of the couch, reading a book.

Jake and Melody sat on the love seat, holding hands. They hadn't held hands in years, but lately, whenever he sat beside her, Jake reached for Melody's hand. Once in a while, he placed a hand on her still-flat belly, which always made Melody smile. She'd dreamed about being pregnant for so long, and now she sat beside Jake, carrying his baby. If only she felt better. She spent part of every day vomiting and found it difficult to eat most of the time. Instead of gaining weight, she had lost five pounds in two weeks, which concerned her, but everyone told her it would pass.

Meanwhile, she sat beside Jake, trying to concentrate on the television and wishing it was time for bed. She glanced at the clock. Fifteen after nine. No, she probably couldn't go to bed yet. Maybe nine-thirty. She yawned and tried to focus on the movie. "Why doesn't he just shoot the guy so Jimmy Stewart doesn't have to?"

"Because Stewart doesn't want anyone fighting his battles for him. That's the point of the movie. Stewart is against violence, but eventually he's forced to learn how to use a gun," Jake said.

"How do you know that?"

"I've seen this movie tons of times."

"Then why do we have to watch it? I didn't know you'd already seen it!"

"Shhhh. Here comes a good part. Watch."

"How's the blanket coming, Mom?" TJ asked.

Clara held it up. It measured about two feet by three feet. "Coming right along. I'm almost done. I can't wait to get my hands on that baby. My first grandbaby! And you'll be an uncle, TJ!" Clara dropped the blanket back onto her lap and continued working on it.

TJ slumped back into the couch. It was weird, sitting here in Jake's house, watching TV with the nurse and his mom. After so many years of constant training, it was odd to spend so much time doing nothing. He was bored. He always felt as if he were wasting his time, as if he should be doing something or going somewhere. But he also knew there might be a day soon when his mother might not recognize him at all. He wanted to spend as much time with her now as possible.

Shifting his weight on the couch, TJ tried to concentrate on the television, but his thoughts returned to Lucy. In some ways, he felt worse than ever. She thought going to the movies with him was not a date, which probably meant she didn't see him as possible boyfriend material. Before he knew it, she'd see him as a friend, and then he'd never have a chance. But, then again, he was going to the movies with Lucy Miller on Saturday. He'd be walking beside her on the sidewalk, sitting next to her in the darkened movie theater. He'd be eating popcorn right out of the same tub. The thought made him smile. Who knew, maybe he could work his arm around her shoulder. Maybe by the time they walked home from the movies, he'd be holding her hand. Maybe he'd kiss her goodnight.

"TJ!" Jake yelled, prompting him to jump.

"What?"

"What in the world are you thinking about? You're sitting over there with a goofy grin. You look like a nut."

"I'm just watching the movie."

"Then we must be watching two different movies."

"I think I'm going to go for a walk." TJ rose from his seat and leaned over to kiss his mother on the forehead. "I'll see you later, Mom. That blanket is looking great."

"Thank you," Clara answered. "Be home by nine.

You've got school tomorrow."

TJ and Jake exchanged sad looks. "Okay, Mom. I will be." TJ retrieved his jacket from the hall closet and left the house.

TJ slipped on his jacket, zipped it, and shoved his hands into the pockets. It was a clear, crisp night. Snow would be here to stay soon. So far, it only appeared and then melted. He hoped it would wait until after Saturday. Overhead, the stars were brilliant white pinpoints in a black blanket. TJ looked for the moon. Full and white, it seemed so small and far away. Somehow, it made him feel sad. TJ wondered how much longer his mom would be able to recognize him. The thought of her not knowing him was more than he could bear, so he shifted his thoughts. The addition would be nice. It would give his mom and the nurse their own bedrooms and an adjoining bathroom, even a little sitting area for his mom to watch television. TJ smiled. He thought she'd like that a lot. Maybe he'd put some fake flowers in there. TJ wondered where to buy fake flowers. Walmart, he supposed. Maybe Melody could pick some out. It was nice, having money to buy stuff now, but it still felt odd.

As he walked, he thought about buying something for Lucy. Maybe he could bring her a little gift on Saturday. But, no, that might look like he was trying too hard. He sighed. All this money in the bank and he didn't know what to do with it. What good was it? Then again, he had been able to help out Cooper. He'd hired a nurse for his mom. He'd paid Jake back for all of the money he had borrowed. And he was paying for the addition to Jake's house. So that was good. When it was done, there'd be five bedrooms. One for Jake and Melody, one for Clara, one for the nurse, one for the baby, and one for him—if he wanted it. Jake had already raised the idea, but TJ wasn't sure he wanted a bedroom at Jake's house. He'd rather sleep on the couch, and maybe in the church once in a while. He wasn't sure about much of anything. Except Lucy. And the only thing he was sure about as far as she was concerned was how he felt about her. The rest was up in the air.

TJ flipped the collar up on his jacket and then shoved his hands back into his pockets and continued walking, with absolutely nowhere to go.

Chapter 25

December

It happened. Libby had been warned it would, that it eventually happened to everybody, but still she had not believed it. It would never happen to her—she was smarter than that.

Libby had been running the same drill press in the factory for more than six months. Six months of going through the same mindless, repetitive routine hundreds of times a day. She picked the part up from a tray on her left, after the person in front of her had done something else to the part and had slid it down the tray to Libby. Libby then put it in her drill press, making sure to orient it in the correct position. She clamped the part in place. She closed the flap that kept the coolant from being sprayed into her face. She placed both hands on two red buttons on either side of her and watched as the machine lowered and drilled the necessary holes. She waited for it to finish, flipped open the flap, unclamped the part, and slid the part down the long metal tray to her right, where another person picked it up and put it in another machine in the assembly line.

When Libby had first been instructed on how to run the

drill press, she was told, "Be sure to close the flap, or you'll get sprayed in the face with coolant. Eventually, everyone does."

At the time, Libby swore she would not be like "everyone." She would never forget to close that flap. Really, how many brain cells could it take? For the next six months she had remembered. Thousands of times a week, she had remembered. And then one day, she didn't. Libby had been thinking about the last time she'd seen Cooper. He was standing in the kitchen of that house Beaulah had showed to TJ, leaning against the counter, looking at her, his dark blue eyes seeing right through her and reading her every thought. She remembered looking at his lips, reminding herself of how they felt against hers, and he had caught her looking. He had known what she was thinking. And, in that moment, he was thinking it too. The look he'd given her—that knowing look, understanding everything she was feeling. Just remembering it caused her breath to slow. In that moment, lost in Cooper's lips, Libby was hit in the face with coolant. It sprayed all over her face and hair, and her eyes were only saved by the safety glasses.

The men running the drill presses adjacent to hers clapped and shouted. One whistled. On another day, perhaps Libby would have thought it funny, too. But not today. Ignoring them, she rushed from her drill press to the women's bathroom, escorted by their laughter and shouting. Once in the bathroom, she dropped her safety glasses in the sink and splashed warm water onto her face. Adding a generous squirt of soap to her hands, she spent the next five minutes washing her face and neck. Drying her face with paper towels, she stared into the mirror. Strands of wet hair framed her face and fell over her forehead. Her skin was red. The eye shadow on one eye had washed off. Streaks of mascara ran down her face. Libby stood, looking at her reflection. She remembered, for a moment, that as a child she had dreamed of being a model. It was a childish dream, true, but the reality of her life was so far from that dream, so far from any dream she ever dreamed. Libby stared into the mirror and did not recognize herself. It was not just the wet hair, red skin, and smeared makeup. It was something deeper. Something becoming permanent. The angry look in her eyes. The downturned frown. The deep line forming between her brows. She tried to remember the last time she had laughed, the last time she'd had fun. She could not.

Turning away from the mirror, she picked her safety glasses up from the sink and washed them, all the time wondering what time it was. It had to be close to three in the morning. Another four hours to go. After drying the glasses, she put them on and returned to her drill press. Just four more hours. Four more hours.

Chapter 26

December

Jake dropped TJ off at the diner just as the first heavy snowfall of the season began. Plump flakes hit the windshield of Jake's car and were pushed away by the wipers.

"Good luck, kid," Jake told his little brother before pulling away in the squad car.

The diner was closed, so TJ made his way to the back parking lot to see if Lucy's car was there. It was not. But, then again, he was early. He passed Sally's car and Cooper's truck and knocked heavily on the back door. After a few minutes, Cooper answered the door. "What's up TJ?" He let TJ into the backroom.

"I'm meeting Lucy here tonight for our d … to go to the movies. She's not here yet, but I saw your cars so I thought I'd say hi."

"Yeah, I came in for a late dinner and hung around. Sally told me tonight was the night."

Sally locked the office door behind her. "Hey, TJ. This is the big night!"

"Just a movie, that's all."

"Lucy seemed excited when she was talking about it today."

"She did? Really?"

Cooper laughed. "TJ! I've never seen you like this. Take it easy, man. She's just a girl."

TJ followed them outside and watched as Sally locked the back door. "What time is she supposed to be here?"

"Any time now."

"Do you want us to wait with you?"

"No. I'm good. Go ahead. She'll be here any minute."

"Are you sure?" Cooper asked.

"Yeah. I'm sure. I'm good."

"Okay. Well, I'll probably see you tomorrow," Cooper said.

"Have a great time." Sally got into her car.

TJ watched them both pull out of the parking lot and wondered what time it was. He wished he had looked at the clock in the back room. It had to be almost ten. The parking lot was covered with snow now. Huge flakes entirely erased the gravel, coating it with a blanket of white that was sullied only by TJ's footprints. Lit by an overhead security light on a telephone pole, TJ paced back and forth, listening for Lucy's car. Time passed. He guessed it was well after ten-thirty. If she didn't come soon, they'd be late for the movie for sure. By now, the previews were probably playing. His hair wet from the snow, TJ brushed the accumulated of snow from his head and then shoved his hands back into his pockets. She'd be here soon. She had to be.

(

Sometime in the middle of the night, Lucy woke up fevered and shaking. She had been so cold after getting out of the shower that she had crawled under the blankets with her robe on and her hair still wrapped in a towel, just for a few minutes. Hours later, she awoke, removed the damp towel from her head, burrowed down into the blankets, and fell back asleep.

In the morning, when Lucy awoke, ill, she realized she had missed going to the movies with TJ. "Mom! Mom!" she called out. "Mom!"

"What are you yelling for?"

"What time is it?"

"Almost eleven."

"Ah! I'm supposed to be at work at noon. I'm sick."

Ivy crossed the room and placed the back of her hand against her daughter's forehead. "Jeez, Lucy! You're burning up. Let me go get the thermometer."

"I need you to call work. Tell Sally I'm sick. Explain about the fever, and tell her to call TJ and tell him I was sick last night. I don't have his number."

Chapter 27

December

"You seem to be feeling pretty good today." Jake wound spaghetti around his fork.

"I do feel good today. Haven't been sick once!" Melody responded. "I think I'm going to go for a walk after dinner, if you don't mind. Brandy and I planned it before I knew Josephine wouldn't be here tonight. Are you okay with that?"

Josephine was having the night off, but was due to return at nine o'clock. No one knew were TJ was, but that was pretty normal. He spent a lot more time at the house now, usually sleeping on the couch at night, but his presence during meals was hit and miss.

Jake stuck a wad of spaghetti into his mouth and chewed, nodding. "Sure." Although that was far from the truth. In fact, he was not okay with it at all. Being home alone with his mom terrified him. What if she messed in her pants or something? What would he do about that? He didn't even know if that was a possibility. Did she still do that? Or was that just a one time thing? He thought back to the day when Beaulah Potts had called him and told him Clara was sitting home alone in a urine-soaked chair. That was the beginning of this nightmare named Alzheimer's. Truth be told, he supposed it began well before that. There were signs that Clara didn't just have memory loss. Jake remembered one time when he went to visit her and found several days worth of mail in her mailbox. He'd thought it strange at the time, but hadn't dwelled too much on it. Another time, he'd found a pair of her socks in the refrigerator. He cringed when he remembered how he had teased her about that. Before she was diagnosed, Clara had seemed moodier too, but again, he easily ignored that.

Jake hadn't been the only one to miss the symptoms. TJ had been living with her and yet managed to ignore them too. The truth was, they were both so caught up in their own lives they hadn't had time to notice their mother was terribly ill. This had been going on for at least two years, maybe more— the thought tore at Jake. For years, his mother had been quietly suffering. And even now, he had to admit, having her in his house felt like an imposition. It was a horrible, selfish thought, but it was true. And the nurse made it even worse. A total stranger in the house, night and day. TJ coming and going at odd hours. And now they were going to add a baby to the mix.

"What do you think?" Melody asked?

"Huh?"

"I swear, Jake, you never listen to me. It's like you're off in your own little world."

"Pass the garlic bread," Clara said.

Jake passed the plate of bread to his mother and then turned his attention back to his wife. "I'm sorry. What did you say?"

"I said I'm thinking about getting a tattoo. What do you think?"

"What? Are you serious?"

"Dumbest thing I ever heard," Clara said in between bites of garlic bread.

"Not a big one. Just a small one. Something cute, like a little butterfly or something. Maybe on my ankle. Brandy has one. It's really pretty. A little red heart on her wrist."

"No, no, no. Don't do that, Mel. I like your skin just the way it is. I don't want some ugly tattoo on you."

"It wouldn't be ugly! Just a little one. Something cute. Maybe a little butterfly on my ankle."

"Why's it so cold in here?" Clara asked. "It shouldn't be so cold. I thought we had global warming. This is the coldest July I can ever remember."

"It's December, Mom," Jake said.

"I'm not stupid. I know what month it is!" Clara snapped.

"Or maybe a flower," Melody told Jake. "A rose! Maybe a rose on my thigh, way up high where everyone wouldn't see it all time."

They all listened to the front door open and close, and TJ breezed into the kitchen. "Spaghetti! All right! I'm starving." He retrieved a plate from the cupboard and started piling spaghetti onto his plate.

"TJ, what do you think? Do you think I should get a tattoo?"

TJ sat at the table and placed his plate before him. He shrugged. "Why not? If you want one, get one," he said before digging into the spaghetti.

"See! TJ thinks it's a good idea!"

A mouthful of spaghetti didn't stop TJ from replying, "Wait a minute. I didn't say that." He chewed and swallowed quickly. "I didn't say it was a good idea. I just said it was up to you." He looked over at Jake.

Jake stared down at his plate. Life should be easier. Why was everything so hard now? Everywhere he turned, there was a problem. That stolen money was still in his bowling ball bag. His mom was getting worse day by day. He had that to look forward to—just watching her get worse and worse, until eventually he supposed she wouldn't even remember him. Melody was sick half of the time with the baby. A baby. He couldn't even imagine adding a crying baby to this household. It was just too much. Everything was a mess. He wanted to fix everything, but he didn't even know where to start. He tried to concentrate on what TJ was saying.

"Why don't you just get a henna tattoo? Those are temporary, and if you don't like it, you won't be stuck with it forever."

"Oh! That's a great idea! How long do they last? Where can I get one?"

TJ added two pieces of garlic bread to his plate. "A few weeks, maybe a month, I think. I don't know where to get one. When I was in high school, some kid did that. Totally freaked out his parents. Maybe you could call a tattoo shop and ask them; maybe they even do them there. If not, seems they'd know where you could go."

"I will. That's a great idea! Thanks TJ. What do you think, Jake? Isn't that a good idea? I could just try it out, see if I like it. What do you think?"

Jake poked at his food with his fork. "Sure. Whatever."

Melody continued talking, something about butterflies and flowers. Jake pushed a meatball across his plate. Maybe he'd just put that money in a box and throw it into the yard of the house he took it from some dark night. But what if someone else found it, or maybe a neighborhood dog? He imagined the box chewed up and the money strewn across the yard. Yeah, that might attract some attention. As he pushed at the meatball, he decided he wasn't going to burn the money. He was going to return it. That was the best answer. If he returned the money, the punks wouldn't be out for revenge—at least in theory. So what if his fingerprints were all over it? It wasn't like they were going to take drug money to the police and ask them to fingerprint it. He just had to figure out a way to get it to them without getting caught.

(

Beaulah had spent the day with Libby, and it had been a wonderful day. They secured two more listings! Beaulah had never had two listings in one day before. They celebrated over an expensive lunch and even each had a glass of wine. As Beaulah drove home, she smiled. She'd never been so busy, and it was all because of Libby. A whiz at marketing and social media, Libby was also great at converting For Sale by Owners properties into new listings. They made a great team. Just that morning, the broker had approached Beaulah and congratulated her on all of the new listings. It felt wonderful. Finally, she was being taken seriously as a businesswoman.

Keeping her eye on the road, Beaulah reached into her purse and dug about for her ringing phone. She looked at the caller ID—Perry. Beaulah dropped the phone back into her purse. He had called several times today, but she'd always been in the middle of something. She'd call him when she got home; he could wait. She imagined telling him about the listings and smiled even wider.

A short time later, Beaulah donned sweatshirt, sweatpants, and an old pair of fuzzy slippers. She'd been cold all day and the warm clothes felt wonderful. A TV dinner was in the oven and would take thirty minutes to cook. She supposed now was as good a time as any to call Perry.

"It's about time you called me back." Perry answered on the first ring.

Beaulah sighed. She had actually been looking forward to talking to him, or at least to telling him about the listings. "I didn't know I was on a schedule. I've been busy. I had two listings today. What do you want?"

"Beaulah, don't you think we should be doing something different?"

"Different?"

"This is crazy, us living apart like this."

Beaulah said nothing. She waited for his apology. Waited for him to tell her how much he loved her, how he realized he had been wrong.

"You're just being stubborn," he said.

Beaulah set her jaw. "I'm being stubborn? *I'm* being stubborn?"

"This makes no sense. And how does it look? I'm the pastor of the biggest church in town and I'm living in my office. People have started to ask questions. What am I supposed to tell them? I don't even know what you're mad about."

"You don't know what I'm mad about?" Beaulah sat down on the couch. She picked up the remote, turned on the television, muted it, and started flipping through the channels, looking for something to watch while she ate.

"Beaulah, as a leader in this community, I can't just let some unfit man open a church and not say a thing about it! It's my duty, as a pastor."

"Who are you to say who can and cannot open a church? Is that up to you? Isn't that up to God? Don't you think He has this under control? And it's not just about Cooper Moon's church. It's more than that. I'm not important to you."

"How can you say that? I love you! I've never even looked at another woman. You know that!"

"What is the first thing I said to you when I called you?"

"What?"

"Right now. This phone call. What was the first thing I said to you?"

"You were mad about me calling you. You said you weren't on a schedule."

"What else?"

"I don't know. You said you were busy."

"I told you I had two listings today! Two listings!"

"No you didn't."

"Yes, I did! It was the first thing I said. I've never had two listings in one day. I told you that, and you didn't even hear me."

"You didn't. You never said a word about a listing."

Beaulah sighed heavily. "You just keep proving my point. You don't take me seriously. You never have. It's you and the church, and I'm just someone who happens to live with you." *The Sound of Music* was coming on in fifteen minutes. Beaulah settled on that channel and placed the remote on the table beside the couch, the sound still muted.

"That's not true! And I've always wanted you to be a part of the church. You know that! I've asked you to get involved in the nursery, or teach classes, or anything at all. You are the one who never wanted to be involved."

"Perry! You aren't hearing me! I don't want to be involved in the church. The church is yours. That is your business, your calling. But being a pastor's wife isn't mine. I love God. I love you, but that doesn't mean I want to stand beside you every weekend and shake everyone's hands as they leave."

"I only asked you to do that once."

Beaulah raised her voice. "Perry, listen to me. Please. Just listen to me!"

"I *am* listening to you."

"No, you're not. You're hearing the words, but you're not listening. Stop being so defensive and listen to what I'm telling you. I'm not attacking you for wanting me to be involved in the church. I'm just trying to tell you how I feel."

"Okay. I'm listening."

Beaulah sighed and tried again. "You say God has a plan for everyone, and I believe that. But I feel as if you've spent your whole life trying to get me to fit into *your* plan, wishing I was the perfect pastor's wife who teaches Sunday School and rocks the babies in the nursery. Don't get me wrong, I enjoyed doing that. In fact, I loved doing that. But it's not all I want to do. It's not what I was meant to do."

"Then what were you meant to do? Sell real estate?"

"Maybe. Maybe I was. I don't know. But I do know that helping a family find a house they want feels good. And when I help people list their houses, that feels good too. I feel like I'm accomplishing something.

"Beaulah, you've never had a sale."

"I will! I've been showing houses to people, even if they aren't buying yet. And how do you know I haven't had a sale? I could have sold something while you've been gone. You already assume I've sold nothing."

"Have you sold anything?"

"No. But I'm getting close! And maybe my work is just as important as yours. Did you ever consider that?"

Perry was quiet for a moment. Beaulah knew what he was thinking. No, her work wasn't important as his. Nothing was more important than his work. He worked directly for God. She wondered if all pastors felt the same.

"That's real good. I'm happy that you're doing something you like. Maybe you did say something about getting two listings earlier. I'm sorry if I didn't hear you. I was so focused on talking to you that maybe I didn't hear you." He paused. "You got two listings? Both in the same day?"

"Yes. Two good listings. Both over two-hundred thousand."

"That's great. Two listings!"

Beaulah rolled her eyes. Why couldn't he have said that at the beginning of the call? "I've got dinner in the oven."

"What are you having?"

"Turkey."

"That sounds good. Mashed potatoes and gravy?"

"Yes." Beaulah didn't mention it was in the form of a TV dinner, but then again, he hadn't asked. She knew he was waiting for her to extend a dinner invitation.

"I've been getting Chinese takeout a lot lately," Perry told her.

"Which one?"

"The one over by the hardware store."

"I thought you didn't like that one."

"I don't, but it's close. And they deliver."

Beaulah began to feel sorry for him. She imagined him sitting in his office, bent over a Styrofoam container of Chinese food, eating it with a plastic fork. But she couldn't invite him over; they couldn't very well split a TV dinner, and she was embarrassed to admit it was a TV dinner. Maybe they could go out to eat, meet somewhere—like a date. The thought excited her. That might be fun! She could just put the dinner back in the freezer. It had only been in the oven for a short time. She hurried to the kitchen, grabbed a hot pad, pulled the dinner from the oven, and slid it onto the counter top. All she had to do was cover it with aluminum foil. And change her clothes.

"Beaulah, I love you. If you told me about the listing I'm sorry I didn't hear you. And, really, I am glad you like what you're doing. I'm sure it is important. I mean, it's not like you are in ministry, but helping people find houses is a good thing."

Beaulah's back straightened. "Just not as important as what you're doing, right?"

"I didn't say that, but you can't compare ministry to real estate."

"So, let me get this straight: God made both of us, but he just made you a little better?"

"No, no. I didn't say that. But not everyone is called to serve God."

"That's not what you tell everyone. You always say everyone in the church is called to serve in his or her own way. The only problem is you don't believe it. You are called to serve, and the rest of us can just help you as we are needed. Isn't that really how you think? You know, I never realized it until this moment, but you not only think you're better than me, you think you're better than everybody!"

"No, no, Beaulah, that's not true. But selling a house and saving a soul isn't the same. You have to admit to that."

"So, God doesn't care about people finding a home in which to raise their family?"

"I'm not saying that…"

"Then what are you saying?"

"Beaulah, let's just drop this. I don't want to fight with you. I'm tired of all of this. It's time for this to be over. It's time for us to live together again."

"And why is that?"

"Because this is stupid, Beaulah! The whole thing is just stupid! You're being stubborn and I don't—"

Beaulah hung up her phone and turned off the ringer. Then she placed it face down on the counter and put the TV dinner back in the oven. She glanced at the clock on the oven. *The Sound of Music* would be starting in a few minutes.

Chapter 28

December

TJ and Cooper had spent the morning working on Jake's addition, saying little, both lost in their own thoughts.

When they broke for lunch and sat on a stack of drywall to eat the sandwiches they had brought, Cooper said, "Hey, TJ. I was wondering something."

"What's that, Cooper?"

"How come you never come to church? I mean, I appreciate you coming for the first service and everything, but you haven't been to one since. Did you think I did a bad job? Is that it?"

"Oh no, Cooper. Don't think that! It's not like that at all. You did a great job. A great job! I just don't see the point in it." TJ took a bite of his sandwich.

"The point in what?"

"Going to church," TJ answered with a mouthful of peanut butter and jelly.

"Really?" Cooper unwrapped his sandwich but still did not take a bite. "Why not? I mean, I'm not judging, I never went to church either—never felt the need—but once I started believing in God, I felt different. Do you believe in

God?"

TJ swallowed before answering. "I guess I believe in something. I think something created the earth. It's just too complex to be some random explosion or whatever, so I think something or someone created the earth. Some kind of God, I guess. I just don't see the whole point of church."

"Well, it's so you can learn about God and the Bible. And so you can meet other people who believe in God. And so you can get together to do stuff for the people in your town."

"Yeah, but I don't see that. There's thousands of churches across the world, thousands of people who believe in some sort of religion, but you don't see a lot of evidence of that. I don't see people out helping each other on a daily basis, do you?

"When something bad happens like a hurricane or something, people come out and help."

"Yeah, but what I'm saying is, if there are so many people out there who claim to believe in God, why are there still poor people? Why is there so much suffering? Why are all of those people in that homeless shelter in Denver, and in every other city across America? I don't see the point of sitting in church on Sunday singing about how great God is. Why not go out and do something about it instead?"

Cooper nodded. "I don't know. I'm still trying to figure all of this stuff out, too. But I've been thinking about that. I think I ought to ask the people who come to church about buying that drunk driving bus we were talking about. I think it's a good idea. And I think that's the kind of thing we should be doing, like you said, helping the people of Timber Lake."

"It's worth a shot."

"Yeah, I think so too. I don't know whether you know it, but both of my parents were killed by a drunk driver. That's how I ended up with my place—used to be theirs. If that drunk driver had ridden a bus home instead of driving, my parents would be here now."

"No, Cooper, I didn't know that. Sorry."

Both men ate in silence for a while. Finally, Cooper asked, "How you doing, TJ? You seem like you're out of it today. Everything going okay?"

TJ shrugged. "I don't know. To be honest with you, Cooper, I was a lot happier last year at this time, before I won Warrior. All this money, you'd think I'd be happier. Don't get me wrong. I appreciate it, and I'm glad I can help people now, but I just feel sort of lost, like I don't have any direction." TJ put the last of his sandwich into his mouth.

"Maybe you need to find something new to do. You used to train for Warrior, and now you don't have anything to do. You need a hobby or something."

"Yeah. Maybe."

"How'd your date with Lucy go? I forgot to ask you."

"It didn't. She never showed up."

"Are you kidding?"

"Nope. I probably waited an hour. She never showed up."

"What happened? Why didn't she show up?"

"I don't know. I never asked her."

"What? TJ! Why not?"

TJ shrugged. "Haven't seen her since."

"Are you expecting her to show up at Jake's house some night, knocking on the door and explaining why she didn't show up for your date? TJ, you need to quit being so passive. Man, you wanted that Warrior contest, and you went for it! I never saw anybody work so hard, for so long, in all my life. And now you're willing to just wait around and see what happens with Lucy? What's with that? Do you want her or not?"

"You know I do." TJ wadded up the cellophane his sandwich had been wrapped in and dropped it into his lunch bag.

"Then why don't you *do* something about it? Go after

her, like you did that Warrior championship."

"It's not that easy. I can't control how she feels. Besides, I think she might have feelings for someone else." TJ stared down at the ground.

"Who?"

TJ looked at Cooper. "You really don't know?"

"No. Who?"

TJ hesitated before speaking. Finally, he said, "Some guy she goes to school with."

"Is she dating this guy?"

"No. She's just attracted to him, I think."

"I don't get it, TJ. You can beat out thousands of guys from all over the world to win a million dollars in a competition, but you just sit around here and wait for Lucy to notice you."

"Yeah, well, that's easy for you to say. Women are crazy about you."

"Hey! I got an idea! Let's go out on a double date—me and Sally and you and Lucy."

"No!"

"Why not?"

"No, Cooper! I don't want to!" TJ got to his feet. "Let's just drop this. I don't want to talk about it."

"Okay, TJ. I was just trying to help."

"No offense, Cooper, but I don't want your help. Not for this."

"Okay. Suit yourself."

Later that night, Violet slept beside Pete, or at least tried to—she had a hard time falling asleep. She turned from one side to the other, flipped her pillow, pulled the blankets up over her shoulder. She concentrated on taking slow, deep breaths. She tried to imagine lying on a beach, tried counting backward from one hundred. All to no avail. She could not fall asleep.

When she finally did, it was a fitful sleep full of

movement and moans. At one point, she dreamed someone was chasing her. It was dark and she could hear him drawing closer. When she turned to look over her shoulder, she could see a man running toward her. Every time she looked, he drew closer. She could not see his face, but she knew it was the man who had attacked her in the parking lot of Bass Turds. She tried to run, but her legs would not move. It was as if her feet were bound by concrete. He came closer. Violet strained but could not pick up her legs. She tried to scream, but she could not find her voice. As he drew closer, Violet could smell him, feel the heat from his body. She looked over her shoulder and saw his hand reach out for her, his face now in full view, contorted by a twisted smile. She screamed, but no sound came out. Her legs would not move. His fingers came closer. He grabbed her shoulder and started shaking her.

"Violet, Violet, wake up. You're having a nightmare."

Violet swung her arms in defense and hit someone, which woke her.

"Violet, it's Pete. You're okay. It's just a nightmare. Wake up." Pete's hand was on her shoulder, gently shaking her from sleep.

Violet sat up in bed and clutched at the blankets, pulling them to her. "I was dreaming?" she asked when she was awake enough to speak.

"Yes. Just a nightmare, that's all. Everything is fine. I'm right here. You're safe," Pete reassured her as he placed his arm around her shoulders.

Violet resisted the urge to lean into his body. She felt disoriented. She gazed around the room and picked out familiar objects. Yes, there was the desk and chair in one corner of Pete's bedroom. There was the yellowed window shade with the tear in it. And, finally, she turned to Pete. Yes, it was Pete, his arm on her shoulder. Violet scooted back down into the bed.

Pete removed his arm and lay down beside her. "Are

you okay?"

Violet nodded, knowing he was watching her. She didn't have to speak. Pete watched her a lot, as if he were always on guard, always ready to protect her—just as he had that night in the parking lot when he had come to her rescue with a baseball bat.

Violet had thought, at first, that she was on borrowed time here, that he might throw her out of the apartment at any minute. But now it was clear that he would not. She wasn't sure why that was true, but it was. She wondered, sometimes, whether Pete was attracted to her? If so, she couldn't tell. But right now, her senses felt off. Everything was being filtered through fear. She was afraid most of the time and the only thing she knew for sure was that she was safe next to him, or at least as safe as she could ever be. No one was ever truly safe; she knew that now. Any semblance of safety or security was just an illusion.

Violet fought against an old memory: her thirteenth birthday, her mother driving, feeling happy and safe. And then, waking up in hospital. Her father dead. Her mother altered. Everything gone in the blink of an eye. *That's really how life is*, she thought. *It can all be taken from you in a single moment.*

Pete asked, "Do you want me to turn on the light?"

"No. I'm okay." Violet stared at the ceiling until it seemed Pete was asleep. Once his breathing was deep and steady, she moved her head closer to his shoulder—inched, inched, inched, until her head was barely touching him. She held her breath. Pete kept breathing. Violet let the weight of her head sink against him and closed her eyes. Soon, she was sleeping soundly.

Beside her, Pete opened his eyes. It was the first time she had ever touched him in bed. He lay awake for over half an hour, staring at the wall and wondering if she would move. She did not. Eventually, his eyes grew heavy and he fell asleep, a slight smile on his lips.

Chapter 29

December

It had seemed like such a simple idea, to build a little white church in the woods, invite a few people and gather on Sundays to talk and learn about God.

But now it was not quite so simple. Ever since TJ had won the World Wide Warrior contest and mentioned Cooper's name on television, it felt as if Cooper was running just ahead of a speeding bullet. Every week, Cooper's congregation had grown. Now, thanks to the attention he was getting from the media, his congregation was almost three hundred. People were crammed into the pews and more were always standing in the back. Cooper had bought thirty lawn chairs at Walmart and placed them behind the last pew, but it still wasn't enough. People started bringing their own lawn chairs from home, forming another row of mismatched chairs behind the first.

Parking was even more of a problem. The small gravel lot in the woods held thirty cars at best. Now, people were forced to park along both sides of Cooper's road and walk to the church, which was a problem when it rained and explained the decline in attendance during bad weather.

"I don't know what to do, Sally," Cooper told his wife. "I don't have enough places for people to park. No one wants to walk down a muddy road in the rain to get to church."

It was a cold night, but the woodstove was keeping the trailer warm. Sharing the same pillow, Cooper and Sally lay next to each other in bed, covered by a light blanket and both staring at the ceiling.

"Build onto the church. Make it bigger."

"But that won't solve my parking problem."

Sally had yet to attend the church. She was at the diner on Sunday mornings, a fact neither of them ever discussed, so she did not fully understand the parking problem. "Well, looks like you only have two options."

"What?"

"Either buy a bigger church with a bigger parking lot, or have two sermons on Sundays so everyone has a place to park."

Cooper groaned. "Oh, I so don't want to do that. It's hard enough, just doing the one service. I can't imagine doing two. By the time I finish one, I'm exhausted. I'd have to stay around and do another one and my whole morning would be shot."

Sally laughed. "You're not sounding like much of a preacher. Isn't that the idea? You're supposed to be willing to do anything for God? Jesus was crucified and you're whining about losing your Sunday morning?"

"Aw, come on, Sally. That's not fair."

"You're the one who wanted to do this."

Cooper groaned again. He hated it when she was right.

Cooper decided against doing a sermon on Christmas Day. He figured people should be at home with their families on Christmas morning, not sitting in church. Instead, he took Sally's advice and planned two sermons for the Sunday before Christmas. As much as he hated the thought of it, he realized he had no other choice. He was going to have to start doing two sermons every Sunday, so he figured he might as well kick it off on that Sunday. It was as good a time as any.

The previous week, Cooper had been at home, working on the sermon, when he was surprised by a knock on the door. Opening it, he found Lucy standing on the concrete steps.

"Hi, Cooper!"

"Hey, Lucy." Cooper looked behind her, trying to see if anyone was with her. No one was, which made him nervous. "What's up?"

"Can I come in?"

"Sally's not here right now. She's at the diner."

"I know. I'm not here to see her. Can I come in? It's cold out here!"

"Oh, yeah. Sure." Cooper stepped out of the way and Lucy walked past him into the mobile home.

"It's warm in here! Your heating bills must be crazy."

"No." Cooper pointed at the woodstove.

"Oh! That's great!" Lucy removed her boots, went to the woodstove, and held her hands above it to warm them. Below her black-and-white plaid skirt, her long legs were accentuated by black nylons. "I hate winter, don't you? I'd love to be lying on a beach somewhere in a bikini, just lying there and soaking up the sun all day. Wouldn't that be great?"

Cooper looked away from her legs and concentrated on the woodstove. "I was sort of in the middle of something, Lucy."

"Okay. I … I won't be long."

Cooper noticed the disappointment on her face, and it made him even more nervous. "I was just thinking it would be nice if the church was decorated for the Christmas service this Sunday."

"Oh. Yeah! That's why you're here?"

"Yeah! I thought it would be cool to decorate the church." Lucy rubbed her hands together to warm them.

"Sally might have some Christmas stuff around here. She's been so busy with the diner that she hasn't really had time to decorate this year."

"I brought my own stuff. I stopped by Walmart this morning and bought a bunch of it. It was on sale, so I got all kinds of stuff."

"You didn't have to do that, Lucy."

"I know. I wanted to! It can be my donation to the church. We can use the decorations every year. It will be awesome!"

"Yeah, I guess that is a pretty good idea. We should have Christmas decorations. I never would have thought of that. Thank you." Cooper put both of his hands in the back pockets of his jeans and looked at the floor. He needed to get her out of here.

Lucy beamed with pleasure. "You're welcome. Let's go out and get started!"

"I ... I'm not very good at decorating."

"You don't have to be—I am. But I'll need your help, and we'll need a ladder. I can't do it all by myself."

Cooper smiled. He had to give it to her: she was resourceful. He raised his head and met her eyes. "Yeah, okay. That sounds good. I tell you what, my ladder isn't here, but I'll go get it. It will only take a few minutes, and then we can get started. Okay?"

Lucy seemed confused. "Well, okay."

"You go ahead and get started. The church is unlocked. Go figure out where you want to put the stuff and by the time you have it figured out, I'll be back. Sound good?"

Lucy nodded. "Sure. Okay."

By the door, Cooper slipped his shoes on and looked down at Lucy's boots. She took the hint and left the stove to put her boots on. Cooper opened the door and went outside to wait in the yard. He wasn't going to stand there while she bent over in a skirt to put on those boots. Nope. He wasn't falling for that one. Of course, he wished he'd grabbed his coat before walking outside, but he needed the cold air.

Lucy stepped out of the trailer, pulling the door closed behind her. "Okay. I'll get started, then. And you'll come back in a few minutes and we'll work on decorating this afternoon? Right?"

"Yep!" Cooper rushed to his truck. "I'll be right back. Ten, fifteen minutes, tops."

"Okay." Lucy walked to her car through the ankle-deep snow. Cooper was already pulling out of the driveway when a thought came to her. "Hey!" she yelled. "I can ride along with you!" But it was too late; he was already driving down the road.

"I don't understand what the hurry was. Why do we have to do this today?" TJ asked twenty minutes later, as Cooper's truck rattled down the narrow lane to the church.

"I told you, I need your help."

"Yeah, but ... hey! That's Lucy's car. What are you up to Cooper?"

Cooper smiled as he parked beside Lucy's car. "The three of us are going to decorate the church for Christmas."

"No! Cooper, I don't want to do this. It's going to be totally awkward."

"It's a long walk home."

"It wouldn't be the first time I walked it."

"Go for it."

Before TJ could respond, Lucy appeared from inside the church and waved at them.

"You can't leave now," Cooper said. "She's already seen you."

TJ reluctantly got out of the truck, slamming the door behind him.

"Hi, TJ," Lucy said as he approached. And there it was. TJ could see it. Disappointment in her eyes. She wanted to be alone with Cooper. It was obvious.

"Hey, Lucy. How's it going?" TJ managed to say.

She did not answer, just watched Cooper pull a ladder out of the bed of his truck and approach the church. "I see you got the ladder. It must have been at TJ's house."

Cooper smiled. "Ready to decorate? We're here to help!"

TJ scowled at Cooper as he carried the ladder into the church.

"Lucy!" Cooper exclaimed. "How much stuff did you buy?"

Twenty red poinsettia plants and fourteen bags of Christmas decorations were scattered about near the door.

Lucy laughed. "A lot! I guess I got carried away, but it was fun. I like Christmas."

TJ smiled. Most of the time when he saw Lucy, she was in her diner uniform, but today she looked like she did in his dreams. She wore a black sweater and a short plaid skirt. TJ had never noticed her legs before, but now he could hardly tear his eyes away from them. She was perfect, absolutely perfect. And she smelled so good. He was suddenly glad that Cooper had showed up at his house this morning. TJ knew Lucy was only at the church to spend time with Cooper, but he was sure glad he got to see her in this outfit.

They spent the next half hour moving poinsettias around the room, and taking lights out of the boxes and stretching them across the floor. At one point, Cooper shouted, "Oh crap! What time is it?"

Lucy pulled her cell phone out of her skirt pocket. "A little after eleven."

"Crap! I totally forgot I was supposed to meet Sally for lunch!" He ran for the door. "I'll be back soon!" he yelled over his shoulder.

After he left, TJ and Lucy exchanged glances. "Well, looks like we're on our own for a while," TJ said. Silently, he added, *Thank you Cooper!*

"Yeah. Looks like it." Lucy smiled back. No look of disappointment—it was a start.

"I like Christmas too. When I was a little kid, I used to help my mom decorate for Christmas. It was always fun," TJ said.

"Me too, when I was little." Sally scooted the ladder over to the back corner of the church. Then, picking up one end of a string of lights, she climbed the ladder. "Do you think you could hand me some of those pushpins as I need them? I want to hang these along the ceiling as far as they will reach."

"Yeah, I can do that," TJ said. *For the rest of my life*, he thought. He grabbed one of the bags, pulled out a package of clear pushpins, and opened them. Then he stood near the bottom of the ladder, behind Lucy, trying to concentrate on the lights she was hanging up, instead of looking up her skirt.

"I don't know how far these will reach, but if we string them end to end, they should go pretty far," Lucy said.

"If we run out, we can always go buy more. I'll pay for them."

"Really?"

"Yeah, sure. I'd be happy to. Like I said, I like decorating. And it's for the church, so that's a good thing."

They worked as a team. Still on the ladder, Lucy stretched her hand to TJ, who placed a pushpin in her palm. He was so close that he could feel the heat from her body. He'd never been happier.

"Did Jake help?" Lucy asked as TJ moved the ladder for her.

"Help what?"

"Help decorate for Christmas, when you were little."

"Oh. No, not much. The three of us would get started on it in the morning, while my dad was at work, but eventually Jake would wander off to his room to play with his toys. Then it'd just be me and Mom. Actually, it got to where I liked it better after Jake left and went to play in his room.

Eventually, over the years, it was just me and mom decorating the tree. It was nice, just me and mom. We did that for years."

"Why'd you stop?" Lucy was on the ladder again, reaching overhead to fasten the lights to the ceiling.

TJ thought. "I don't know. I don't even remember when we stopped. Maybe when I was a teenager? I can't remember. I just know that eventually we didn't do it anymore. I'd come home and the tree would be up."

"That's kinda sad."

All of a sudden, TJ felt like crying. He blinked, and fought it. "Yeah. It kind of is. How about you? Do you decorate with your mom?"

"Yeah. We still do. But it's not the same as when I was little. We used to make a big deal of it and bake cookies the night before. Then we'd get up in the morning and get a big plate of those cookies and two glasses of milk and get started on the tree. We'd listen to Christmas music and the fire would always be going. It was nice." Lucy climbed down from the ladder. TJ moved it, and she climbed back up.

"What kind of Christmas music?"

Lucy laughed. "Elvis. My mom is a big Elvis fan."

"Why'd you stop doing it? I mean with the cookies and the music and all?

"Cookies are so fattening! And I got tired of Elvis."

They both laughed and continued to hang the lights.

After a while, Lucy said, "Oh, hey! I never did get a chance to apologize for not going to the movies with you that time."

"Oh, yeah. No biggie."

"I was so sick. That was terrible."

"You were sick?"

"Yes! Didn't Sally tell you? My mom called the next day and told Sally about me being sick and for Sally to let you know what happened."

TJ felt as if a weight had lifted from his shoulders. "I

never got the message! I didn't know you were sick."

"Oh, jeez. I feel terrible about that. I'm sorry. I took a shower that night before I was supposed to meet you, and I was so cold that I got into bed for a few minutes to warm up. The next thing I knew it was the next morning and I had a terrible fever. I was sick all the next day."

"Man, that's terrible," TJ said, a huge smile on his face. "Nope. I never got the message. Sally must have forgotten to give it to me."

"Or my mom forgot to tell her."

"Yeah, maybe. Well, whatever. I know now. And that's good."

"Maybe we can try it some other time, going to the movies?"

TJ cleared his throat. "Yeah. That'd be good. Sure. Whenever you want."

"You need to give me your cell number. If I'd had it that night, I could have called and explained."

"Yeah. I don't have it with me right now, but I'll get it to you."

On the ladder, Lucy reached into her skirt pocket for her cell phone. "What's your number?"

"Oh, yeah. Um … you know, I can never remember. I'll have to give it to you later." TJ vowed, at that moment, that he was definitely going to buy a cell phone as soon as possible.

"Okay." Lucy went to put her cell phone back into her skirt, but missed the pocket. Fumbling with the material, she leaned backward on the ladder, and, in doing so, lost her balance and tumbled straight backward. "Whoa!" she shouted before falling.

TJ dropped the pushpins and reached out to catch her, accidentally grabbing one of her breasts in the process. He quickly put her down and released his grip, then threw his hands into the air. "Sorry! I didn't mean to … I didn't on purpose … I mean … I didn't feel anything … well, I did. I don't mean you don't have anything to feel, you clearly do, I just mean … I didn't feel anything … I didn't do that on purpose!" He stood there, flushed, his mouth open, staring down at her and feeling like an utter fool.

Lucy smiled. "You caught me, TJ. I would have really hurt myself otherwise. I know you didn't … do that on purpose. Thank you." She laughed and blushed slightly.

TJ nodded and searched his surroundings for something to comment on. It was a couple of moments before he came up with, "We're almost out of lights."

"Yeah, we are. And where's Cooper? He should be back by now." Lucy leaned over and picked her phone up from the floor. "It's 1:30! It doesn't take that long to eat lunch."

"Maybe he had to do something else. Or Sally wanted him to do something at the diner."

"Yeah. Maybe." Lucy looked down at the two remaining boxes of lights. "You want to go to the store and buy some more lights?"

"Yeah! Sure! Let's go!"

They gathered up their coats and walked out the door.

"You know what we ought to do?" asked TJ.

"What?"

"We ought to buy a Christmas tree! We could set it up in the front of the church!"

"That's an awesome idea! How big a tree should we get?"

"Whatever will fit in your car."

They got into Lucy's car, smiles on their faces, discussing what kind of ornaments to buy for the Christmas tree.

By the end of the day, TJ had spent five hundred dollars on Christmas decorations and the little church was aglow with tiny white lights. A twelve-foot tree stood in the center of the back wall, surrounded by red poinsettias and lit with slowly blinking white lights. Cooper had not returned, and both times they drove past the mobile home, going to the store and returning from the store, his truck was not in sight.

They worked well into the evening before Lucy stood, her hands on her hips, to survey their handiwork. "We have three more boxes of ornaments to put on the tree, but we're out of hooks, and I really should be going home. I'm getting tired."

"Yeah, me too," TJ lied.

"Do you want me to take you home?"

"Yeah, that'd be great."

"Do you think you could put the rest of the ornaments up before Sunday? You'd have to get some more hooks, but it wouldn't take long. I'm just too tired to mess with them tonight," Lucy said. "And I have to work tomorrow."

"Yeah. I can do that."

"Are you sure you don't mind?"

"I don't mind at all." Didn't she know that he'd do anything for her? Anything!

"Good. I'm tired. I didn't think this would take so long."

"Yeah, me neither. But it was fun," TJ said as they gathered their coats from a chair near the door.

"Yeah. It was. I had fun, TJ," Lucy said.

His name sounded sweet on her lips.

Chapter 30

December

"You didn't tell me we had to stop at the store, TJ. What are you up to? Where are we going?" Jake pulled over and parked in Walmart's parking lot.

"Jake, come on, quit being so grouchy. This will be fun. I'll be right back." TJ got out of the car and ran to the store.

"You should have told him to get milk while he was in there," Clara said from the back seat.

"Really?"

"We might have enough for breakfast, but that's about it."

Jake looked out the window at the parking lot. It was a cold night, crisp and clean. Snow was falling—fat, lethargic flakes that meandered on the breeze, taking their time to reach the ground. He wondered if they actually were out of milk. His mom seemed good today, but it was so hard to know when to believe her anymore. He pulled his cell phone out of his pocket and texted Melody. *Do we need milk?*

Her response was quick. *Yes. Please get some.*

Okay, will do. How do you feel?

Better. Brandy should be here any minute. Gotta go.

Okay. See you later.

"I'll stop at the gas station and get some on the way home, Mom."

"All right. But it would have been cheaper in the store."

(

Melody set her phone down on the coffee table and returned to wrapping the Christmas present she had bought for Brandy. She glanced at the clock as she added a few final pieces of tape. Almost seven. She'd be here any minute.

Melody had thought everyone would be home when Brandy arrived, but at the last minute TJ had asked Jake to take him and Clara somewhere; he wouldn't say where. Melody had planned on introducing Brandy to Jake. She had to admit, though, it had not broken her heart when they'd all left after dinner. It would be nicer this way. She had already lit some candles and, thanks to Josephine, freshly baked cookies sat on a festive Christmas dish on the coffee table. Melody couldn't say she liked the nurse, but she did enjoy it when Josephine baked, which was at least a couple of times a week.

The doorbell rang. Melody positioned the wrapped present in the middle of the coffee table and rushed to the door. Brandy was standing outside, holding a small present. "Brrrr! Feels like winter! I'm not ready for this."

"Come in, come in. I know! I guess we should be ready by now. It is December, but I still hate to see it coming. Give me your coat. I'll hang it up for you."

Brandy slid out of her winter coat and handed it to Melody. "You're adding on to the house!"

"Yeah. We've lived here forever but it's getting crowded."

"I didn't know cops did so well."

Melody hung the coat in the hallway closet. "They don't. Like I said, we bought it years ago. We probably couldn't afford to buy this house today. Come on into the living room. I'll be glad when the addition's done. I'm so tired of all the noise." The women exchanged small talk and nibbled on cookies until, eventually, they got around to opening the presents. Melody opened hers first, pulling off the ribbon slowly. "You know, it's silly, but I still feel like a little kid every time I open a present."

"I know! Me too! I love it when they're wrapped. That's the best part."

Melody pulled away the paper until a white box was revealed. Inside was a gift certificate to Eddie's Tattoos. "Oh my gosh! This is awesome!"

"When we were talking about tattoos a while back, I realized this would be the perfect gift. Now you can go get your Henna tattoo and try it out. Or if you are really feeling brave, go for it and get a real one!" Brandy laughed.

"Jake would kill me if I got a real one."

Brandy shrugged. "Once you've got it, there's not much he can do. Tell him to quit being so cheap."

Melody laughed. "It's not a matter of money. He just doesn't want me to get one."

"Must be nice to not be worried about money. I've worried about money my whole life."

Melody glanced down at the gift certificate. "Now I feel bad. Maybe we shouldn't have exchanged gifts."

"No. I didn't mean it that way. I just mean, I wish me and my man were as secure as you and Jake, that's all." She started unwrapping the present Melody had bought for her. Inside was a long, thin box, obviously from a jewelry store. "Melody! What did you do? You shouldn't have done this." Brandy opened the lid to reveal a delicate gold bracelet. Brandy gasped. "Melody! It's beautiful!"

Melody smiled. "I'm glad you like it. I thought you might."

"But, really, I can't accept this. It's too much." Tears gleamed in Brandy's eyes. "I just can't."

"Of course you can! I got it on sale. Really, I didn't pay

that much for it. About the same as your gift certificate," she lied.

"Really?" Brandy wiped her eyes.

"Yeah, really. Honestly, Brandy, I loved buying it. I haven't had a proper friend in a long time. I wanted to get you something nice. Here, try it on." Melody scooted over on the couch, took the bracelet from the box, and helped Brandy clasp it onto her wrist. "Oh, good. It fits. It seemed so small, but your wrists are pretty tiny."

Brandy turned her wrist back and forth. "It's beautiful! And it fits perfect." She wiped at her eyes again. "Really, though, I feel bad."

"Not as bad as Jake is going to feel once I get that tattoo!" Melody said, and both women laughed.

(

TJ brought the cold air into the car with him. "Okay! Ready to go."

"Where we going?" Jake asked.

"I'll point the way. Turn left out of the parking lot."

TJ continued to give Jake instructions until they reached Cooper's road. "We're going to Cooper's house?" Jake asked.

"Keep driving."

"Nobody else lives down this road, and it's a dead end. Why are we going to Cooper's?"

"Drive!"

As they approached Cooper's driveway, Jake put his foot on the brake.

"Nope. Keep driving," TJ told him.

"We're going to the church?"

"Yes."

"Oh, for goodness sake, Jake," Clara said from the backseat. "Quit being such an old fuddy-duddy. Just do what your brother says. This is fun!"

TJ laughed. "Yeah, Jake! Quit being such an old fuddy-duddy."

Jake shook his head, but he had a smile on his face as he turned into the lane that led to the church. The woods were covered with snow and the tires crunched on the lane as they drove. "Cooper better get out here and get this plowed out before Sunday," Jake said. "We're supposed to get more snow."

As they turned the final bend of the lane, the little church came into view and Clara gasped. "Oh! Look at it! It's all lit up inside. It's beautiful!"

In the darkness of night, the church glowed from within, every window spreading joy into the black woods. Jake pulled up directly in front of the church and parked. Silently, they all walked the short distance to the front door and TJ inserted the key and swung the door open.

Clara was the first to enter. "Oh, TJ! It looks like a dream."

Twinkling white lights outlined the high ceiling. Candles illuminated every arched window. Gold bows decked every pew, lining the center aisle. Centered along the back wall, the Christmas tree twinkled, covered in slowly blinking lights.

"Come on, Mom." TJ took Clara's hand and helped her up the aisle and over to the tree. On the floor near the tree were three boxes of ornaments. TJ reached into his pocket and withdrew a Walmart sack. He pulled out a box of ornament hooks and handed them to his mother. "We're going to finish decorating the Christmas tree, just like we use to when me and Jake were little. All three of us."

Clara closed her fingers over the package of hooks and looked up at her youngest son. "Oh, TJ," was all she could say.

For the next hour, as snow nestled into the dark woods, Clara decorated the Christmas tree with her sons, just like they used to so many years ago.

Later, as they drove home in the dark, they sang Christmas songs. They had not done that since they were kids either.

"Thanks," Jake told TJ when they pulled onto their street. "This was a really great night."

"Sure was!" Clara agreed from the back seat.

TJ smiled. "It *was* a great night. One of the best."

A car was backing from their drive. Jake touched his brakes and waited on the road. "Must be Melody's friend."

Brandy backed onto the road and waved as she passed. She wore a winter hat and her collar was pulled up, making it difficult to see much of her face, but Jake waved and smiled before pulling into the driveway. "Yep," he told TJ as he waited for the garage door to slide open. "This was a perfect night."

Chapter 31

December

Shortly before closing, Frank Collette strolled into the diner. "Where is everybody?" he asked Sally.

"Just me and Lucy closing up. It's been dead since about eight. I guess everyone is out doing last minute Christmas shopping. I should have shut down then." Sally was standing in front of the counter, wiping it down. She left the cloth on the counter and rested her hands on her hips. "What are you doing tonight?"

"Just delivering Christmas presents."

"No hot date tonight?" It was common knowledge, by now, that Violet was living with Pete in his apartment above Bass Turds. It was also common knowledge that Frank was wasting no time mourning the demise of his marriage. He had been seen out and about with much younger women, and seldom the same one twice.

"No. No hot date."

"I thought you'd have some pretty little thing on your arm, taking her to some Christmas party at the bank."

"No. I've got something more important to do tonight."

"What's that?"

Frank reached inside his coat and brought out a small gift-wrapped box. "Give you your present."

"Frank!" Sally said in surprise. "What'd you get me a present for? You didn't have to do that."

"Yes, actually I did. Here, take it. Don't you want to know what's in it?"

Sally smiled and accepted the present. "I love the wrapping paper. It's beautiful. It seems a shame to open it."

"Open it."

Sally pulled at the bow, slipped a fingernail under the wrapping paper, and ripped it open to find a small white box. Pulling off the lid of the box revealed a long gold chain. Sally's mouth fell open and she looked up at Frank. "Frank! I can't accept this necklace. It's too beautiful. It must have been very expensive. Really, I can't—"

"Shhh," Frank told her as he reached for her neck. "You will see. It is very practical. His fingers moved under her collar and took hold of the shoestring she wore around her neck to safeguard her safe key.

Sally laughed. "How did you know that was there?"

"The ends of the shoestring are always sticking out the back of your uniform, through your hair."

Untying the shoestring, Frank then removed the key and slipped it on the gold chain. "Let me put it on you." He placed the necklace over her head, brushing his hand against her neck as he dropped the necklace into place. "There! It looks beautiful!" he told her with a smile. "It's a crime for a ratty shoestring to be around that stunning neck."

Sally's hand went to the necklace. "Frank, really, I shouldn't keep it. It's not … right."

"Why not? We're friends. It's Christmas. Don't be silly."

"I … I …" Sally said, but Frank interrupted her.

"You think too much. Just relax, Sally. Relax and enjoy. Merry Christmas! Now give me a Christmas hug!" he said before taking her into his arms.

Sally tensed, but then softened. It was just a hug after all. But, just for a moment, she remembered a time before she knew Cooper, a time when she had a crush on Frank Collette, the star football player of Timber Lake High. She relaxed into his arms and hugged him back, just for a moment.

Lucy watched Frank and Sally through the crack of the slightly open kitchen door. Carefully, she pulled back and closed the door. Then she tiptoed across the backroom, grabbed her coat off one of the hooks by the door, and slipped out into the night. She thought about driving straight to Cooper's house to tell him, but she had no way of knowing how long Sally would be here. No, she'd wait; it was just a matter of time before Cooper found out about Sally and Frank, and when he did, she'd be there to pick up the pieces.

(

Libby sat on the couch, all of her lights off, eating a bowl of popcorn and watching a movie with her feet up on the coffee table. She was exhausted. Between working for Beaulah and her job in the factory, she was putting in more than ninety hours a week. She couldn't remember the last time she had taken any time off, but this afternoon she called in to work and told them she was sick and couldn't make it. It was true. She was sick—sick of work. She hung up the phone, took a long bath, and put on pajamas and slippers. Now, hours later, she was still in pajamas and was enjoying every minute of her day off, except for all of the Christmas commercials on television; those were annoying.

Her double-wide was clean and tidy, everything in place, and lacking any trace of anything related to Christmas: no tree, no presents, no decorations at all. Libby didn't celebrate Christmas. She hadn't celebrated it in years. After her parent's double suicide, she had spent a few years in foster homes. Every Christmas found her in a new home, and every year there was a present for her under the tree, always some cheap thing she didn't want. Always an awkward moment. She had always smiled when she opened the gift, often while the "real" children of the family were surrounded by heaps of gifts. The gifts varied—a cheap sweater, a robe, slippers—but they were all merely tokens. Libby would have preferred nothing at all. So, when she got out of the foster system and was on her own, that is exactly what she did— nothing at all. Christmas came and went. No celebration. No gifts. Just another day.

The rumble of an exhaust caught Libby's attention. She froze in place, in the middle of grabbing another handful of popcorn, and listened. It was approaching. Libby jumped from the couch and hurried for the door, tripping over the leg of the coffee table and sprawling across the floor. The table tipped over, sending popcorn flying across the carpet. "Shit!" Libby screamed. "Shit! Shit! Shit!"

Outside, the truck slowed down in front of her house, and then sped away.

She scrambled to her feet and ran to the door. Pulling it open, she searched for the truck's taillights. Was it Cooper? She couldn't be sure. Was he coming to her house? Maybe he had a Christmas present for her! All of her lights were off. He probably thought she was sleeping! "Stupid!" Libby shouted. *Why didn't I leave the lights on?*

Her keys. Where were her keys? If she hurried, she could catch him. She ran into the bedroom, hunting for her purse. Where was it? Not next to her bed. Not in the closet. She ran back into the kitchen. Not on the counter. "Come on!" Finally, she spotted the strap of her purse sticking out from the upended coffee table. She rushed into the living room, flipped the table back onto its feet, grabbed her purse, and sprinted out the door. As soon as her slippered foot hit the icy concrete steps, she tumbled the rest of the way down them and landed on her butt, sitting in the snow, her pajama bottoms getting wet. Still clutching her purse, Libby got to her feet and hurried to her car. Her knees were a little sore, but other than that, she seemed okay. She dug through her purse for her keys and quickly unlocked the doors, jumped in the truck and followed the truck.

If it were Cooper, he'd turn right at the crossroad. Lucy pushed on the gas and the rear end of her truck slid a little on the slick pavement. She reminded herself to buy some sandbags at Walmart and put them in the truck bed to help with traction. Her speedometer climbed to fifty, then sixty, then seventy. She could catch him; he'd probably be driving slower because of the snow and patches of ice. At the crossroad, she stepped on her brakes lightly. No oncoming traffic, so she rolled through the stop sign and made a right. Now there was nothing but a straight stretch of country road in front of her. She pushed on the gas. Taillights shone in the distance. Was it Cooper's truck? She couldn't tell. It was too far away. Libby sped up. They looked like Chevy taillights.

In a split second, her truck was sliding sideways down the road on patch of ice. She stepped off the gas and tried to correct the truck, but the wheels caught on the pavement. The front tires hit the ditch, bouncing Libby out of her seat and slamming her head against the windshield. She held on to the steering wheel, turning the truck out of the ditch and up into a field on the side of the road. Hitting the brakes, she slammed to a halt, within six inches of sideswiping a telephone pole.

Libby sat in the truck, her head wobbling on her neck as she struggled against passing out. She couldn't pass out here. It could be a long time before anyone drove by here. Libby rolled down her window and stuck her head outside to get some air. Her reflection in the cracked glass of the side mirror shocked her. Blood streamed down her forehead. She raised her hand to touch her head. A wide gash was gushing blood, soaking her hair. She touched it, thinking she would need stitches, and then everything went dark.

Jake was on the way home when he got the call. He was tempted to ignore it, except that he was so close. He hesitated for a minute and then turned his squad car around.

Dumb ass probably speeding, he thought as he got out of the car on the side of the road, his lights flashing.

The tires of the truck were buried deep in the cornfield, which was a good thing. If the ground had been frozen, the truck surely would have hit the telephone pole on the driver's side. Jake hurried up the road and pulled his flashlight out, shining it directly at the truck. He could see the driver's head tilted out the window. "Hey! Help is here. How are you doing?"

There was no answer.

Shit, Jake thought to himself. *Two days before Christmas*. He hoped the guy didn't have little kids. Jake struggled to make his way through the ditch and held on to some saplings to pull himself up the other side. The smell of gasoline filled the air; that wasn't good. He approached the truck, tapping gently on the side with his flashlight. "Hey." Jake pointed his flashlight at the driver and realized it was a woman. Dressed in pajamas, blood pouring from her head. The smell of gas grew stronger. *The tank's probably ruptured*, Jake thought. He leaned inside the truck and placed his hand on her neck to feel for a pulse. She was still alive, but there was no ambulance in sight. His training told him to leave her there; the paramedics would arrive soon. She might have internal injuries and moving her would only make them worse. But his instinct told him to get her away from this truck. It was hot, and it was dripping gas—never a good combination. He looked down the road once more. Nothing.

Jake dropped the flashlight into his jacket pocket and hurried to the other side of the truck to open the door. He didn't have enough room to get her out of the driver's side. The telephone pole was too close. He would have to pull her through the truck, out the passenger door. He leaned through the truck and checked for a seatbelt. She wasn't wearing one. Jake climbed into the truck and placed his arms under her back and legs, scooting her across the seat toward the passenger door. She made a soft moaning noise, as if in pain.

"It's okay. I've got you." Blood covered her face, pouring from her wound. It crossed Jake's mind that he might be too late. He wondered how long she had been sitting here. She felt cold, and what in the world was she doing out in this weather wearing pajamas? He pulled her to the passenger side of the truck and then stepped out. As he leaned over, he pulled her across his shoulder, performing a fireman's carry—no small task under the circumstances. Thankfully, she didn't weigh much, but the snow made it rough going. Jake was already breathing hard and he'd barely stepped away from the truck. *I'll never make it through the ditch with her on my shoulder without falling.*

He tightened his grip on her and walked along the edge of the cornfield. Just a short distance away, he could see the spot where the farmer had driven his tractor in and out of the field. It was further away than he'd like, but it would be a lot easier than trying to navigate the ditch with her on his shoulder.

"I've got you. You're going to be fine. I've got you," he told her again. The scream of an ambulance pierced the night. "Do you hear that? They're coming for you. They'll be here any minute. You'll be in a warm hospital bed in just a few minutes. Do you hear me? You hang on. Help is coming."

Jake's original plan was to walk back to his squad car, but with the ambulance arriving, that didn't make sense. When he reached the tractor path, he stood beside the road, his legs shaking under the strain.

The ambulance slid to a stop, red lights flashing, siren wailing. Two men jumped out and pulled a stretcher from the back of the ambulance. As they took the woman from Jake's arms, they asked, "Anyone else in the car? Any identification on her?"

Jake, winded and unable to talk, shook his head. He watched as they strapped her down and slid the stretcher into the back of the truck. One man clambered into the back with her and the other slammed the doors shut.

Finally, Jake found his voice. "Do you think she'll make it?"

"Hell, yes!" The driver flashed a smile before speeding away, red lights flashing, the siren echoing into the still night.

Jake watched the ambulance fade into the distance. He could hear it long after it vanished from sight. He felt dazed. It had all happened so fast. He didn't know what to do next and took a couple of minutes for his head to clear. There was probably some form of identification in the truck. Her registration was probably in the glove compartment, and maybe her purse was in there too. Jake took a couple of shaky steps back toward the truck.

With a loud boom and a flash of fire, the truck exploded, sending flames and sparks arcing into the air.

Jake sprinted down the road to his squad car, knowing he had to move it before it caught on fire too. Running past the truck, he could feel the heat of the flames. Almost there, he told himself as he ran harder. Jake jerked the squad car door open, put the vehicle in reverse and slammed on the gas, putting a safe distance between himself and the burning truck before pulling to a stop.

He called in the fire and sat there, waiting for the fire truck to arrive, wondering if the woman were still alive.

Chapter 32

December

It was Sunday, Christmas Eve. Cooper had already performed one service and was preparing to do the next.

He'd much rather do one and be done with it, but he had to admit that it cleared up the parking situation. And he'd even seen a lot of new faces. He supposed some people only came to church twice a year—on Christmas and Easter—which was two times more than he used to come.

He wasn't sure what to do between services. He'd already said goodbye to everyone and now he was waiting in an empty church. He'd hoped to see the old guy he had talked to once, the former preacher, Troy. He attended most Sundays, but Cooper still hadn't had a chance to talk to him again. Cooper picked up some twigs from the floor and threw them away. *Should I be standing in the church when people start to walk in?* he wondered. *Or will that look weird?* Usually, he made a sort of entrance from the back door, so it felt odd to just sit there waiting for everyone. Maybe he'd be better off waiting in the back. There was a small folding chair by the back door, in the alcove. He supposed he'd go back there and wait. He glanced up at the clock on the wall.

Fifteen more minutes before the next service.

At the back of the church, Cooper sat down in the alcove. He had recently added a small clock on the wall beside the door. Fourteen more minutes now. He sighed. He'd have to think of something to do back here. He couldn't just sit here every Sunday. In nice weather he could just walk back over to the trailer for a short break between services, but today the woods were covered with snow and it didn't make much sense to wade back through it. He looked over to where his boots sat in a puddle of muddy water. He always kept a clean pair of shoes in the church to change into. He thought about getting a pair of those boots that slipped over your shoes. What were those called? He couldn't remember. They were black and had buckles on them. The word *goulash* came to mind. That couldn't be right, could it? That was a dish made of noodles and hamburger. He looked at the clock again. Thirteen minutes. He needed to get a magazine or something. This was stupid. And a waste of time.

The clock continued ticking until, eventually, Cooper heard people filling the church. He walked out one minute early, unable to stand sitting back there any longer.

"Welcome, everybody. Thanks for coming, especially since it's the Sunday before Christmas. I know you all probably have stuff to do, so it means a lot to me that you've chosen to spend this time together. And from now on, it looks like we're going to be doing two services a week." The congregation clapped and somebody whistled. Cooper smiled. "Who woulda thought, huh?"

Laughter filled the room.

And then Cooper spotted her, sitting in the front row. Sally. Suddenly, he couldn't see anyone else. He smiled at her and she smiled back. Finally, she'd come to his church! Her mouth formed the words, *I love you.*

"I love you too, Sally," he said. Sally's face flushed with embarrassment. She squirmed in the pew, certain everyone in the church was staring at her. And they were. Necks craned. Heads turned. A few people pointed. Sally shook her head at Cooper.

He smiled again, and then refocused his attention. "When I was thinking about what to talk about this weekend, I was thinking I should come up with something really good, with it being Christmas and all. I spent the better part of the week looking through the Bible and searching for verses I thought would be right for today. But the more I looked, the more I got confused. I couldn't come up with anything. It wasn't until I came across Book Two of Matthew that I settled on something. And I figured I couldn't improve on it, so I'm going to just read it straight out.

"In those days Caesar Augustus issued a decree that a census should be taken of the entire Roman world. (This was the first census that took place while Quirinius was governor of Syria.) And everyone went to their own town to register.

So Joseph also went up from the town of Nazareth in Galilee to Judea, to Bethlehem the town of David, because he belonged to the house and line of David. He went there to register with Mary, who was pledged to be married to him and was expecting a child. While they were there, the time came for the baby to be born, and she gave birth to her firstborn, a son. She wrapped him in cloths and placed him in a manger, because there was no guest room available for them.

And there were shepherds living out in the fields nearby, keeping watch over their flocks at night. An angel of the Lord appeared to them, and the glory of the Lord shone around them, and they were terrified. But the angel said to them, 'Do not be afraid. I bring you good news that will cause great joy for all the people. Today in the town of David a Savior has been born to you...'"

Cooper looked up from the Bible and stopped reading for a moment. He smiled at the people gathered before him. He had not admitted this to the first service, but he thought

he would go ahead and admit it this time. Why not? It was
kind of funny. "I'm embarrassed to admit this, but when I
first read this, I realized it sounded familiar. I'm reading the
Bible, and all of a sudden I think, *Hey! This is right out of
Charlie Brown!*"

The entire room laughed.

Cooper laughed too. "Remember? Linus says it in the
Charlie Brown Christmas show. I know, pretty pathetic, but
true. Okay, back to the original."

"'He is the Messiah, the Lord. This will be a sign to you:
You will find a baby wrapped in cloths and lying in a
manger.'

"Suddenly a great company of the heavenly host
appeared with the angel, praising God and saying, 'Glory to
God in the highest heaven, and on earth peace to those on
whom his favor rests.'

"When the angels had left them and gone into heaven,
the shepherds said to one another, 'Let's go to Bethlehem
and see this thing that has happened, which the Lord has told
us about.' So they hurried off and found Mary and Joseph,
and the baby, who was lying in the manger. When they had
seen him, they spread the word concerning what had been
told them about this child, and all who heard it were amazed
at what the shepherds said to them. But Mary treasured up
all these things and pondered them in her heart. The
shepherds returned, glorifying and praising God for all the
things they had heard and seen, which were just as they had
been told."

Cooper closed the Bible and stood before the
congregation. They clapped for a long time. Cooper waited.
He smiled over at Sally. She smiled back. *Thank you, God*,
he said silently. *Thank you so much.*

Chapter 33

December—Christmas Day

Pete placed a small, gift-wrapped box into Violet's lap.
"Pete! I didn't think we were exchanging gifts."

"We aren't. I just got you something small. I hope you like it." They were sitting on Pete's couch, and Pete was watching Violet's face intently, anticipating her response.

"I feel bad."

"Don't feel bad, just open it."

Violet tugged gently at the wrapping paper, wanting the moment to last. Removing the paper and lifting the lid revealed two things: a key and a card. Lifting the key from the box, Violet looked at Pete in question. "What's this?"

"It's a key."

"Ha, ha. I can see it's a key! A key to what?"

"It's a key to this place."

Violet smiled and then reached into the box again and pulled out a plastic card. "A gift card?"

"Yes. It's for a clothing store in town. You didn't bring much stuff with you, so I thought you could use it."

"Tell the truth! You're tired of me wearing your sweatpants and sweatshirts."

Pete reached over and touched the sleeve of the sweatshirt she was wearing. "You look cute in my sweats. I just thought you might like some new clothes. You didn't bring that many from home."

"And, if you bought me a gift certificate, I'd have to leave the apartment, right?"

"Well…"

"It's okay, Pete. I know what you're trying to do, and I appreciate it."

"It's not good, you staying inside so much. I'm worried about you, Honey." Pete caught his breath. He hadn't meant to call her that.

"I know. I'm worried about me too," Violet said.

Emboldened, Pete took her into his arms. He could feel her tense up immediately, so he kissed her lightly on top of the head and released her. She'd be all right, he told himself. It was just a matter of time. He almost believed it.

(

It was a tradition—every Christmas, Cooper and Sally woke, opened their presents, and then watched *It's A Wonderful Life*. Cooper didn't really like the movie, but Sally did, and she cried every time, without fail. As soon as George Bailey started running through the town back to his house, snow falling and Bedford Falls all lit up, she started sniffling. Cooper loved that about Sally, that predictability. He knew how she would react to most things most of the time. Whenever she saw a puppy, whether in real life or on a TV or movie screen, she smiled. If a Sarah McLachlan song came on the radio, she always turned up the volume. When he asked if she wanted to get pizza for dinner, she always said, "Sure!" Before she fell asleep every night, the last words she spoke were always, "I love you, Cooper."

Cooper watched Sally as George Bailey crossed the bridge, as George recognized the old tree he had run his car into, and then, as he started running down the streets of his hometown. She sniffled. And then, sure enough, a hand went to her cheek to wipe away a tear. Cooper pulled her closer.

(

"There are leftovers in the refrigerator. And we have all kinds of snacks. I have my cell phone with me if you need us," Ivy told her daughter, as she and Drake stood on the doorstep.

"Mom! Go! Have fun," Lucy said.

"She's right. Come on, Ivy. We're going to be late."

Lucy hugged them both and then locked the door behind them. She was just steps from the door when the doorbell rang. Lucy spun around and opened the door. "What'd you forget?"

Ivy smiled. "Nothing. Why don't you get dressed and come with us?"

"Mom! I don't want to go to a Christmas party with a bunch of old people."

"Thanks!"

"You know what I mean. Seriously, I don't mind being home by myself."

"But it's Christmas. I feel bad."

"Mom. Go! But thanks for thinking of me. I love you." Lucy gave her mother a quick hug. "Now, go! Dad's waiting in the car."

"Are you sure?"

"I'm sure."

"Okay. See you later. We probably won't be gone that long, but we have to go, you know that. It's all of your dad's suppliers. You sure you don't want to go with us?"

"Yes!"

"Okay. Lock the door." Ivy turned away from the door and walked back to the car.

"Be gone as long as you want. I'll be asleep before you even get home," Lucy called after her. Locking the door again, Lucy then settled on the couch, covering herself with a nearby throw and picking up the remote.

(

The only sign of Christmas in the entire Barnes' house was the wrapped Christmas presents Jake, Melody, Clara and TJ were now opening. Everybody but Josephine, who was spending Christmas with her own family, was gathered in the living room. Melody tried to concentrate on the presents, and on holding a forced smile on her face. Her "morning" sickness had become worse. She was now vomiting several times a day, and today was no exception.

"Do you want to open it?" Jake asked her, picking up the present from TJ.

"No. You go ahead."

Jake unwrapped a small box, pulled out a piece of paper, and began reading it.

"It's a college fund for the baby!" TJ said.

Jake's brows furrowed. "TJ! This says there's fifty thousand dollars in the account!"

TJ nodded. "Yeah, hopefully that will get the kid through college in eighteen years. And it will gain interest every year. So in eighteen years, there should be a pretty good chunk of money in there."

"Fifty thousand dollars!" Melody exclaimed. "TJ, that's the nicest thing anyone has ever done for us. First you put the addition on our house, and now this! Thank you so much." Melody got up from the couch, crossed the room, and hugged him.

"Melody, we can't keep this," Jake said.

"It's already done, Jake. You don't have a choice. The account is set up. You just need to add the baby's name and social security number to it when it is born."

"Don't be silly, Jake," Melody said. "Of course we will accept it. It's a gift. How would we ever put the baby through college on your salary?"

Jake put the piece of paper back in the box and turned to his mother, hoping to find some support there. "What do you think, Mom? Do you think it's okay for TJ to give us so much money for the baby?"

"What baby?" Clara asked.

(

Beaulah was determined to have a "normal" Christmas, even if Perry was no longer living with her. Her house was fully decorated, she had seen to that, and she had spent Christmas morning cooking all of the dishes they usually had on Christmas: ham, mashed potatoes, green bean casserole, corn, deviled eggs, and even cherry cheesecake for dessert (Perry's favorite). Beaulah placed all of the food on the table, lit a candle, and filled a plate.

She was done eating in ten minutes.

Blowing the candle out, she refrigerated the leftovers in plastic containers, loaded the dishwasher, washed the pans, and went to bed. It was a little before eight.

As she walked to her bedroom, she realized Libby had probably eaten alone today, too. She regretted not calling her and inviting her to dinner. *Oh well*, Beaulah thought. *Maybe I'll give her a call tomorrow and invite her over for leftovers.*

(

Perry walked through the empty church, his hands stuffed in his pockets. He whistled, just in case someone was hiding somewhere. He'd never admit this to anybody, but he was afraid to be in the building alone. There were so many places for an intruder to hide. As he walked through the dark church, he tried to relax. It was silly; he knew it, and he wanted the feeling to go away. So, every night, before he retired to his office for the evening, he walked through the entire building, room by room. He whistled or jingled the keys in his pocket and he told himself that, eventually, he'd be able to walk through the entire building silently in the dark, and without fear.

Perry had completed five Christmas services today, and he was exhausted. After a quick walk through, he was going to return to his office, make a bed on the couch, and watch a little television. Since he had moved into the office—or perhaps, more accurately, since Beaulah had thrown him out of the house—he had bought a new television for his office. All in all, it was a pretty comfortable arrangement.

When he made it back to his office, Perry noticed that something smelled funny. He frowned, wondering about the odor. It didn't take long to find its source. Across the room, in his trashcan, he spotted a container of Chinese food takeout. Perry picked up the trashcan, walked down the hall and placed it in the main office; he'd take it out to the dumpster tomorrow. The offices were closed until January second anyway. He'd have plenty of time to get to it.

(

Frank Collette sat in his living room. A box of cold pizza from the refrigerator and a can of beer sat on the coffee table before him. The remote was in his hand and he flipped through the channels in search of something to watch. It was another perk to Violet being gone: he could watch whatever he wanted. Actually, life didn't seem much different with Violet gone. They had hardly talked anymore anyway, and their sex life had been almost non-existent. The only thing Frank missed was having groceries in the cupboards. He hated going to the store and mostly lived survived on takeout. It would be nice to have some chips or something to snack on. Soon, he'd be out of beer and be forced to make a grocery run.

Pulling open the drawer under the coffee table, Frank grabbed the wad of cash and counted it. After giving Sally the fifteen grand to pay Annie, he had less than two thousand dollars left. He'd have to do something about that soon. Maybe he'd send another blackmail note to Cooper. The first time worked like a charm. Frank tossed the money back into the drawer and smiled. Cooper was such a dumb son of a bitch. Sally was being stolen away from Cooper right under his own nose, and stupid Cooper Moon was even paying for it.

Later that night, Jake sat at his kitchen table, rubbing his sore shoulder muscles and unable to sleep. Everyone else was asleep. For once, the house was quiet. He thought about the woman who had crashed her truck. He had not heard anything about her, and as far as he knew, she still had not been identified. *Someone should have been able to ID her by now*, he thought. The truck had burned to a crisp, but they still should have been able to identify the license plate, burnt or not. But, then again, it was Christmas and a lot of people were probably not working. He guessed it was to be expected.

He had called the hospital earlier in the day. They said she was in stable condition, but heavily sedated, and no one had called the hospital looking for her. Jake wondered where her family was. Surely, someone was wondering where this woman was. No missing person reports. No calls to the hospital. It was weird. Maybe he'd go check on her; he couldn't sleep anyway, so he might as well.

A short time later, Jake was entering her hospital room. It was past visiting hours, but he flashed his badge and the nurse at the front desk let him in. Her room was dimly lit; he supposed to make it easier for the nurses coming in and out. An IV was in her arm and a couple of machines monitored her vitals. Jake stared at one of the machines for a minute and watched a green line jump with the beat of her heart.

Her eyes were bruised and swollen, and a bandage was wrapped around her head. Her face seemed swollen too. Jake looked at the name tag on her wrist. *Jane Doe*. So, she still had not been identified. Jake wondered if she had a husband. If she did, he must be frantic with worry. He thought of Melody. *What if it were her lying here, hurt and alone?* The thought sickened him.

He felt like he should say something, do something, but he didn't know what to say or do, so he just turned and went back down the hall to the elevator. As he passed the nurse's station, Jake spotted a bowl of candy canes on the desk. He pulled one out of the bowl and returned to the room. Tiptoeing in, he placed it on the bedside table.

When he turned, a nurse was standing behind him, smiling.

"I thought maybe she'd see it when she woke up," he whispered.

"Are you a friend?"

"No. I don't know her." When she gave him a strange look, he figured he better explain. "I'm a cop. I was at the accident."

The nurse nodded. "Oh. I see."

Jake hesitated at the door. "Will she wake up?"

"Yes. Right now she is in a drug-induced coma, just while she recovers and the swelling goes down. But as we reduce the meds, she should wake up in a day or two. You can come back then and see her if you want."

"No. No. I was just wondering if she was okay. Thanks," he said before walking out of the room.

Back home, he undressed and crawled into bed behind Melody, wrapping his arms around her.

"What time is it?" she mumbled.

"After three. Go back to sleep. You need your rest." He kissed her shoulder and settled onto his pillow.

"What have you been doing? Watching television?"

"No. I went to the hospital to check on that woman who was in the wreck."

"Oh, that's nice. How's she doing?"

"Okay, I guess."

Jake rested his hand on Melody's belly. "I love you," he whispered.

"I love you too."

Chapter 34

January

Libby awoke up to the sound of someone talking.
"Come on, it's time to wake up. Come on, you can do it. Wake up, Honey. Wake up."

She opened her eyes. A woman dressed in white stood before her, patting her arm and holding her hand. "There you go. Good girl! You're in the hospital. You had a bad wreck but you're going to be just fine now."

Libby could not hear well; something was covering her ears. She reached up and felt her ear. It was wrapped. Her whole head was wrapped. Her head ached. "Where am I?"

"You're in the hospital. You were in a car wreck, but you're going to be fine. You are healing real nice. Your head is bandaged. You had a nasty bump and had to have some stitches. Can you tell me your name?"

"Libby. Libby Cartwright."

"Okay, that's good. We weren't sure. We traced your plates and figured you were the one driving the car, but I had to ask to be sure.

Libby squinted against the light of the room.

"You want me to close those shades?"

"Yes, please."

"Was anyone hurt in the wreck?"

"Just you, hon." The nurse moved to the window and began closing the shades. "You slid on the ice and ended up in a ditch. Amazingly, you don't have a single broken bone. Could have been a lot worse. You just missed a telephone pole. Someone was looking out for you." She returned to Libby's bedside and placed a hand on her lower leg. "Can I get you anything? Are you hungry? Would you like a drink?"

"No. I can't remember, did this happen this morning? What time is it?

"Oh, no. You've been here for several days. You came in a couple of days before Christmas, and it's the sixth of January."

"Does anyone know I'm here?"

"I guess so. Look at all of these flowers! And you've had a visitor every single day."

For the first time, Libby noticed the flowers in the room. Her head hurt too much to turn, but even without turning it, she could see six bouquets of mixed flowers. One had a balloon attached that read, *Get well soon!*

Cooper! It had to be Cooper, Libby thought. *He must be so worried about me.* "Where's my cell phone?"

"You came in here with the clothes on your back. I'm not sure about your phone."

"My purse?"

"I don't know, hon. Let me go ask at the desk. I'll be right back."

Libby suddenly felt very lonely. She wanted Cooper. She needed his arms around her. In that instant, she remembered—she'd been chasing him when her truck spun out of control on the ice. The last thing she remembered was sliding sideways. It seemed so stupid now. But then she imagined telling Cooper: *I was trying to catch up with you when I slid on the ice.* Maybe he'd feel sorry for her. Maybe he'd see how much she loved him.

The nurse returned. "I got bad news for you, hon. No cell phone and no purse. Your car caught fire after you were taken away in the ambulance. Nothing was saved from it."

"My truck caught on fire?" Libby tried to absorb the information. "While I was in it? I don't understand."

"No. You got into a wreck, you were taken away by the ambulance, and then your car, or I guess it was a truck, caught fire in the field. Burned completely up."

"My cell phone, my purse, all of my ID…"

"Hey, all of those things can be replaced. It's just an inconvenience, that's all. You could have been in that truck when it caught fire. Remember that!"

"Yeah, I guess you're right." Libby glanced over at the nearest bouquet. "Is there a card on there?"

The nurse crossed the room and plucked a card from the center of the bouquet. "Sure is."

"Would you read it? My head is killing me."

"It says, 'Get well soon, Libby. Love, Beaulah.' You want me to read the others, too?"

"Sure."

The nurse bustled around the room, gathering and reading cards. Every bouquet was from Beaulah. Not one was from Cooper. *Does he even know I'm in here?*

(

Jake eased off the gas and coasted past the house. There were no cars in the driveway and no lights on. It was the drug bust house, where Jake and his buddy, Danny, had helped arrest a meth gang just a few months ago, where Jake had pocketed over fifty-two thousand dollars, now hidden in his closet. But after TJ had won World Wide Warrior and came home with half a million dollars and signed several lucrative endorsements that had netted him even more money—and Jake didn't even know (or want to know) how much those had brought in—the money hidden in Jake's bowling ball bag seemed ridiculous. And dangerous. He'd risked his career and his reputation while his little brother swung through an obstacle course to haul in money by the bucket load.

More than anything in the world, Jake just wanted to get rid of that money.

He drove past the house, considering just dressing in black some night and walking up to the back of the house, breaking a window, and throwing the money through. His fingerprints were all over it, but so what? It wasn't like the drug dealers were going to call the police and report money being thrown through their window.

Jake's radio crackled and a call came across reporting an armed robbery in progress at a convenience store. He replied that he was en route and flipped his lights on. It was only minutes away.

Pulling up in front of the convenience store, Jake flipped his lights off and looked through the window. He could see a young guy standing in front of the counter. He wore a dark sweatshirt with the hood pulled up. His right arm was extended across the counter and he pointed a gun directly at the frightened cashier, a young girl of about twenty. Jake put his hand on his door handle, but then, instead of pulling it to open the door, he held on to it, suddenly feeling as if he might fall out of the car.

He watched the guy's hand shaking as he pointed the gun at the girl, motioning for her to hurry. Jake felt his body start to tremble. A fine trickle of sweat ran down his temple. The kid was just minutes away from spending the rest of his life in jail, over some money—a damned stack of paper. The kid's life, as he knew it, was coming to an end. He was going to prison over a mistake that took less than a minute to make. Jake tried to pull the door open, but the trembling snaked through his body and down his arm. His heart pounded, his breath came in quick gasps, and he was beginning to feel light headed. Sweat poured from his body and he could feel his shirt clinging to his chest.

Jake Barnes had to get rid of that money, even if it meant burning it up. He didn't want anything to do with it. Suddenly, overwhelmingly, the implications hit him square in the face. What was he thinking? He'd never done anything dishonest—ever! His entire life, he had been nothing but a straight shooter, but now, stashed in his bowling ball bag, he, Jake Barnes, had stolen money from a drug bust. He was no different to that kid he was watching through the window.

Reaching across the counter, the kid grabbed a pile of money, turned and ran for the door, stuffing the money into his pocket as he pushed his shoulder against the door and ran into the parking lot.

The guy hesitated briefly, stunned by the sight of Jake's squad car, and looked up directly at Jake. His hands now shaking violently, Jake reached over and pulled the door handle with both hands. It opened. Jake looked at the kid, and for a couple of seconds, they both seemed to wonder what the other one was going to do next. Then the guy ran, disappearing around the corner of the convenience store and into the night.

As Jake watched, the scene began to tilt. He wondered, briefly, how could that be? It looked like the guy was running sideways. And then Jake tumbled from the squad car onto the pavement of the parking lot, and everything went black.

Chapter 35

January

Cooper could not get past the thought that Violet had dared to come to the Sunday service. What sort of person did that? Came along as if nothing had happened? He decided enough was enough. It was time to pay Violet a visit and talk about this blackmail note. He had to have her assurance she would not send any pictures to Sally or the press. He walked into Bass Turds and settled into a booth. Pete looked at him questioningly because Cooper always sat at the bar. Cooper turned sideways in the booth and put his leg up on the seat. "Twisted my knee, and it's hurting," he lied.

The last couple of times Cooper had been in, Violet had been upstairs in Pete's apartment and he had never seen her. Today, she was waiting on tables. "Hi, Cooper. Would you like something to drink?" Violet approached him with a small pad of paper and a pen.

"Yeah. I'll have a Coke."

Violet nodded and turned away before Cooper could say anything. He glanced over at Pete, who was placing a coaster under some guy's drink, somebody Cooper didn't recognize. How was Cooper going to talk to Violet with Pete standing right behind the bar? Pete couldn't hear Cooper from over there, but he'd be sure to wonder what Cooper was talking to Violet about. Cooper tried to come up with something plausible but could not. He frowned. He used to be much better at this type of thing. He was getting out of practice.

Violet returned with the Coke and set it on the table.

"Hey, Violet. I need to talk to you."

"About what?"

"About the letter you sent me. I paid you, so now I want those pictures."

"What?"

"The pictures of us," Cooper said in a low voice.

"I have no idea what you are talking about. Do you want something to eat?"

"Violet, I'm not playing with you. I'm serious."

Pete surprised him by stepping up beside Violet. "Is there some sort of problem, Cooper?"

Yeah, you might say that. Your girlfriend is blackmailing me, Cooper thought. But he said, "No problem. I was just telling Violet how I twisted my knee. Was walking through the woods and stepped right into a hole."

Violet frowned and looked confused. "Do you want something to eat?"

"No. You know, I just remembered something I have to do." Cooper got up from the table, leaving his Coke untouched.

Pete watched him walk away, noticing that Cooper was not limping at all. "What was that all about?" he asked Violet.

"I have no idea."

When Jake awoke in hospital, Melody was beside him. At first, he was telling the truth when he said he couldn't remember what had happened. But after a few minutes, he recalled passing out in the parking lot of the convenience store. Another anxiety attack, at least that's what he thought it was. But he was too embarrassed to tell Melody that. Besides, he wasn't a doctor, so maybe it was something else. He'd wait and see what the doctors found out.

"What if something is really wrong with you, Jake?" she asked.

"There's nothing really wrong with me, Melody."

"How do you know? You passed out. They found you lying in a parking lot. That's not exactly normal. Maybe there's something wrong with your heart or something."

The same thought had crossed Jake's mind. He had been having chest pains off and on for a while. "Well, if there is, the doctors will figure that out. We just have to wait and see what they say."

Melody moved closer to his bed and leaned in next to him. "But, Jake, what if it's something really bad? What about the baby? What will I do?"

"What do you mean?"

"Jake, what if you had died or something? What would I do? Clara is living with us and I have a baby on the way! I can't do all of that, Jake."

Jake's mouth opened and his brows furrowed. "Melody, I'm not planning on kicking the bucket any time soon. Man, you're not exactly making me feel better."

Melody pulled her chair closer. "I'm sorry, but really, what would I do? Just imagine if you were gone tomorrow. What would I do? What about the baby?" She gripped the bedrail that ran along the side of the bed.

Jake took a moment to look at her. She looked tired and almost frantic. "Mel, why don't you go home and get some sleep. I know you didn't get much sleep last night. If I find anything out, I'll call you right away."

She looked down at the floor for a moment and then back at Jake. "You wouldn't mind?"

"No. Not at all. I'm just lying here. I've got plenty of

people to take care of me. You go home and get some sleep. I promise I'll call you if I need you."

Melody stood and leaned over to kiss him. "Okay. If you're sure you are okay with it."

"I am. Go home."

"I'll be back in later tonight."

"No, really. Go home and get some rest. Come back in the morning."

"You promise you'll call me if you need me?"

"Promise."

She kissed his cheek. "Okay. I'll see you in the morning." Turning, she then hurried out the door.

Cooper Moon was walking in as she walked out, and they bumped into each other. Melody's hands flew protectively over her belly. "Watch where you're walking!" she snapped. "Oh, sorry. I didn't mean to bump you." Cooper turned to watch her walk down the hallway before walking the rest of the way into Jake's room. "I barely touched her. Honest."

Jake shook his head. "I know. Don't worry about it. She's wound a little tight right now. The baby, I guess, and worrying about me."

Cooper stood by Jake's bed. "How are you? I ran into TJ and he told me you were in the hospital so I thought I'd stop by and say hi." In truth, when TJ had suggested Cooper stop by the hospital to visit Jake, Cooper's reply had been, "What for?" Then TJ reminded Cooper that he was Jake's pastor and that's what pastors did. "Crap," had been Cooper's reply. "I didn't even think about that." And he hadn't. But he was here now, and he figured that had to count for something, especially since he didn't like hospitals.

"I'm all right. The doctors are doing some tests, but I don't think it's anything to be worried about."

"TJ said you passed out. Fell right out of your car."

"I don't remember much."

"Good thing you weren't driving!" Cooper said with a

smile.

"Yeah. Could have been worse, huh?"

A nurse entered, and immediately noticed Cooper. "Excuse me," she said as she scooted between him and the bed. Jake looked at Cooper, brows raised. Cooper shrugged and took a couple of steps back.

"There's two sides to this bed," Jake said with a smile.

The nurse ignored Jake's comment and checked his IV. "How are you guys doing tonight?" She smiled at Jake, and then smiled even longer at Cooper.

Cooper took another step backward and shoved his hands into the back pockets of his jeans.

Jake laughed. "Well, I've been better."

"Are you in any pain at all?"

"No. I'm fine."

She leaned over Jake's bed slightly and examined the scrape across his face. "Looks like that's healing nicely. If you need anything for pain, just push your nurse's button and I'll come running. If you need anything at all"—she looked in Cooper's direction—"my name is Allison."

Cooper nodded awkwardly and then stepped over to the window to peer into the parking lot.

Allison took the hint and left the room, her nurse shoes making a grateful, silent exit.

After she had left, Jake started laughing. "It must be good to be you, Cooper."

Cooper ran a hand over his chin and returned to Jake's bedside. "It used to be a lot more fun than it is now. Being a pastor kind of changes things." Cooper smiled and shook his head. "You know, that's the first time I've said that. The first time I've actually called myself a pastor. Feels kind of creepy."

Jake looked toward the door. "Yeah, speaking of that … Would you close the door?"

Cooper closed the door and returned to Jake's bedside.

"Cooper, as a pastor, as my pastor, I can talk to you,

right?"

Cooper sat in the chair beside the bed. "Sure. You can talk to me anytime, Jake."

Jake glanced over at the television that hung from the ceiling. A sitcom was playing but there was no sound. "I mean, if I tell you something, you wouldn't tell anyone, right?"

"No, Jake. You can trust me."

Jake stared straight ahead at the television. "I told the doctors and Melody that I don't know what happened to me, but I remember. I got called to a convenience store, a robbery in progress. I parked in front of the store, and I saw the guy run out of the store, but I couldn't do anything. I started shaking and … I think I had an anxiety attack. I think I've been having them for a while now. I mean, it could be my heart or something, but from what I've read on the Internet, I'm pretty sure it's an anxiety attack. And now I'm afraid that if they find out I'll lose my job." Finally, he turned back to Cooper.

Cooper ran his hand through his hair and then rested his hands on his legs. "Shit, Jake. That's terrible. Does TJ know?"

Jake shook his head. "I haven't told anyone but you."

"How long has this been going on?"

"Maybe a year. I'm not sure. Maybe less. Honestly, I don't think I noticed it much at first, but then the attacks kept getting worse and I started having chest pains."

"Maybe it's your heart."

"Maybe. But I don't think so. I think I'm just going nuts."

"Man, I don't know what to say. Maybe you should tell someone in here. Talk to a doctor, or a psychiatrist or something."

"I'm afraid it would get back to the station. I'd lose my job for sure. No one wants a whacked-out cop running around town with a gun."

"I think you should tell somebody."

"I just did. I told my pastor."

Cooper sighed. "Yeah, and I'm no help at all. I don't even know what to tell you, Jake." Cooper thought for a moment, "But I do know this. Most of the misery in my life has been caused from hiding things from Sally."

"Cooper, I'm not running around on Melody. I'm having anxiety attacks and I'm afraid of losing my job. That's different."

"I'm not so sure it is. Lying is lying. Tell Melody; that's what I would advise you. Whatever your problem is, you'll be better off if she knows about it and the two of you are working through it together."

Jake shook his head. "No. Melody isn't like Sally. She's more ... fragile. Especially now, being pregnant and all." Jake blinked a couple of times and bit the inside of his lip. "Cooper, I ... there's something else I haven't told anyone. Maybe if I told you, maybe I'd feel better. Maybe you could even help me figure out a way to ... fix it. But ... I'm not sure. I don't know..."

"What?"

"Hypothetically, what if someone told you they did something that wasn't exactly ... legal. Would you keep that a secret? How does that work? Would you have to tell?"

Cooper got to his feet. "Jeez, Jake. I don't know." He crossed the room, opened the door, peeked outside, and then went back to stand next to Jake. "Hypothetically, I'd tell the person not to tell me until I find out." He peered out the window. "I don't know how to find out. One of these days we're gonna have to break down and buy a computer. Couldn't you look that up on your phone?"

"That's nothing I'm ever going to do a search on. You know that stuff can be traced."

Cooper nodded. "I'll find out and get back to you. I might know someone I could ask, someone who wouldn't say anything. I'll act like it's just a question I have, in case something like that ever comes up."

"Thanks, Cooper. I appreciate it. I think it would help to talk about this." After a moment, he added, "Hypothetically."

(

In the hallway, Beaulah walked alongside Libby, whose wheelchair was being pushed by a young man dressed in white. Libby was being released today, and although she had protested about the wheelchair, the orderly had insisted, claiming it was hospital policy.

"Well, at least you're getting out on a nice day. It's gorgeous outside. Cold, but nice and sunny," Beaulah said.

"Right now, I wouldn't care if it was pouring rain. I just want out of here." All of Libby's bandages had been removed, most of the bruising had gone from her face, and the stitches had been removed from her head. She'd have a large scar, but it was on top of her head and her hair would cover it. They passed one of the hospital rooms and Libby turned her head. Cooper? Did she hear Cooper's voice? As they continued down the hall, she convinced herself she must be hearing things.

Cooper left the hospital and drove straight to Timber Lake Community Church. He couldn't think of anyone to ask such a question, except for Perry Potts. Perry had been a pastor for years, so Cooper figured if anyone knew the answer to this question, it had to be Perry Potts.

It was after seven, so Cooper was afraid the parking lot would be empty. He figured they were probably out of there by five, six o clock, at the latest. Surprised to see a car in the parking lot, Cooper parked his truck and hurried inside.

The halls were dark and no one was in sight. The offices were also dark, but he could see a light coming from the direction of Pastor Potts' office.

"Pastor Potts?" Cooper called. There was no answer.

Cooper walked through the dark outer office and down the hall to the open door of Perry's office. "Pastor Potts?" he called again.

As Cooper stepped into Perry's office, Perry stepped out from his private bathroom located at the rear of the office. He was wearing plaid green pajamas.

"Oh, sorry," Cooper said. "I saw the light. I didn't know…"

Perry tugged at the front of his pajamas and stood straight. "I … I … I'm sleeping here tonight."

Blankets and pillows were stacked on the couch, and Cooper could smell popcorn. A large television hung from the wall; Cooper didn't think it had been there the last time he had visited Potts.

"How can I help you?" Potts asked.

"I'm sorry. I guess this is a bad time. I didn't mean to…"

Potts walked around his desk and sat down. "How can I help you?" he said again.

"You sure you don't want me to go?"

"Mr. Moon, for the third time, how can I help you?"

Cooper sat in the chair on the other side of the desk. "I won't stay long. I just wanted to ask you something. As a pastor, if someone tells you something, you're supposed to keep that a secret, right?"

"Unless doing so would harm someone or risk someone's life, yes."

"What if someone told you about something they did that was illegal?"

"Again, unless someone's life were at risk, you would be bound to confidentiality. And, of course, if a child is involved, then it goes without saying you are required to do whatever you need to do to protect the child. That would include notifying the authorities."

"No, no. It's nothing to do with a kid, I don't think. And, really, I'm just speaking hypothetically. It's just so I know, okay." Cooper nodded. "Well, that's good to know. What if that person had an important job? Would that make a difference?"

"Well, obviously, there could be extenuating circumstances, but again, you always want to ask yourself if confidentiality might put someone else in harm's way?"

Cooper stood. "Okay, okay." He nodded. "Well, I guess that answers my question." At the door, he hesitated. "Do you come across that sort of thing a lot, people telling you secrets?"

"It's part of being a pastor. You might want to do some research on it. Look up pastor confidentiality on the Internet. You'll find lots of information on it that should help you."

"You wouldn't have a book on that, would you?"

"No, I don't think I do." Perry stood. "But, like I said, you'll find lots of information on the Internet."

"All right, will do. Well, thanks. I really appreciate it. Have a good night."

Perry nodded and Cooper left. As Cooper walked back through the darkened office, he heard the door lock behind him. He made his way through the building, wondering why Pastor Potts was sleeping in his office, and feeling bad for walking in on the guy while he was wearing his pajamas.

(

That night, Libby sat on her couch and watched television. After they had left the hospital, Beaulah had taken her to the cell phone store and to the car rental place. A new cell phone sat beside Libby on the couch, and a rental car was parked in her driveway. She was feeling much better, although still a little sore from the accident. Thanks to the wreck, she had to buy another car and replace all of her ID. She tried not to think about it. Tonight she was going to rest and relax in front of the television. Soon enough, she'd have to worry about all of life's details and jump back into her regular routine back at the factory. Tonight, she could put that off a little longer and just breathe. She felt depleted. She wasn't sure if it was because of the accident or because she had not seen Cooper since November. Since then, Thanksgiving, Christmas, New Year's Eve, and a life-threatening accident had all passed—all spent without him. While Libby had spent her nights alone, spent day after day in the hospital alone, Cooper had been at home with his wife.

When she thought about it, it was silly of her to expect him to come to the hospital to see her. No one would have contacted him to tell him. Why would they? She wasn't really a part of his life. If she had died that night, he wouldn't even know until he saw it in the paper or someone mentioned it in passing. The only person who had come to see her in the hospital was Beaulah. As far as she knew, Cooper still didn't know about the accident, and she had no way of contacting him while she was in the hospital. His phone number was unlisted. It had been in her cell phone, but she couldn't remember it. All of her numbers had been restored to her new phone today, but she still hadn't called him.

Maybe it was time she faced reality. Maybe it was time to give up on Cooper Moon. She didn't know. All she knew was that tonight, just tonight, she needed to rest.

Chapter 36

January

Cooper was up early the next morning and was ready to leave before Sally even got out of bed. He leaned over and kissed her forehead. "Bye. I'll see you later. What time do you get off work?"

"I'm leaving at seven."

"Want to get pizza tonight?" He sat on the edge of the bed and pulled on his socks.

"Sure!"

Cooper smiled. "Okay, I'll call it in. You pick it up on the way home."

"Where you going so early?" Sally yawned and stretched against the sheets.

"Going to visit Jake in the hospital."

Sally sat up in the bed. "You're kidding. In hospital? Are you serious?"

"Yeah. I was there yesterday too. Just thought I'd check in on him."

"You hate hospitals. You never visit anyone in the hospital."

"I'm a pastor now. It's part of the job." Cooper grinned

at her, looking a little embarrassed.

"Cooper Moon, you never cease to amaze me."

Cooper stood and walked around to her side of the bed. "That's the idea, woman." He pressed his lips against hers and kissed her passionately. Both of them lingered, lost in the kiss, sliding into desire. Cooper pulled away. "I gotta go," he whispered. "But I'll be waiting for you when you get home tonight." He kissed her forehead once more and left her. Both of them smiling.

Cooper drove to the hospital, feeling productive. He wished his radio worked. He would have liked to listen to some music this morning. He was a pastor. A pastor! He grinned as he drove. And he was doing something good today. Visiting Jake was a good thing. Sally was right, he did hate hospitals, but this was part of his job now, and he was going to do it more often. Cooper wondered if anyone else in his church was in hospital. He wondered how he could find that out. Maybe he should say something this Sunday, tell people that he was available to visit them in hospital if they wanted him to. He supposed he could just give them his home phone number. Maybe he could pass it out at the end of the service. Yeah, maybe he'd do that. That sounded like a good idea.

Jake was pushing food around his plate when Cooper entered his room. "Hey Jake. How's it going?"

"Okay, except for this food. It's enough to make a person sick. Why would they give this to anyone?" Jake poked at a pile of scrambled eggs that wiggled back. "I'd give twenty bucks for some of Sally's biscuits and gravy right now."

"I could go get an order for you."

"Are you serious?"

"Yeah! Why not? It's just down the road. I'll be back in ten minutes. You got your cell phone with you? You can call the diner and order it to go. It'll be ready when I get there."

"Nah. You don't have to do that."

Cooper walked to the door. "I'm on my way. Call. The number is six five eight five. I'll be right back."

"No, you don't have to do that," Jake said, but Cooper didn't hear him; he was already out the door and down the hallway. Jake reached over to the bedside table and picked up his phone. "Six five eight five. Six five eight five." He dialed the number and ordered his food.

As he was hanging up, Danny Bennett entered the room. "Are you kidding me? You're still laying here on your fat ass?"

"Yeah. And it's about to get fatter—just ordered some takeout."

Danny stood at the end of the bed. "Man, you got the life, Barnes. You get a little dizzy and you spend two days in the hospital ordering takeout and getting pretty nurses to wait on you hand and foot."

"Hey, what can I say? Some guys know how to work it."

"Seriously, for a minute there, I thought our friends might have got to you."

"Our friends?"

Danny closed the door. "Culver has had someone following him for two days. And Harman said someone's been parking in front of his house during the day when he's not home. He caught them yesterday and he recognized the guy. Said it was one of the guys we busted on Miller Street, already out of jail."

"What'd the guy say?"

"Well, he had it all worked out, had a quick excuse. He had a map on his lap and said he just pulled over to read it, but Harman's wife said the guy had been there for hours. They're definitely watching us. I don't know how they're figuring out everyone's home addresses."

"Not that hard. Internet. Or just follow us home from work."

"Yeah, I guess. All I know is, it's bullshit. I don't like

the idea of these punks sitting in front of Harman's house or following any of us around."

"They'll hang themselves. It's just a matter of time."

"Yeah. I just hope they do it soon. I still can't believe they're telling everyone we stole a hundred grand from them. You and I were the ones who did the walkthrough. You didn't steal a hundred grand in drug money, did you?"

Jake laughed and tried to keep a smile on his face, but his facial muscles felt tight and he couldn't be sure whether he was smiling or not. "Yeah. As soon as I get out of here I'm gonna go buy a Lamborghini."

"You probably couldn't even get a Lamborghini for a hundred grand."

Jake tried to keep smiling. He imagined someone sitting in front of his house while he was here in this hospital bed. Maybe he shouldn't have sent Melody home. He clenched his teeth and held the smile. This was all his fault. If he hadn't taken that money, none of this would be happening. He had to make this right. But how? "So, who do you think is behind all of this?" he asked.

"Looks like it's the brother. I told you before, remember? He lives right next door to the house where we did the bust. Dumb ass has taken over the family business and is cooking meth and dealing it. We'll have him soon, too. And this time, we'll have so much evidence that none of them will get out. In the meantime, we just gotta be careful. I'm not real worried about it. They're just a bunch of punks. But when they start sitting in front of our houses, that just pisses me off. I catch someone in front of my house and they'll wish they had found some other place to park."

Shortly afterward, a nurse came in and removed Jake's food tray, commenting on how little he ate. Then his doctor came in and told him he was being discharged. The doctor said all of Jake's tests looked good, and that it was probably dehydration that had made Jake pass out. Jake was glad there was nothing wrong with his heart, but he knew it wasn't dehydration. It was those damned anxiety attacks. They were getting worse. Everything was getting worse. And it wouldn't get any better as long as that money was still in his bowling bag. He had to get out of here and take care of that.

Soon after, just as Danny was leaving, Cooper returned with the takeout order. Jake was standing by the bed, buttoning his shirt.

"You leaving?" Cooper asked.

"Yep. I've been sprung."

"What'd they find out?"

"Doc said it was probably dehydration, said that can make you pass out."

Cooper sat the food on the wheeled table positioned over Jake's bed. "Well, it's good that it's nothing serious.

Jake sat back down and started eating. He nodded and continued chewing.

"I've got an answer to what we were talking about yesterday," Cooper said.

Jake looked at him in question, still chewing.

"You asked, hypothetically, whether if someone told me they did something illegal, I could I keep it a secret."

Jake swallowed. "Oh. Never mind about that. I was just asking you for one of my buddies, but everything is straightened out."

"Oh." Cooper said. "Are you sure?"

Jake nodded. "Yeah. It's all good. Hang on and I'll pay you for this."

"No. You don't need to. No charge."

"You sure?"

"Yeah."

"Well, thanks. I sure appreciate it. This really hit the spot."

At the door, Cooper hesitated. "Jake, if you ever want to talk about anything—"

"I'm good." Jake cut him off. "But thanks, Cooper, and thanks for going to get me this food."

"Sure," Cooper said. "I'll see you around."

Cooper walked down the hospital hallway feeling like a food delivery boy. He'd felt like a pastor when he had arrived. Staring at the floor, he pushed his hands into the pockets of his jeans and slouched toward the exit.

Maybe he wouldn't pass out his phone number to the congregation. Maybe that was a dumb idea.

Chapter 37

January

A few days later, TJ found Cooper in the church, sweeping the floors. "Hey, Coop. What's up?"

"Not much, TJ, but I'm glad to see you. I'm starting to go stir crazy. I've never spent so much time alone."

"I have an idea."

"What's that?"

"What do you need?"

"A new truck?"

"No. Well, yeah, but what else?"

"I give up."

"A bigger church."

"Yeah, well, that's not going to happen any time soon." Cooper swept a pile of dirt into a dustpan and then dumped it into a trashcan in the alcove.

"And what do I need?" TJ asked as he followed Cooper.

"A haircut."

"No! Cooper, I'm being serious."

"So am I! You need a haircut!"

"No! I need something to do with my time. I need some

sort of goal or purpose. I just go through the days, one after another, with no end in sight. I got nothing to look forward to. If I stayed in bed all day, it wouldn't matter to one single person."

"That's not true." Cooper leaned the broom and dustpan against the wall in the alcove.

"No, really it is. But what could solve both of our problems?"

"No idea."

"What contest did I just win?"

"What's with you and all of the questions?"

"World Wide Warrior. And, all across America, heck all across the world, guys are training for that. They are trying to train in their backyards and trying to build their own courses, just like I did. What if they had a place where they could come and train every day? Maybe even a one-week camp or something like that? A place with obstacles like the ones they're gonna face at Warrior? And what if you used that same course as a place for local kids to come and have fun? You could have safety nets in place, and safety harnesses, so the kids wouldn't get hurt, but they'd have a chance to crawl around and have some fun too."

"You're going to build an indoor obstacle course?"

"No. I'm going to put one in an existing gym. And where is there a gym for sale?"

Cooper shrugged, getting annoyed with all of the questions.

"First Baptist, Cooper! First Baptist has a gym!"

"Hey, you're right. I forgot about that. But what are you going to do with the rest of the building?"

"Cooper! Duh! You're going to put your church in it. I'll buy the building and then lease the church part out to you, and the office space, too. Although, I might need one office. I don't know. I haven't thought this all the way through."

"I can't afford a lease!"

"I'll give it to you for a dollar a month. When the

church gets huge, you can pay me more."

"TJ, do you know how much all of that would cost? Buying the building and then remodeling it to build the kind of gym you're talking about."

"Who cares? I'm loaded."

"Yeah, but TJ, that money isn't going to last forever. I keep telling you that. You're going to run out if you keep spending so much."

"So? What if I do? I've been broke before. Who cares? Why not take a chance? What good is this money just sitting in the bank? Besides, this could make more money. I could charge guys to come to a week-long camp and I could teach it. And then we could let the little kids come for a reduced rate, or even free if they couldn't afford it. And you'd have that whole big auditorium, or whatever you want to call it, for your church service on Sunday. You could go back to one service. You'd never fill that thing up. It's huge!"

"Are you serious, TJ?"

"Would I tell you this if I wasn't serious?"

"I guess we could go look at it again. I know it hasn't sold yet. I drove past there the other day and the sign was still up."

"I already called Beaulah. We're supposed to look at it at six."

Cooper looked at the clock. "That's less than an hour away. What if I hadn't been home?"

"Then I'd go and look at it by myself, and give the church space to one of my other friends who needs a bigger church."

A short time later, TJ and Cooper were looking around the church gym with Beaulah.

"Where's Libby?" TJ asked.

"She's at home. She'll probably be ready to work again by next week."

"Is she sick?" Cooper asked.

"Oh, no. Sorry, I thought maybe you'd heard. She was in a bad wreck, totaled her truck. She was in the hospital a couple of weeks."

Cooper stopped walking and faced Beaulah. "Is she okay?"

"Oh, yes. She'll be fine. No broken bones, but she got a bad bump on the head. She was out of it for almost two weeks in the hospital. They had her on so much medication that she just slept. I guess they were worried about injury to her brain. But she's fine now. A little bruised, that's all."

Cooper nodded and continued to follow Beaulah through the church. "Who's been taking care of her? Can she get around?"

"Sure, she can get around. Like I said, her head injury was the worst of it. She's supposed to go back to the factory today or tomorrow. I forget which. And I've been stopping by every day." Beaulah turned her attention back to the church, pointing out the benefits of the building to the two men. After they had looked at every room, she left them alone in the two-story to talk things over.

"What do you think, Cooper?"

"It's a great building. There's no doubt about that. You know I wanted to buy it when I looked at it the first time, but it's a lot of money, TJ. I don't know what I was thinking. I could have never made the payments on something like this. And even though you won Warrior and have all that money from endorsements now, I'm afraid you're going to end up broke. And if the gym doesn't do well and you need to sell the place, it could be years before you get your money back—maybe never. It's been on the market a long time now."

"Yeah, I know. But we only go around once. Why not go for it? This gym is huge. I'd have all kinds of room for obstacles." TJ walked across the gym to a door and turned the doorknob. "Hey, this leads outside to the parking lot. It wasn't even locked. That's weird." TJ opened the door and peered outside. "You have to be kidding!"

"What?"

TJ pointed into the parking lot. Cooper went to the door and looked outside. An old sky-blue school bus was parked outside. The words First Baptist Church were emblazoned on the side. "There's our drunk driver bus," TJ said. "It's a sign."

"You think so?"

"No. Probably not. But I want to buy this place. With the endorsements, I can swing it. Let's do it."

"TJ, you might be crazy."

"Wanna be crazy with me?"

"Yeah, what the hell. Let's do it."

TJ and Cooper returned to the foyer.

"Well, what do you think? It's a beautiful building, isn't it?"

"I want to make an offer. I'm offering a million and a half," TJ told her.

"Really?" Beaulah said, sounding surprised. "Well, that's wonderful," she managed to say after she pulled herself together.

"I want them to throw the bus in, too."

"The bus?"

"There's an old school bus out back. I want it."

"Oh, all right. Sure. We'll put that right in the offer. Let me go outside and get the paperwork," Beaulah said.

Beaulah hurried to her car. She couldn't believe it. Finally! Her first sale! She was sure the sellers would take any reasonable offer, and TJ had the money. She was actually going to make a sale! She picked her briefcase up from her seat, but then put it back down. Reaching over, she pulled her cell phone from her purse and dialed Libby's number.

"Hi, Beaulah," Libby answered.

"Guess what I just did!"

"I don't know. What did you do?"

"I just sold First Baptist to TJ Barnes!"

"Beaulah! Are you kidding?"

"Nope. He just said he's making an offer. A million and a half. I'm standing outside the church right now getting ready to take the paperwork in to him, but I just had to call you first."

"Oh my gosh, Beaulah, that's amazing!"

"Do you know what kind of commission I'm going to get from this sale? It will be huge! Libby, this sale is actually going to happen! TJ has the money, everyone knows that. And the bank is dying to unload this church. They'll take the offer. I know it. We have our first sale!"

Libby laughed. "Congratulations, Beaulah. This is so exciting!"

"Libby, listen to me. I want us to be partners. I'm more organized than I have ever been. Right now, I have ten listings and you brought me eight of those. I don't know a thing about social media, and I don't want to learn. You can do all of that for me. And once you get your license, you'll be able to do listings on your own. We'll be able to be twice as effective!"

"Partners? But I don't have my license, and what if I can't pass the test? I wasn't very good in school."

"Don't be silly! Of course you can pass the test. If I can pass it, you can. I'll help you in any way I can. And there's one more thing."

"What?"

"If this sale goes through. No, *when* this sale goes through, I'll give you half of the commission, but I want you to quit your job."

"But I can't have my license by then."

"It doesn't matter. I'll give you half of the commission anyway. I believe in you, Libby. You need to get out of that factory. You deserve better than that. And I need a partner. So, what do you think?" Beaulah waited. Libby was silent on the other end. "Are you still there?" Beaulah asked.

"Yes."

"Yes, you're still there, or yes, you want to be my partner.

"Yes to both!"

"Oh! That's great! Now, I gotta go. I gotta get this offer written up. Talk to you later, partner."

Libby placed her phone on the arm of the couch and stared at it. One call and her world just shifted. Originally, she had planned to keep working both jobs until she had enough money saved for herself and Cooper to leave town. Lately, though, she'd been wondering if she should give up on Cooper. It was taking so long to save money. By the time she had enough, he might have forgotten about her. Now, though, she wondered if she should quit the factory and spend all of her time selling real estate. With just a few sales, they could leave this summer. She'd lose her insurance, but it might be worth the risk.

Could she actually quit the factory? Just like that? She'd imagined it a million times—taking her gloves off right in the middle of the shift, dropping them to the floor and walking out the door. Maybe shouting, "I quit!" as she passed her supervisor. She'd been waiting for that day for so long. But really, she could do it right now. She didn't even have to go in again. No more terrible shifts. No more metal shavings in her hair. No more coming home and changing her clothes at the front door because they reeked of the factory and were full of shavings. She hesitated. She'd always fantasized about doing it in person. She wanted to see the look on their faces when she walked out, but the thought of never going into that building again was too much to resist. She picked up the phone and dialed the number.

A woman answered.

"Hello. This is Libby Cartwright. I work in plant three. And I quit. I quit! Right now, this second. I'm never coming in again! I quit!" she said, her voice getting louder with every sentence.

"Could you hold for one moment?" the woman said.

Libby hesitated for just a second, this time controlling the level of her voice before she spoke. "No, actually, I cannot hold. I have stuff to do." A huge smile on her face, she hung up the phone.

Libby rose from the couch and strode to the door. A cardboard box sat there, a pair of steel-toed work boots inside. They were oily, smelled bad, and sparkled with embedded metal shavings. With her fingertips, Libby picked up the boots and carried them her trashcan. Lifting the lid with one hand, she then dropped the boots into the can and moved to the sink to wash her hands.

As she washed them, she laughed aloud. It was frightening, the thought of giving up a weekly check, but liberating too. She laughed again. This summer—that was the new goal—this summer she'd be driving out of this town, Cooper at her side.

Chapter 38

February

Violet had planned on buying something red to wear for Valentine's Day. But January came and went, and then the first week of February came and went too, and still Violet had yet to use her gift card for clothes. On several occasions, she had showered and put makeup on in preparation for a trip to the store, but she had never made it beyond the door. She had walked up to it, even touched the door handle once, but that was as far as she'd made it. Pete had been watching, the time she touched the door handle. "See you later, Violet," he had said, hoping that would give her the extra push she needed. But it had not.

"Oh! Darn! I forgot my car keys," she had said. Avoiding eye contact with Pete, Violet had walked past the bar, through the kitchen and the backroom and up the stairs leading to the apartment. After dropping her purse onto the couch, Violet had gone into the bedroom and pulled one of Pete's sweatshirts and a pair of his sweatpants from the closet. Changing quickly, she then grabbed the television remote and a blanket off the bed, and settled into the couch for the night.

Although she still had not made it to the store to buy something red for Valentine's Day, she had found an old red shirt that didn't look too bad. Violet was excited about Valentine's Day, more excited than she had been in a very long time. She had talked Pete into trying something new, so they were advertising two-for-one Valentine's dinners. They were also featuring four new drinks—all with umbrellas. Pete had to go buy those, which took some talking on Violet's part.

"Pete! Half of your customers are women. And if you offer cute little drinks, women will buy them." Pete was skeptical, but it was the first time Violet had expressed an interest in the bar, so he was more than happy to go buy a few umbrellas and some extra ingredients. He just hoped she wouldn't be discouraged when the drinks didn't sell. And he still wasn't sure about the two-for-one dinners. Giving away food didn't make much sense to him, especially steak dinners, which had also been her idea. *Well, hell*, Pete thought to himself. *The worst that can happen is I lose some money, or we end up with a freezer full of steak.* He was willing to give it a try, for Violet.

The flowers, though, that was another thing. At three o'clock, a kid from Fanny's Florals strode into the bar and approached Pete. "I got a delivery for you. Where do you want me to put them?"

"There must be a mistake. I didn't order any flowers."

Violet came from the back of the room. "Oh, yes! Those are ours. Bring them right in here."

"Flowers?" Pete asked.

"You said I could do some decorating for the Valentine's Day Special."

"Well, yeah, but flowers?"

"Yes! You can't have Valentine's Day without flowers."

Pete started to argue with her but then realized that he probably should have bought her flowers, too. It was so odd, their relationship. He never knew quite where he stood, or what to do. All Pete knew was that he loved her.

"How many flowers did you order?"

"I ordered a vase of three roses for every table, and I ordered five dozen long-stemmed roses. I thought we could give one to every woman, maybe bring it with the check and thank her for spending Valentine's Day with us. And, I used my credit card, so don't worry."

"You shouldn't have done that, Violet."

"I wanted to. It was my idea, and it's fun. Oh! I have to go get the candles!"

Pete watched her hurry away and smiled. Who would have thought? Roses and candlelit steak dinners at Bass Turds.

TJ and Lucy arrived at Bass Turds a little after six. TJ was wearing a dress shirt and slacks, and his shaggy hair was slicked back. Pete did not recognize him until he spoke. "Hey, Pete. How's it going?" At the bar, he introduced Lucy.

"Happy to meet you, Lucy. Welcome to Bass Turds."

Lucy wore a red spaghetti-strap dress, and TJ hovered around her as if he could not believe his luck.

"Bass Turds? That's quite the name," Lucy said.

"Yeah. It's a long story."

"Two for dinner tonight?" Violet greeted them.

"Yes, two!" TJ said, beaming.

As they followed Violet to one of the booths, Lucy said over her shoulder, "I'd like to hear that story, Pete."

Pete smiled and nodded. Did she mean that? Was he supposed to walk over there and tell her the story now? Women were so hard to figure out.

"Oh! Pretty flowers," Lucy said once she and TJ were seated at a booth. "And I love the candle!"

Violet smiled. She knew it! She hoped Pete was listening. "We have some specials tonight." Violet handed them a piece of paper listing all of the specials and the new drinks. "And we also have some special Valentine's Day drinks. You'll see those at the bottom of your menu sheet."

"Oh! A Cosmopolitan! I want one of those," Lucy said.

"Lucy, you're not twenty-one, are you?" TJ asked.

"I am today." Lucy reached into her purse, pulled out her driver's license and showed it to Violet.

"A Valentine's Day baby," Violet said as she looked at the date on the license. "Do you want a drink, TJ?"

"Uh, yeah. I guess I'll have one of those, too."

"A Cosmopolitan?"

"Yeah. Sure."

As she walked away, Violet looked across the room at Pete and gave him a thumbs up. Two drinks already! This was going to be great!

"I didn't know it was your birthday!" TJ told Lucy.

"How could you know?"

"I don't know. But I feel bad. I would have bought you a present if I had known."

"You're buying dinner. And drinks!" Lucy laughed. "Gosh, this is fun! I know this sounds stupid, but I feel like such a grown up."

"It doesn't sound stupid at all. Lucy, you never sound stupid."

Lucy looked at him, as if trying to decipher his words. TJ looked away.

Later that night they strolled down the street, Lucy holding a long stem rose and TJ trying to muster enough courage to hold her hand as they walked to the car.

"What a great night!" She held the rose to her nose, inhaling its aroma. "I don't want to go home yet."

TJ wondered if it was the Cosmopolitans talking or whether she was enjoying his company. Whatever it was, he wasn't going to question it.

I like your car," Lucy said when they reached the vehicle.

"Thanks." TJ didn't know much about cars. When he had bought the car, he'd taken Cooper along with him to the car dealership. Cooper picked out the car and told TJ it would be good on gas and mechanically dependable. Cooper had also talked the dealer down in price. TJ merely signed the papers and paid cash for the car. "I guess Toyotas are supposed to be pretty good cars. What do you want to do? Go to a movie?"

"No. I'm not in the mood for a movie."

"Uh ... we could go for a walk," suggested TJ.

"Too cold."

"A drive?"

"Okay. Let's do that. Are you okay to drive? You've been drinking."

"That was a couple of hours ago. And I didn't even finish the drink—too sweet."

"Okay. If you're sure that you're okay, let's go for a drive in your new car."

TJ drove through the night, cruising through the streets and heading out into the country.

Lucy looked out the window and sang along with some of the songs on the radio. TJ imagined that she was singing to him.

"TJ, do you ever wonder why you're here?" she said as she gazed out at the starlit sky, humming along to a song.

"All the time."

"I look up at that great big sky and I feel so small. I wonder if I have any significance at all. Am I just a blip in some chain of life? Or am I important in some way? Sometimes I feel like I have all of this stuff stored up inside of me, like I'm destined to do great things. But most of the time, I feel like I don't matter at all—like a squirrel that gets run over on the street. People look at it and just drive right over it. And that squirrel doesn't matter at all."

TJ opened his mouth to say, "You matter to me," but he could not release the words; they clung inside his throat. "I think that too sometimes," was all he could manage.

"Oh my gosh! How can you say that, TJ! You won a million dollars on World Wide Warrior! You were on television and in magazines. You're all over the internet! You're famous!"

"Well, it was less than that after taxes, and all the rest of that stuff, it doesn't mean anything. It's just something for people to talk about for a while. I'm no different. I'm still the same guy everyone used to make fun of. Only now, those same people want to be my friend. It's just the money, not me."

"That must be hard, wondering whether people truly like you or whether they just want to get close to you for your money."

TJ shrugged, but Lucy was still gazing out the window and did not see the gesture. "Sometimes it is. But I've never had a lot of friends. I don't see why that should change just because I have some money now. And, that money won't last forever. It's just temporary too."

They drove through the night, winding down dark country roads and seeing few cars. "Where are we going?" Lucy asked.

"I don't know, just driving." TJ thought about it. He couldn't take her to Jake's house. Well, he could, but you never knew what was going to be going on there. The last thing he needed was for Lucy to experience some awful scene with his mom. He supposed he could take her to a bar and have another drink, but he wasn't much of a drinker and he thought maybe she'd already had enough. "Hey! I know! We could go to the church. I have a key."

"The church?"

"Cooper's church." As soon as he said it, he wished he had not. Why did he have to bring up Cooper's name when things were going so well? Now she would be thinking about him!

"Sure! Let's do that. Sounds good. Maybe we could

stop by their house."

"Well, I don't know about that. Sally goes to bed pretty early. But, we'll see." There was no way he was doing that. He hoped their lights were off when he drove past.

"We could call them, see if they're up. Shouldn't we call them anyway? If we drive by their house to get to the church won't they hear your car and wonder why someone is back there? It's a dead end."

"No. I go there sometimes to sleep. Cooper is cool with that."

"Oh," Lucy said, sounding disappointed.

"But maybe if their light is on. Let's just play it by ear."

When they drove by the mobile home, not one light was on. *Yes!* TJ thought. "Looks like they're not home. Cooper's probably spending Valentine's Day at the diner with Sally."

"Yeah, probably," Lucy said quietly.

TJ drove the rest of the way down the road and pulled into the unmarked gravel lane that led back through the woods to the little white church.

"It's so pretty back here with all of the snow, like a Christmas card. Remember that night we decorated for Christmas?"

TJ smiled. "Yeah. I remember." They rounded the final curve and TJ parked the car.

"Why do you sleep here?" Lucy asked as they approached the door.

"I don't anymore. I used to. Lately, I've been staying at Jake's house. With my mom being sick and everything, it doesn't make much sense to be away from her."

"Yeah, I heard about that. Your mom being sick. Sorry."

TJ unlocked the door and pushed it open. He flipped on the lights. "Here we are."

"Why did you sleep here?"

TJ shrugged. I don't know. I like it here. It feels like home to me. Maybe because we spent so much time building it. And I trained for Warrior out in the woods. So it all feels familiar."

"Where did you sleep?"

"I've got a cot. Come here, I'll show you." Lucy followed him to the back of the church. Moving behind the stage, he went to a closet in the alcove near the back entrance and opened the door. "See." He pointed to a fold-up cot standing against the wall. "Let me show you." TJ pulled the cot out of the closet and carried it to the corner where he always slept. Unfolding it, he set it up. "Here. Lie down."

Lucy raised her eyebrows.

"No, really, lie down. I want to show you something."

"I've heard that before."

TJ laughed and then blushed. "No, really. Lie down."

Lucy kicked off her shoes and sat on the cot.

"Lie down!" TJ said as he ran back to the entrance door. At the front wall, he flipped all of the light switches off and the church went dark except for the light streaming through the windows. TJ ran back up the aisle in the dark. He sat on the floor beside the cot and leaned back against it. He could feel the warmth of Lucy's body behind him. "Can you see the moon?" He pointed out one of the arched windows. "No, I guess you can't right now, maybe it's too cloudy, but a lot of times I could see the moon at night right through that window. I used to lay here and look at it and just think."

"What did you think about?"

This was it. It was his chance. He opened his mouth and then closed it. And opened it again. Finally, he said, "You."

They were both silent for a moment. Lucy reached out and put her hand in the back of his hair, gently stroking it.

TJ closed his eyes.

"I know, TJ," Lucy said. "I know."

Chapter 39

April

It was early afternoon, in between the lunch and dinner crowds, and the diner was empty except for a couple of women who were sitting at a booth and talking. Sally was the only waitress on duty. Bruce and Mike, the cooks, were in the backroom taking a break and playing poker. So far, Bruce was winning, but he always won, because Mike always tipped his cards, making it possible to see his hand every time. Everyone knew this but Mike, who received a lot of invitations to poker parties.

Sally leaned against the counter and listened to Frank. "I've been thinking about this, Sally. The business is doing great. I know you want to put that addition on. Let me help you with it. Basically, it's just one big room. It shouldn't be that expensive to build. I'm friends with a lot of contractors in the area. I bet we could get that room built for less than twenty thousand dollars."

"I don't have twenty thousand dollars; that's why I wanted Cooper to build it."

"You don't need Cooper. I can get this built for you and it won't cost you a thing."

"How is that possible?"

"I've got some money put aside, and I've been looking for a good investment. How about I invest in the diner? I'll pay for the addition and you can pay me back a little at a time. Maybe ten percent of your income per week? With the addition, you will make more money each week, so you'll never notice that ten percent."

"Why would you do that?

"Why wouldn't I? It's a good investment. If it makes you feel better, I'll charge you interest. How about ten percent? I'll loan you twenty thousand dollars, and you pay me back twenty two thousand dollars, a little at a time every week. I'll make ten percent income on my investment and you'll make more money every week as soon as that addition is up. It's a win-win."

"Ten percent of my income every week? That's after expenses, right?"

"Sure. I'll make up a simple contract stating just that, have it notarized, and then we're all set. We can start building soon. What do you think?"

"I still don't know why you'd do this?"

Frank gazed into her eyes. "Sally, you know why."

Sally's body tensed and she pulled back slightly.

Frank realized he might have crossed the line. "I believe in you! I think you're a smart businesswoman and I know a good investment when I see one. Plus, I wouldn't mind making some money!"

Sally smiled and relaxed. "But what if business went bad for me and I couldn't pay you?"

"It's ten percent. Some weeks that will be more, some weeks it will be less, depending on how business is. If you had a bad week, then we'd just skip that week. But that won't happen, Sally. Once you put that addition on, you'll have so much money you won't know what to do with it all."

"Do you really think so?"

"Hey, would I risk my hard earned money on something

that could fail?"

"I guess not." Sally looked down and drummed her fingers against the counter. She bit her bottom lip, deep in thought. Finally, she said, "No. I can't."

"Why?"

"Cooper wouldn't like it. You know that."

Frank shrugged. "Seems a shame to me. You're letting him hold you back, Sally."

Chapter 40

April

It was a relatively mild winter, and by the end of the first week of April, the snow was not only gone, spring flowers were poking from the ground, redbuds were filled with purple blossoms, and apple trees were dressed in white. The front yard of First Baptist was flush with yellow daffodils. Inside, TJ and Cooper were working in the gym. The obstacle course was nearly done, just a few details here and there. They had built replicas of most of the Warrior obstacles and a vast network of sturdy webbing ran under every obstacle so that anyone who fell would be safely caught. In addition, for the kids, was an overhead series of cables hooked to safety harnesses that every child would be wearing. Anyone under the age of fifteen was wearing a harness, no exceptions.

There was even a mini obstacle course in one corner for toddlers. It was fenced off from the rest of the gym and included a ball pit as well as seating for moms and dads.

TJ was on top of one of the obstacles, securing a cargo net. "You know, Cooper, we're almost ready to open and we don't have a name for this place. What in the world are we going to call it? We need to have a sign made."

"I don't know. What do you call a place that has a church *and* a gym?"

"I've been thinking about it, and I can't come up with a thing."

"Sally came up with an idea the other night. At first, I thought it sounded kind of dumb, but the more I think about it, the better it sounds."

"What's that?"

"She says we should go to all of the schools in town and give away free passes to the gym. At the same time, we say we are having a contest to name the gym and church and that the kids should put their idea for the name on the back of the pass. Just write it down on there. And then when they bring in the free pass, we take it and put it into a big fish bowl or something and then have the drawing on a certain date. Maybe we can even get a local radio or TV station to cover it."

"Man! That's a great idea, because we'll have all of those kids wanting to come in here and their parents will have a chance to see the gym. It could be great for business! Sally came up with all of this?"

Cooper nodded. "Yeah, it sounded kind of dumb at first, but the more I think about it, the better it sounds."

"I think we should do it. While we're printing up the passes, maybe we should ask Sally if she wants us to print up coupons for her. Something like one free ice cream with any paid dinner or something; that way, she'd be getting something out of this too, since it is her idea. And it would drive people to her diner."

"Great idea. I'll ask her about it and see what she thinks."

By late April, they were ready for their grand opening. It was to be on a Saturday. The previous Thursday, they had held a private opening for friends and family and had also drawn out the new name of the church and gym. All of the local radio and TV stations had sent reporters and several camera crews were in place. As he often did, TJ underestimated the clout his name carried. Even one of the national news channels was there to cover the event.

They held the drawing in the auditorium, so they could use the stage. All of the cameras were set up on stage or right below the stage, and the auditorium was about one-third full. Even though TJ and Cooper had only invited friends and family (a relatively small number of people), they had also told everyone to feel free to bring some friends, and evidently, they had. There were three times more people attending than they had expected.

TJ and Cooper stood on the stage, a large goldfish bowl on a tall wooden stool between them. "We want to thank everyone for coming," Cooper said. "We sure appreciate all of you spending today with us. It's a pretty exciting day." Cooper looked over at TJ, hoping he would step forward and say something. He did not. He had already told Cooper he was not going to speak because he hated speaking in public, but Cooper had hoped TJ would change his mind in the moment. "We want to say a special thank you to all of the kids who participated in this naming contest. We had over one thousand participants."

Many of the kids in the audience cheered. TJ and Cooper looked at each other and smiled. "And we also want to thank Sally Moon, owner of Sally's Diner, who came up with this idea. Thank you, Sally!"

Seated in the front row, Sally beamed and gave Cooper a little wave. She had to admit, it was a great idea. Every day she had families with a free coupon coming in to the diner to eat. Since opening under her name, business was up twenty-five percent. So far this month, the average was even higher. She was beginning to feel like a successful business owner. Now, she was even giving advice to other businesses. So far, it had been a great year!

"Okay, I guess it's time!" Cooper scanned the audience and spotted a little girl of about seven with curly blonde hair. He walked over to the edge of the stage, pointed at her, and asked, "Would you like to help me pick the winner?"

Beside her, her parents nudged her into nodding yes. When she did, her mother pushed the child from her seat, encouraging her and pointing toward the stairs at the side of the stage. As the little girl made her way to the stage, the crowd broke out in applause. She put one of her fingers in her mouth and walked slowly up the steps and across the stage to Cooper.

"What's your name?" Cooper asked, holding the microphone down to her mouth. "Anna," she whispered as she looked over at her parents. They smiled at her and she seemed to relax. "I'm in first grade!" she added.

Cooper laughed. "Well, come on over here, Anna the first-grader, and pick a winner for us." Cooper handed the microphone to TJ, picked up the bowl and lowered it down to the child. "Just reach in and pull out one of those pieces of paper—only one, though. Kind of like trick or treating."

Anna reached deep into the bowl and pulled up three entries. Reaching in with her other hand, she chose one of them and handed it to Cooper, letting the other two drop back into the bowl. "Thank you, Anna," Cooper said. "You can go back down to your mommy and daddy now." The child skipped across the stage, waving at her parents as she did. Laughter rippled through the crowd.

Cooper took the microphone back from TJ. "How about a hand for Anna? Didn't she do a great job?" The audience applauded again, this time even louder than the last. "And doesn't she have the prettiest curly hair you've ever seen in your life?" The audience clapped louder and someone whistled. Meanwhile, Anna slowly descended the steps and then skipped over to her parents and sat down. Both of them were laughing, and her mother wiped a tear from her eyes.

Cooper walked back over to stand next to TJ. "And our

new name is … Holy Balls!" Cooper looked over at TJ.

TJ's mouth fell open.

A few people in the crowd laughed. Someone from behind a camera motioned to Cooper to keep going. "Uh … that's from Bobby Walker, a third grader from Timber Lake Elementary. Thank you, Bobby. Now, we'd like to invite everyone over to the gym to try it out for free tonight. Have fun everyone!"

The people in the crowd got to their feet and made their way to the gym. One of the reporters stuck a microphone in TJ's face. "TJ, are you going to stick with the name? You advertised this as a contest to name the church and gym, are you going to honor that commitment?"

"Uh … yeah, I guess. Cooper?"

Cooper stepped forward and the reporter immediately smiled. "What are your thoughts on this, Mr. Moon?"

"Cooper. It's Cooper. Yeah, we are going to honor that commitment. And little Bobby also just won a free one-year membership to the gym." Cooper looked over at TJ, who gave a little nod. "Thanks for coming. Be sure to check out the gym," Cooper said before turning and leaving the stage.

TJ turned and followed Cooper, ignoring the reporters' questions. Catching up with Cooper, he walked beside him through the auditorium. "What are we going to do?" he asked in a whisper.

"What can we do? We have to go with it."

"Holy Balls? Can you imagine seeing that on a sign out front?"

Cooper shrugged. "You gotta admit, it's an eye catcher."

"We should have pulled out ten and picked the best name from those ten."

"Well, yeah, now you come up with that idea! That's not much help."

TJ laughed. "Can you imagine the tee shirts?"

Chapter 41

May

Every night for a week, Jake had driven past the drug house from which he had stolen the money. There was always a different car in the driveway, and it seemed as if someone was always home. Getting rid of the money had become his number one priority. He could think of little else. Nothing in his life would be right until that money was gone. Now, he just had to think of a way to make that happen. He vacillated between wanting to destroy it and wanting to return it. There seemed to be no easy answer.

Jake eased off the gas and coasted past the house. It was a little after nine and there were five cars in the driveway of the house next door. Every light in the house seemed to be on. Jake wondered about the little kids who were there the night of the bust. They should be in bed, warm and smelling like soap, with someone reading a story to them, instead of living in a house full of people who probably gave them less thought than they would a stray dog. Maybe the kids had been taken out of the home and placed with foster care. Jake sighed. Sometimes he hated people.

He drove past the house and cruised through the

neighborhood, driving along in a blind sort of daze, seeing little that he passed. Maybe he ought to just burn the money, completely destroy the evidence. He liked the idea of that. But where would he burn it? It wasn't like they lived out in the country. Burn anything in his subdivision and someone was bound to call the fire department. He couldn't even burn leaves without it drawing some sort of complaint. Maybe the grill? He could burn the money in the grill. He imagined a gust of wind coming along while he was burning the money and carrying half-burnt bills off on the breeze, scattering them about the neighborhood. That might be hard to explain.

Part of the problem was that his fingerprints were all over the bills. Most of the time, he told himself he was silly to even worry about that. At other times, he obsessed about it. He wondered how to get fingerprints off bills. He supposed he could look it up on the Internet, but then he imagined some guy on the Computer Forensics Team tearing apart his hard drive and reporting the results to a jury. Maybe he could do the search, take out his hard drive, throw it away, and then get a new one. Of course, he didn't know how to take out a hard drive, and he wasn't even sure if that got rid of everything on a computer. It was getting harder and harder to get away with anything these days.

Maybe he could, literally, wash the money. Jake wondered what money was made of. He didn't think it was really paper. It had some sort of fiber or something in it, like cloth. He could put all of the money in the washer on the gentle cycle. But then he remembered what his cash looked like when he forgot to take it out of his pants pocket—all wadded up and crumbled into a ball. Maybe not.

He could wash the money in the kitchen sink. Just swish it around a little in some hot soapy water and then lay the bills out on the counter to dry. He could wear rubber gloves so his fingerprints wouldn't get back on the bills. But how could he lay the money out on the counter to dry when someone was always home? He imagined Josephine and his mother walking into the kitchen while he was spreading the cash across the counter. He suddenly realized that he was never home alone anymore—never.

Jake wiped beads of sweat off of his forehead and turned back toward town. There had to be some way to get rid of that money! Maybe he could find a deep lake somewhere and drop it off a bridge, right in the bowling bag. He could poke some holes in the bag so it would sink more quickly. But then he imagined divers finding the bag full of soggy money and a bowling ball with *Happy bowling, Jake! Love, Melody* engraved in it. That wouldn't work. He could go to a second-hand store and buy an old bowling ball to replace his. Or he could just buy a brand new bowling ball and bag, switch the money over to it, drill holes in it, and then throw it into the water. Yeah! That idea had some merit! A brand new ball and bag. And by the time anyone found the money, his fingerprints would be washed off! Jake smiled as he drove past the courthouse. That sounded like a good idea.

Jake's cell phone trilled in his pocket, startling him. He pulled it out and looked at it. Melody. "Hey, Mel, what's up?"

"I've got a flat tire. I'm sitting on the highway, just down the road from Walmart."

Jake sighed. "Okay. I'll be there in a few minutes. Lock the doors."

"They're locked."

Jake flipped on the lights and drove toward Melody. It looked like it was going to rain. He hoped it held off until he had the tire changed. He remembered the last time he had changed a tire for someone it had been pouring down rain. Earlier in the year, he had come across a woman trying to change her own tire in the pouring rain. At first, he thought she was a teenage boy. Her long wet hair had fallen out from under her hooded sweatshirt, heavy and dark, and her clothes had been muddy. She'd been soaking wet, and still she had argued with him about changing the tire. Even when Jake had taken the jack handle away from her, she had stood beside him in the rain as he changed the tire. He wondered where she was now.

Pulling up behind Melody, Jake got out of the squad car and surveyed the situation. Right rear tire. At least he wouldn't have to worry about someone clipping him along the side of the road. Melody's window rolled down and she handed him the keys. She was pissed off, he could tell. He took the keys and walked to the back of the car, popping the trunk open and wondering why in the world she was mad at him. It wasn't like he'd stuck a nail in her tire or something. It wasn't his fault she had a flat tire. Of course, she had been telling him she needed new tires for most of the last year, but new tires for her car were pretty low on the list of things they needed. As Jake pulled out the tread-bare spare tire from the trunk, he thought maybe they needed to move new tires up the list.

Before he could get the lug nuts loose, Melody was out of the car, standing by his side. He had hoped she would stay in the car. "I told you I needed new tires, but no, you won't listen to me."

"I know you need new tires," Jake said as he struggled to loosen a lug nut with the tire iron.

"And now, here I am, sitting alongside the road. Eight months pregnant and I'm sitting here in the middle of traffic."

"Melody, you're not in the middle of traffic. You're off the side of the road. And I'm changing the tire for you. What more do you want?" Jake remembered how that woman, muddy and wet, had stood beside him, holding the lug nuts in her hands and handing them back to him one at a time as he replaced them on her spare tire. Most of Melody's words seemed like white noise as Jake moved back and forth between the tire and the trunk—getting the jack, jacking up the car, removing the old tire, putting on the spare.

"Are you even listening to me, Jake?"

"I'm listening."

"This is ridiculous. Your brother is buying churches and building gyms and you won't ask him for a penny. Meanwhile, your wife and unborn child are in danger. Does that make sense to you? Why should I be driving around in a car with bad tires when your brother is a millionaire? And it's not like you're not close to him. He lives with us! It wouldn't kill him to throw a little of that money our way to make our life easier."

Jake clenched his jaw. "He just paid to have an addition put on our house. He is paying for a nurse for Mom. He gave us money for the baby's college fund. And I know he gives you money for groceries all the time. I've seen him do it!"

"That's not the point, Jake! We have expenses. We need things! And it's only going to get worse once the baby comes. We can't make it on what you make. We need help!"

One by one, Jake picked the lug nuts up off the ground and put them back on the car to hold the spare tire in place. Standing up, he then moved back to the trunk, threw the tire and tire iron into it, and slammed it shut.

"Are you going to ask your brother for some money, or not?"

"No, I'm not."

"Then I will! I'm going to ask him for money!" Melody walked back around the car and over to the passenger side.

"No! You're not! You're not asking him for a penny!" Jake slammed his fist against the trunk.

Melody's mouth fell open. She slowly walked back to the trunk and looked at it. "You just put a dent in my trunk!"

Jake swiped his hand over the trunk. "Shit," he said as he wiped at it. "I didn't mean to do that. I'm sorry."

"Oh, it's no problem, Jake! I'll just take it to the body shop and have it fixed! Right after I buy those new tires at the tire store!" Melody stomped back to the driver's side, got in, and slammed the door behind her.

"I'll buy you new tires!" Jake yelled as she started the

car and put it in gear. "I'll buy you new tires!" he yelled as she stomped on the gas, sending gravel flying and squealing the tires as they caught on the pavement.

Jake stood there for a moment watching her taillights fade into the traffic. His hand was beginning to hurt from hitting the trunk. *That was a dumb thing to do*, he thought to himself as he turned around and got back into his squad car. Flipping the lights off, he pulled into the traffic, no longer able to distinguish the taillights of his wife's car from the many others.

(

Cooper and Sally lay in bed, entwined in each other's arms. They had just made love and their breathing was slowing and returning to normal. One of Sally's legs was flung over Cooper's thighs, and he had an arm wrapped around her, his hand idly playing with a strand of her hair. It had started raining about an hour ago, so as they lay there, Cooper listened to the rain plopping into the pans in the kitchen and thought he needed to fix that roof. Maybe he could get TJ to help him with it. It was odd, though, that he'd come to like the sound of the water plopping into the pans on rainy nights; there was something familiar in it. And comforting. Sally didn't feel quite the same.

"You need to fix that leaky roof," she said.

"I know. I was just thinking about that."

"It's been leaking for years, Cooper."

"I know. I'll fix it. I'll get TJ to help me."

"I'd be nice to have those pans back. Hopefully, I can get that creosote smell out of them."

"Your hair is soft."

Sally smiled.

Sleep began to creep up on Cooper. He sank into it willingly. He loved this time the best—falling asleep right after making love. Sometimes, Sally wanted to talk afterward, but he always wanted to sleep. It was the best sensation, falling asleep beside her, knowing she was content. Knowing he had pleased her. He sank into the sheets, into the mattress, into sleep, weightless and unaware of his body.

Sally's voice startled him and brought him back into the room.

"What?" he asked.

"I said: are you happy?"

"Of course I'm happy, Sally." Cooper roused himself from sleep and yawned. "Why would you ask that?"

"It's hard to tell sometimes."

"What do you mean, it's hard to tell? You can't tell that I'm happy?"

"No. Not really. I mean, you've always seemed happy, even when we were having … problems. You've always seemed happy. Sometimes I think you'd be happy with anyone."

Cooper pulled back and propped himself up on his elbow to gaze at Sally in the darkness. "How can you say that, Sally? The only reason I'm happy is because I have you. Can't you see that? I've been happy ever since we met. That's why you've never seen me unhappy. You made me happy, Sally. You still do."

"Then why…" Her voice trailed off, but she didn't need to finish the sentence. Cooper knew what she was asking.

"Sally." He could find no words. He moved his hand to her face and ran his thumb down the side of her cheek. "I don't know. I don't know why I cheated on you all those times. I … to be honest with you, Sally, until I started believing in God last year, it just didn't seem like that big a deal."

Sally pulled her head away from him and gazed over at the wall. Cooper gently pulled her face back to his. "I know that sounds awful, but it's true. I walked into Bass Turds that night before I started believing in God and I thought I was a good person. I've always thought that. But then I prayed and, just like flipping a switch, I could see the truth of it—I was a horrible person. I used all those women, and more importantly, I had hurt you. Until then, I just couldn't see it. I know that's hard to believe, and if someone else was telling me this story, I wouldn't believe it either." Cooper sighed. "I love you, Sally. I love you more than anything in the world. You are my world. Without you, nothing matters. I'm sorry. I'm so sorry. But those are only words. I know that. And you don't even have to believe them. But if you give me the chance, I'll spend the rest of my life proving it to you." Cooper kissed her lips gently. Then he reached up and wiped away a tear that was sliding toward her ear. He kissed her cheek. And when his lips brushed against her neck, and then found their way down to her shoulder, Sally forgot every time he had broken her heart.

Chapter 42

May

Memorial Day weekend found TJ and Lucy at the church on Sunday, looking for paint. The old bus needed a paint job, and today seemed as good a time to paint it as any. Cooper said he would be there, but so far he had not shown up. TJ suspected this might be another of Cooper's ploys to get TJ and Lucy to spend some time together. TJ did not object.

Initially, when Cooper came to TJ and told him that Lucy had applied to work at Holy Balls, TJ had been against it. He knew she only wanted to be closer to Cooper. But the more TJ thought about her working here every day, the better it sounded. At least he'd get to see her more often. Once in a while they went to a movie or ate together at a restaurant, but it always felt very casual and not "like a date." TJ hoped for more, but he was afraid to push it. Neither of them ever spoke of the night they visited the church after the Valentine's Day dinner. TJ had come close to declaring his love for her. She had come close to acknowledging it. Yet they stood right on the edge, perhaps even backed away from that edge, and remained silent—

Lucy trying to erase the knowledge, TJ grateful to spend any time with her and afraid of pushing her too far. He knew that if he did, if he declared his love for Lucy and asked about her feelings for him, it would not end well. TJ knew she was in love with Cooper, or at least she thought she was. It was better to hover on the hope of all that was possible than to push things to a sad culmination. If they worked together, she would have to spend time with him. It was better than nothing.

"So where's the paint?" Lucy asked.

"Cooper said there's all kinds of paint in the storage room, more than enough to paint the bus."

"Have you ever painted a bus?"

"No, but it's not like we're painting the whole bus, just the long part on the side where the name goes."

But don't we need some sort of special paint? Isn't some paint for wood and some for metal?"

TJ shrugged and flipped on the light, and the two of them walked into the large storage room. The room housed various items left by First Baptist: folding chairs and tables, assorted boxes of props used in Christmas plays and sketches, snow shovels, rakes, and brooms. Along the back wall ran shelving full of cleaning supplies and assorted cans of paint. TJ picked up one of the cans, and started reading from the can. "This says it's good for wood and metal, so it should be all right, and here's some brushes. We have spray paint and regular paint. We should be set." He looked at Lucy. "What color do you think we should use?"

"I don't know. Let's take a bunch of them and we can decide later. Here!" Lucy picked up a couple of empty five-gallon buckets from the floor. "We can put a bunch of cans in these buckets and then decide when we get out there."

"How are we going to write the words on the bus? We can't do it with spray paint, can we?"

"I have stencils. We can paint the background and then use the stencils to paint the words. We'll need masking tape."

TJ pulled a large roll of tape from the top shelf.

"Perfect!" Lucy said.

An hour later, they were standing beside the old baby-blue school bus. Empty cans of black spray paint littered the parking lot. They had painted over the long, narrow strip down both sides of the bus that read First Baptist Community Church in black and now they were waiting for the paint to dry so they could tape the stencils in place and begin with the lettering.

"What name are we putting on it?" Lucy asked.

"Last Call."

"Really? I thought he was kidding."

"Nope. That's it."

"Well, it's memorable."

"He's going to have business cards made up and put them in the bars. They're going to say: *Make us your last call of the night*."

"Hey, actually, that's not bad."

"Better than some of the other ones they came up with."

"Like what?"

"Drunk Bus. Pub Crawl. Dry Heave Express. Stone Pony Express. Blow Chunks Bus. DUI Buster," TJ told her.

"I kinda like DUI Buster."

"Yeah, me too."

TJ reached up and touched the fresh black paint. "I think it's dry enough to tape the stencils on."

Lucy picked up a can of spray paint. "It's a shame to have all of these different colors and only use black and white paint. Maybe we could paint a little color here and there. This bus is so boring. I hate the blue."

"I don't know. Cooper might not like that. He didn't say anything about painting the rest of the bus, just the name."

Lucy shrugged. "Well, he said he'd be here soon, so let's see what he says. Maybe I will do a little painting on the other side while you work on this."

They exchanged looks, but TJ said nothing. Lucy smiled, grabbed a couple of cans of spray paint, and walked to the other side of the bus. Both of them knew Cooper would not be showing up, even though he had said he would. His numerous attempts to bring TJ and Lucy together were becoming more and more obvious. He found projects for them to do together, like painting the bus, and said he would join them. He never did. There was always an excuse of some kind—he overslept, his truck did not start (which was always a possibility), or something else. The end result was always the same: TJ and Lucy spent more and more time together.

While TJ worked on the stenciling, he listened to the sound of paint being sprayed on the other side. Once in a while, Lucy returned to retrieve more paint. If it were anyone else, TJ would have stopped them. But the truth was, Lucy could do anything she wanted, just as long as TJ could be near. If she wanted to burn the bus to the ground, he'd find her some matches. As he was finishing the last letter, Lucy came around the bus and touched his shoulder. "Come here and look at what I've done."

"I have to finish this. I'm on the last letter."

She took his hand in hers and TJ felt his heart lurch. "Come on! Come look!" she insisted.

Despite pulling back slightly and feigning annoyance, TJ let her lead him around the back of the bus.

The once solid-blue conservative church bus now looked like a hippie bus headed to Woodstock. Assorted daisy-like flowers floated across one side in a haphazard fashion, as if a gust of wind were blowing them across the surface of the bus. Butterflies flew amid the flowers in varying sizes and colors. Ladybugs crawled across the surface of some of the flowers and a wisp of a white cloud was beginning to form under the sponge still in Lucy's hand.

"Lucy! I didn't know you could paint! Cooper is probably going to be mad as hell, but this looks really cool.

You're some kind of an artist."

Lucy laughed. "Nah, not really, although I did love art in school. It was always my favorite class. And I took all of the art classes in high school."

TJ walked backward and then stood in place to take in the whole bus. "Lucy, seriously. This is good."

"No. It really isn't. But it was fun. You think he'll be mad?"

"What's your major in school?"

"I'm still undeclared."

"It should be art. You should be doing this for a living."

Lucy shook her head, but her eyes glowed with pleasure. "There's no money in art. What would I do for a living? I'd just be wasting my time."

"Everyone told me I was wasting my time with the World Wide Warrior contest. I spent years training for it and everyone thought I was crazy. But I won."

"Yeah, but I don't think I'm going to win a million dollars from painting."

"Do you love it?"

Lucy looked at the bus for a moment. "Yeah, I guess I do. I always have."

"Then you should go for it. Don't let anything get in your way. If something is important to you, you should pour your heart into it."

Lucy looked at TJ and took in what he was saying. He was sincere in his encouragement—she could see that—but as they continued to look at each other, his words began to take on a new meaning, and they both realized it. Lucy looked away.

TJ cleared his throat and looked back at the bus. "What are we going to do about the other side? Are you going to paint it, too?"

"Do you think I should? I never meant to paint this one. I was just going to paint one little flower, but I kind of got carried away." Lucy laughed and they were able to look at one another again.

"I think you should do the whole thing. Maybe he won't be mad. Cooper is pretty cool." TJ did not add that he was the one who had actually paid for the bus, and if he needed to, he would insist on Lucy's artwork staying on the bus. "I'll go ahead and work on stenciling the name on this side while you keep painting."

"Are you sure?"

"Yes, I'm sure. I love it." His words began to take on new meaning again. They both looked away this time.

"Okay," Lucy said. "But if he gets mad, I'm blaming you."

Lucy did not notice her mother's car. Ivy drove slowly past the church, her attention caught by the now-colorful bus parked in front of the building. She eased off the gas and watched as Lucy disappeared around the other side of the bus. Ivy could see her car parked nearby. Clearly, Lucy was not working at the diner today, which is what she had told Ivy. And just yesterday, another day when Lucy was supposed to be working, Ivy had driven by the diner and had not seen Lucy's car there. At the time, Ivy hadn't thought much of it. She figured Lucy must have gone somewhere on her lunch break. But now, she wondered why her daughter was lying to her about work. Ivy scowled and looked for Cooper's truck as she passed. She didn't see it, but it could be parked in the back. That TJ kid was there, too.

Ivy pulled into the parking lot of a nearby gas station, took out her cell phone and looked through the numbers she had dialed. She never cleared her phone, so it took her a few minutes to find Sally's number, but there it was. She called the number and waited.

"Hello, Sally's Diner." Sally answered.

Ivy hesitated. She supposed Cooper's wife had heard about Ivy pouring oil over his truck. The last thing Ivy needed was an argument with Sally right now. "Hello. I'm friends with Lucy Miller and I'm trying to leave a message for her. She's not answering her cell. Could you give her the message?

"I'm sorry, but Lucy doesn't work here anymore. She works at Holy Balls. It's in the old First Baptist building. You might want to give them a call. Do you want the number?"

Ivy sat silent for a moment and then hung up. Lucy had lied to her about working at the diner. How long had she been working with Cooper? And why was she lying about it unless there was something to hide? Ivy had a sick, anxious feeling in the pit of her stomach. The thought of Lucy spending her days with Cooper Moon was horrifying. It was only a matter of time before she ended up used and discarded. No. If it were not too late, she would refuse to let it happen. She'd do something about this.

Ivy pulled out of the gas station and drove past the building again, seeing nothing but the wildly painted bus. She imagined Lucy inside the church, in the arms of Cooper Moon. The thought made her physically ill.

(

That same afternoon, someone else was getting ready to paint. As Beaulah drove home from the hardware store with a gallon of red paint, her thoughts turned to Clara. Beaulah tried to visit Clara at Jake's once a week, but she didn't always make it. Truth was, it depressed her. She hated seeing her friend in decline, but she also felt guilty about that. Before, she would have called Clara on such a morning and the two of them would have painted the door together. It would have been so much fun. They used to do that—share domestic chores. Planting flower bulbs, or cleaning out closets, or having a garage sale. It was always so much more fun to do together. Beaulah missed their talks. They used to talk about everything: complain about husbands, brag about children, or just talk about a TV show they both watched. Sometimes, she felt closer to Clara than she did to Perry. But maybe that wasn't so odd. Clara could never break her heart. Perry could. Good friendships were like that. Invaluable. Endless. Comfortable.

When she came to the spot where she was supposed to turn toward her house, Beaulah turned toward Jake's instead. Half an hour later, she and Clara were painting the door side-by-side, just like the old days. It had taken her a while to talk Jake into letting Clara out of the house without the nurse, but Beaulah had prevailed. She had promised to keep her cell phone with her and to call if anything went wrong. By the time they left the house, Beaulah wondered whether she had made a mistake. Jake was so worried. Was Clara worse than Beaulah realized? But after a few minutes in the car, she relaxed. Clara was having a good day.

"Oh!" Clara exclaimed. "It's so good to be out of that house!"

"Well, I figured you'd be the perfect person to help me paint my door."

"What color are you going to paint it?"

"Red!"

"Oh, Perry's not going to like that."

Beaulah smiled and said nothing. She had told Clara, several times, that Perry was now living in the church. But it didn't matter; the sun was shining and they were going to have a great day.

"That nurse drives me crazy! Always hovering over me. Always fussing. Can't even go to the bathroom without her following me down the hall. I don't even know why she's there."

Beaulah wondered whether she should say anything. What was she supposed to do? Just let things slide or correct Clara? She should have asked Jake. "Clara, Jake got that nurse for you because you have been forgetting things."

"What? That makes no sense at all. Everybody forgets

things."

"The doctors say you've got Alzheimer's, Honey. The nurse is there to help you if you need it."

"Alzheimer's? I don't have Alzheimer's! That's the craziest thing I ever heard of. I'm going to talk to Jake about that when I get home. He's just wasting money on that nurse if that's what he thinks."

Shortly afterward, they were both painting Beaulah's front door bright red. The May sun was warm on their shoulders and tulips poked tentative heads out from the soil not far from their feet.

"I don't know about this red," Beaulah said. She stepped back and looked at the door, which was now about halfway painted. "It's so … red!"

Clara laughed. "Yeah, red is kind of like that. So red."

"Well, I'm stuck with it now, so I guess we should just finish. Maybe once it dries it will look better. If not, I can always paint it another color, I guess."

"Perry is going to hate it."

"Perry is staying at the church. We aren't living together right now, remember?"

"You never told me that!" Clara stopped painting and faced Beaulah. "What in the world? What's going on between the two of you?"

Beaulah dipped her brush into the paint can and raked it across the edge to remove surplus paint. "Honestly, at this point, I'm not sure. All I know is that I don't miss him that much. We had gotten to the point where we didn't talk much. Sure, we said the everyday stuff, but we never really talked about real stuff."

Clara turned back to the door and continued to paint. "I don't know. Seems like you guys always had a good marriage. And the everyday stuff is real life."

"I don't know. Maybe I'm not explaining it well. I just feel like we don't connect anymore. All he thinks about is the church. I'm just someone who shares his house. It's like we've just become roommates, not even friends. Friends share stuff. We don't do that anymore. And I don't agree with him speaking out against that Cooper Moon. It's wrong. I don't care what he says. Sometimes, it just feels like Perry thinks he's better than everybody else, including me."

"Did you ever tell him that?"

Beaulah frowned. "Tried to once. But, it didn't work out."

"Well, tell him again. Men understand less than we give them credit for. We think they're ignoring us when we're hurt about something, but I think most of the time they don't even notice."

"Maybe." Beaulah continued painting, now wondering why she had even bothered painting the door. It just seemed spiteful now. And she didn't even like the color. Actually, it was terrible. Maybe she should go and talk to Perry. Maybe Clara was right. Maybe he deserved another chance. Maybe if he really understood how she felt... Her thoughts were interrupted by Clara's urgent voice.

"I can't get this to work! I can't get this to work!"

Beaulah looked over. Clara had shoved the paintbrush all the way into the bottom of the can, burying most of her hand in the paint as well.

"This won't work!" Clara shouted.

Beaulah pulled Clara's hand out of the paint bucket and pried the paint-covered brush from her fingers, letting the brush drop back into the bucket. Paint streamed from Clara's fingertips onto Beaulah's concrete steps.

Beaulah tried to catch the drips with her hand. "Here, Honey, here." Beaulah reached for a nearby roll of paper towel and wrapped Clara's hand. Guiding Clara off the steps and into the yard, Beaulah tried to wipe the paint from her friend's hands.

"My paint thing won't work! It broke! And now I've made a mess. Look at all the spilled paint!"

"It's okay. Don't worry about it. It will all clean up.

Come on, let's get you inside the house and wash your hands."

"I'm sorry. I don't know what happened. It was working and it just stopped."

"I know. I know. That happens sometimes," Beaulah told her friend as she guided her around the front of the house and toward the garage entrance. "Happens to me all the time. Don't worry about it."

"I can't do anything. I can't do anything anymore."

"No. No. That's not true. Your ... paint thing just broke, that's all. Not your fault at all."

"Maybe I better go home now. I'm getting tired."

"Okay, Honey, but let's get you cleaned up first." Beaulah carefully guided her dearest friend into the garage, and tried not to cry.

Chapter 43

June

After closing up, Sally called Cooper from the diner. "Hello," he said after the third ring.

"Hi. I forgot to tell you something this morning."

"What's that?"

"I'm going to be a little late tonight. Violet Collette asked me to stop by Bass Turds. She wants to talk to me about something."

Cooper immediately thought of the pictures Violet's blackmail note had mentioned. She was going to show them to Sally! Even after he paid her off! "When are you going?" he managed to say.

"Now. Then I'll be home right afterward. See you soon."

She hung up before Cooper could respond.

Sally was on her way to talk to Violet and there was nothing Cooper could do about it—nothing. He looked down at the phone, feeling like a condemned man.

In the back of Bass Turds, Violet sat at a table, drumming

her fingers against the wood. Yesterday, she had sent a note to Sally. She'd asked TJ to deliver it, and he assured her that he would. So now, it was just a matter of waiting. It was almost 9:30, the time she'd asked Sally to meet her. Violet tried to tell herself it didn't matter. If Sally showed up, that was fine. If she didn't, that was fine too. But that wasn't true. Violet really wanted Sally to show up. She couldn't remember the last time anything had meant so much to her. She stared at the door.

"Hi, Pete," Sally said as she walked through the door. "Violet sent me a note and asked me to meet her."

"She's back there." Pete pointed to the back corner. "You want something to eat or drink?"

"No thanks." Sally started for the back, but halted. "On second thought, bring me a coffee."

"Sure thing."

Sally closed the distance between herself and Violet and sat down opposite.

Violet spoke first. "Thanks for coming. I wasn't sure if you would."

"I almost didn't. What's this about?"

"Business—a business opportunity." Violet watched Sally. She seemed to sink into her chair, relax a bit. Violet wondered if Sally had thought this meeting was going to be about Cooper, something about their past together. That was the last thing Violet wanted to discuss. If she could, she'd erase that entire part of her life. "I've been helping Pete run the place and we've done a few promotional things that have worked out great for us. And I know business is great for you, too. So, I was thinking maybe we could do some kind of double promotion between both of the businesses."

Pete set a cup of coffee in front of Sally and left. Sally took a sip, watching Violet over her cup. "What kind of promotion?"

"Well, I thought maybe we could discuss it. I have a few ideas, but I'm open to trying anything. And I think Pete will go along with whatever we decide. One of the things I'm thinking we could do is offer coupons for each other. Like, with every dinner we serve, we give our customers a coupon for something free at your diner, and you do the same. Or, if you don't want to do free, we could do coupons, like twenty-five or fifty percent off any meal, something like that."

"Why would we do that? Drive customers to each other's business?"

"Because we have a different clientele. You have a lot of morning and lunch business. We have more nighttime business. You get more families and we get more singles and couples. So, we'd both be fishing in new pools, so to speak. I bet most of our customers don't come to your place, and vice versa. If we offer something that would be sure to get them through the door, maybe we'd both have a chance of picking up new customers. Maybe some of our customers would go to your place for breakfast or lunch. Maybe some of your customers would come here when they want a night out away from the kids."

Sally took another sip of coffee and then set her cup down.

Violet rushed ahead, unnerved by the silence. "We could put a time constraint on it. Like this coupon expires in thirty days or something. And it would be easy to track to see if it worked. Just keep the coupons and count them up at the end of the month. Maybe we could even add a question to it that they have to answer—something easy. Like, for your coupons, we could print on the bottom, *Have you been to Sally's Diner in the last year?* Just have them check yes or no to answer it. Then we'd know how many new customers we are bringing in. People wouldn't mind doing something as simple as that. And we could have our waitresses make sure the customers answer the question. If they don't, the waitress or cashier could ask them directly and mark the box. It would be simple."

"Are you living here now?"

Violet nodded. "Yeah, I guess I am."

"Are you and Frank getting a divorce?"

"I don't know if he has filed or not, but it's just paperwork. Our marriage is over. Honestly, I guess it has been over for years. I didn't treat Frank very good."

Sally's brows raised at this admission. "I thought maybe that's why you wanted to talk to me—something about Frank. He's been helping me out a lot at the diner."

Violet shook her head. "No. I didn't even know that. We don't talk."

"Or I thought maybe you'd want to talk about Cooper."

"No. No reason to talk about him either."

Sally stared at her, making Violet squirm. Almost a full minute passed before Sally spoke. "I think this dual promotion is a great idea. I love it. Let's do it."

"Really? Oh, I'm so excited!" Violet started laughing. "And I'm so relieved. I was afraid to ask you. I thought you'd think I was crazy or something. But I think it's an excellent idea. And it will be fun! I love doing this kind of stuff. I did a Valentine's promotion here for Pete and it turned out great."

"Yeah. I heard about it. Heard it was very nice."

"Really? You heard about it?"

Sally nodded. "One of my waitresses, Lucy, came in here with TJ. I think it was their first date. She said you had decorated the place beautifully and the food was great. She loved it."

Violet beamed. "It did turn out good! We're going to do it next year too."

Sally looked at the clock on the wall. "I gotta go. Cooper will be wondering where I am. But I can stop by here tomorrow at about the same time if you want to work out the details. Or you could stop by the diner, if you want. But, honestly, there's more room here, unless we meet in the back office at the diner."

"No. I'd rather you come here, if you don't mind."

"I don't mind." Sally took a last sip of her coffee and then placed the mug on the table a final time. Standing, she hesitated, as if looking for something to say. "I ... I ... Thanks. Thanks, Violet. I think this is a great idea. Thanks for thinking of me."

Violet stood and extended her hand and the two women shook on it. "Thanks for coming here. I wasn't sure if you would, but I'm glad you did. I think we'll make a great team."

"Maybe," Sally said. "Maybe."

When Sally reached the mobile home, Cooper was waiting for her.

"I was getting worried," he said.

"Sorry. It took a little longer than I thought it would," Sally unbuttoned her clothes as she made her way down the hallway.

Cooper felt a pounding in his ears. He swallowed hard. "What did she want?"

"Just a business idea. I'm gonna take a quick shower, be out in a few minutes."

Cooper sat on the couch, wondering if he should follow Sally into the bathroom to talk. *What did Violet say to her? Did she tell Sally about the naked pictures? About the blackmail money?* he worried. No, that didn't make sense. Sally would have been furious.

"What kind of business idea?" he poked his head into the bathroom and asked Sally, who was already in the shower.

"She came up with the idea of us offering coupons for each other's restaurant. She'd hand out coupons for my diner, and I'd hand out coupons to Bass Turds. It's a good idea. I think it might work."

Cooper leaned against the doorframe, flooded with relief. "Yeah, sounds like a good idea."

"Why don't you join me in here?"

Cooper pulled his shirt over his head and dropped it on the floor. "Another great idea," he said, so grateful for this moment.

Chapter 44

June

While Cooper and Sally were making love in their shower, Ivy sat at her kitchen table with paper and a pen. She waited until she was sure Drake and Lucy were both asleep. Ivy wanted to get this done tonight, so it could go in the morning mail. Every day that Lucy worked with Cooper she was in danger of ending up in his bed. Ivy would not let that happen. Her daughter would not be used and cast aside. She wrote carefully:

Dear Sally Moon,

Your husband, Cooper, worked on an addition on our home earlier this year. At that time, he tried many times to seduce me into bed. I refused his advances, but after my husband found out about it, he fired him on the spot. I don't know what he told you about being fired, but I bet he did not tell you the truth. Now my daughter (and your former employee) Lucy is involved with him. I have reason to believe he is actively pursuing her and trying to get her into bed. Maybe he already has.

I also know he has slept with many other women in the

last year, all the while pretending to be some kind of preacher. I will not name those women. That is your problem. But my daughter is my problem. I do not want her working with your husband. I would suggest that you talk him into firing her. If he does not, I will go public with all of this, which would not do your business or his church any good.

Ivy Miller

Ivy put the letter into an envelope, put the diner's address on it, and stamped it. After leaving the house, she trotted across the street to the mailbox and put the envelope into the box. Then she shut the door and raised the red flag. There. It was done. The mailman would arrive before Drake and Lucy were out of bed. She slipped back into the house and locked the door behind her. She knew Lucy would probably be fired and that she might be broken-hearted, at least for a short time, but it was worth it if she could keep Lucy away from Cooper Moon. Ivy would need to plan something to distract her. Maybe she'd suggest a trip to Chicago to go shopping. Lucy always liked to shop. Maybe she'd make the suggestion tomorrow, after Lucy woke up. That way, when Lucy got fired a couple of days from now (maybe even tomorrow!), the suggestion would not seem strange. In fact, it would be a welcome diversion. Ivy walked toward her bedroom, certain she was doing the right thing.

Chapter 45

June

Libby sat at her kitchen table and wrote checks to pay her bills. This month, she had not only paid all of her bills, she had money left in her checking account—even after paying the last of the hospital bills. Quite a bit of money left over—more than eight thousand dollars. Normally, after paying her bills, Libby was down to two digits. Libby looked at the balance in her checkbook, resisting the urge to go over the figures again. She had added and subtracted everything twice; she knew the numbers were correct. But still, it was easier to believe in the possibility of a mathematical error than in the possibility that she actually had this much money in the bank. And two more sales were scheduled to close next week. She'd have over ten thousand dollars saved by then.

Libby had even splurged and bought some new clothes, a couple of pairs of shoes, and a new laptop bag during the last month. Her new car (still a used car but "new" to her) was much better on gas than her truck had been, so she was even saving money on gas every week, despite driving more. Soon, she'd have enough money to leave town. Was ten thousand dollars enough? Maybe it was. Soon. She wasn't sure how she was going to make that happen, but she was sure it was going to happen. She had to believe it, else there was no reason to get up in the morning.

Libby had passed the exam for real estate licensing. It had actually been easier than she thought it would be. And she liked working with Beaulah. At this point, she considered her a friend. She'd miss her.

Of course, Libby wasn't sure how she was going to get Cooper to leave with her. She hadn't seen him since she and Beaulah had closed on First Baptist, and that was just across a desk. They hadn't spoken privately. But she could still remember how he had looked at her that day. His blue eyes gazing so deeply into hers that she was sure he knew her every thought. He'd had to look away, and he'd avoided looking at her the rest of the time they were in that office. Yes, he still loved her; she knew it.

But how was she going to get him to leave with her if they never talked? She stared out the window. The clump of orange daylilies at the end of the driveway was starting to bloom. The summer would be over in the blink of an eye. She needed to be more proactive, but how? Cooper didn't carry a cell phone. He rarely answered their home phone. It wasn't as if she could send him a letter.

And then it hit her. When the notion struck, she wondered why she had never thought of it before. She'd attend his church. Everyone was welcome in church, right? It's not like she'd run into Sally. Libby had heard she never attended because she was always at the diner. Libby smiled. This was it! She could sit right there in church every Sunday. She could catch Cooper's eye, maybe even talk to him after the service. She closed her checkbook. Yes, that would work.

(

"I still think it's kind of weird. What's your mom going to think?" Lucy asked as they stood on the sidewalk in front of Jake's house.

"She's not going to think anything. We're friends. I just want her to meet my friend, that's all." *Before she is totally gone*, TJ thought to himself. He wanted his mom to meet Lucy. It was important to him. It couldn't wait. Every day now, they lived in fear that today, this moment, would be her last moment of coherence. She seemed to be getting worse much faster now. When TJ had asked Jake about it, Jake told him the doctor said she's probably had Alzheimer's much longer than they realized. Now, her mental capacities were diminishing rapidly. They needed to spend as much quality time with her as possible, the doctor had advised.

TJ wondered what constituted quality time? Any time when she recognized him? Any time she made sense? That was now quality time. He reached for the door and hoped his mom was having a good day. "Anyone home?" he called, but it was a silly question. Someone was always home now.

"We're in here," Josephine called out from the kitchen.

TJ motioned for Lucy to follow him. "I brought company," TJ warned. Again, he hoped his mom was having a good day. He rounded the corner and saw her standing over the table, rolling out dough with a rolling pin. "Good! The more, the merrier! We're making pie!"

Josephine stood at the stove, stirring something that smelled a lot like apples.

"Apple pie?" Lucy guessed.

"You bet! My favorite!" Clara said with a smile.

"My favorite, too," Lucy said. And this, just this, made TJ so happy.

"Who's your friend, TJ?" Clara put her rolling pin down and wiped her flour-covered hands on her apron.

"This is Lucy, Mom."

"And, Lucy, this is my mom, Clara."

Clara shook Lucy's hand and then placed her other hand over the top of Lucy's. "TJ's never brought home a girl before. You must be pretty special."

Lucy's mouth opened, but she said nothing.

TJ jumped in before she could. "Mom! Lucy and I are just friends. That's all. Just friends."

Clara leaned in closer to Lucy and whispered. "He's not fooling me. He's crazy about you. It's all over his face. Look at his eyes. Oh, no doubt about it, he's in love."

TJ flushed. "Mom!" he pleaded.

Josephine chuckled as she stirred the mixture on the stove. "Sometimes I just love you, Clara."

Lucy looked from person to person, not quite sure what to say. Finally, she uttered, "Yep. Apple pie is my favorite."

Clara let go of Lucy's hand and picked up her rolling pin. "Why don't the two of you go out on the porch and swing? The pie won't be ready for an hour or so. We'll call you in when it's done."

"Okay, Mom. We'll see you in a while." TJ pushed Lucy back out of the room and toward the front door. The introduction had not gone as planned.

"I'm sorry about that," he said as they left the house. "She says all kinds of weird stuff. Doesn't make sense most of the time."

Out on the porch, Lucy looked for a porch swing; there was none. "Where's the swing?"

"There isn't one. We used to have one when we were kids, at our old house, not this house. But even that one has been gone for years."

"So, we're not going to swing on the porch swing, then?" Lucy asked with a smile.

His face still red, TJ walked down the front steps and onto the sidewalk. "Funny. Very funny," he said. He wondered whether Lucy would swing with him if they did have porch swing, or was she just teasing him? He had no idea. All he knew was he wanted to put some distance between them and his mom. He couldn't bear any more of those kinds of comments. She'd scare Lucy away for sure.

(

Sally didn't get much personal mail at the diner, so when a letter arrived with her name handwritten across the front, she took notice. Right away, she had the feeling it was a portent of bad news. She stepped into the office and left the door slightly ajar. Her hand shook slightly as she slipped a fingernail under the envelope flap and as she read the letter.

Leaning against the desk, Sally pressed the back of her hand against her mouth. It was too much. Too much. Lucy and Cooper? Surely, he wouldn't stoop that low, would he? But Lucy had quit working at the diner, and now the girl was at the new church with Cooper every day. And Sally knew Lucy was crazy about Cooper. Maybe it wasn't such a stretch of the imagination after all. But she was so young!

Still clutching the letter, Sally walked through the kitchen, pushed the door open and peeked into the diner. Frank sat at the far end of the counter. Sally stepped into the diner. "Frank?"

Frank turned in her direction and Sally motioned for him to come to her. She turned back into the office and sat on the edge of the desk. Her hands were shaking so hard she could hardly grip the letter. She had to crumple the edge just to keep from dropping it.

"What's wrong?" Frank asked.

Mechanically, Sally raised the arm still holding the letter. Frank took it, but Sally had a hard time releasing her hold. Maybe she shouldn't show it to Frank.

"You are shaking like a leaf. What in the world is wrong?"

"Read it," Sally said, finally able to uncurl her fingers.

As Frank read, the letter became more real to Sally, more believable. Of course Cooper was sleeping with Lucy; Cooper slept with everyone. He would never change. Church or no church, he was still the same. She had been such a fool. Sally reached into the desk drawer, pulled out her cell phone, and dialed Lucy's number.

When Lucy answered, Sally began screaming. "Don't you ever come near me! Do you hear me? Never. If I ever see you again, I'll snatch every hair out of your head!" Sally threw the phone across the floor and the battery popped out, both pieces sliding into the corner.

Frank reached over and closed the office door, sure everyone in the kitchen had heard everything.

"I'm so stupid," she screamed at Frank. "I'm so damned stupid! What is wrong with me? Why do I do this? Why do I keep believing him? Why do I have any faith in him at all? What is wrong with me?" Her arms flailing, hatred in her eyes, pacing in the small office space while Frank listened, Sally ranted, recounting the many times she had caught Cooper cheating. Frank tried calming her with soothing words, but she couldn't hear him. Finally, he gave up and just let her rant. It seemed as if she would never stop screaming, but almost half an hour later, she did. Spent, exhausted, Sally stopped in the middle of the room, her shoulders suddenly sagging under the weight, defeated.

Frank moved in, wrapping his arms around her, stroking her hair with one hand. "It's okay, baby. It's okay. At least you know now. Shhhhh. It's okay. I'm here. I'm here for you."

The office door opened and Lucy started to enter. "Sally, what..." she said, freezing as soon as she saw Sally in Frank's arms.

Sally broke free from Frank and lunged in Lucy's direction, but Frank grabbed her around the waist and held tightly as Lucy recoiled and backed out of the office.

"Get the hell out of here! I swear, I'll kill you! I'll kill you!" Sally lunged and swung at Lucy, but Frank held tight.

Lucy backed out the door and hurried to her car, where TJ was waiting for her. That was it, the last straw. She was telling Cooper about Sally and Frank. He had to know about Sally. Sally was crazy. He deserved better.

(

Sally finished her shift. She was pleasant to customers, and she didn't even cry on the way home. But by the time Sally pulled into the drive that night, her hands were shaking so much she had difficulty removing her keys from the ignition.

Cooper was slouched on the couch, watching TV, his socked feet on the coffee table. Sally dropped the letter into his lap.

Cooper slid his feet from the table and sat up. He looked up at Sally, holding the edge of the envelope as if it were on fire, a stricken look on his face. He swallowed a couple of times before asking, "What's this?"

Standing in front of him, looking down on him, Sally did not answer.

Cooper pulled the letter out of the envelope and read it. He sighed. "Oh, this is nothing." He smiled.

"Why do you look so relieved? What did you think it was?"

Cooper was not about to tell her that he thought it was another blackmail letter, or naked pictures. "I don't know. You were so mad. I thought it was something bad."

"It is something bad. And I'm still mad."

Cooper shook his head. "No, Sally. Ivy Miller's crazy. That's all. She's just crazy."

"Why would she say this if it wasn't true?"

Cooper shrugged. "I don't know. I guess she's pissed because I didn't sleep with her. That's why she fired me. She came on to me and I turned her down. Remember? She poured oil all over the tools in the bed of my truck."

"That's not what you told me."

"I was afraid you wouldn't believe me."

"So you lied?"

"Yeah."

"And how do I know you are telling me the truth now? You lied then, so how do I know you aren't lying now?"

"I'm not!" Cooper stood and reached out to Sally. She stepped back and avoided his reach. "Sally! I didn't do anything with Ivy Miller."

"And what about Lucy?"

"Sally! She's just a kid."

"She's not a kid."

"She's TJ's girl, or at least that's what he's working on. Sally, I'm faithful to you. I know I haven't been in the past, but I am now. I am, Sally. I haven't cheated on you ever since I started believing in God. I haven't. I swear it. I promise."

"Cooper, I'm telling you. This is it! This is it! I can't do this anymore. I won't! Do you hear me?"

Cooper stepped toward her. Sally stepped back and held her hands up between them. "Don't touch me."

"Sally."

"I mean it, Cooper! Don't touch me! I swear to God, if you do, I'll slap you right across the face."

Cooper let his hands fall to his side. "Sally." He lowered his voice, using a tone Sally often found difficult to resist.

"No, Cooper. No." She turned and walked back to their bedroom, slamming the door behind her.

Cooper sank back onto the couch, heaving a sigh of relief. Could have been much worse. He imagined Sally opening an envelope and finding pictures of him and Violet together. He pushed his hair back and sighed again. Yes, could have been much worse.

Chapter 46

June

Libby had never attended church. If there were a God, she never would have come home to find both of her parents dead. It was as simple as that. She was under no illusion. No loving God was watching over her. Libby Cartwright was on her own—at least until Cooper was hers. Then it would be the two of them against the world, and nothing could stop them. She'd be happy. Finally.

She entered the church and settled into the back row. It was a large room and most people sat in pews near the front. The back half of the church was empty. Only one other person was sitting in the back row on the other side, an elderly man with a cane, who stared at the floor.

She still found it hard to believe—Cooper, a pastor. Until that moment, she had never thought about what leaving town with her would mean to him. He would lose his role as pastor. But, really, how important could that be to him? Surely, it was just some passing phase. He couldn't be serious about all of this. Libby had always assumed this "church thing" was something to fill his time, something to do while Sally was away working at the diner. If he had

Libby in his life, he wouldn't need anything else to fill his time. Maybe he could get a real estate license too; they could be a team. Libby started imagining him showing houses with her. Then she imagined him showing houses without her—empty houses to other women, women who would gladly throw themselves at him. Maybe real estate was not for him.

Maybe firewood? He did that now, but it seemed to be hit and miss. Maybe they'd move somewhere and buy a place with a woods, so he could cut firewood, maybe somewhere out west, somewhere far from here. A place where no one knew them. She imagined walking down the sidewalk, holding Cooper's hand. Maybe a charming little mountain town. People would need firewood there. Maybe somewhere where the real estate market was hot.

Libby tilted her head and gazed at the ceiling. Must be thirty foot tall, at least, she thought. It was covered with beautiful wooden planks and she wondered how much that cost. If she were TJ, she was sure she could think of better things to spend money on than this great big old building. If she were TJ, she'd be on a beach somewhere sipping a cocktail and listening to the whisper of the ocean waves. Maybe she and Cooper would move to the beach; she'd like that. Beachfront property was crazy expensive. There'd be some good commissions on beach houses. But what would Cooper do all day? She imagined bikini-clad beauties parading up and down the beach in front of Cooper while she was at work. The mountains were sounding better and better. Maybe Colorado. Maybe they could get a little place in Aspen, just an apartment at first, but once she started making some sales they'd get a cabin nestled into the side of a mountain, somewhere down a long and winding road with no neighbors. Just her and Cooper. She smiled. Yes, that was it, Aspen.

Cooper walked out from behind the stage, into the spotlight, and Libby caught her breath. He was so handsome—even more so under the light. The most beautiful man she had ever seen in her life. Easily. Hands down. Absolutely gorgeous. He smiled at the crowd and began talking. Every pore of Libby's body responded. He would be hers soon, all hers. He spoke, but she could not hear him. Soon. Soon.

Libby imagined the moment. She'd tell him everything she'd been planning and he'd take her into his arms. She wondered when he would want to leave—maybe that very afternoon! The thought made her heartbeat quicken. As she watched him speaking under the spotlight in the darkened church, a slow smile slid across her face. *Tonight. Oh, yes! Let it be tonight!*

Although she never took her eyes off him, she heard little of what he said. The reality of the situation was finally hitting her. They could leave tonight! She could drop the keys off to Beaulah and ask her to sell the place. None of her furniture was worth keeping. All she had to do was fill up some suitcases with her clothes and they could leave. She'd have to stop at Walmart and pick up some more suitcases, and stop at the bank to withdraw all of the money out of her accounts, but none of that would take very long. She could be packed and ready to walk out the door in an hour, two hours at the most. She wondered if Cooper even had a suitcase. Probably not. It wasn't like he and Sally ever went anywhere. They could buy him a couple of suitcases too. She didn't imagine Cooper had many clothes. She wondered what else he would want to take. Probably his chain saw, and some tools, she supposed. All of that would fit in her trunk. Maybe she could talk him into leaving it all behind. Everything. She'd buy him new clothes and a new chain saw. The thought of him going home to pack made her nervous. What if he changed his mind? What if Sally came home and caught him packing? Plus, he could just leave his truck behind; it couldn't be worth much and it would never make the drive to Colorado.

After they settled in Aspen, Cooper could call Beaulah

and tell her to sell his place. Of course, he'd have to file for divorce, too. She wondered how much he owed on the trailer and land. She hoped not much. Maybe he'd even clear a little money. That would be nice. Or he could just sign the whole thing over to Sally; Libby didn't care. Things would be tight in the beginning, but once she started getting some sales, they'd have enough money to buy a place of their own. Maybe they could even use those new suitcases and do some traveling. She'd heard that houses out in Aspen sold for millions. Libby sat in the church, trying to determine what her commission would be on a two-million-dollar house.

Libby sat there, so lost in her own thoughts that she was startled when the lights came on and Cooper walked off stage. He was done! It was time.

Libby hung at the back of the crowd and slowly followed everyone else to the door while Cooper stood there shaking hands and thanking people for coming. As she shuffled along, Libby opened her purse and withdrew a small piece of folded paper bearing a simple note: *Please come to the high school parking lot as soon as you can get out of here. I need to talk to you. It is very important. I will be waiting for you in a blue car. It's a matter of life and death.*

Libby felt a little guilty about the last sentence, but only a little. It was a matter of life and death—sort of. If Cooper wasn't in her life, she might as well be dead; she had nothing to live for.

Libby was one of the last to leave. Cooper reached out his hand to shake hers before he even looked up and recognized her. When he did, he froze in place, his hand not fully extended. Libby stepped closer and reached her hand out to him, holding the folded note discreetly. "Great sermon," she said. She placed the note in his palm and whispered, "Read this." Then she smiled and walked out the door before he could respond.

There! She'd done it! The first step had been taken.

Within minutes, Libby was sitting in her car waiting, all of her windows rolled down. It was a perfect June afternoon and a light breeze wafted through the car. The radio played softly. Cooper would be here soon. The high school was just down the road from his new church. Libby felt as if her life was just beginning—finally!

Cooper strode out to his truck in disbelief. He couldn't believe Libby had walked right into his church and handed him a note in front of everybody. He wondered if anyone saw it. Surely, they saw her. And Timber Lake was a very small town. First Violet starts blackmailing him, and now Libby shows up at church and passes him notes like a schoolgirl! He really didn't need this. Cooper wished he'd never had anything to do with either of them. What in the world was he thinking?

As he approached his truck, he noticed a piece of paper stuck under his wiper. Shaking his head in frustration, he assumed she left another note there. He jerked the note from under the blade and unfolded it.

I hate to hurt you like this, but you need to know. Sally is having an affair with Frank Collette. I'm sorry, but you deserve better than this. A concerned friend.

Cooper looked around the parking lot. Most of the cars were cleared out, just a few remained, and he didn't recognize any of those. He got into his truck and read the note again. He pulled Libby's note out of his pocket and compared them. Maybe Libby wrote them both. The handwriting was totally different, couldn't be her.

Cooper put both notes in the glove compartment and started his truck. By the time he reached the spot where Libby had told him to meet her, he had a headache, and he never got headaches. He pulled up beside her car. Libby was out of her car and into his truck before he even turned off the ignition. "What's this about, Libby?"

She turned to face him, and Cooper caught a whiff of

her perfume. She looked beautiful. He had never seen her look more beautiful, at least not with clothes on.

"I need to talk to you. This is important."

"Is something wrong? Do you know something about Sally?"

Libby's brow furrowed for a moment. "No. This is not about Sally." She took a deep breath and her face relaxed. "It's about … the future. Cooper, I've been working with Beaulah on selling real estate. I've got my real estate license now, and we are a good team. In fact, I'm making more now selling houses than I ever was working in the factory."

"That's great, Libby, but I don't understand what this has to do with me." Cooper glanced around the large lot. A few cars were there, but they were quite a distance away, parked in front of the school. "I need to go, Libby."

"Cooper, let me finish. Please, listen to me. This is very important—for both of us. I've been saving money. I have quite a bit saved. Over ten thousand dollars."

"Must be nice. That's a lot of money."

"It is. It's enough money to get a new start somewhere else. Enough for two people to get a start."

"Libby…" Cooper turned toward her, a look of surprise on his face.

"Listen, please. Please." She blinked away tears and took another breath to compose herself. "I've been thinking about this. Please, hear me out. I love you, Cooper. I love you more than I have ever loved anyone in my life. I'll never stop loving you. Never. And I could make you so happy if you'd just give me a chance. The two of us could leave here. We could leave tonight. We could start all over. Just pack up and leave. I'd make you so happy, Cooper." She reached over and placed her hand on top of his on the seat between them. "Cooper, this is our chance to be happy. I know you aren't happy with Sally. If you were, you wouldn't cheat on her. You would have never made love to me. Remember, Cooper? Remember how good it was between us? That wasn't just sex. It's love, Cooper—pure love. And I'll never let you down. Never. We could be so happy."

Cooper gazed through the windshield. He had to admit: it was tempting. He thought about the note in his glove compartment. Could it be true? Could Sally be having an affair with Frank? Maybe she was. Maybe for the past few months, while he'd been determined to be faithful to Sally, she had been cheating on him. It was becoming a possibility. She had been acting odd for a while, and she had lied to him about buying the diner, about saving money behind his back. Maybe it wasn't the only thing Sally had been lying about. And Frank seemed to always be at the diner. Cooper rubbed at his eyes and then rested his head against the back of the seat, eyes closed.

Libby scooted over to nestle her head against his shoulder. Her leg rested against his.

She smelled so good. She was so close.

"I love you, Cooper. I love you so much. Come away with me. Let's go. I was thinking maybe we'd move to Colorado, in the mountains. Maybe Aspen. It's beautiful there. I could sell real estate and you could cut firewood. We could get us a log cabin on a mountainside—just me and you. It would be perfect. I'd make it perfect for you." She placed her hand on his thigh. "Just give me a chance."

Cooper lifted his head from the back of the seat and leaned it against hers. Her hair was so silky. He loved her hair. It was wild and unruly and silky soft, just like her.

"Just me and you," she whispered. "We'll get away from this town and never look back. I love you so much. And I know you love me too."

Cooper sighed. That was it—*that* was the problem. He didn't love her. He cared for Libby. He cared for Libby more than any other woman he had ever slept with. He remembered how she kissed. How she started at his mouth, her lips sliding over his neck, and then working her way down. He remembered how she liked to lie beside him afterward, running her hand gently through his hair. He remembered how she always looked when he left: sad and a little hurt. He did care for her, but he loved Sally.

And even now, with Libby inches away, willing to leave town with him, and smelling like seduction, his thoughts kept returning to his wife. Sally and Frank? No, no. It couldn't be possible, could it?

Cooper pulled his right arm from between them and wrapped it around Libby's shoulder. She started crying, instantly. "Libby, I…"

Libby reached up and put her fingertips on his lips. "No. Don't say it. Don't say anything."

Cooper pushed her hand away. "I have to. Libby, I care about you. I really do. You … you're beautiful, Libby. You really are. Any man would be lucky to have you."

"Apparently not." Libby wiped at her eyes, but her tears continued to fall.

"I should have never…"

"No! Don't say that. Please. I'll never regret…" her voice trailed off as her breath caught in her throat.

"It comes down to one thing: I love Sally. I do. I haven't always acted like that, but now I'm trying to. I love her more than I have ever loved anyone. I could never leave her. Or leave here. I can't. She's part of me. I can't imagine ever waking up without her beside me. I can't imagine ever spending one day without her in my life. I'm sorry. I'm so sorry."

Libby shook her head. "No," she said, sniffling. "No. Please, don't say that. I'm not sorry." She fought to control her breathing, to stop the little gasps of breath between her words. "And I don't regret anything. I do love you, and I'll never stop. Never."

Parked on the side of the road that ran behind the high school parking lot, Frank Collette could not believe his luck. He had been following Cooper, hoping to snap a photo of

Cooper and Lucy Miller together. Surely, that would be enough to drive Sally over the edge. But this was even better. Initially, he had not recognized Libby's new car. But as soon as she got out of it and walked toward Cooper's truck, Frank started snapping photos. This might be even better! Sally already suspected Cooper was sleeping with Lucy. Now, here was proof that he was involved with Libby Cartwright too! Surely, Sally would leave Cooper now. Cooper had stolen Violet, and Frank was only too happy to return the favor. He kept snapping shots. All he had to do was send them to Sally. It was so easy. He grinned.

(

Libby pulled away from Cooper and wiped her eyes. "I won't do this again. I'll never say another word about this. Or call you. But … if things ever change for you." She tried to add another sentence, but could not. Libby scooted over in the seat and opened the door. Reaching behind her without looking, she found his hand resting on the seat and held it for a moment before exiting the truck.

(

Frank took some more pictures of Libby leaving Cooper's truck and then drove in the direction of the diner. He was going straight to Sally with these. He wondered if she were working. Probably. So easy. Moon totally screwed himself this time. Frank laughed aloud. He couldn't wait to show the pictures to Sally. She couldn't forgive Cooper again, could she? But what if she did? She might even turn against Frank after he showed her the photos. No, that was no good. He eased off the gas. There had to be a better way. And then, suddenly, it came to him. "Perfect!" he said, pushing back down on the accelerator.

Chapter 47

June

Cooper woke up Monday morning to find a note on Sally's pillow. *Working a long shift today. Be home late tonight.* Relieved, he lay back against his pillow. Just for a second, he had thought she'd left him. She was still mad about that crazy note from Ivy. *Would talking to Ivy make things better or worse?* He wasn't sure. Soon, he fell back to sleep, waking hours later.

He spent the day in the woods, cutting and stacking firewood for the upcoming winter. Late in the afternoon, he decided to shower and drive to the diner for something to eat. He knew Sally was mad, but it would give him a chance to keep an eye on Frank—maybe even to straighten him out if he was hanging around Sally again today.

Cooper parked in an empty spot near the front of the diner. Just as he was about to pull open the front door, he caught a glimpse of the newspaper box that stood on the sidewalk, just outside the front door of the diner. The headline caught his attention: *Local Pastor Caught in Tryst.* Cooper stepped back and stared at the photo under the headline. It was him and Libby. Someone had taken a photo of them in his truck yesterday. Cooper's arm was around Libby, her head resting against his.

Stunned, Cooper stared at the photo. *This can't be happening! This can't be real!* He wondered, just for a moment, if he were dreaming. He bit the inside of his lip. It hurt. No, this wasn't a dream. This was his life. He jerked open the diner door and rushed inside, scanning the building for Sally. She was not in sight. "Where's Sally?" he asked one of the waitresses.

"I don't know. Haven't seen her since lunch."

Cooper rushed past the booths and pushed open the door that led to the kitchen. "Where's Sally?" he asked one of the cooks. "Don't know. She left some time ago."

Cooper ran back through the diner, out the door, and down the sidewalk. Then he jumped into his truck and sped home. When he did not see Sally's car parked there, he hurried inside and used the house phone to call her cell. It went directly to voicemail.

Frantic, he spent the next two hours driving through town looking for her. He drove past Libby's house, past Lucy's house, past Frank's house, past every restaurant in town, through the local parks, and twice through Walmart's parking lot. No trace of her anywhere.

Who could have done this? Why? What would be the point? Violet? She already said she had pictures of herself and him. Could she be behind this? But why involve Libby? None of it made sense. Well, he told himself, only one way to find out.

After parking in front of Bass Turds he hurried down the sidewalk. Another newspaper box greeted him at the front door. Had this always been here? He didn't remember ever seeing it. But then again, it was easy enough to ignore if your picture wasn't on the front cover. He dug through his pockets for some change. Depositing the change into the newspaper box, he opened it and pulled out an issue. Then he slammed the palm of his hand against the door and charged through, scanning the dark bar for Violet.

She was wiping down a table at one of the booths. Cooper strode over to her and slapped the paper down on the table. "Did you do this?" he shouted. Stepping closer to her, he shouted again, his words bending her backward. "Did you do this? I want to know!"

Violet started shaking. "I don't know what you're talking about."

Cooper grabbed the paper from the table and shook it in her face. "This! This!"

Violet glanced at the paper briefly. "I never saw it. I don't know what it is."

Pete was at her side instantly. He grabbed Cooper's shoulder and spun him around.

In reflex, Cooper raised his fist.

"Don't even think about it," Pete growled. "Get out, Cooper."

Cooper turned back to Violet, pointed at her. "You're not getting another cent from me. Not another cent. I don't care how many pictures you have! Do you hear me? Not another cent."

Violet's hand flew to her mouth and she cowered against the booth, shaking her head, confused.

Cooper strode out, flipping a chair over and sending it flying as he passed it.

"What the hell was that all about?" Pete asked.

Violet shook her head. "I don't know." Shaking violently, she looked as if her legs were about to buckle.

"Sit down," Pete told her. "Sit down." They both sat in a booth and Pete wrapped an arm around her shoulders. "That's it. He's never coming in here again. Never." He looked down at the table and spotted the headlines. Orienting the paper so he could read it, he read the headlines again and glanced at the photo. "He's lost his mind. This has nothing to do with you. What the hell is wrong with him?"

Cooper drove his truck down the street, feeling as if he

might explode. He wanted to hit someone—anyone. But the image of Violet cowering against the booth kept flashing in his mind. Maybe she didn't know anything about the picture in the newspaper, but she sure as hell had been blackmailing him, so she deserved to be yelled at. Still, he felt as if he had just tortured a bunny rabbit.

He continued to drive, looking for Sally, until he noticed red lights in his mirror. "Shit!" he said as he slammed his fist against his steering wheel. He pulled over and turned off his truck. Could the day get any worse?

Jake Barnes approached the side of his truck. "Hey, Cooper. How's it going?"

"Pete call you?"

"Yep. Said you were raising hell over at his place. What's that all about?"

"Did you see today's paper?"

"No."

"I'm on the front page—with Libby Cartwright. We were talking in my truck yesterday, just talking, I swear Jake. She was all upset and I put my arm around her, just for a few minutes. Well, somebody got a picture of us and it's on the front page of today's newspaper."

"What's that got to do with Violet?"

"I don't know. I thought she might be behind it, but maybe not. Hell, I don't know. And I can't find Sally anywhere."

"When did you last see her?"

"This morning, before she left for work. Before this hit the newspaper."

Jake shook his head and rested one hand against the roof of Cooper's truck. "Man, Cooper. You're in the middle of a shitstorm."

"Looks like it."

"Oh, Pete says for me to tell you to stay away from his place. Said he'll file a restraining order if necessary. I think he means it. I'd stay away from there if I were you. He's really pissed."

Cooper slumped in his seat. "Oh, man. This just keeps getting better."

"Go home. Stay there. Stay away from Bass Turds."

"Yeah. That's where I'm headed: home. Maybe Sally is home by now."

When he got there, her car was not in the driveway. Cooper went inside and walked from room to room searching for Sally. When he reached the bedroom, he saw a crumpled yellow piece of paper on the dresser. He picked it up and smoothed it out. He recognized his own handwriting. It was a note he had left for Sally on the kitchen counter some time ago. It depicted an awkward heart with two words written inside of it - *Cooper + Sally*. Cooper placed the note back on the dresser and then ran his hand over it again to smooth the wrinkles.

With a sigh, he returned to the living room to wait for Sally.

It was a long wait.

Later that night, Perry called Beaulah. "Did you see today's paper?"

"Yes."

"I told you that man can't be trusted. I told you! Now what do you think of Cooper Moon? Still think he should have his own church?"

Beaulah hung up. She looked down at the newspaper on her own table. She had tried to call Libby several times, but Libby had not answered. That was unlike her. The last time Beaulah had called, a recording said her message box was full.

Late that night, Sally rang Frank Collette's doorbell. When he answered the door, she asked, "Can I stay here tonight?"

"You bet," Frank answered. "I'll put the garage door up. Go ahead and pull your car in and I'll close the door behind you."

Chapter 48

June

TJ was showing a small boy how to climb a cargo net in the children's section of the gym when he was approached by a reporter. "TJ, what do you have to say regarding the story about Cooper Moon?" Another man stood beside him, operating a video camera.

TJ kept his hands near the child's waist as he climbed back down. "Great job, Jimmy," he told him before giving his attention to the reporter. "I don't know what you're talking about."

The reporter handed TJ a copy of the paper, the camera still rolling. "Cooper Moon, your business partner and the pastor of this church, was just found with another woman. Do you have any comments?"

TJ looked at the paper in confusion. Was this really Cooper? Who was he with? TJ scanned the text and then quickly handed the paper back to the reporter. "Get out of here."

Lucy joined him, stood near him.

"Do you know the woman? How long has this affair been going on? Is she a church member?" the reporter asked.

TJ pushed the camera away from his face. "Get out. You have no right to be here."

"This is a public gym."

"You're not a member. Get out before I call the police." He looked over at Lucy. "Lucy, do you have your cell phone?"

Startled, Lucy reached into her pocket, withdrew her cell phone, and held it in the air.

"Go. Now!" TJ said. He walked to the door, motioning for them to leave as the reporter kept asking questions. TJ ignored every question and kept repeating, "Out!" until they were, indeed, outside the door. TJ glanced out at the parking lot and saw two vans with the names of local television channels on the side of them. A woman and two more men with cameras were approaching. TJ reached down and locked the door. "Make sure all of the other doors are locked," he told Lucy. "Hurry!"

While Lucy checked all of the doors, TJ hurried back into the gym. "Hey everyone, I need your attention!" Many of the gym patrons turned in his direction, but several more continued working on the obstacle course. "I need your attention!" he yelled. Now he had everyone's attention, even those still on the course. "We need to close down. I'm sorry about this, but something has come up and we need to close the doors. To make up for it, I will give everyone here an extra month of membership for free." A couple of people clapped, but most of them grumbled on their way out. A few expressed concern, but TJ remained vague. "I will explain more later. I just can't right now. Sorry. Thanks for understanding."

After they had left from the building, TJ taped a sign to the window—*Closed Until Further Notice*—and turned off all the lights. Standing in the near dark, he and Lucy silently absorbed the news.

"Gotta be a mistake," TJ said, but he wasn't sure he really believed that.

"Yeah, probably. If it isn't, this is really bad." Lucy's eyes belied her words. And broke TJ's heart. In those beautiful kind-of-blue, kind-of-green eyes that TJ adored, he saw it: the unmistakable look of hope.

(

Jake stopped by home to check on Melody. Now that the baby was due in two weeks, Melody was on his mind most of the time. Stopping by to check on her during the day always made him feel better. True, he was only a phone call away, but he always felt better after seeing her in person.

When he walked in, Melody was lying on the couch, sound asleep. He stood there for a moment looking at her and then walked into the kitchen where Josephine was reading a magazine at the table. "Where's Ma?"

"Asleep. I guess it's naptime for everybody but me. Never could sleep during the day." She continued flipping pages as Jake pulled the refrigerator door open and peered inside.

"Well, I won't wake Melody. But tell her I stopped by, okay?" He pulled out a bottle of water and closed the refrigerator.

"I'll tell her. While you're here, though, we need to get something clear."

Jake unscrewed the lid and took a drink. "What's that?"

"I was hired to care for your mother, not watch a baby."

"We'd never expect you to watch the baby."

Josephine licked her finger and kept turning pages. "Mmmmm, I don't know. Melody don't seem like the motherly type to me. Some women take to it and some don't. If I had to guess, I'd say she was going to be in that last group. So, I'm just letting you know, I wasn't hired to care for a baby. Watching your mother is plenty of work for me."

Jake frowned. "No, you don't understand. Melody has wanted a baby for years. She's dreamed about this baby for so long. She's going to be a great mom."

"Okay. Just as long as we're straight on this."

"We are. And, I guess we don't tell you enough, but we do really appreciate you, Josephine. We really do. You've made a huge difference with Mom. I don't know what we'd do without you."

Josephine finally looked up from her magazine. "Thank you. I appreciate that. It's good to hear. I like your mom. She's a sweet woman. I'm happy to be here to help her out. And you're a good son. You've got too much on your plate in my opinion, but you're a good son."

Jake cleared his throat and then scratched his temple. "Thanks. Well, I gotta go. Be sure and tell Mel I was here."

"Will do."

Chapter 49

June

L ibby hated her parents. She had hated them for years. Hated them for committing suicide and leaving her. She could not fathom how they could have been so selfish, how they could have left her to fend for herself in this world. She'd been just a kid, barely thirteen years old. Today, though, she hated them a little less. Libby could almost see how someone could be so tired of hurting that they just wanted the pain to stop. She could almost see how suicide seemed like an easy answer. Almost.

After leaving Cooper the day before, Libby had come straight home, pulled her clothes off, and crawled into bed. That was more than a day ago and she had only gotten out of bed to use the bathroom a few times. The only thing she had accomplished was that she had finally stopped crying. Beside her bed, on the floor, waded up balls of toilet paper were testament to a long crying jag. She had cried well into the night, woken up, and cried some more this morning. Now, well into the afternoon, she was cried out—at least for the moment. But her head was killing her. She knew she should probably get up and eat something, but she didn't have the energy; perhaps a drink of water.

She got up from the bed, walked to her dresser, pulled out an old pajama shirt and tugged it over her head. Slowly, she made her way down the hall, running her fingers against the wall as she walked. She felt dizzy and her head pounded with each step. At the kitchen sink, she turned on the faucet, leaned over, and drank from it. Straightening, she wiped her chin and turned off the faucet. Libby thought about taking something for her headache but didn't feel like making the effort to look in the cupboard.

Her phone sat on the counter. She picked it up and listened to the first three messages, but didn't bother to listen to the rest. The first had been Beaulah. "Libby, I'm worried about you. Please call me back. I'm assuming you saw the picture of you and Cooper Moon on the front page of the newspaper? I'm sure there is a reasonable explanation. Whatever the explanation … well, I love you Libby. And you can count on me. You hear? You can count on me. I'm on your side. Call me back."

The second message was not as kind. "I saw you in the paper, you filthy tramp. You home wrecker! How dare you go after a man of the cloth, you filthy—"

Libby deleted it.

The third message was more of the same. "How does it feel to be the town tramp? Do you know what you've done? You—" Libby hit delete. She then switched her phone to off and dropped it in a drawer.

She had thought she was all cried out; she was wrong. Tears slid down her face as she walked back down the hall and crawled into the cocoon of her blankets.

Driving by the house on Miller Street had become Jake Barnes' obsession. He thought that if he drove by, if he was close to the house, then one day he'd come up with a solution—he'd figure out how to return the money. But still the money sat in his closet, hidden in his bowling ball bag.

Lately, he'd been thinking about leaving the money in one of the cars parked in the driveway. There were always several cars parked there, most with their windows rolled down. He could just drop the money in one of the cars and take off. But what if the person took off with the money and didn't return it to the people in the house? Then he'd be in the same boat he was in now, but even worse because there'd be no money to return.

As he turned into the street near the house, he spotted something in the road. Initially, he could not identify the object, but as he drew closer, it became clear. A little boy, maybe two or three, was playing in the middle of the road, lying down on the pavement and pushing a car. Jake slammed on the brakes and jumped out of his car, looking both directions down the road for oncoming traffic. There was none—so far. "Hey, buddy. How's it going?" he asked the child.

The little boy sat up, his blonde hair shining in the sun, his blue eyes sparkling. "See my car." He held the car up at Jake in his little fist.

"Yeah. That's a nice car, buddy. Let me see that." Jake moved slowly and bent over to scoop up the child. "That's really a nice car. I wish I had one of those."

"Mine."

"Yes, that one is yours. Where do you live? Where's your mommy?" Jake asked, scanning the surrounding houses to look for anyone in a yard. There was no one. "Where's your mommy? Can you point to mommy?"

The little boy pointed to the house that was now a target of investigation, the house next to the one where they had carried out the drug bust—the house that belonged to the brother of the meth dealer. And now Jake was walking up to the front door of that house, carrying a child. He knocked hard on the door and heard a dog bark inside. He looked back at his squad car. He'd jumped out so quickly that he hadn't even turned off the lights. Now, his car was parked in the middle of the road, the door hanging open.

A young woman came to the door and opened it. With a look of confusion, she reached for the child.

Jake did not release his hold on the boy. "Are you his mom?"

The woman withdrew her hands and looked at Jake, suddenly panicked. "Yes. How did you get him? I don't understand."

"He was lying in the middle of the street, playing with his car. He could have been run over, do you realize that? Or someone could have taken him. What if it hadn't been me that found him?" Jake attempted to keep the anger out of his voice.

The child began to whimper and reached out for his mother. She reached back to him, but Jake held him firm. "Oh my God," she said. "My God! Thank you! Thank you so much." She began crying. "He was just sitting here playing cars on the floor, I swear it. The baby woke up and I walked in there to get her. Her diaper was dirty. I was changing her diaper when you rang the doorbell, I swear it. Five minutes! I couldn't have been out of the room for longer than five minutes!"

"How'd he get out the door?"

"I don't know. I guess he opened it."

Jake looked at her skeptically.

"He can open it by himself. I always keep it locked. My husband must have left it unlocked."

The child was squirming now, his entire upper body leaning in the direction of his mother, his little arms reaching out for her. Jake handed her the child. As she reached out to take him, a flash of gold on her wrist caught his attention—a bracelet, and under the bracelet, a red heart-shaped tattoo on her wrist. He stared at her face. Yes, this was the woman he had seen backing from his driveway just before Christmas, the woman Melody had given a bracelet to for Christmas. Melody's friend with the heart-shaped tattoo! Brandy. Only she wasn't Melody's friend. It was suddenly clear—she was a plant! She'd been in his house. Melody considered her a friend. But all along she'd been married to the drug dealer's brother and no doubt trying to find the money in Jake's house.

Jake felt nauseous. He put a hand against the doorframe.

The woman wrapped her arms around her child and asked, "Are you okay? You don't look so good."

"Don't let this happen again," Jake said as he pulled away from the doorframe. "Get a deadbolt, and use it." He turned and hurried back toward his squad car, feeling light-headed. He struggled to slow his breathing and to take deep breaths.

"Thank you!" she called after him. "Thanks so much. It won't happen again. I promise!"

Jake got into his car, closed the door, and then pulled away. He turned the air on full blast and turned the air vents to face him. "Relax, relax," he told himself. "It's okay." But that was a lie. Even as the nausea lifted and he started to feel better, Jake still couldn't buy that lie. It wasn't okay at all. They were in his house. In his *home*! Melody, his unborn baby, Clara, TJ—none of them were safe, and it was all his fault.

He jumped as his cell phone rang.

"Jake," Melody told him. "Come home. I'm in labor."

He flipped the lights and siren on and pushed down on the gas pedal.

Chapter 50

June

"Thanks for dropping me off. But you don't have to stay if you don't want to," TJ told Lucy as he took a seat in the waiting room of the maternity ward.

"Well, I didn't think you should drive. You were pretty rattled when you called me. I'll stay for a while. I don't have anything else to do since the gym is closed."

"I don't even know why I called you. I was just so excited after Jake called me and told me Melody was in labor. I had to tell someone. Thanks again for driving. And I'll pay you for this time off. It's not your fault that the gym is closed. I just can't deal with the press right now. I had my fill of them after I won Warrior."

"Have you heard from Cooper?"

"No."

Lucy picked a stray hair from her sleeve and dropped it on the floor. "Seems like he would have called you by now."

"He will eventually. I'm sure he has a lot on his mind right now."

"Maybe he will stop by here."

"I doubt it." TJ noticed the disappointment on Lucy's

face.

A nurse walked up to them. "Mr. Barnes?"

TJ stood. "Yes?"

"Your brother has asked me to tell you that you can come into the delivery room if you would like to."

TJ's mouth fell open. It took him a moment to speak. "In the delivery room?"

"Yes. Your brother asked me to give you the message."

"Is the baby here now?"

"Oh no. Mrs. Barnes is still in delivery. Would you like me to show you the way?"

TJ shook his head and sat down. "I'll just wait here."

"Okay. If you change your mind, they are in room 140. It's just down that hall. Last room on the right."

After the nurse left, TJ turned to Lucy with a bewildered look on his face. "Why in the world would Jake want me to go in there?"

Lucy laughed. "You're hilarious. You should see the look on your face right now. They're not asking you to deliver the baby, TJ, just to be in there when it's born."

"You think I should?"

Lucy shrugged. "It's up to you. I don't have a brother or sister, but I think if I did, I'd want to be there when my niece or nephew was born."

"But what if I pass out, or get sick or something?"

"They aren't going to lock you in there. You can leave if you feel bad, I'm sure."

Jake interrupted them. "TJ, come on. They say the baby should be here soon! You can come too, Lucy." He turned and hurried back to Melody's room.

TJ's head whipped toward Lucy. "Now what do we do?"

"You should go."

"I'm not going unless you go too."

"I'm not going! I'm not family!"

TJ stood and stretched out his hand to Lucy. "Come on.

Come with me. I'm serious. I'm not going unless you do."

Reluctantly, Lucy stood, her face scrunched in a frown. "I don't see why I have to go in. I should have just dropped you off!"

TJ pulled her down the hallway and they tiptoed into the room. A small leather couch was positioned just inside the door. They both sat in it immediately. On the other side of the room, Jake gave them a small wave from Melody's beside.

"This won't be bad," TJ whispered. "You can't really see anything." It was true. Melody's body was covered in a white sheet, although it was clear that her legs were up in stirrups. From their viewpoint, parallel to Melody's bed, but some distance away, TJ and Lucy would be able to see the baby shortly after it was born, but not much else. "Thanks for coming in with me."

Lucy nodded, absorbed in watching Melody and Jake.

Jake stood beside Melody, brushing her hair from her eyes and talking to her in soothing tones. "You're doing great, Mel. Keep it up. It won't be much longer now. Keep it up. You can do it."

The doctor stood at the foot of Melody's bed with a nurse beside him. "Push, that's it," he told Melody. "Push now. Now, now, now, now. Okay, stop. Stop, Melody. Hang on. Don't push." He was busy doing something.

TJ and Lucy exchanged looks.

"Is something wrong, Doc?" Jake asked.

The doctor did not look up and kept working. "Hang on, Melody. Don't push. The umbilical cord is wrapped around the baby's neck."

"Is that bad?" Jake asked.

"It can be," the doctor said.

Minutes passed.

Jake held Melody's hand and watched the doctor.

Melody's eyes were closed and her soft moans sounded more animal than human.

TJ and Lucy said nothing, both intently staring at the doctor as he worked behind the sheet.

"Okay, push now. Push. Come on! A big push!" the doctor urged. "There, there! Almost! Almost! One more time! Ah … a little girl."

"Do you want to cut the cord, Jake?" the nurse asked.

"No." Jake waited, hoping to hear a baby cry.

TJ and Lucy exchanged looks again. Silence. Lucy wiped a tear from her eye.

More minutes passed.

Melody said nothing. Her eyes closed. Exhausted.

"Shouldn't the baby be crying?" Jake asked.

The doctor did not reply, his focus on the baby. More silence.

And then … the sweetest sound in the world—the quivering cry of a newborn.

Smiles spread around the room, except for Melody. Exhausted, she emitted a soft moan.

The doctor patted her on the knee before leaving. "You did good, Melody. You've got a beautiful baby girl. I'll be in to see you in the morning."

The nurse cleaned the baby, wrapped it, and then laid her across Melody's chest. "There you are, Mama."

Jake reached over and touched his daughter for the first time. Tenderly, he stroked the side of her face with his fingertip. "She's so small. Look at those tiny little hands. Oh, Melody, look how cute she is."

Melody tilted her head up to look at the baby. "I can't see her very well."

Jake turned on the light over Melody's bed.

"She's a funny color," Melody said.

"That's normal. It will go away real quick," the nurse assured her. "Your little girl is just fine, right as rain."

Jake looked at Lucy and TJ. "Come over here and see her!"

TJ and Lucy both kept a respectable distance from

Melody's bedside.

"She's so little. I thought she'd be bigger," TJ said.

"Big enough!" Melody said, prompting laughter around the room.

"Look!" Lucy said. She's got so much hair! I think I was bald when I was a baby. You could put a little bow in her hair already."

The new baby squirmed on her mother's chest, yawned, and then began to cry.

"Could you take her?" Melody asked the nurse. "I need some rest."

"Sure, Honey. I need to finish cleaning her and get all of her stats. I'll bring her back later. You get some rest." The nurse scooped up the baby and put her in a wheeled cart near the bed.

"Where are you taking her?" Jake asked, wondering whether the drug dealers were even watching his family in the hospital?

"Just down the hall. I'll bring her right back in a few minutes."

"Okay," Jake said, but he wasn't sure it was a good idea.

"What's her name?" the nurse asked.

"We haven't decided yet," Melody said.

"Well then, I'll call her Beautiful until you give me a name," the nurse said. She left with the baby and the room suddenly seemed much larger, much emptier.

"We better think of a name," Jake said.

"I will. But now I really do need some sleep," Melody said.

Goodbyes and congratulations were exchanged and then Jake, TJ, and Lucy left the room together. "I think I'm gonna spend the night here with them," Jake told Lucy and TJ as they rode the elevator down to the lobby. As they exited the elevator, a huge stuffed Panda bear in the window of the gift shop caught Jake's attention. "Wow! Look at that bear! I'll see you guys later. I'm gonna buy that for the baby." Jake thanked them for coming, exchanged an awkward hug with TJ, and then hurried into the gift shop.

"He's going to be a great dad," TJ said with a smile as they continued toward the parking lot.

"Yeah, I think so." Lucy smiled. "I guess it's a good thing that I stayed. You need a ride home."

"Yeah, guess so." TJ glanced in her direction. He wanted to tell her that he loved her, tell her she looked beautiful under the lights in the hospital parking lot, tell her that she was his favorite scent. He stopped near her car. "Thanks for hanging out with me tonight."

"Sure! Happy to, TJ. I've never seen a baby being born; it was pretty cool. Congratulations!" She stepped forward and gave him a small congratulatory hug.

It surprised TJ. He hugged back and savored that brief contact. When she let go, he held on for a moment longer. Just a moment. Then he stepped back and smiled down at her.

"Do you have tears in your eyes?" Lucy asked.

"Yeah, guess I do. I'm pretty stoked about being an uncle." TJ was a bad liar. They both knew the look on his face had nothing to do with his new niece, and everything to do with the girl standing before him.

"Well, let's go," Lucy said as she turned and opened her car door.

TJ walked to the other side of her car and got in, already reliving the memory of holding her in his arms.

Chapter 51

June

When Melody brought the baby home, Clara thought it was a ham. "Spread some brown sugar on it and spear some pineapple slices on top with toothpicks," Clara told her daughter-in-law as Melody walked through the front door carrying the newborn.

Melody looked at Jake and whispered, "She's not touching this baby. Do you hear me?"

Jake nodded, but he was sure his mother would come around soon and welcome the baby into the home. She did not. The baby was home for two full days before Clara became aware of her granddaughter's presence.

It happened in the middle of the night, while everyone was sleeping.

Clara's eyes opened wide. Feeling a sense of urgency, she left the bed, pulled her robe on and tiptoed past Josephine's room where the nurse was snoring softly. She continued past the door, to the baby's room.

Lit by a small night-light, the nursery smelled of baby powder and lotion. The huge panda bear Jake had bought in the hospital was slumped in the corner, staring into the middle of the room. In the crib, the new baby, still unnamed, defenseless and content, made little wet noises as it sucked its thumb.

Clara edged into the room. It had been so long since she had tiptoed into the bedroom of a sleeping child. Down the hall, Melody and Jake slept soundly. A monitor was in their room, but Clara made no sounds to wake them. Taking small steps, she moved to the crib. Reaching in, she picked up the baby and a tangle of blankets and left the room, the baby making soft grunting sounds as she carried it down the hall. Clara moved into the kitchen, opened a drawer and pulled out a pair of scissors. Gently, she placed the baby on the counter. It squirmed briefly, and then relaxed. Clara leaned over the baby, the scissors in her hand. Lifting a tiny arm, Clara slid the scissors under the hospital wristband still on the baby's arm, and snipped it off.

"There, that's better," she whispered as she placed the scissors and wristband on the counter. The baby's feet poked from under the blankets. As she had done so many times with her own babies, Clara fussed with the blankets, straightening them, and then wrapping them around the child, creating a soft cocoon. She picked the newborn up, placing the tiny infant against her shoulder, and left the kitchen.

In the dark living room, Clara took a seat in the new rocking chair in the corner. The child rested against Clara's shoulder, sucking its thumb, its soft head touching Clara's cheek. Clara started rocking, the satisfying heft of a baby against her body; she whispered a song of love to her first grandchild.

"Rock-a-bye baby in the tree top..."

She rocked the child through the night. When morning began to break, the black sky fading into dusty periwinkle, a small and tenacious moon still in the sky, Clara crept back down the hall and returned the child to the crib. She adjusted the blankets and rubbed the child's back. "Goodnight, precious. Your grandma loves you. Sweet dreams."

Then she made her way back down the hall to her bedroom, unaware that this was to be her very last lucid moment.

The End

About the Author

Cheryl Shireman lives in the Midwest on a beautiful lake with her husband, Bruce. She has three adult children and one adorable granddaughter. Cheryl is the author of several novels, including the Life is But a Dream series, Broken Resolutions, and the Cooper Moon series. She is also the author of the Curious Toddler series of books, and the non-fiction book, You Don't Need a Prince: A Letter to My Daughter. Cheryl is also the organizer of the popular Indie Chicks anthologies.

Follow on twitter.com/cherylshireman

Follow on facebook.com/cherylshireman

Website: www.cherylshireman.com

For more information on the four-book Cooper Moon series, check out the Cooper Moon website at www.coopermoon.com

www.ingramcontent.com/pod-product-compliance
Lightning Source LLC
Chambersburg PA
CBHW062016170626
46813CB00001B/185